OAK BABY

OAK BABY

G.W. REYNOLDS III

Rutledge Books, Inc. Danbury, CT

Copyright © 2000 by G.W. Reynolds

Cover artwork and illustrations by Steve Robertson

ALL RIGHTS RESERVED
Rutledge Books, Inc.
107 Mill Plain Road, Danbury, CT 06811
1-800-278-8533
www.rutledgebooks.com

Manufactured in the United States of America

Cataloging in Publication Data
Reynolds, G.W., III.

Oak Baby

ISBN: 1-58244-140-5

1. Fiction.

Library of Congress Catalog Card Number: 00-106774

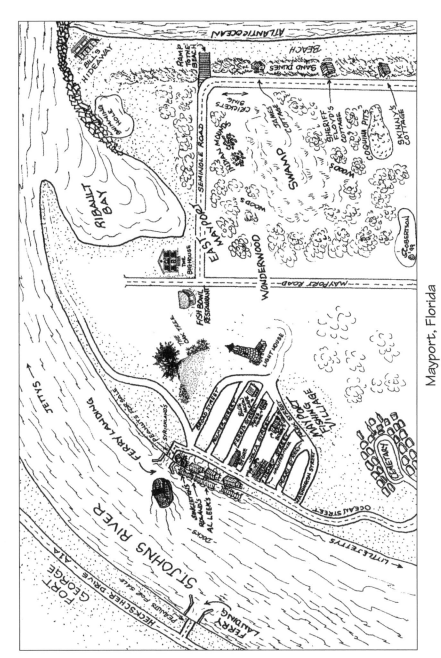

Mayport, Florida

PRELUDE

THE SOUTH JETTY ROCKS, AT THE MOUTH OF THE ST. JOHN'S RIVER, HAD been extended out into the Atlantic Ocean. The big ships would have to go farther out before turning south into the open sea. There would be less trash on the beach as the river emptied deeper than before. The work was over and the huge flat top working barges were gone, along with the others that carried the big red rocks. The small shuttle boats were also gone and Mr. Leek's dock had returned to being a normal fish house. It had been a great year for the workingmen in Mayport.

The men, who had spent the last year at the rocks, were either working on shrimp boats, gill net fishing, or looking for work "on the hill". Any work away from the water and boats was considered "on the hill". Some of the young men had even taken regular jobs driving trucks or with a construction crew. The Coca-Cola Bottling Company and Royal Crown Cola in Jacksonville were both hiring and that was good news for some of the young men. They wouldn't work "on the hill" very long; they never did. Life on the water would eventually lure them all back. There was a strange hold on anyone who had felt the freedom of working on the water. They would never have any money, but they would always have their freedom.

Jason met Sofia at the foot of the sand hill. Her big beautiful blue eyes widened to their fullest when she saw the baby Jason was holding. Sofia's face lit-up with pure joy as she reached out and took the child into her arms.

"Oh Jason! Look at this beautiful baby." Jason loved Sofia. She always said the right thing.

"This is my son, Billy." Sofia held the child to her body and once again she knew what to say. "He has his mother's eyes." Jason smiled. He did love Sofia. He always had.

Jason sat with Sofia and Billy in the front seat of Uncle Bobby's truck for over an hour. He told Sofia how he had found Tom Green, but lost Jessie. Jason was different and knew more than he had known before. Sofia listened to every word coming from Jason. Her eyes would fill with tears then she would smile the tears away as Jason told of his adventure into another world.

Sofia knew how special Jason was from the first time she met him, but she knew he was even more so, now. Jason was the talker and Sofia was the perfect listener. She was perfect in every way: eyes, teeth, hair, skin, lips, body and now ears.

Jason showed Sofia the magic carousel and asked her to keep it at her house for him until he was settled. He wasn't sure how his mother would react to such a treasure and he knew Sofia would take care of the wonderful gift and she would understand how precious the antique truly was. She loved the trust Jason had shown in her. She would hide it in her bedroom and add the new secret to the other secrets she and Jason shared from the past. Jason started the truck and drove away from the great oak tree.

Sofia loved being with Jason, but she was puzzled and fearful that her dream had moved her to go to the sand hill that very morning. Jason was at the tree in her dream and it was unsettling that he was really there when she visited the tree. She was happy Jason was home, but she knew he was different. He had a son and had been through another one of his wild adventures. Sofia loved Jason and wanted to be with him, but she knew their moments together had been strange and as frightening as moments could be. She had her worries that they were destined not to be together. She usually didn't have negative thoughts about such things, but her relationship with Jason had proven to be disastrous so far. Sofia would continue to nurture her feelings for Jason, but she would move with caution. She knew his impulsive nature and she was afraid she would wake up one morning and he would be gone again. Sofia's heart was too fragile and it could easily be shattered by her love for Jason. She also knew he would not hurt her on purpose and she felt he did love her in return. Even though she loved him dearly, she would always be prepared for a strange moment. Not knowing what was next would be the hardest part of a relationship with Jason. Jason drove Sofia home and she lay Billy on the seat of the truck next to him.

"Thank you for listening to me. You are so special and you always make me better than I am." Sofia looked deep into Jason's eyes and thought, "What a wonderful thing to say to someone." She continued her stare. He had more to share.

"I know all this is hard to take in. I just hope we can spend time together after all is settled."

Sofia smiled and thought again to herself, wondering if it would ever be settled. It was strange that Jason had returned to Mayport with a son, a story about the death of the child's mother and a magic music box. When it came to Jason, could it ever be settled? Sofia leaned over the baby and kissed Jason on the cheek as she picked up the carousel. "It is so beautiful. It will be safe with me, I promise." Jason smiled at the kiss and Sofia's promise. "I know it will." She ran into her house.

CHAPTER ONE

MARY C. SAT ON HER FRONT PORCH SWING AND FELT THE WARM JUNE morning air touch her face. She held her infant grandson in her arms, surrounding him with the sleeves of her white terry cloth bath robe. She was excited and happy her son, Jason, had returned to Mayport, but she wasn't sure if she was holding a bundle of joy or a bundle of trouble against her body. She looked down at the child's face and could see nothing except his green eyes. Jason walked from inside the house and joined her and the child on the porch.

"He's beautiful, ain't he Mama?" Mary C. looked up at Jason and smiled. "He has Jessie's eyes. It's not that he has eyes like hers, it's like he really has her eyes." Jason smiled too.

"I know. I think they are her eyes." The smile left Mary C.'s face.

"And that ain't spooky to you?" Jason kept his smile.

"Mama, this whole thing is spooky. You will never know how spooky, but he's my son and he's your grandson; spooky or not." Jason stepped closer to the two swingers. "Ain't his head perfect? His skin too? Ain't his head round and perfect? Babies ain't never got perfect heads. I ain't never seen a baby with a perfect round head, have you?" Mary C. didn't look down at the child, but she did change the subject.

"Why'd ya name him Billy? We don't know no Billies, do we?"

Jason shook his head and smiled again. He did love his mother. She didn't wait for his answer. Mary C. had to be Mary C.

"You know ya shouldn't of run off like ya did, don't ya?"

"Mama, you know we talked about me leavin'. It was just hard to tell you I was goin'."

"I'm ya mama, you should be able to tell me stuff."

"Well, that ain't the case sometimes. Ain't he beautiful?" They both looked at Billy.

"He is just that." Lester "Hawk" Hawkins opened the screen door and stepped out onto the front porch to join the morning family conversation. "I ain't never seen a baby that beautiful before. And his head's perfect." Jason's smile was the biggest of the morning. He knew Hawk had been listening to the earlier conversation and his support was welcome and appreciated. Mary C. couldn't help herself. There was a new center of attention.

"I never heard such carryin' on by full grown men over a baby. And stop sayin' he's beautiful. He's handsome. Don't ya'll know nothin'?" Hawk and Jason both smiled and shook their heads. They both did love Mary C. Hawk put his hand on Jason's shoulder.

"You alright?"

"Yes suh, I am. It's all so sad, but sadness with happiness. It's hard to explain. They shouldn't go together, but I guess sometimes they do. It's just hard to explain." Hawk moved away from Jason and sat next to Mary C. and Billy on the swing. Jessie's beautiful face flashed in Jason's head. He made no effort to stop the vision. He wanted it to linger. The newly created family was quiet for a moment. Only the swing made any noise. It was as if Hawk and Mary C. allowed Jason his moment with Jessie.

Lester "Hawk" Hawkins had left the work at the rocks even before the job was completed. It was not in his character to do such a thing, but he had done many things out of his character since he had fallen deeply in love with Mary C. She had used her favors on him and taken advantage of his true love for her as she persuaded him to leave the barge and start shrimping the Mary C., her brother Bobby's shrimp boat.

Mary C. had arranged for an old friend of the family to work with Hawk on the shrimp boat until Hawk was able to run the boat himself. Hawk knew about boats and he learned fast, so it wouldn't take long before he would be on his own. Mary C. was hoping Jason would join Hawk in the shrimping business now that he had returned home. As usual, Mary C. had everybody's life planned out for them. She was a master of manipulation.

Uncle Bobby's first mate on the Mary C., and the best fisherman around, had agreed to make Lester "Hawk" Hawkins a "shrimpin' man." The people of Mayport called him Chichemo. His real name was Earl, but that name was seldom used, unless maybe his mother called to him. He knew all there was to know about fishing and shrimping. He had shrimped the Gulf of Mexico off the coasts of Texas, Louisiana and Florida. His favorite shrimping grounds were out of Ft. Myers, Florida, as far down as the Dry Tortugas and into the Mexican waters. Chichemo had an interesting pet and best friend. The spider monkey's name was Bosco and wherever Chichemo went, Bosco would sit on his master's shoulder as if they were one. Hawk liked Chichemo and respected him for his knowledge of the sea and his taking the time to help Hawk become what Mary C. wanted. Bosco was a different story. Hawk wasn't very fond of the funny little spider monkey, but he was a tolerant man to a point. Mary C. broke the silence on the porch.

"It gives me the creeps, us all bein' so quiet. This is a happy day. Jason's back where he belongs and he can help you on the boat." Neither of her men responded to her attempt to direct their lives and she really didn't care if they responded or not. She had stated her position and what she wanted. She was fine with the silence at the moment; mainly because, she had more to say. " Do you know how proud Bobby would be if you and Hawk made the Mary C. the best boat in Mayport? Can you imagine?" Jason did love her dearly.

"Mama, I'll try and work the boat with Hawk, but I can't make you any promises about us being the best boat ever. I need to work and take care of Billy. I know what I have to do."

Mary C. was excited and yet she was still Mary C. "What about the baby? Who's gonna take care of this baby? I can help out some, but I can't just be here everyday waitin' on him to grow up. I ain't that young anymore." Jason shook his head again.

"I didn't think you would take care of Billy all the time. I can hire someone to help us. I don't want you to change anything because of us." Hawk had his thoughts too.

"Mary C., you have got to help out at first if you want Jason to get started right away on the boat. I'm sure you remember what it sounds like to have the patter of little feet around the house." Mary C. didn't like Hawk's challenge and statement.

"Well, I don't remember what it sounds like. I didn't hardly get to hold Jason 'til he was about four. I was so young when his daddy died. Daddy Bob and Mama just flat took over the boy. It was as if I was there like a big sister or somethin'. I really ain't never raised up or took care of no little baby. Hell, I'm over forty years old. I'm too old to be raisin' and tendin' to a little infant like this." She looked down at her grandson and could see only his beautiful eyes.

"And these eyes of his are too much for me. It's like that girl's lookin' deep into my soul and tellin' me to take good care of this child." She looked up at Jason and her man, Hawk. "This is a special boy in my arms. Spooky or not, there is something special in this child." Mary C. stood up from the porch swing and walked past the two, now silent and shocked, men in her life. She held Billy close to her body as she opened the screen door and walked into the house. The two men said nothing to Mary C. or to each other. They had no words. Mary C. was always full of surprises and contradictions. They both smiled to themselves. They did love her.

Mary C. placed Billy on her bed and lay her terry cloth robe covered body down next to him. She opened the thin blanket that had been covering the child, exposing his naked little body. She smiled a grandmother's smile. Billy was perfect from head to toe, especially his head. She hummed a sweet song as she touched her cheek to his cheek. It was a great moment for a woman like Mary C. Hawk's voice ended the moment.

"We're gonna go down to the boat. Y'all gonna be alright for a while?"

"Y'all go on, we're just fine."

Margie stood next to the oak tree. She had to be at the store in a few minutes to relieve her mother, but she was compelled once again to visit the tree. Like her young sister, Sofia, a dream she had during the night had sent her to the tree. Her three failed attempts to "breed" under the tree with Jimmy Johnston had her frustration level at its peak and she was even more determined to plan a successful sexual encounter with her more than willing partner. If she had known at the time that Jason was back in Mayport, he would have been in her new plan to "breed."

Margie couldn't help herself as she once again climbed up onto the lowest limb and pushed the front of her body against it. She straddled the huge limb, as she had done before, and rubbed her lower body back and forth as she pressed down. Then she lay forward so her upper body could do the same. Her movements became harder and harder as she sat straight up again, continuing her aggressive lower body movements. Margie gripped the limb with both hands and rotated her hips and pelvic area keeping contact with the tree. She felt it coming from her toes as her stomach muscles contracted and her body fluids exploded from within her. It was too much for her and she actually screamed with pain and delight.

The Croom twins, Chuck and Buck, and their friend, Rusty, were playing near the light house and turned toward the sand hill when Margie's scream was carried to their ears. Chuck was first.

"What the hell was that?" The other two boys continued looking toward the tree, but couldn't see Margie from where they stood. Buck was next. "It's them ghosts up there or maybe them oak babies cryin'." Chuck wasn't sure. "Them oak babies don't cry in the daytime." Even Rusty had to say something. "Maybe they do cry in the day. I'm scared." All three boys continued their wide-eyed stare with the oak tree. Chuck had to act brave. "Let's go up there and see." The other two boys rejected his idea immediately and in stereo.

"We ain't goin' up there." Chuck laughed at them both, but he knew he wasn't going up there either. He followed his two brothers toward home and away from the tree.

Margie didn't realize her sounds of pleasure had traveled on the wind or that she had become addicted to her sexual ritual with the tree. She dismounted slowly and felt her weak and fatigued leg muscles quiver in the sand beneath the tree. Margie also didn't know she was standing on the sand where Jake's body had been buried. His bones were only a few feet below the surface where she stood.

During her two attempts to "breed" with Jimmy Johnston, the two midnight lovers lay in the sand over Jake's grave. Jake would have liked watching the "breeders" roll their naked bodies in the soft white sand. Margie moved down the grape arbor side of the sand hill and tried to hurry to the store to relieve her mother. She was late, but it was worth it. She saw the three Croom brothers turning into the little alleyway near Mr. Pickett's store, but she had no idea her scream had ended their activities at the lighthouse. The boys would tell their few friends about hearing the scream of an oak baby during the day. Margie entered the store, sounding the bell on the door.

Margie's mother, Miss Margaret, was sitting at a small table talking to her youngest daughter, Sofia. They both turned to the door when the bell rang. Margie didn't wait for her mother to speak.

"Mama, I'm sorry I'm late. I really am." Sofia smiled at Margie's same old "song and dance," but didn't say anything. Miss Margaret was next. "Is it time for me to go? I had no idea it was that late. I've been so busy this morning and then we got to talking and I just don't know where the time goes." Sofia looked at Margie's now relieved and smiling face and shook her head at her older sister's luck when it came to getting out of any trouble. Margie knew not to say anymore and went directly to her cleaning chores. Miss Margaret added to the moment.

"I've done most of the extras. I just really felt like working today. You know how a person just loves to work hard sometimes? Well, that was me today." Sofia looked at Margie as if to say, "No Mama, Margie has never had that feeling. " And Margie looked at her mother as if to say, "No Mama, I have never had that feeling." But, neither girl said a word. Sofia and Miss Margaret left Margie at the store.

Jason and Hawk entered Mr. Leek's fish house and walked toward the dock where the boats were tied. Hawk was excited to have Jason with him. Jason was easy to like. Hawk had liked him from the first day he saw Jason working on the jetty barge and now Hawk's feelings for Mary C. made him care for Jason even more.

"You're really gonna like the way the boat looks. We've cleaned her up and I know Bobby would be proud." Jason liked the way Hawk talked. Jason had always liked Hawk too, and he remembered for a moment how his Uncle Bobby had told the story of how Lester Hawkins became the "Hawk." Jason was still amazed at the people and things his Uncle Bobby knew about. He just seemed to have his hand in everything. Jason liked his return to the past and a moment with Uncle Bobby. The two men stepped out onto the wooden dock and there she was, the Mary C. A chill went through Jason's body when he saw Uncle Bobby's beautiful boat. She was almost sparkling as the morning sun bounced off the water. She was freshly painted in her original colors and any sign of age, wear or tear was gone. Her hull was white and all the large trim was a deep blood red. Her name, Mary C., was written in blue and all the smaller trim and riggings were blue as well. It was a beautiful sight for Jason's eyes to behold. He was speechless and he savored the moment. Hawk could see the look of pure pleasure on Jason's face. He savored the moment, too. There was a new bond between them and it was another Mary C. A welcome and familiar voice ended the Mary C. trance that held Jason and Hawk.

"You fellas know a beautiful woman when ya see one, don't ya?" Jason knew Mr. Leek was standing behind them. He was excited again as he turned to greet his good friend and past "partner in crime." "Mr. Leek!" Jason didn't hesitate to embrace Mr. Leek as if they were father and son. Mr. Leek returned the heavy hug and the excitement was clear on his face too. It was a great moment for the two friends.

"It's good to see ya, boy. I've been thinkin' 'bout ya quite a bit,

Bosco

lately." Jake's face, with his eyes bulging out of their sockets, flashed in Jason's head, but he was quick to shake free of the unpleasant memory. There was too much good around him to linger in the past. Mr. Leek's words helped him. "Ain't she about the prettiest thing you've ever seen floatin' on the water?" Jason nodded his head in agreement as he turned back to look at the Mary C. once more.

"Hawk and Chichemo have done a great job gettin' her lookin' good and back into action. Everybody wants to buy her." Another voice broke into the moment.

"Are ya gonna just stand there gettin' mushy or are ya comin' aboard?" The three on the dock all turned to see Chichemo standing on the clean deck of the Mary C. with his companion, Bosco the spider monkey, sitting on his right shoulder. "Ya growed up good, Jason. Ya mama was right. Ya made into a good lookin' man." Jason smiled and stepped down off the dock and onto the railing of the Mary C. Hawk followed.

"Hey, Mr. Chichemo, it's good to see you again. I was a little boy last time you were here. I see ya still got Bosco with ya." Chichemo touched Bosco's little hand with his fingers.

"Yeah, I guess we'll be together 'til one of us drops dead." Chichemo kissed Bosco on his little head. The monkey wiped off the kiss with one of his little hands. "How ya like her?"

Jason knew Chichemo was talking about the boat. "She's beautiful. She's never looked so beautiful. I know Uncle Bobby's happy right now." Chichemo smiled a huge grin.

"Well, as long as he don't show up and want to take her back, I'll be just fine. I ain't never liked bein' near the ol' King place. Me and ghosts don't get along so good. I loved your Uncle Bobby and all, but once you're gone ya need to stay gone. That's just the way I feel about it." Jason had forgotten how funny Chichemo and his monkey were. He liked seeing them again. Hawk had been quiet, as usual, as the others talked. He liked seeing Jason's reaction to the boat. Bosco jumped off Chichemo's shoulder onto the top of the boat's wheelhouse and disappeared to the other side of the boat. The monkey's exit didn't seem to concern Chichemo at all, so no one commented on his departure. Jason was given the grand tour and he loved every step he took on the boat. He knew Uncle Bobby walked with them, but he didn't mention that fact to Chichemo.

Like most infants, Billy was asleep. Mary C. left him on her bed and had placed pillows on both sides of him so he would be safe from falling off the bed. She had decided to cook one of Jason's favorite meals in honor of his return. She didn't know what to think of the new family member. Her emotions were mixed and unsettled. One second she wanted to be his loving grandmother and the next second she wanted it all to be a dream and she was waking up.

Officer Jimmy Johnston walked through the door of Miss Margaret's store. He knew Margie was working and he was compelled to see her. He didn't like it when he desired her so deeply. He knew it made him very vulnerable to her every whim. He didn't want to be like that, but it would hit him every now and then and he couldn't help himself. He had to see her. Margie was standing behind the front counter when he entered the store.

"Well, well, look what the wind blew in." Jimmy didn't know if her greeting was good or bad for him. She continued. "I thought you had forgotten about me." He wasn't sure how to respond to her comments. He had talked to her the day before and she seemed to be in a good mood. He wasn't sure how to read her greeting. He did his best with his own greeting.

"I couldn't go another minute without seeing you. You've been on my mind during the day and in my dreams at night. I just had to see you." Margie liked his greeting, but she would not let him know. It was her selfish and most foolish game.

"On your mind and in your dreams, huh? Very romantic. Where did you read that?" Jimmy knew her games and he didn't care because even though she had her attitude and somewhat smart remarks, she would always end up with him for a night out on the town or sometimes just an hour of wild sex in his patrol car, at his single wide trailer, or in the sand beneath the oak tree. He would allow her to toy with him.

The Magic Carousel

"I asked you where you read that little gem you were spouting so elegantly."

"I didn't read it anywhere, Margie. I just thought you would like to know how much I think about you. Don't worry, I won't bother you again with such foolishness. Sorry I interrupted your work. I'll see ya." Jimmy Johnston pushed the door open, ringing the bell, and walked out of the door. Margie was shocked and really didn't know what to do. Her pride kept her behind the counter too long and when she decided to run after her boyfriend, his patrol car was moving away. She was too late; he was gone. Margie was alone at the store and it was her own fault.

Lester "Hawk" Hawkins sat on the stern of the Mary C. as Jason and Chichemo finished the tour of the boat. He watched the ferry crossing over to Mayport from the Ft. George side of the St. John's River. He felt good about being part of the rejuvenation of the boat and his future as it's skipper. He was glad Jason was back because it made Mary C. happy. He liked the thought of being part of a family and having others depend on him.

The injuries Hawk had sustained during the fight with Big Zeke Shackleford had, for the most part, healed. His bite was still off from the broken jaw which was not healing properly and he had a hard time breathing if he turned a certain way in bed during the night. The beating he had taken would have killed a normal man. But there was nothing at all normal about a man like Lester Hawkins.

Sofia sat alone on her bed looking at the most beautiful carousel music box in Gibsonton or Mayport, or perhaps the known world. Jason said it was a magic box, but didn't say much more about it when he asked her to keep it safe in her room. She took it off the bed and placed it on her dresser. Sofia stepped back to admire the unusual item. She was startled by a knock on her bedroom door.

"Sofia, are you in there?" She recognized her mother's voice.

"Yes, ma'am." She moved quickly to the door.

"You were so quiet and locked up in there, I thought you were gone." Sofia stood at the door.

"No mama, I'm fine. I was just tired and I was resting."

"With the door locked? What is it?" Sofia knew she had to open the door and respond to her mother. She put the music box on the floor next to her dresser where it was hidden from view and opened the door.

"Well, I was worried about you. Are you sure you're alright? You're not getting sick again are you?" Sofia smiled and hugged her mother.

"No ma'am I'm not sick at all. In fact I feel great. I was just resting. I'm sorry I didn't hear you at the door." She kissed her mother.

"I get worried when one of my girls needs to rest during the day. But, if you say you're fine, I'll take your word for it." Miss Margaret stepped out of the doorway and walked away. Sofia closed the door and hurried to hide the magic box back in the closet. She would investigate the mysterious box later.

The boat tour was over and after saying good-bye to Mr. Leek, Jason and Hawk left the dock and headed home in Uncle Bobby's truck. During the ride home, they passed Mr. John King's haunted house. Mr. King was standing on his front porch as usual, but he had company. There was a huge man standing next to a white car. It was a fancy car with black tinted windows, but Jason didn't know what kind it was until Hawk told him.

"I ain't never seen a car like that in Mayport. Jason look! That's a Mercedes Benz. That's a damn Mercedes Benz." They both looked at the car as they drove within ten yards of the white machine. Jason's eyes zeroed in on the huge man standing next to the car who seemed as if he was guarding it from spectators. He was dark and looked like an Indian of some kind. He wore a white turban on his head. The sight of the turban was new for Jason. The man's eyes met Jason's and he did not smile or nod. Jason knew a mean and evil face when he saw one. And he knew he had just seen one. Hawk didn't seem to notice the big man. He was too interested in the car. Jason had slowed the truck down to a snail's pace for a better look. Jason's eyes refocused when he saw Mr. King walking down his steps, arm in arm with a woman. She was dressed in black; stylish and expensive black. She had a black hat on her head with a red scarf draped down her shoulder from the hat. Hawk noticed her also and he was glad Jason was driving slowly. Mr. King was escorting the woman to the Mercedes Benz where the huge man opened the back door for her. She stood next to the car talking to Mr. King for a moment then turned to slide into the back seat of the car. Jason and Hawk could both see her plainly now. Hawk was taken by her real woman's figure and her exotic facial features. Jason was taken by her beauty, but he was also taken by the thought that he knew her, or he had seen her before. He felt like he was in a dream for a moment, but she got into the Mercedes Benz and the big man closed the car door. Jason had driven the truck past the house, but he stopped as the Mercedes Benz drove away. Jason watched Mr. King walk back up the steps to his porch. Hawk brought Jason back from his Mercedes Benz trance.

"Jason! You alright?" Jason's fog cleared. It was a fog he had not experienced one time in the last eight months. "Are you alright? You look like you just saw one of John King's ghosts."

Jason looked at Hawk and smiled. "No, I thought I knew that lady from somewhere."

Hawk smiled. "A good dream perhaps." Jason smiled too. Hawk wanted to talk about the strange encounter they had just experienced together.

"Jason, do you think seein' that car and woman was a little spooky?" Jason thought of his mother's words about Billy.

"Not you too. Mama said the word spooky this mornin'."

"Well, I don't know what to say. It was odd, wasn't it?" Jason wasn't used to Hawk talking so much and his being puzzled.

"I'm not sure what to say, either. I didn't like the way the man, standing at the car, looked. And I thought I knew the woman, but I don't know why, so I guess it is spooky." Hawk had more. "I didn't see anything or anybody but that car and that woman. It was like they fit and belonged together. She was beautiful, but distant. Like she was untouchable. I wonder why she was with Mr. King. You don't think John has a new girlfriend, do ya?" The comical statement took their minds off the encounter and they both laughed. Jason shook his head. "Not hardly. Or, I hope not. Now that would really be spooky." They both laughed again at Jason's uncharacteristic joke. Jason stepped on the gas peddle and they headed home. They would both think about the woman later, but separately and privately.

Mary C. was setting the table when she heard the truck drive up to the house. The aroma of country fried steak filled the front yard as her two men walked up onto the front porch. They both recognized the smell in the air. They had big grins on both their faces as they entered the house.

"Boy, Mama, it sure smells good in here." Jason walked into the dining room where Mary C. was placing the glasses of iced tea next to the three plates.

"Well, it's about time you two decided to come home. I was about to eat without y'all." Jason smiled and looked for Billy. Mary C. knew what his roaming eyes wanted.

"He's in my bed and leave him alone. He's been sleepin' good. He don't need for you to wake him up just because you missed him." Jason kept his smile and walked to her bedroom. Billy was still sleeping between the pillows. He had not moved at all. Jason did what Mary C. suggested and let the child sleep.

The three adults enjoyed a great meal together. Mary C. had outdone herself with her usual country fried steak, mashed potatoes, string beans and those little Merita, brown and serve, dinner rolls. Mary C. dominated the conversation, talking about how wonderful it was going to be with Jason and Hawk shrimping together. For once, Jason agreed with his mother's plans. He liked the idea of working on the boat with Hawk, Chichemo and Bosco, the spider monkey. He liked the idea of being home, having a son, seeing Sofia and having the Mary C. not be a "ghost boat." He would honor his Uncle Bobby by making the Mary C. the best boat in Mayport.

Jason knew he would have to overcome one serious problem; his chronic sea sickness. He didn't just get sea sick. He got deathly sea sick, usually lasting for days. Jason actually suffered from an inner ear disorder called vertigo, causing his equilibrium to run-a-muck, but who knew or cared about that? He would suffer on the high seas and honor his mother's wishes and Uncle Bobby's memory.

Neither Jason nor Hawk mentioned the woman in black walking with Mr. King or the Mercedes Benz. Jason knew Hawk was taken by the woman and his mother didn't need to hear about a new beautiful mysterious lady in Mayport. It just wouldn't make for good dinner conversation. Hawk appreciated Jason's silence and he also appreciated the kind of man Jason had become. They would be good friends.

Margie stood outside the door of Miss Margaret's store. She was looking for Officer Jimmy Johnston's police car. She would never admit it, but she was sorry she had been her usual sarcastic self. She wanted him to come back to be with her. Officer Jimmy Johnston would not return to Mayport that night.

There was a quiet sadness in the atmosphere at the Giant's Motel in Gibsonton, Florida. Jason, Jessie and Billy had given new life to the group of strange individuals who had chosen to live their lives out in the tiny South Florida town. They all missed the handsome young couple and their desire to learn more of the world.

They missed the new life that was born in the magic carousel room. No child had ever been born at the motel. Big Bob, the Giant, missed Jason's strong handshake and the young man's acceptance of all mankind. Black Beulla, the Fat Lady, missed Jason's handsome face and southern manners. Tom Thumb, the World's Smallest Man, missed Jason's manliness and bravery and Jessie's beautiful face and legs. He fantasized about the tongue lashing he had given her thigh. In his perverted mind, he thought Jessie would have eventually joined him and Helga in their sexual activities. Helga, the Amazon Warrior, missed talking to Jessie as they worked together. She liked Jessie's beauty and the fact that Jessie reminded her of herself in her younger days. Norman, the Skeleton Man, just missed them both. And Beth, the Werewolf Girl, still wanted to mate with Jason to continue her species. Beth had left Jason alone and did not pressure him to mate out of respect for Jessie. Beth knew Jason's loss was devastating and she was an honorable creature. Beth believed in her heart that in time Jessie would have given her blessing for Jason to mate with her. She was sad and surprised when Jason left unexpectedly with Billy and returned to Mayport. It was a hitch in her plan, but she considered it a small hitch. She would create her own destiny.

The "Welcome Home Jason and Billy" dinner was over. Mary C. and Jason were washing the dishes and Hawk had taken the trash of the day out to the fifty-five gallon metal drum that was buried in a hole in the woods behind the house. When it was full, a screen would be placed over the top of the drum and the trash would be burned until the drum was empty again. There was no garbage pick-up in Mayport. Jason liked helping his mother and listening to her talk. She never said anything with much substance to it, but he did love hearing her voice. There was a beautiful noise that interrupted Mary C.'s voice. Billy was awake.

Big Bob, the Giant, formally known as Big Bad Bob, a name which was changed when he left the circus life and decided to go into the motel business, stood on the stage of the Big Top Lounge. He was trying to calm a screaming and clapping audience that had just heard a Brenda Lee song medley from the Siamese Twin singing sensations, Ming and Ling. The Twins had performed the medley as a second curtain call encore and, as usual, the crowd was in another encore frenzy for more of the hypnotic sounds from the Asian duo. They were a strange and wonderful mixture of beauty, talent and affliction; they were true wonders of the world.

Big Bob knew the audience would continue the wild ovation for a long time. They did so every night the sisters performed. The Twins had already returned to the stage twice and they were through for the night. Big Bob knew he would have to wait for the crowd frenzy to burn itself out. He always allowed the Twins to end the evening's performance because the customers would stay late, eat heartily and drink heavy as they waited for the finale. He also knew that the other acts could not follow the Twins. They had to be last.

Big Bob stood on the stage in the soft blue spot light, shaking his head and smiling at the wild spectators as the noise level began to drop and the audience realized Ming and Ling were not coming back out.

"Thank you very much. The girls appreciate your excitement and enthusiasm. Thank you! Thank you!" The spot light went out and the house lights lit up the dining room and lounge areas. About half of the customers began to gather their coats, hats and other belongings and headed for the exit doors. They were still humming with the excitement left behind by the Twins and many continued eating and drinking. Every bar stool was filled and Norman, the Skeleton Man, was up to his bony elbows with those fancy mixed drinks the Big Top had become famous for. Black Beulla, the Fat Lady, was drawing draft beer from the tap for the beer drinkers and assisting Norman with the easier bar drinks. Norman could concentrate on the Flaming Zombies, High Wires and Fuzzy Monkeys. Everytime Norman lit the 151 proof rum on top of a Zombie, he thought about how Jessie loved to make a Zombie. He also remembered how she loved to drink one too. He smiled at his memory and missed his two young friends, and the infant they had brought into his life. Big Bob stepped up to the bar.

"You alright Norman?" Norman filled three tall Zombie glasses full of the potent mixture.

"I can handle it now that Beulla pitched in. Where's Beth, anyway? She was supposed to work with me tonight. It isn't like her not to show." Black Beulla stepped up behind Norman like a huge black tanker ship floating up next to a one man row boat.

"I haven't seen Beth since early this morning. Now that I think about it, she was very quiet when we were cleaning and breading the shrimp for tonight. She's never that quiet." Beulla stepped away to serve a few more beer drinkers on the other side of the oval shaped wooden bar. Norman went back to his bartending duties and Big Bob made sure the remaining customers were happy with the service they had received from his staff.

Big Bob looked over at the doorway of the lounge and smiled when he saw the beautiful and voluptuous belly dancer, Ana Kara. He had a soft spot in his huge heart for the exotic beauty. Big Bob had never expressed his feelings, but Ana had her suspicions. Ana seemed to be troubled and in a hurry as she approached the 8 feet, 3 inch tall giant.

"Bob, look at this." Ana handed Bob a piece of paper. Bob's height gave him the wonderful advantage to be able to look down Ana's already extra low cut blouse. He took the paper, but didn't take his eyes off her big round and fully packed breasts that were moving up and down as her rapid breathing made them come alive with their own perky personality. The movement invited all eyes to gaze upon her physical attributes. Ana's raspy voice broke Big Bob's "big breasts" trance.

"I found this on Beth's door. I went by there to see if she was finished with my hair dryer and this was on the door." Big Bob unfolded the sheet of paper and recognized Beth's handwriting. A mousy little voice cut through the air as Tom Thumb, the World's Smallest Man, stepped up behind Big Bob, then moved next to Ana Kara. "Read it Bob. What's it say." Ana Kara stepped away from the little intruder as Big Bob read the note.

> *My biological clock is running down. I know in my heart I am the last of my kind. I also know in my heart what I have to do for us to survive. I know he will save us. I will be careful with the truck. I love you all.*
> *Beth*

Tom Thumb looked at Big Bob. "Can Beth drive? I don't think I ever seen her drive. You ever seen her drive? I know I haven't. I'm tired of hearing about her damn clock tickin' or what ever's runnin' down. Ain't you tired of all that 'her kind' talk?" Big Bob was too pressed to deal with Little Tom's verbal rambling.

"Tom, please stop asking questions and be quiet for a moment. Can you do that, please?"

"Oh! You can ask me questions, but I can't ask you questions. Well, just how fair is that, can you answer me that one last question? Just how fair is that?" Black Beulla couldn't help herself. "Shut the hell up, you little pigmy rat, before I stomp you into a grease spot." Big Bob would not allow such threats. "Beulla, please, he's just nervous about our friend Beth. He talks too much, too loud and too fast when he's worried. You should know that by now." Beulla looked at Tom like she could easily bite his little head off. He gave her an evil smile.

"That's right, ya fat hog, don't ya know nothin'?" Tom hesitated and thought about Big Bob's words for a second. "Hey wait a minute! I don't talk loud or fast. And I ain't nervous about anything. And who the hell cares about that moon howlin,' big tittied, pile of hair, anyway? If I was worried, it was about the truck. Y'all can all kiss my pigmy ass." Tom shot everyone in the room a double defiant bird with his two middle fingers and walked out of the room. They were just two little birds.

Beth was driving North on U.S. Highway 41. The trip to Mayport would take her two nights, mainly because she planned to travel only at night and hide off of the road during the day. She was afraid of how people would react to her on the open road during the day, so night travel would cause her less trouble. Her driving skills were limited and that was another good reason for her driving during the night. The trip usually took about ten hours, but it would take Beth much longer because of her situation. Big Bob's fishing truck was headed to Mayport, Florida, U.S.A.

It was midnight in Mayport, Gibsonton and all the other Florida towns. Margie was in her bed thinking about another attempt to breed at the oak tree. Officer Jimmy Johnston was in his bed staring at the ceiling of his single wide trailer, parked on a lot in Wonderwood. Margie was still in his head.

Mary C. was wrapped around Hawk and had just began to work her magical, sexual Mo-Jo on a more than willing participant. Jason was standing over a number 10 galvanized wash tub that was lined with a soft blanket. It was Billy's make-shift bassinet for the night.

Big Bob and his unusual family sat at the tables in the main dining room of the Big Top Restaurant and Lounge. The customers were all gone and the family, including Tom Thumb, had finished the end of the night clean-up duties. It was time to discuss Beth and her untimely and unexpected departure. Every member of the family knew Big Bob would be in control of the meeting and discussion. Even Little Tom would be quiet and respectful.

"We have a serious problem with this situation of Beth's. We can throw out the possibility of her being rational and returning on her own. I think we all know that." They all nodded in agreement. "She feels her predicament is crucial to her survival. The threat of extinction is real to her. I am sure she is not the last of her kind, but I'm also sure she believes she is, and it is not an easy task to be Beth." Beulla had a thought she needed to share.

"It's not easy to be any of us, but it is true that Beth has the biggest cross to bear." All the family members nodded their heads again, silently supporting Beulla's statement. All except Tom, who rolled his eyes, but didn't say anything. Big Bob noticed, but ignored Tom's facial expressions.

"As Beth's family we all have to decide what to do. Do we have someone go after her? We have a good idea where she's headed and what her intentions are. Who should go to find her and if they find her, what then? My good friends, we do have an interesting dilemma to deal with." Norman Bates, the Skeleton Man, had a novel idea for the interesting dilemma.

"We have always been stronger and better as a group together. We talk all the time about going out into the regular world. We really need to get away. I say we all go to Mayport to find Beth. We need to see where Jason and Billy live." Big Bob was surprised at Norman's suggestion as another dilemma was created.

"And just how do you propose we all go? We have responsibilities you know?" Their eyes were on Norman and they liked his suggestion.

"We always talk about a vacation, but all we do is just talk. Beth, in her strange way, has given us a good reason to do something away from here. I say put up a gone fishin' sign, lock the doors, gas up the old circus bus and let's go on a new adventure, compliments of our dear, dear Beth."

Norman's words sent chills through every member of the family. All eyes were wide open and fixed on Big Bob, waiting for his response. The room was quiet. The only noticeable movement and noise was from Ana Kara, and she was just breathing.

Bob looked into every face of each family member. Big Bob wanted to rescue Beth from herself and he did not want to disappoint the
people he loved. He looked directly into Norman's empty, receding
eyes. "Do you think the old bus can make the trip?" The room
exploded with yells, cheers and laughter. They all looked at each
another with excitement and disbelief.

Norman hugged Beulla, as far as he could reach his arms around
her huge body. Ana Kara hugged Big Bob with her beautiful face
against his waistline and her full round breasts pushed against his
lower pelvic area. He put his huge hand on her back and gently held
her body against him. It was a great hug.

Little Tom lost himself during the excitement and wrapped his
short arms and legs around one of Helga's long legs in the ride position. Helga was excited, but she was not interested in Tom's idea of
celebrating. She pushed him away and made him stand at a distance.
Tom turned to hug another family member and found himself facing
the huge knee cap and shin bone of Black Beulla. He was smart and
quick with his decision not to attempt his infamous sexual ride with
the Fat Woman. He would keep his excitement to himself.

Sofia had gone to bed at ten-thirty but her sleep was uneasy
because of her recurring dream where she rode a merry-go-round,
but was not able to catch Jason on a horse ahead of her. Sofia woke
up and sat up in her bed. It was midnight. She looked toward the
closet where Jason's carousel was hidden. Sofia didn't know why, but
she wanted to see the strange and beautiful music box Jason had
given her for safe keeping.

Sofia got out of her bed, opened the closet door and took off the
blanket which she had hidden the box under. The moonlight coming
through her bedroom window guided her back to her bed. She sat
Indian style on the bed with the magic music box in front of her and
pulled the small lever switch. The carousel lit up instantly and began
to turn. The movement startled Sofia at first, but it was a delightful
scare. The circus music began to play as a thousand spots of colored
light began to bounce off of the walls and ceiling in her dark bedroom. Sofia's bedroom was transformed into a wonderland of music,

colors and lights. She was speechless and became swept up in the magic around her. Sofia shifted her body so she could lie on her side next to the carousel with her cheek supported by her hand, so her face could be closer to the lights. The lights reflected off of her beautiful blue eyes. Her eyes actually became one of the hundred lights. The moving musical spectrum was soothing and hypnotizing to Sofia's young, sensitive and creative mind. Sleep took her when her head slid off her hand and fell softly onto her bed. It was magic.

As Sofia fell asleep the white Mercedes Benz pulled up to the front of John King's house. The Indian stepped out of the driver's side and opened the back door of the car. The mysterious woman in black stepped out onto the ground. She wore black leather boots with chains and spurs on the heels. Mr. King walked out onto his front porch and assisted the woman into the house as her Indian servant followed them with a large black trunk he held across his huge muscular back. Mr. King had visitors who were spending the night.

Jason was asleep in his own bed for the first time in eight months. It was only a matter of time for one of the usual Mayport dreams to overtake his resting mind. He saw himself as a child on the porch at the Big House in East Mayport. Someone was sitting across the porch from him on his Daddy Bob's porch swing. It was dark, but he recognized that it was a figure of a woman. He thought it was his mother. The boy walked to the swing to be close to his mother and, perhaps, have a moment alone with her in the comfort of the swing.

The woman in the swing had her head down and seemed sad as he approached her. She lifted her face and, if you could actually scream during a dream, Jason's scream would have been blood curdling. He found himself eye-to-eye with Eve Klim, the evil woman who killed her husband, Ray Klim, and assisted Charlie Klim in killing Jason's grandfather, Daddy Bob. As a child, Jason knew she could change her face from woman to devil when she wanted to summon the evil inside her. Jason also realized the mysterious woman in black he had seen at John King's house was the evil female nemesis from his childhood. He could not remove himself from the awful dream as Eve's face transformed into the face of the devil. The swing moved back and forth with the child Jason, frozen with fear, standing in front of it. The devil's face would come close and be eye-to-eye with Jason when the swing moved forward, and then the evil face would turn back to a woman's face as the swing moved away; swing forward, devil face; swing away, woman's face; over and over again. Jason could not close his eyes to relieve the pain and fear he was feeling. The child Jason, in the dream, screamed again and the adult Jason sat up in his Mayport bed. He was sweating, panting and afraid. Eve Klim, from his past, had been added to his welcome home party. It was all unsettling and Jason had not felt so afraid or weak in a long time. The presence of evil and the emotional drain took it's toll on Jason's fragile stability.

Mr. John King led his two strange guests up his staircase and stopped outside one of the twelve bedrooms upstairs in his, once a boarding house, home. He opened the door as Eve walked past him into the room. Mr. King was excited.

"I hope this will be comfortable enough for you. It's so good to see you Eve, I didn't think I would ever see you again. This is a wonderful surprise and I'm honored to have you stay here."

"Thank you, John. You have always been a good friend to me and my family. My father thought the world of you. I can't count how many times you scared me when I was a child, and how you enjoyed it." Mr. King smiled at her kind words and the memory moment. He looked at the huge Indian, wearing the white turban. "And the gentleman may choose from the other rooms. They are all in order." Eve turned to her old friend and touched his cheek gently with a soft gloved hand. "My dear John, his name is Sandeep Singh. He is a Punjab warrior. He is a soldier-saint who upholds the highest virtues of dedication, loyalty and bravery. He believes all men and women are equal in the eyes of God. He wears a turban during the day because he has never cut his hair and if he has to use his warrior skills his hair would impede his effectiveness." The soldier-saint walked past Mr. King and Eve and placed the black trunk on the floor of the bedroom as Eve continued her strange and informative introduction to a wide-eyed and attentive Mr. King.

"He has no understanding of fear or hatred. He would give his life so another could live. He has the highest form of human discipline on the Earth. His baptism was of the sword and this makes him invincible as long as there is no hate in his heart. Sandeep is an expert in all manners of self-defense and he is a master in the use of the Kirpan sword, but it is seldom unsheathed. His people have the most wonderful philosophy. They believe that where goodness and sacrifice cannot avail, violence has to be met with violence. And when affairs are past other remedies, it is justifiable to unsheathe the sword." Eve smiled at Mr. King. "Now John, don't you just adore that way of thinking?"

The master storyteller was at a complete loss for words. His head was swimming with Eve's formal introduction of the servant-soldier-saint. Mr. King looked into Sandeep's eyes and could only think of one thing to say. "Would you like to select your room, now?" Sandeep didn't speak and he turned away to open the large black trunk he had carried from the car.

"John, you are really something special." Eve touched his face again. "Sandeep will stay in this room with me. He is here to protect me and to pleasure me as well. He is a great warrior and a great lover. You do know about how love and war go together, don't you? Good night, John." She closed the door. Mr. John King would enjoy the sounds of pleasure and pain that echoed through his huge haunted house that night. The ghosts must have enjoyed it, too; they were still and quiet.

Sofia was in the deepest and most pleasant sleep her young body had ever experienced. Her dream was full of all the colors of the carousel and her blood was warm, giving her a comfortable feeling throughout her body. She was lying in the soft white sand beneath the oak tree. Her back was against the warm sand and she could see the moon and stars in the night sky above the oak tree. Sofia was not afraid at all. The feeling she was experiencing was too comfortable for any fear to enter her thoughts. A single hand fingered its way from the sand and touched her left shoulder. She moved her head from side-to-side as the single hand massaged one shoulder. Then a second hand came out of the sand and gently pinched her other shoulder, causing her head to move again. Sofia had never had such a feeling. A third and fourth hand kneaded her thighs, causing her to quiver with delight while two more hands cupped and squeezed her firm young breasts. The index finger and the thumb of the hands pinched and rolled her sensitive, erect and hard nipples. She felt hands beneath the sand squeeze her buttocks and she pushed her butt cheeks downward for more pleasure. The hands were moving all over her body in a rubbing and kneading frenzy. A last single hand came up from the sand between Sofia's legs, placing the palm of the hand against her womanhood. One of the fingers on the lone hand moved forward and penetrated inside Sofia's trembling body. Her stomach muscles contracted at the first touch and she felt a rush of blood and body fluids racing to combat the intruding digit. It was natural for her to move her hips up and down, causing the finger to penetrate deeper inside her. She screamed with uncontrollable, but pleasurable, stomach muscle spasms, as the finger went deeper and the other hands continued to squeeze, pinch and rub the rest of her body.

Sofia opened her eyes to see the lights from the magic box still bouncing off her bedroom ceiling above her. She realized she was lying flat on her back in her bed. She also realized the finger deep inside her body was her own. She felt it deep inside and moved it for a last moment of pleasure. Her finger was wet, her panties were wet and the bed was wet. The carousel stopped spinning, the music stopped playing and the tiny lights stopped bouncing off the walls. Sofia wiped her hand on her sheet and then placed a pillow between her wet legs. She wasn't sure what had happened to her, but she knew she liked it. She would wish for the same dream again, but it would not come without the magic of the carousel.

CHAPTER TWO

Jason slept very little that first night home. He spent most of the night checking on Billy and thinking about the return of the devil woman, Eve Klim. He hoped she was just passing through, but in his heart he knew that wasn't true. She had a reason for being in Mayport and it made him uneasy and concerned. He knew first hand, Eve was an evil murderer because he had seen her beat her husband with a water hose and then drown him when he was unconscious from the beating. She was also there when his grandfather, Daddy Bob, was lying in his own blood with an ax in his chest. He hated the woman he had seen that day at John King's.

Jason didn't hear any movement in the house so he knew his mother and Hawk were still sleeping. He had moved Billy into the bed with him during the night. He changed the baby's cloth diaper and took off his tiny white t-shirt. Billy's skin was smooth and dark, like Jessie's. He was perfect.

Jason thought of his other family in Gibsonton, Florida and how he missed Tom Green. He also missed the comfort, safety and wonderful dream filled carousel room at the motel. His night of evil dreams and memories was not what he expected or wanted. He felt obligated to his mother, Hawk and his Uncle Bobby. He wasn't sure why he had taken the child to the tree as soon as he returned home. He wasn't sure why he had agreed to shrimp the boat with Hawk.

The only thing he was sure of was that a new evil presence was in Mayport, perhaps that's why he had to return. He had only been home one day and he was already a prisoner again.

Sofia woke up with the sound of circus music in her sleepy ears. She smiled as she thought about her wonderful sexual dream and then realized the magic music box was running again without her turning it on. She sat up in her bed to see her oldest sister, Margie, sitting on the floor next to the bed with the carousel next to her. Margie had taken it off the bed, placed it on the floor and turned it on. Sofia couldn't believe what she was seeing.

"What are you doing? Turn that off! How dare you come into my room!" Margie didn't look up from the spinning carousel.

"Where did this thing come from? It is the most beautiful thing I've ever seen. Where did you get this?" Margie still didn't look at Sofia.

"Turn it off, please! I can't believe you just came in here like this!" Margie reluctantly turned the box off.

"I didn't come in here to find your little secret. I needed a clean blouse and I was going to borrow one of yours. I wouldn't have even looked at you if you hadn't been moaning and groaning, with that silly smile on your face. When I looked at you I saw this thing on the bed. It wasn't my intention to find anything, but a blouse. What were you dreaming, anyway?" Sofia dropped her eyes and didn't answer her sister's question. Margie didn't care for an answer.

"This thing is so beautiful, I just had to take a look. Where did you get such a thing?" Sofia was disgusted with her sister and didn't want to betray Jason's trust, but it was her own fault for taking it out of the hiding place she had selected.

"I won't tell on you. Did you find it? Did someone give it to you? Who?" Sofia knew Margie would continue until the truth was known so she knew what had to be done.

"I'm keeping it for someone. It's not mine. I promised to keep it safe until they needed it back. Now, that's all I can tell you. Please, don't ask me anymore, please." Sofia's pitiful plea meant nothing to her sister. It only made Margie more determined to know all there was to know. Sofia knew the look on Margie's face. "Please Margie, I'm begging you. Just leave it alone. This once, please. Allow me to keep my promise. I know you can make me tell, but don't please. I'm begging you." Margie was too mean and cared nothing about Sofia's promise.

"This thing must be worth a fortune. I'll bet it's an antique of some kind from a far away place." Sofia knew she was doomed.

"I don't know anything about it. I just know it's beautiful and it's suppose to be magic." Margie's face lit up at Sofia's new information. "Magic? What do you mean, magic? For someone who doesn't know anything about it, that's an interesting comment to just throw out there, don't you think? What does it do?" Sofia was sorry she had used that word, but she had. She knew she had to tell Margie everything. She actually knew she would tell from the beginning. "Jason gave it to me to keep for him." Margie's face lit up again.

"What did you say? Who gave it to you?"

"Jason asked me to keep it safe until he could decide what to do with it." Margie couldn't believe her ears. "When did this all happen?"

"Yesterday. He came back yesterday. I had a strange dream about the oak tree and I went there. When I got there, Jason was there, too. He was showing his son, Billy, to the tree." Margie's head was spinning like the carousel.

"Hold on a minute. Let me see here. You're telling me that you had a dream that made you go to the oak tree, a place you have never been." Sofia nodded her head as Margie continued.

"And it just so happened that when you got there, Jason was there, too. He had returned that very moment. And on top of that he had his son with him and he asked you to keep this thing for him until he needed it? Is that what you're telling me?" Sofia nodded her head again. She didn't say anything because she could tell Margie was somewhat beside herself as the strange, but true, story unfolded.

"This is really too crazy. Oh, and this thing is magic? Jason told you that?" Sofia's head continued to move up and down. "Stop nodding your head like that! You look like one of those stupid dogs in the back window of a car. Stop it!" Sofia stopped nodding. She knew it was time to talk. She didn't want to, but she did.

"Jason came back yesterday. Jessie had his son. Jason named the boy, Billy, after that boy who saved Jason at the oak tree when they played that awful game, Duckin.' Jessie died during the child's birth in a town called Gibsonton, Florida. They found a friend of Jason's named Tom Green and some circus people took care of Jason and Jessie until the baby was born at a Giant's Motel. They both worked at the motel until Billy was born. Jessie died there. Jason brought the baby here to show the oak tree, just in case all that oak baby stuff is true. Jason isn't too sure about all that. He didn't want his mother to see the music box so he asked me to hide it somewhere safe, and now I've betrayed him, like everybody else." Margie had had enough.

"Stop! Please stop! Don't tell me anymore, please. I've heard enough. I can't take anymore at the moment. Perhaps when I recover and wake up from this ridiculous dream, we will laugh about this, but for now, just stop. And put this thing back in its hiding place. Don't worry I will surely not tell anyone about it. Go back to sleep."

Margie left Sofia's bedroom and continued talking to herself as she moved away down the hall. Sofia jumped out of her bed and put the magic carousel back into the closet. She knew Margie would have more questions later.

Everyone at the Giant's Motel was getting the big circus bus ready for the trip to Mayport, Florida in search of Beth, the Werewolf Girl. The bus had not been driven in a year or so, but Norman had started the engine every week just to make sure the battery was charged in case it would be needed. Norman was pretty handy with cars. Beulla was sweeping the aisles and under the seats while Norman was washing the outside. Little Tom was scrubbing the tires while Big Bob wiped the windows from the outside. Ming and Ling would make the trip, but they were not required to do much of the physical labor. It was hard enough for them to move about, much less work. They had tried to work a fruit stand on the road outside the motel, but it was just too difficult for them to assist the customers properly. They did their share by singing on stage twice a week. All

The Bus

the others understood and they loved them dearly. Even Little Tom was always respectful of the Twins; he knew their plight was a heavy one and he would never belittle them in any way.

The bus was a strange contraption from the circus in the 1940's. The three inch thin rubber tires encircled a five prong star-like rim with mud flaps front and rear. The bottom section was like a regular school bus with a single driver's seat to the front left, and up and down sliding windows on each side of the bus. Each seat would hold two adults comfortably with a wide middle aisle between the two rows of seats. The novel addition to the bus was another seating area on the roof of the regular bus. It was a double-decker with ten double rows of seating on the roof. The upper section had arm rails, but no roof. The weather would have to be pleasant in order for the passengers to enjoy the ride on top. If the speed of the bus exceeded twenty-five miles an hour, the top passengers would also have to contend with insects, birds and other airborne objects of the open road. There was a narrow spiral staircase on the back of the bus leading up to the upper level. A capacity crowd could be seventy passengers.

The Giant's Motel family would only count eight, so no one would have to sit on top for the ride to Mayport. The bus was deep Easter egg purple with yellow trim and had "Barnum and Bailey Circus Bus Tours" written on each side under the windows. On the destination display window above the front windshield was written, Gibsonton. It was a great bus.

Beth, the Werewolf Girl, had driven Big Bob's truck off the main highway onto a narrow dirt road. She had put two containers filled with extra gasoline in the back of the truck so she would not have to stop at a gas station. The less she made contact with others, the better chance she would have to complete her mission. She knew she didn't need to bring any unnecessary attention to herself. She poured the contents of one container into the gas tank of the truck. Beth had seen road signs telling her she was on Highway 301 in a town called Baldwin. The map she had, directed her to turn east and she would be on her way to the Atlantic Ocean, the St. John's River and the town called Mayport. She hadn't planned to ride during the daylight hours, but that biological clock, in her head, kept ticking too loud and made her make irrational decisions. She was taking a serious chance driving during the day, but her mission overshadowed her logic. She left the dirt road and headed east.

Jason, Hawk, Chichemo and Bosco would work on the Mary C. one more day before they made their first trip. Mr. Leek's dock crew would add the finishing touches before the boat would begin a new era of shrimping in the Atlantic Ocean. She would be fueled and iced and prepared for a two day trip as the first time out. The longer trips would be later when Hawk and Jason knew what Chichemo knew, or at least half of what he knew.

Jason and Hawk both were excited about their new endeavor and they listened to Chichemo's words of wisdom. Neither one liked Bosco. The spider monkey was more of a nuisance than a pet and Chichemo gave the nasty little animal a free run of the boat, including the galley and the food cabinets. Jason and Hawk knew Chichemo and Bosco were a temporary situation and they did appreciate the extra training they were receiving from the master fisherman. They would tolerate those little monkey hands in the cereal box for a while.

Jason and Hawk had seen the white Mercedes Benz in front of Mr. King's house when they drove to the dock that morning. Hawk had mentioned the car still being there, but Jason did not tell that he knew who the mysterious woman in black was; his childhood devil woman. Eve from east Mayport had returned.

Mr. John King had been up since six A.M. He had eaten breakfast, completed his household chores, sat on his front porch for an hour, watched the Mayport folks move about the small fishing village and listened to the ferry horn at least a dozen times. It was almost noon and he had heard nothing from his house guests, Eve and her strange companion Sandeep, except for the noises they made during the night. He knew they were still there because the white Mercedes Benz was still parked in front of his house. He had no thoughts of disturbing them.

Sofia had the early shift at the store. She had relieved her sister Peggy at seven that morning. Her sister, Susan, was to relieve her at one o'clock, then Margie would work that evening. Sofia was surprised when the bell on the door sounded and her sisters, Susan and Margie, both walked into the store.

"I didn't know both of you had to work. Are we expecting a crowd today?" Margie had the answer.

"I'm not here to work. Susan's relieving you a little early and we're going to see Jason's son. I've been thinking about this all morning. I think we're going to see a true oak baby. I want to see one." Sofia couldn't believe her ears.

"What are you talking about? There is no way I'm going to Jason's house with you to see his son. Not with you talking about oak babies. You'll embarrass me and I'm not going to let you do that." Margie shook her head.

"We're not going to talk about him being an oak baby. We're just going to welcome Jason and his new son back home and congratulate him on the birth of his son and say we're sorry about Jessie. Good friends and neighbors do such things. We've had a lot to do with Jason and his family and it will be the proper thing to do. If you're with me it will even be better. You seem to be in with the family." Sofia didn't like Margie's sarcasm and wanted to refuse to go along with her neighborly visit.

"I'm afraid you'll say something about the tree and all that stuff you believe. You've always been real forward when you talked to Miss Mary C. and that really worries me. I would simply die if you said that stuff about the boy being an oak baby to Miss Mary C."

Sofia's oak tree dream filled with hands in the sand, flashed in her head. She felt as if the blood flow in her young body had changed directions and that warm pleasant sensation raised the peach fuzz hair on the back of her neck and on her slender arms. There was a tingling between her legs. She knew her face was flushed. Sofia took a deep and gain control breath and hoped her sisters didn't realize she was experiencing such a new sensation. Margie continued to talk, so evidently she saw no change in her little

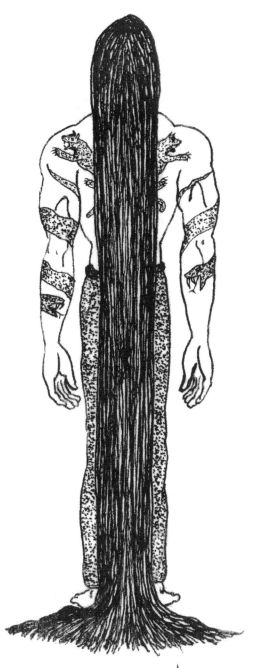

S ROBERTSON
© 4/2000

Sandeep Singh

sister's appearance. Sofia didn't realize the change was from within and not outwardly visible.

"You have to go with me. It's obvious, Jason likes talking to you and his mother likes you, too. I'd look foolish going over there alone. Now, are you going with me or not? I promise I won't mention the tree and embarrass you in any way. We'll just be friends wanting to see the new baby." Sofia looked at her other sister, Susan.

"Hey, leave me out of it. I think the whole thing's scary. I think our dear sister, Margie's scary and getting more scary all the time." Margie rolled her eyes at Susan's comment as Susan continued. "I think the fact Jason's been gone for a long time is strange. I think him leaving with that black girl was strange. Now, he comes back with a baby boy and the black girl's dead. The whole thing is scary to me. I wouldn't go over there if you paid me. So don't look at me." Margie had to add her two cents. "There you go again. Everything is scary to you, but I'd bet you my next pay check that if Jason asked you to breed under that oak tree with him you'd be naked in the sand waiting on him." Susan's eyes lit up at Margie's crude remark. Sofia had another change in her blood flow direction, as the dream of sandy hands flashed again in her head. Susan had a reply. "You'd lose your money this time, sister dear. I'll admit I'd like to be with Jason just like you, but not under that tree. You would lose that bet." Margie appreciated the strong and determined reply from her sister. Sofia recovered from her dream flash.

"You two stop talking like that. We never talk to each other that way. You two apologize to each other right now." Margie and Susan both looked at their little sister and screamed with laughter. Margie was first. "Sofia, you are the funniest thing I know. Please don't turn into Mama. I couldn't take it." Susan agreed. "Me either." They both laughed again as Margie moved to the door. "You coming or not?"

Mr. John King was still sitting in his wicker chair on the front porch of his haunted house. He looked over the smoke from his long cigar when the screen door of his house opened. The master of fright could not believe his own eyes. The Indian, Sandeep, walked out onto the front porch. There was no turban on his head. His never-been-cut raven hair ran down his muscular back like a shining black waterfall. The ends of the massive growth passed the backs of his calf muscles and actually touched the wooden boards of the porch floor. Sandeep was wearing a pair of long pants made of black silk, tied at a tapered waist with a red braided cord. He wore no shirt, exposing a chest that looked like it was chiseled from a granite rock, with arms that looked like legs. He was an outrageous specimen, but the most unusual sight of all to touch John King's eyes was the hundreds of tattoos covering Sandeep's chest, arms, shoulders and back. There was no visible skin. He was completely covered with colorful art-work of animals, demons and creatures, Mr. King didn't recognize.

Sandeep walked to the edge of the porch and stood by the rail-ing. He did not look at his stunned and speechless host. Sandeep said nothing. John King said nothing. He could not see all the tattoos on the Indian's back because of his long mane of thick black hair, but it was obvious they were there. Mr. King's visual trance was lifted when Eve's voice cut through the Mayport air.

"Isn't he a marvelous creature, John?" Mr. King turned and looked at Eve, but she knew he had no words for her. "If he had lived in Greece in ancient times, he would have been considered a god and he would have been a son of Zeus or perhaps he would have been Zeus, himself. He is one of a kind and there are no others. He has no peers. I love to fix his hair. I consider it an honor. He keeps it in the turban so it will not impede his mobility and ability to maneuver. He doesn't like it hanging down, but he does take the turban off at night. I do love fixing it."

Mr. John King had taken his eyes off Sandeep and they were now glued to Eve, as she moved toward her saint, lover, servant, warrior. She wore a black skin tight body stocking type outfit. It hugged her every bulge and curve. It was easy to see she wore nothing under-neath the apparel. Her body was that of a young woman; hard and firm in the right places and big and round in the other places. Her breasts and nipples were visible and Mr. King could see the crack of her butt through the black material. Mr. King had to look away when he saw Eve's crotch area pushing against the thin material. He could tell she had shaved her pubic hairs and the black material was pressed against her mons de Venus. He looked away as Eve moved closer to Sandeep.

The Indian sat in one of the porch chairs as Eve moved behind him. His hair lay in a huge circle around the chair and on the floor of the porch. Mr. King turned his eyes back to Eve and enjoyed the sight of her as she moved her body and braided Sandeep's massive mane. He puffed on the big cigar as if the three of them were having sex on the front porch of the haunted house.

Eve added to Mr. King's fantasy. "I think we scared a few of your ghosts away last night, John. They were awful quiet. I hope we don't scare you too much while we're here." Mr. King took the cigar out of his mouth and took a deep breath. "Not a chance in hell, Eve; not a chance." They both smiled. Sandeep smiled, too.

The bell rang on the door of Miss Margaret's store when Margie and Sofia walked outside, leaving Susan alone. They were going to see Jason's son. As they walked to the front corner of the building Sofia looked in the direction of Mr. King's house. She held her arm across the front of Margie's body to stop her forward motion. "Look over at Mr. King's. Look at those people. What is she doing?" Margie focused her eyes on Sandeep at first.

"Oh my God! What is that?" Sofia saw him, too.

"It's a man. Look at his hair. That can't be his hair." Margie couldn't take her eyes off the Indian.

"That is his hair and she's braiding it. What is she wearing? She looks black." Sofia disagreed.

"I don't think she's black. See, her face is white. She's wearing something that makes her skin look black. I think you can see through it. She looks naked from here." Margie pulled Sofia back to the edge of the building.

"They're going to see us gawking at them. Let's go over there and see what's going on. We'll say hey to Mr. King." Sofia's eyes widened to their fullest at Margie's brave thoughts.

"Are you crazy? We can't just go over there like that."

"Why not? Mr. King's sitting with them. He must know them

and he's letting them stay with him. Look at that car. What is it? Maybe they're famous or even movie stars. I'm going over there. You and Susan can be scared of everything if you want, but not me. I want to know all I can know. No more being scared for me. I told you that months ago." Sofia had a final thought.

"I don't know if Mr. King knows any movie stars or not, but he does know some ghosts. And these just might be two of them." Margie shook her head.

"Well, if that's true, they'll probably be gone before I get there. I don't think ghosts hang around when people show up. And I don't think they sit on the front porch in the daylight. Come on." Margie walked out into the open and headed for Mr. King's front porch. Sofia stood next to the store and watched her brave oldest sister cross the road and stop next to Mr. King's front steps. Mr. King saw Margie first. "Mornin' Margie, or should I say good afternoon?" Margie stepped up on the first step.

"It's a little after noon, Mr. King. How are you today?"

"I'm good as I can be." Mr. King noticed Margie had her eyes on his two strange guests.

"Allow me to introduce you to my friends." Margie's mouth fell open when she noticed Sandeep's upper body was covered with muscles and strange tattoos. "This is Miss Eve, an old friend of my family's, who use to live in east Mayport, before the Navy took her home." Eve looked at Margie as Mr. King continued." Eve, this is Margie, Miss Margaret's oldest daughter." Eve smiled and nodded at Margie. "How do you do, Margie?" Margie nodded back as Mr. King had more to say.

"And this is Eve's friend, Sandeep. He's not from around here." Margie and Mr. King both smiled at his little humorous moment. Eve and Sandeep didn't smile at all.

"Nice to meet you both." Margie noticed Eve's exposed body parts through the thin black material that didn't cover her assets at all. Margie tried not to stare at either one of them, but it was an impossible task for the young and curious Mayport girl. Her eyes were bouncing from Eve to Sandeep and back again. She was keeping her pledge not to be afraid.

"I've never seen anyone with hair that long before, especially a man. Forgive me if I stare." Eve smiled and was quick to respond.

"No need to be sorry. I would be concerned about you if you didn't stare at such a man. He is the most a man can be and then he is even more than that. He is a soldier saint, a warrior priest, if you will. It is a true privilege for you to see such a man and be near him. Your life is better because your eyes have seen him." Margie didn't know what to say after Eve's strange comments about Sandeep. Eve had a new interesting topic for Margie's ringing ears.

"Your mother, Margaret, did not like me when I lived here." Margie was surprised with the odd and quick change in the subject at hand. To move from Sandeep's godliness to Miss Margaret's feeling toward Miss Eve was very disturbing to Margie. She would not be afraid.

"Perhaps you are mistaken. My mother has always liked everybody. That's one of her serious faults as far as I'm concerned. I actually wish she did dislike someone. It seems unnatural to me to like everybody; don't you think? It just doesn't seem real to see good in everybody, now does it?" Eve smiled again. She liked Margie's open and brave reply.

"Well, I assure you there was a time when your dear mother didn't like everyone, especially me." Margie wouldn't accept Eve's belief. "If mother didn't like you, that was a long time ago. She'd probably have no bad feelings toward you now. I'm sure of it." Eve liked the way Margie defended her mother to a stranger.

"Perhaps you're right. Maybe we'll see if what you say is true before we leave. That would be interesting to see, wouldn't it? Which of us is right. I have a sure feeling you like being right." Margie didn't hesitate with her part of the aggressive conversation.

"I love being right, who doesn't? Don't you?" Eve smiled again.

"Yes, I do. Very much so." Eve looked at Mr. King. "John, I do like this young lady. Please tell her that at one time I was in love with her father and her mother hated me because I tried to steal him away from her, so she will see she is quite wrong. Her mother will never be my friend, but you know I will never blame her at all." Margie's throat went dry and her stomach burned. She looked at Mr. King for help that wasn't coming. He could see her struggle, but he had to follow Eve's lead. "She's telling you the truth, but I'm not sure why. It is true there has been bad blood between Eve and your mother, but I have to agree with you. That was a long time ago. And I must say with all due respect, Miss Margaret is probably not troubled by the past." Eve never took her eyes off Margie.

"Oh John, you are such a dear. Forgive me if I have upset you or the young lady. Sometimes I am just too outspoken for my own good or anyone else's for that matter. Both of you please forgive me. I am your guest here and I should have kept my feelings from the past out of this pleasant conversation. Just forget I ever said anything and let's just start fresh." Eve went back to her braiding duties.

Margie was stunned. What she thought was brave curiosity had opened a strange door of unwanted information she didn't need to hear. She wanted to run away from the nasty woman dressed in black sheer, showing her body to the men on the porch, or any other passer-by. Margie knew Eve was sinisterly evil and too much for Margie's twenty-two years of sheltered living to handle. Miss Margaret's oldest daughter was sorry she had been so brazen when she crossed the street to Mr. King's porch. She knew she had to retreat and lick her wounds.

"I didn't mean to interrupt your day. I guess my curiosity got the best of me. I hope you enjoy your visit to Mayport. Good day Mr. King." Margie nodded and Mr. King nodded back with a half-smile and a look of "I'm sorry," in his eyes. Margie turned to walk away. Eve was not finished with her first of many Mayport victims.

"You do know that old saying about what curiosity did to the cat? There are many dead curious cats in this world." Margie didn't look back or reply. She just wanted to get far away from the evil woman who was staying at Mr. John King's haunted house.

When Margie turned to escape Eve's troubling words, her sister Sofia had crossed the street and was walking up to the porch. When she realized Margie was talking to Mr. King and the strangers, she decided it was safe to join her sister. "Sofia, what are you doing here?" It was easy for Sofia to see Margie was upset and didn't want her there. Mr. King interrupted their meeting.

"Well, if it isn't the youngest of the family, Sofia. Two sisters in the same day. I haven't had this many visitors during the day in quite awhile. How are you?" Sofia looked at Sandeep, she couldn't help it. He looked directly into her beautiful blue eyes. She was unable to respond to Mr. King 's "How are you,"question. Sofia saw nothing but the soldier saint's black eyes. Margie looked at Sofia, then at Sandeep.

Sandeep surprised everyone on the porch when he stood up from the wicker chair. His hair fell down around his shoulders and onto the floor. Eve was the most surprised because he walked away from her as she was holding his hair in her hands. Sandeep walked to the edge of the porch and stood next to the railing, continuing his stare with Sofia. Eve didn't move, she only watched her companion like the others. Mr. King was silent and concerned about Sandeep's strange and sudden movement. He didn't want the Indian to scare the young sisters, but he remained in his wicker chair. It was unusual for Mr. King not to want somebody scared, this was daytime and this was different.

Sandeep left the railing and walked down the stairs until he stood in front of Sofia. Margie backed away from the stairs as he came toward her and her little sister. Sofia did not move as Sandeep approached her. In a few seconds he was only a foot away from her. Margie was afraid but could do nothing.

The Indian took Sofia's right hand into his huge right hand. Sofia did nothing to stop him, she only continued her stare. He kissed the back of her small snow white hand like a French gentleman. The unfastened braids from his hair and the life-time growth covered his shoulders, back, butt, legs and some of the ground. It was as if he wore the cape of a super hero.

Then the strangest thing of all took place. All eyes watched in amazement as Sandeep dropped to one knee, causing his hair to cover even more of the ground at Sofia's feet. He bowed his head to Sofia in a humble and respectful fashion. For the first time since the two strange visitors had arrived, Sandeep spoke. His voice had no god-like thunder. In fact it was mild and smoother than most other men's. Mr. King was surprised when he heard the voice of a normal man. "I am honored to be here with you. Thank you for allowing this moment." Margie looked from Sofia to Sandeep to Eve and back to Sofia. She could tell Eve was not sure what was happening either. Sandeep stood up and bowed to Sofia as if she was royalty. As Sandeep's head dropped, Sofia added to the surprised faces around them.

"I am proud to be here with you, too. Thank you for your kindness." Sandeep lifted his head.

"I am Sandeep Singh. As the good Mr. King will tell you, I am not from around here." Sofia smiled. The others couldn't believe the conversation they were hearing. Sandeep turned to Margie. Her eyes widened. "You must be proud of your younger sister. She is a true gift to the world. If she was in my country she would be showered with gifts of gold and jewels. I know you are most proud." Margie was stunned and had no reply. Sandeep ended the one sided conversation. "I must return to my duties and the lady, Eve. I am a better Punjabi because our eyes have met. Thank you." Sandeep turned and walked back up the stairs. He returned to the chair where Eve was still standing. He looked into Eve's questioning eyes. He had his back to the others and whispered to her. "The child is the purest of the pure; complete goodness. She walks with God, but does not know it. She is in the wrong place; the wrong world. She will not be protected much longer. I can only pledge myself to one and that is you. There will be no one to save her from this place. She is from another time. How she got here, I have no answer. At the time you choose to release me or at the time of your death, I will devote myself to this child. I will honor my promise to you, but I am bound to tell you my thoughts. I'm sorry about the braids falling. I know it is difficult to prepare my hair." Sandeep sat in the wicker chair with his back to Eve. She hated the young beautiful woman who had taken the attention of her soldier, lover, saint.

Sandeep was surprised when he turned around and the two sisters were gone. He didn't change his facial expression, but he did look across the street and saw Margie and Sofia arm-in-arm, walking away quickly. In fact, Margie was actually pulling on Sofia and making her keep walking. Mr. King noticed Sandeep's interest and visual search. "They just took off while you were talking to Eve. You kinda come out your shell there, didn't ya boy? I didn't know ya could even talk. I thought maybe ya didn't speak the language; you bein' from another country and all. I'm glad to know you can understand what's bein' said. It makes me feel a whole lot better, I can tell ya that much. I think ya scared them two girls pretty good. They ain't used to people like you two. Eve scares Margie the oldest and then you kneel down in front of Sofia like ya did. Hell, you two are sendin' out some real mixed messages here, ain't ya?" Sandeep heard only one thing Mr. King said, and that was Sofia's name. Sandeep surprised his host again. "My path of life has never crossed such as Sofia. I was compelled to acknowledge her." Mr. King looked in the direction of Miss Margaret's store. "Well, I'll be damned."

Margie held on to Sofia's arm as they walked past the store and in the direction of Jason's house. When they were out of sight of the three porch dwellers, Margie pulled Sofia behind Mike Rady's gill net boat. "Are you alright? What was he doing to you? I'm scared." Sofia was calm.

"I'm not sure what happened, but I don't think he was trying to scare us or hurt me. He seemed to like us." Margie thought Sofia's statement was a drastic understatement.

"Oh really? And when did you think he liked you, when he fell to his knees and kissed your hand or was it when he thanked you for being there? He seemed to like you a bunch, don't you think? I didn't know what he was going to do next. I was scared." Sofia kept her calm smile.

"I thought we were not going to be scared anymore, remember?"

"You didn't hear that awful woman talk to me. If he's so nice why is he with that woman?"

Sofia didn't understand. "She didn't say anything to me. What did she say to you?" Margie was ready.

"She said our mother hated her when she used to live here and that she was in love with our father and tried to take him away from Mother. She said Mother would still hate her today."

"What a rude thing to say to a stranger." Margie couldn't take Sofia's calm reaction to the warrior priest.

"Sofia, we need to tell Mama about this woman and man. This can't be a secret. This is all too crazy." Sofia nodded and agreed.

"Do you want to go home now and tell her what happened or do we go see Jason's son first?"

Margie had forgotten their intended mission before her curiosity interfered with her plans.

"Yes, let's go see the baby, then we'll tell Mother."

The boat was ready. Chichemo and Bosco would stay on the boat until that night and be ready when Jason and Hawk arrived for their first attempt at shrimping since Jason returned. Mr. Leek had come out of the fish house and sat on the dock talking to Jason about Jessie's sad death, the baby and Jason's adventure at the Giant's Motel.

"My friend, is your life always going to be full of unusual things and so much sadness. You have lived as full a life as any hundred year old man. Each time happiness appears, something takes it away from you. I hope and pray it all can calm down for you, so you and Billy will be able to have the life you deserve. I'll pray for you both."

Jason knew Mr. Leek would never talk about that night on the sand hill when Mr. Leek killed Jake to save Jessie's life. With Jessie gone, only Jason and Mr. Leek knew what happened that awful night. It was as if it never happened. They both knew no one else would ever know they had killed and buried Jake, the Mayport phantom vampire, under the oak tree.

Beth, the Werewolf Girl, had driven through the city of Jacksonville, Florida without the other drivers on the road paying her any attention. She wore, what could be considered a disguise. She tied a scarf around her neck and head. A straw hat covered her head and the top of the scarf. A pair of bug eyed sunglasses completed her attempt to hide her strange and disturbing appearance. Her decision to drive during the day had caused no real problems. One time when she stopped at a red light, two young boys in the back seat of a station wagon looked at her and realized she looked strange. Beth saw them looking and talking about her so she pulled down her glasses to display her unnatural yellow eyes and smiled, exposing her long canine teeth. The boys yelled at the driver, but he must have thought the boys were playing because he did not look back or turn the car around. Boys will be boys. Beth kept moving.

She passed a place called Beach Road Chicken and almost stopped when she smelled the fried chicken cooking. There was a long line of people waiting their turn to eat. Beth wished she could stand in that line for some of that chicken. She was only about a half hour's ride from her destination of Mayport, Florida, U.S.A. She just didn't know it.

The "We're on vacation" signs were up and in place at the Giant's Motel. The bus had been cleaned, serviced, packed and was ready to roll. Norman Bates, the Skeleton Man, was in the driver's seat and had just pulled the arm lever to open the door for his passengers. He wore a chauffeur's hat and driving gloves covered his bony hands. He was a sport. Black Beulla, the Fat Lady, was the first to come aboard. "Your destination ma'am?" Beulla would always play the game. Her sense of humor was as big as her, down from a thousand pound, six hundred pound body. "Mayport, Florida, sir, and do drive carefully. I'm much too delicate for a bumpy ride."

"I'll do my best ma'am. Watch your step there." All the passengers would have a single seat to themselves, but Beulla would be the only one who needed one. Helga, the Amazon Warrior, was next to climb the bus stairs. "Watch your head there, lady." Helga ducked low so she would not hit her head as she entered the bus.

"Thank you kind sir. I don't think of that sometimes." Helga's six feet six inch muscular female frame moved past Norman and found the seat she wanted. Tom Thumb, the World's Smallest Man, was next.

Norman knew the little pigmy would be near Helga. Tom put his hands on the bottom step of the bus and pulled himself up to chest level and then threw one of his short legs up onto the same step. He rolled up onto his stomach and stood on the first step. Norman watched the tiny man's struggle. Tom did the same pull up, leg up and stomach roll for each of the steps, until he stood on the floor of the bus next to Norman in the driver's seat. Norman couldn't resist.

"Watch your head." Tom looked at the sarcastic driver. He couldn't resist either.

"Kiss my ass." Tom walked slowly back to the seat were Helga was sitting. He was fatigued from climbing the stairs. It took a great effort for him to climb into the seat with her, but she knew not to help him. When he was in the seat, he lay his little head on her big thigh and she rubbed his little head while he rested.

Ana Kara stepped up onto the bus steps with her cleavage leading the way. Norman smiled and never took his eyes off the line of flesh separating her full, firm and tanned breasts. He was too preoccupied to give his usual bus driver's greeting. Ana Kara broke the breastful hold she had on the Skeleton Man. "Love the hat, Norman." He was lost in his own titty heaven.

"I love 'em, too. I mean thanks." Ana smiled and passed by Norman, walking to one of the last seats at the back of the bus. Helga nodded at Ana as she passed, but Tom didn't open his eyes. He was truly physically spent. Beulla touched Ana's arm as she walked by the Fat Lady's seat.

"Hey, sugah. You look so pretty all the time. I do wish I had your figure. You need to be in the movies, like in "Gone With the Wind." You'd make a real southern beauty if we could get you to say y'all more often." Norman was watching Ana walk down the aisle in the rear view mirror. There was movement near the bus door and it took his attention from Ana. He looked at his next passenger and loved what he saw.

Ming and Ling, the Siamese Twins and singing sensations, were making their way to the bus. Ming was walking and Ling was riding on her sister's back. Their faces were identical but Ling was smaller than the stronger Ming. They were attached at the center of their backs and Ling looked like a hiker's knapsack on Ming's back and shoulders. Norman jumped off the bus to assist and protect the Twins as Ming made her first careful step onto the bottom step. Norman stood behind them facing Ling. She was much smaller than her sister and her feet did not touch the ground. Norman's position behind them allowed him to keep Ming from falling backwards if she lost her balance. He would not allow them to get hurt.

Ming took the first step with Ling hanging behind her. Norman stepped up as close as he could get to the suspended Ling. Norman smiled at her beautiful face and she smiled back. Then Ling puckered her red lips and stuck them outward in Norman's direction, making a kissing sound. Norman smiled and did the same, pressing his puckered lips against hers. Ming took a second careful step and the kiss ended. Ming realized the activity behind her. "Oh, thank you both velly much. I do all work, you get all kissy, kissy. Same ting all time. I work, she kissy. Somebody kissy me soon." She took the last step onto the bus and moved only one seat down the aisle. Ming maneuvered Ling slowly and gently so she would not hit the metal on the seat. They sat sideways in the seat with Ling facing the window and Ming facing the isle. Ming had a request, or better yet, a command. "Somebody need kissy me, now." Norman moved to Ming and they both puckered and kissed the same way he and Ling had done on the steps. Ming smiled at Norman. "O.K., we both get kissy." Ling smiled, too.

Little Tom lifted his head up off Helga's thigh as Norman stood up after the kiss. "Hey Norman, I need kissy, too. Whata ya say? How 'bout one more pucker, you pile a spare ribs." Helga pulled Tom's little head back down as Norman turned to respond to the mean little pigmy's insult. "Don't pay him any attention, he's just nervous about the trip. He's probably worried about getting bus sick. You know how he suffers from motion sickness. He doesn't mean to be mean." Tom's head popped up again.

"Will everybody stop talkin' for me. I ain't nervous 'bout anything. I ain't gettin' sick. I do mean what I say and he is a rack of bones." Norman waved Tom off and took his place back in the driver's seat. He decided not to allow the mean little man to ruin the excitement of the trip and the two wonderful kisses he had been privileged to get.

Big Bob was the last of the family to climb aboard the Gibsonton to Mayport Express. He had completed his final lock down of the motel and hung the informational signs for the potential customers and the regular lounge crowd. He hoped they were doing the right thing, but he was just as excited as the others. Big Bob knew it was time for a new adventure for his family and he knew they had to find and help Beth during her time of need. The entire family was on the Barnum and Bailey Circus tour bus. Norman fired up the twenty year old engine as Big Bob found him a seat with the others. Norman turned the dial over his head and the destination display sign flipped over and read Mayport. The strange residents of the Giant's Motel were officially on their vacation and on their way to Mayport, Florida, U.S.A.

Mary C.'s House

CHAPTER THREE

Margie and Sofia found themselves standing in front of Jason's house. They were only a few steps from the porch. Sofia put her foot on the bottom step and stopped her forward motion when she heard a voice. It was Mary C. She stepped out of the house. "Oh my goodness! Look who's here. Sofia, how are you? Ain't you as pretty as ever. Even prettier than the last time you were here." Mary C. hugged Sofia and looked past her at Margie. "And this is Margie, right? Welcome, both of you. Please come in or we can sit out here on the porch." Mary C. hadn't given either of the sisters anytime to say hello or say anything for that matter. Margie didn't care if they talked or not, she just wanted to see the baby. Mary C. had more.

"Did ya see Jason yet? He's back home, ya know." Mary C. finally gave someone else a chance to talk and Sofia took it. "Yes ma'am, I saw him yesterday. I saw the baby, too."

Mary C. had a surprised look on her face. "Really. He didn't tell me that. I guess he's been so excited he didn't think to mention that to me. I gotta get on that boy." Sofia had more, too. "I told Margie how beautiful the baby was and she just had to come see for herself. Babies are fun to see, aren't they?" Sofia did have a way about her. Mary C. liked the way the youngest sister talked. Mary C.'s next comment surprised the sisters, but it was typical Mary C.

"He's a pretty little thing, but he's pretty spooky, too." Both sisters realized in an instant that Mary C. was not going to be your everyday grandmother. Margie couldn't believe her ears but she was intrigued. Her curiosity was in full gear. "Why do you think he's spooky?" Mary C. couldn't wait to tell someone what she thought.

"Well, first of all, his eyes. They belong to his mother, that Jessie girl. I don't mean they look like her eyes. I think they are her eyes. They left her and jumped into his head. If we dug her body up right now, I'll be willin' to bet she ain't got no eyes." A chill ran down Sofia's spine. Margie took a deep breath. She didn't like what she had just heard, but she refused to react or be afraid. Sofia's eyes did meet Margie's for a moment as much as to ask, " I don't believe she said that, do you?" The sisters shared the thought mentally and not out loud.

Margie wanted to see the baby even more now that Mary C. had given her strange and twisted opinion. Margie had to speak up. "May we see him?"

"Sure you can. Come on in. He's in my bedroom." The two sisters followed Mary C. into the house and walked with her to her bedroom. Billy was once again surrounded by pillows to keep him from falling off the bed.

The baby was wide awake and seemed to be staring at the ceiling of the room. Mary C. spoke first. "He's been a good baby so far. He lays there and looks around at everything. He moves his arms and legs a lot, but he don't cry much. Now that I think of it, he ain't cried at all. Now, ain't that another spooky thing?" Mary C.'s strange choice of words was unsettling for the two visiting sisters. Margie stepped closer to the bed and leaned over toward him, bringing her face close to his.

He was the most beautiful baby Margie had ever seen. She was silent as she looked into Billy's big deep green eyes. Margie reached out her hand and touched his smooth and naturally tanned skin. Billy was perfect and Margie knew she was seeing an oak baby for the first time. She had no doubt it was all true. She broke the silence of the room. "He is the most beautiful baby I've ever seen. His eyes are so big and beautiful." Mary C. interrupted Margie's moment of praise.

"They're so big 'cause they ain't baby eyes. They're grown up eyes. They're her eyes I tell ya. And she's watchin' us." Neither sister liked Mary C.'s eery comments about the beautiful baby before them. It was so unnatural to the two loving sisters for the grandmother of the baby to be saying such things. But, they also knew Mary C. would not be a normal grandparent. She was different and there would always be controversy around her. Mary C. had more ungrandmotherly thoughts for the two good neighbors to hear. "One good thing is that he does have Jason's blood in him, too. If that girl wasn't lyin' 'bout Jason bein' the daddy. He seems to believe it so I 'spose he was with her in that way." Margie rubbed Billy's little arms as Mary C.'s next comment opened the door Margie had been waiting for.

"Jason hasn't ever said it but I have a feeling she got him up to that tree and that's when it happened. Bobby used to tell me about folks breeding under that tree to have special babies, but I never put much stock in all that mumbo-jumbo. But, Jason liked that girl and I'll be willin' to bet that's where it happened." Sofia's eyes popped open wide when Margie took Mary C.'s lead.

"Then you don't believe there are oak babies?" Mary C. shook her head.

"Not at all. Never have. Didn't even know much about it 'til Bobby told me." Margie had more.

"You do know everybody thinks Jason is an oak baby, don't you?" Sofia looked at Margie. Mary C. smiled. "I've heard that, but if that was true I would have had to be with his daddy under that tree and I ain't never been under that ugly tree." Sofia didn't like it, but her big sister had more. "If you did do it there, you couldn't tell anyone, anyway. You would have to deny it or Jason would lose the power. You must realize how strong Jason is and that's why people think he's an oak baby. They think the tree protects him. He seems to always win and he is always the last one standing. Maybe you know that his strength comes from the tree and you can't tell it." Mary C. smiled. "If that's what you and the other folks want to think, then that's up to you. I can't convince you otherwise. You want it to be true, so you make it true. I will admit Jason's different and he has a certain way about him, but it ain't from that tree 'cause his mama ain't layed under no tree with no man. It's from bein' who he is. I know that sounds simple to you and most people would say I'm simple for sayin' it, but all the things that have happened to him makes him Jason. Nobody can be like him unless they have lived the same life and taken on the same hardships and victories. It ain't got nothin' to do with that tree. I don't believe in things like that. Now, I do think this baby's mother could have been a witch and she put a spell on my Jason." Sofia looked at Margie and Margie looked at Sofia. Mary C. was the most incredible contradiction on the face of the earth. She was as rare as they come and the two sisters were completely enthralled with her words and anticipating the next gem of absurd wisdom.

"You see, you like Jason. You like the mystery of that tree. Maybe you've become one of the believers. It would be much better for you if the magic was true." Sofia had a dream flash back in her head and saw those magic hands coming up out of the white sand. Margie remembered her last attempt to breed under the tree with Jimmy Johnston. Mary C. had no idea the sisters mentally left the room so she continued. "Just think if this baby is one of the oak babies and the power of that tree runs in his body. What does that mean? What do we do? What does the baby do?" It was three question time, but Margie was ready.

"It means he would be like Jason. It means he would be better than others. It means he will show others the way to be. It means he would touch many hearts and the world would be better because he is here." Nothing really ever moved Mary C.

"My goodness. That boy of mine does move a woman's heart. I don't know where he got that talent from, the damn tree I guess." Mary C. looked at Sofia, then at Margie, then in her own way changed the subject. "I'm not sure why these things seem to happen to Jason. I want to help him with this baby, but folks will start talkin' soon enough and even though I ain't never cared what people said about me, I don't know how things will be with this baby and I don't want things said. The word's spreadin' fast and I know trouble's comin'. I just don't know when." Sofia hadn't said anything until then. "Whenever you need someone to help with Billy, please call me and let me know. I would love to help you and take care of him sometimes. I'm sure this is difficult for you, having to take care of a little baby unexpectedly. It would be a shock for anyone. With Jason working, you'll need some help. Please don't hesitate to call me." Mary C. sure liked the young beautiful blue-eyed blonde girl and the way she talked.

"That's very nice of you and I'd like that. Did ya'll notice how perfect his little head is?" Mary C. was as big a mystery as the tree.

The Barnum and Bailey Circus Tour bus was rolling north on Highway U.S. 41. The sign to the left read, Ybor City. Helga broke the silence on the bus. "I love to eat at the Columbia Restaurant over there. We haven't been there in a long time." Little Tom opened his eyes. Helga remembered. "The last time we were there was the first night Jason and Jessie stayed at the Motel." Big Bob joined in the memory moment. "That's right. They were the nicest couple. She was scared and wide-eyed and he was brave and ready to see the world. I do love the way that boy shakes hands." Beulla couldn't help but add her thoughts. "When I first saw them at the breakfast table I knew they were something special. She was a real natural beauty and he was my handsome Rhett Butler talkin' southern gentleman. 'Yes ma'am' just rolled off of his lips." Little Tom's head popped up from his comfortable position with Helga. "Damn, woman, you gettin' a little excited there ain't ya? Course you don't do nothin' little now, do ya?" Beulla turned toward the little sarcastic pigmy. " Don't start with me, Tom. I haven't said anything to you and I'd like to enjoy this trip without us being at each other's throat. You always have some smart ass remark to make to me. Can't we just have a truce until this thing is over?" The entire bus was silent after Beulla's plea. They all looked at Tom, waiting for his reply. Tom knew all eyes were on him. Even Norman kept one eye on the road and the other eye on Tom through the rear view mirror. Beulla had made a serious challenge to her arch enemy and he knew he had to respond. "Damn woman, lighten up, will ya? Don't be so serious. You act like you ain't been part of the bickerin'. It's a truce, hell yes." Tom lay his embarrassed head back down on Helga's thigh. Bob smiled at Beulla in an acknowledgment of the stand she had made. The bus was silent for a number of miles. Everyone seemed to be enjoying the scenery and the freedom of the road.

Margie and Sofia could not bring themselves to leave Mary C. and Billy. They were completely mesmerized by the baby, but more so with the unusual statements and conversations they were having with Mary C. The two sheltered sisters had never heard the likes of Mary C.

"If his mama was half black and half white. And his daddy's all white. What does that make him? I know he's mixed, but how mixed is he. Just how white is he?" Sofia looked at Margie. Mary C. went on. "That girl did have white blood in her, you could see that. And we know Jason has all white blood in him. So does he have most white blood and a little black blood? I just don't know how to figure such a thing." Sofia had to share her thoughts.

"Miss Mary C., he's just a beautiful baby, with wonderful blood in his veins. He's Jason's son and your grandson and nothing can change that or make it wrong. Just think how much fun you'll have watching him grow and the things Jason will teach him. This is a wonderful thing. I'm sad his mother had to die." Mary C. tried to make a reasonable reply.

"I don't know about all that, but ain't his head a perfect shape?"

Beth stopped Big Bob's truck on a ramp, leading to a sandy beach. The Atlantic Ocean was directly in front of her. To continue driving would have put her and the truck into the Atlantic surf. She had to be careful not to be seen. She knew her appearance would cause a major problem and disturbance. Beth hadn't realized she missed the Mayport turn off to U.S. Highway A1A until she saw the ocean. Then she new she had gone too far. She had not seen a sign with directions to Mayport. Beth took the map out again and it didn't take her but a few seconds to see how she had to backtrack in order to head in the right direction. Beth fixed the scarf and straw hat and put the sunglasses back on. She was as disguised as a Werewolf Girl could be.

The ocean tide was at its lowest level and there was over sixty yards of open solid sandy beach. Beth drove off the ramp and turned north. She had heard Jason talk about the beach near Mayport and she knew from the map it would be in that direction. She was creating her own destiny.

Mary C., Margie and Sofia were all three sitting at Mary C.'s kitchen table. The neighborly sisters had been visiting for over two hours. Mary C. had said some wild things to the two young girls. They had never talked at length to such a strange woman. They had never seen such strength and such ignorance in a single personality. Mary C. was easy to like and easy to fear. She was a true contradiction on the earth, or at least in Mayport. Margie stood up and took the three empty coffee cups Mary C. had made for them to the kitchen sink.

"I'll get those. You're my guests. Just leave those alone." Margie put the cups in the sink.

"I can wash these. We do it all the time. Where does it say visitors can't help with the clean up. Guests can clean up, too." Mary C. smiled

"You girls are so nice all the time. Your mama sure has done good with you girls." Margie smiled, too and looked out the small window above the kitchen sink. Neither Mary C. nor Sofia could see the blood leave Margie's face. They didn't know she was as white as one of Mr. King's ghosts.

Margie's voice quivered when she was able to speak. "Miss Mary C., I think you need to look out this window." Mary C. and Sofia knew right away Margie was serious and something was very wrong. Mary C. moved to the sink, stood next to Margie, and looked out the small window. "Oh my God!" Mary C. left the window and ran out of the kitchen. Sofia took Mary C.'s place next to Margie and took her turn looking out the small window. "Dear God, what are they doing?"

"I don't know, but I'm scared." Margie had been scared two

Mary C.'s Cannon

times within a two hour period. Her vow, not to be afraid, was definitely being challenged. Both girls turned from the window when they saw Mary C. move past the kitchen area. She was carrying a big double barreled shotgun. Margie saw the gun first. "Oh my god! She's got a gun!" Margie followed Mary C. and Sofia followed Margie. Mary C. pushed open the screen door leading to the porch and stepped out of her house. The girls followed.

She raised the gun as she stepped onto the porch. Mary C. and the two sisters were greeted by at least fifty black residents of Mayport. It looked like every black man, woman and child who lived in the small town was standing in her front yard. Mary C. raised the gun to her shoulder and aimed the two big barrels at the crowd. "I don't know what's goin' on here, but if anyone of you comes any closer to my house, I'm gonna empty this cannon in the next one of y'all stupid enough to move." The crowd went silent and they stopped moving forward. The two sisters stood behind Mary C. They couldn't believe they were standing behind the wild Mary C. and there was a strong possibility she was going to shoot somebody. One of the bigger men became the first talker from the crowd. "Miss Mary C., they call me Truck. I know your son, Jason. We didn't mean to scare you and we mean you no harm. I didn't know this many would come. I know it looks bad, but like I said, we don't mean you no harm." Mary C. held the gun in place.

"What would you think if a mob of white folks showed up in your front yard with no invite at all? You'd be gettin' a gun, too."

"Yes ma'am, you're right. I really didn't know this many would come. We're just all too excited. Sad, but excited. We're sad 'cause we lost a real treasure when Jessie had to leave us, but we're excited and happy 'cause of what was left behind. We just want to know if it's true, that's all." Mary C. kept the gun in place.

"What the hell are you talkin' 'bout boy? I want all of y'all off my property or I'm gonna start clearin' the yard myself." The young black talker made one more effort.

"Miss Mary C., we just want to see the baby. We have to know if he's really from the oak or not." Margie and Sofia couldn't believe they were part of what was going on around them. When it came to Mary C. and Jason, the adventure never ended. Mary C. didn't like the black man's words. "You ain't gonna see nothin' but the flash of this blaster if you don't get movin'. You are makin' a big mistake if you think I won't use this thing. Y'all are trespassing on my property and I've asked you to leave. Now, I am considering your actions as a serious threat against me and my friends. I will shoot you if you are not leaving in the next five seconds. One....Two..." The crowd started to back up and move away from the house. "Three..." Truck had not started moving like the others. "Four...." Mary C. pointed both barrels at the talker.

"You are a fool, Mister....Five." Mary C. pulled the trigger of the shotgun, sending at least a hundred round metal BBs into the air directly at Truck and the retreating crowd. When the gun exploded Sofia and Margie both screamed and a number of the crowd screamed, too, as they ran. It was small bird shot and the majority of the pellets hit the ground near Truck, but at least a dozen or so hit him in his legs, tearing holes in his dungarees and penetrating his skin. He knew he was hit, but didn't fall to the ground. He backed away, hoping Mary C. would not empty the other barrel. "Please don't shoot anymore, we're leavin'." Truck began to limp away with the moving crowd. Margie and Sofia were both in shock. They had just watched Mary C. shoot another human being and perhaps she hit others.

As a few of the male members of the crowd moved to assist

Truck, a horn sounded from the road. It was Jason and Hawk. Jason was blowing the horn on Uncle Bobby's truck to move the crowd so he could drive closer to the house. The crowd opened a pathway as Jason drove slowly through the intruders. Hawk looked at the faces in the crowd. "What the hell's goin' on here? This don't look good. Oh my God. Your mother's got a gun." Jason jumped out of the truck, leaving the door open. He moved quickly through the remaining crowd, making his way to the porch. He ran up the steps and took the gun from his mother. "Mama, what are you doin'?"

"I'm protecting me, these girls and your baby. What the hell does it look like? You don't think it's a little strange that every nigger in town's standing in our front yard? We ain't havin' no barbecue, ya know? They came for the baby." Hawk joined Jason at the steps. Jason handed Hawk the gun and turned to the crowd. He saw Truck sitting on the ground with a woman tending to his wounds. Jason moved quickly to the bleeding young man.

"You're hurt. Is that you, Truck?" The young man grimaced in pain as he nodded his head.

"We come to see the baby. I'm sorry so many came. It just got out of hand. I guess we scared your mama." The woman was dabbing the blood spots on Truck's legs with a cloth as he talked.

"Mama shot you?" Truck nodded his head again.

"I think she was tryin' to scare us. Once she said she was gonna shoot, she couldn't back down. We shoulda been smarter 'bout comin' over here. We all got too excited about the baby and didn't think what it would look like when we marched into your yard. I'm sorry 'bout Jessie. I know she wanted to be with you. We was all happy when ya'll left this place. I was worried Jake had tried to find y'all, but I guess if he did go after y'all he didn't find ya. He must still be lookin', cause ain't nobody seen him since that night y'all left. He's probably crazy enough to keep lookin'. He'll be back one day." Jason didn't respond to Truck's statement, but he knew for a fact, Jake wouldn't be coming back.

Jason was on one knee next to the young black man. Truck wanted Jason to know more. "You know how a lot of folks feel about the tree. I ain't sure about it myself, now that I know more about life, but when you are taught something as a child it's hard to let it go. The tree has such a hold on us and we still have certain thoughts, just in case it is all true. What if oak babies are real and this boy of your's and Jessie's is the purest one ever? This could be a great day in our time." Jason knew he had the same thoughts, but didn't know what to do. Truck went on.

"I don't think there have been many true oak babies. I think folks have done the breeding with no truth in their hearts. Maybe there's a true one once every fifty or a hundred years. And just what if this is one in our time and it's your son? You have to know." Jason was excited and moved by Truck's words

"What do we have to do? How will we know?" Truck was excited, too, at Jason's question. He struggled to his feet.

"We have one true believer with us and another who has certain ability and can help us." Truck limped toward the porch. Mary C. saw Truck's movement and she tried to take the shotgun back from Hawk. Hawk held it tight and would not release it to her.

"If you ain't gonna give me that thing, you shoot the son-of-a-bitch." Jason stepped to the porch with Truck behind him.

"Mama, stop please. Nobody else is gonna get shot. Not today." Mary C. was mad.

"They want the baby, can't you see that? They're probably gonna cook 'em and eat 'em. They think he's from the tree. I don't know how that girl got you up there to do this thing. I just don't know."

"Mama stop! Hawk, please take her in the house." Jason was surprised to see the two silent and in shock sisters, Margie and Sofia. Hawk maneuvered Mary C. toward the door.

"I want them out of my yard. What the hell is wrong with all y'all. They can't be in my yard like this. Somebody shoot another one maybe they'll get the message." Mary C. could be heard as Hawk moved her into the house. Jason looked at the two sisters.

"One of y'all get Billy." Truck's eyes widened and a chill ran through his aching body. He couldn't believe his ears. Sofia's eyes widened, too, as she looked at Jason. "Bring him out here?"

"Yes. Bring him to me." Margie and Sofia, both followed Jason's request and entered the house. Hawk had moved Mary C. to the living room couch. She was boiling mad and watched the crowd of unwanted visitors through the window.

"What kinda men are you two, anyway? This ain't bein' handled right and you know it. That girl's done somethin' to Jason when they was gone together. She was a witch, I tell ya, a voodoo witch. They gonna do somethin' to that baby. You mark my words." Hawk had to respond.

"We have to trust Jason in this. It is his son and his decision." Mary C. was furious now.

"He ain't thinkin' right, can't you see that? Hell, you ain't thinkin' right. It's voodoo I tell ya. I seen it before. They ain't rubbin' no chicken feet on my grandson." Hawk knew how serious the situation was and that a man had been shot, but he almost smiled at Mary C.'s chicken feet protest.

Mary C. heard a noise behind her and turned to see Sofia carrying Billy toward the door of the house. "Oh my God! What are you doin'?" She moved toward Sofia, but Hawk stopped her.

"I'm sorry Miss Mary C. Jason told me to bring Billy to him." Sofia didn't know what to do as Mary C. made her plea.

"Please don't take him out there. This is crazy and something is seriously wrong. You must feel it, too. Jason's not himself. He's under a voodoo spell." Sofia had a strange dilemma on her delicate hands. Jason ended Sofia's moment of indecision when he walked into the house and took Billy from her. Jason didn't say a word as he took the baby. Mary C., Hawk, Sofia and Margie followed Jason out onto the front porch.

The crowd began talking when Jason stepped onto the porch holding the child. Truck had moved to the bottom of the steps. Jason stood above him. "What happens now?" The crowd went silent as Truck turned toward them. There was movement in the crowd, but no talking. A big heavy black woman stepped forward from the crowd and began walking toward the porch. She reminded Jason of Miss Bell, the woman who Jessie thought was her real mother for most of her life.

The woman wore a big simple straight cut, flowered dress with sleeves clinging tightly to two fat arms. Her eyes were big and round with her cheeks puffed up under those eyes. Jason remembered thinking Miss Bell's head had to weigh at least a hundred pounds. This lady had a ninety pounder. She was barefoot and made deep footprints in the ground and soft grass as she walked toward the porch. When she stopped next to Truck there was more movement in the crowd as another woman emerged and walked toward the porch.

She was a tiny woman in contrast to the other. She was skinny and had eyes that sank deep into her skull. She reminded Jason of Norman Bates, the Skeleton Man, from the Giant's Motel. Her one outstanding feature was a large silk scarf that she had wrapped around her head. The wrapping was much larger than her head. It was extremely large for the size of her little head. It looked like a child had made a large paper mache replica of planet Earth and placed it on the woman's head. There was something under the wrapping besides her head and hair. Whatever it was must have been very light in weight, because the skinny little woman was able to walk easily and balance the huge round object on her head. She stopped next to Truck. Truck turned to Jason and introduced the two strange women. The big woman was first.

"This is Macadoo. She is the truest of the believers and she knows many things of the tree. She is Miss Bell's cousin and helped raise Jessie. She will know the child by his feet." The big black woman bowed to Jason.

"I am so sorry about the Lord takin' our Jessie. Sometimes He don't let many oak babies walk the earth at the same time. It's a chance they take." Everyone on the porch was quiet. Even Mary C. Truck made the second introduction.

"This is Voo Swar. She knows of the tree, as well. She does not claim to be a true believer because of her own religion, but she has special gifts and powers we need here today." The skinny woman looked at Jason.

"I will be able to feel if he is special or different. I have been able

to recognize the golden children when they needed to be found."
Mary C. couldn't stand there any longer.

"She's voodoo, can't y'all see that? She's got roots and leaves,
and God know what else, on her head. Don't ya'll know nothin'?"
Jason turned to his frustrated mother. Voo Swar had more.

"She's right about what I am. But, there will be no voodoo here
today; there is no need." Mary C. was beside herself.

"I can't believe you're gonna let this crazy nigger touch that
baby." Jason hated that word.

"Mama, you have to stop. Please. They will not hurt Billy."

"And you think you can guarantee that?"

"Yes ma'am I do."

"Well, you just remember what I've said here today when something awful happens."

Mary C. turned away and walked back into the house again. All
eyes were on Jason and Billy. Jason walked down the steps. Without
Mary C. and her gun the crowd was quick to move and try to re-
establish positions closer to the porch. Truck held up his hand to stop
the sudden movement of the excited crowd.

"Please don't come up here. It's scary enough for these folks to
have us all here. We don't have to add to their fears. I didn't know it
was going to get like this. Miss Mary C.'s right. If any of our yards
filled up with white folks with no invite, we'd be sayin' the Klan was
there and we'd be afraid too. So stand where you are and respect
Jason and the baby." All forward motion of the crowd stopped. Truck
turned to the two special women and Jason. Margie and Sofia had
been mesmerized by what was taking place around them. They knew
no one would believe the stories they would have to tell. Truck had a
question.

"Can we see the baby?" Jason pulled back the blanket that covered Billy's head as Truck, Macadoo and Voo Swar stepped closer to
the child. The women observed the child in silence, but Truck was
moved.

"Look at his eyes. He has Jessie's eyes. It's easy to think of her
when you look at him."

Margie, Sofia, Jason and Hawk all thought, "Don't say that to Mary C." Truck had more to add to the tension filled situation.

"Jason, if you don't mind, could you hold the baby up so the women can have a good look at him and the others will not have to come closer." Jason didn't know why, but he put both his hands under each side of Billy's arms and held the child up toward the two gifted observers.

Billy's little legs dangled under him as Macadoo stepped up and put the palms of both her hands against the bottoms of Billy's little feet. As Macadoo held her hands in place, Voo Swar placed her thumb on the child's navel and held it there.

"The navel is the center of man, where life begins. It may very well be the center of all things." Sofia and Margie could not believe their eyes and ears. All the spectators began walking forward for a better look at the non-voodoo oak tree baby ceremony. Voo Swar made a moaning noise deep in her throat as her thumb remained on the child's small navel. Her hand began to quiver slightly, but the others were quick to notice the movement. There was noise in the crowd. Macadoo closed her eyes as if to swoon from the contact with the baby's feet. With her eyes still closed, Macadoo was the first of the two to make an audible sound.

"Oh, my dear sweet Jesus. Thank you for lettin' me be here." Voo Swar joined in the thanks and praise, as her bony hand shook even harder.

"Praise and glory be." Jason continued holding Billy in both hands like he was presenting the new born king to the throng of subjects. It looked scary to Sofia and Margie, but they were too caught up in the moment to talk to each other about their strange feelings. They would do that later. Beads of sweat formed on Macadoo's forehead and swollen cheeks. Something was happening, but no one was sure what it was. Margie and Sofia were both locked into the mystique of the strange moment.

Hawk had his doubts about the true talents of the two women, with the quivering hands and praises to heaven. He didn't believe in the magic or voodoo that seemed to hover over Mayport.

Hawk had seen many things in his life and he had seen little evidence at the moment, or any past moment, that any of the world's superstitions had much substance. He knew folks liked to believe in the more mysterious side of life. It was more exciting that way. Two old black women touching a baby and shaking didn't prove much to Hawk. He would need much more than that.

Macadoo took her hands away from Billy's little feet, smiled at Jason, and turned to the waiting crowd. There was an instant silence in the yard. A silence of anticipation. Macadoo took a few steps toward the others and raised both her big arms above her big head as a gesture to the heavens above them.

"This child is a true acorn. He has the seed of the great tree. This child will never cry. He will have no reason to." It was strange to Jason, Hawk and the two sisters that the crowd remained silent after Macadoo's proclamation of the child's origin. The strange silence remained as Voo Swar took her trembling hand and thumb off Billy's navel. Like Macadoo, Voo Swar moved away from Jason and the child and walked toward the still quiet and waiting crowd. All eyes were glued to the Voodoo woman with the skinny hands and oversized head dress. She was not as dramatic as Macadoo.

"I do not know his destiny or what purpose he has. I do know he is a golden child and one of a kind among us. If you follow him, you will be better for it. If you protect him, you will be protected. I for one am glad he is with us. This child is the truth."

On Voo Swar's last word the silent crowd exploded with cheers, clapping and laughter. Macadoo and Voo Swar walked back into the crowd and left Mary C.'s front yard, followed by the excited Mayport black folks. Truck walked a few steps from Billy and Jason.

"Thank you for allowing this to happen. I know it took great strength and courage." Jason was still concerned with Truck's injuries.

"Let me take you to the doctor. Your leg looks bad." Truck replied, but kept walking away.

"I'll be alright. I'm sorry we scared Miss Mary C. We didn't think about that. I've been hit with stingers before. I'll be sore, but I'll live.

I don't think she was trying to kill me. She was scared and wanted to scare us, too. Tell her she did what she set out to do. We were plenty scared. Keep the child safe." Truck joined the excited crowd as they moved on away from the house and on down the road. They were gone and out of sight in a matter of a minute.

Sofia and Margie were sitting on the front porch swing in a state of shock at what they had witnessed. They couldn't wait to get to their other sisters, Susan and Peggy, and to Miss Margaret or whoever they could find to tell. Hawk walked into the house and Jason held Billy close to his chest as he joined the sisters at the swing.

"I never got the chance to say hello to you two and ask what are you doing here?" Margie was always the one with the quick answer.

"We came to see your son. Sofia told me how beautiful he was and I wanted to see him. We were having such a great time talking to your mother and being with Billy. Then they came up and you know the rest. This was pretty interesting , if you don't mind me saying so." Jason smiled at Margie's ability to simplify the situation.

"I guess interesting is as good a word as any. You're right it sure was interesting." Hawk's voice cut into the air as he walked back out of the house and joined the others on the porch.

"Mary C.'s locked in her bedroom and ain't takin' any visitors." Margie took Billy from Jason and held him against her in the swing. Sofia touched the child as she and Margie made the swing move by pushing their feet on the boarded floor of the porch. Hawk wanted his thoughts to be known.

"I don't want to offend anyone, but I don't think I believe in this oak baby stuff." Jason smiled.

"It is difficult to take it all in. I'm not sure either, but I keep thinking about the possibilities and it worries me to think I might overlook it all and it will be real." Hawk nodded.

"I guess anything is possible, but I just don't see it. I ain't been one for the superstitions of the world." Margie couldn't wait to join in.

"You do know that most of the myths and superstitions around the world are all based on some truth. And like you said, anything is possible. We should all keep an open mind. People don't like things they don't understand. It may not be all true, but something or somebody started this oak baby thing a long time ago and they did it for a reason, that's for sure." Jason sat down on the top step and leaned his shoulder against the porch railing. Sofia had been quiet while her sister had the porch floor, but now it was her turn.

"It would be wonderful to have a son that was special and different; a child blessed more than others in some way, with special talents, or powers. But, the truth of the matter, as we can know it, is that you have a beautiful and exceptional son. He is beautiful in every physical way, because that is all we can judge at this time. Time will show his abilities, intelligence, as well as his personality. What he becomes depends on what he is taught from this day until he is a man. This is a great responsibility for anyone to have. It means you are charged with the life of another and what you do is what he will be." Sofia's philosophical moment had possibly been too much for the three others on the porch to absorb. Hawk still thought Sofia was the most mature young person he had ever seen and her little gem of wisdom didn't diminish his admiration toward her. Jason liked what she said and how she said it. He always loved hearing her talk. Margie wanted to tell her little sister to stop acting like everybody's mother, especially their mother, Miss Margaret. Another voice cut through the air. Mary C. had emerged from her bedroom.

"Well, what kinda curse are we all under from that root headed, skinny voodoo woman? Hell's fire, her damn name's got voodoo in it. Y'all checked the baby for red spots or bleedin' gums?" Margie and Sofia both made a face at the same time. Margie moved the blanket off Billy so she could look for red spots. Mary C. wasn't finished by a long shot.

"I don't know what happened here tonight or why, but you can bet all your asses, it ain't over. Now that they know they can come into this yard and see this child, they'll be comin' round on a regular basis. You gave them an open invitation to stop by whenever they please. And if they think the baby can do somethin' for them, like healin', they'll be lined up in this yard like we was given away free bottles of gin. This is far from over, I tell ya. Far from it." Jason had waited long enough.

"Mama, you didn't have to shoot the man." Mary C.'s eyes lit up.

"You were not here. We looked out the window and there they was. It looked like a Tarzan movie out here, 'cept they was dressed." A little smile cracked Sofia's serious look and Margie held back a laugh. They both thought Mary C. was a rare breed of woman and grandmother. She was on a roll.

"I'll aim higher next time and I'm tellin' you there will be a next time. What would you have thought of me if I let them come into this house and take that baby? I didn't know what they was goin' to do and they didn't give me any time or warning to decide, so I chose to defend what was mine. I protected your son. I'd do it the same way again, if need be. If y'all don't like it, I don't care. Y'all can all kiss my ass. Good night girls, thank you for bein' here with me. I would have been even more scared if y'all hadn't been with me. It was nice seein' y'all again. Come back when ever y'all want to. Maybe next time I won't have to shoot nobody. Kinda ruins your day." Sofia and Margie had no words for the interesting Mary C. They both smiled and nodded their heads as Mary C. walked to the swing, bent down, and kissed Billy on his little forehead.

"He is beautiful, ain't he? The sisters were perfect in their simultaneous reply.

"Yes ma'am he is." Mary C. turned to walk back into the house, but she had a thought so she whispered to Hawk.

"Take me to bed. I need to get this tension and rage out of my body." Mary C. looked back at the others one more time.

"Good night again girls. Good night son." Mary C. turned back to Hawk.

"You shoulda shot somebody."

CHAPTER FOUR

THE YOUNG BLACK MAN CALLED TRUCK, THE MAN MARY C. SHOT, SAT AT A corner table in the Blue Moon Tavern, the only black honky tonk in Mayport. Barbara Lewis' voice was coming from the juke box on the other side of the room. Truck had his leg propped up on a chair as a young girl cleaned and bandaged his wounds. Three other men sat at the same table, as well as, the skinny voodoo woman, Voo Swar. Truck made a face as the young girl dabbed one of his small opened cuts.

"Easy there pretty, that's a bad one there." The girl stopped her first aid.

"I'm sorry I hurt you. I'm not very good at this. This one's deeper than the others. Maybe you should see a doctor."

"Just do the best you can. I'll try not to complain no more." The young girl smiled and continued dressing Truck's injuries while he turned his attention to the others at the table.

"When we take the baby, I want that crazy white bitch dead." One of the other men responded.

"What if the tree protects them, like folks say? What then? You yourself said they seemed hard to kill. Like something was keepin'em safe."

"I know what I said. Once we get the baby, we'll be the one's protected." Another man spoke up.

"I don't think I want anything to do with killin' her. It's true she's crazy and all and I'm sorry she shot you, but killin' her's another thing. I just don't know." Truck had more.

"First of all you ain't gotta kill nobody. I should have said when we take the baby, I'm gonna kill that crazy white bitch. We can't let no crazy white whore raise that child. No tellin' what he would become with her around him everyday. And that daddy of his is just as bad. How Jessie ever got wrapped up with him and his mother, I'll never know. And now Jessie's dead. Who knows what really happened to her. I know I don't know. She shoulda stayed here with us. Ain't it strange how folks just seem to keep dyin' around those awful people. We can't let that baby be in that kinda danger. Tree or no tree, they'll find a way to kill him and won't even know they did it. Just bein' near them brings death. I'd like to kill'em all before something happens to that child." Voo Swar was ready to join the conversation.

"It has to be done at the right time. You have to be smart. Be sure that one man is not there. You do not need to face him." Truck wasn't sure he liked her instructions.

"It doesn't matter who's there. If we have to kill'em all, we will." Voo Swar shook her tiny head, causing her scarf covering to move and tilt to one side for a second and then move back in to its balanced place.

"Don't be a fool, because you are hurt and angry. This man, Hawk, is a bad man. Listen to me. This man knows death and has faced it many times. When he has faced it he has never been afraid. The woman has softened him, but he will remember his strength if she is in danger. You are all brave young men, but this is no normal man. You have not seen one like this before. Nothing protects him. He is on his own, yet he will not be easy to kill or maybe he will not die at all. Be careful of this man, Hawk. Be smart."

Jason drove Margie and Sofia home after the wild ordeal at his house. The two sisters held Billy during the short drive. They couldn't wait to get home and tell the rest of the family about their day full of adventure. Actually, it all started early that morning when Sofia woke from her dream and Margie was introduced to the magic carousel. They would not share that part of their story with anyone else.

They would, however, tell of the devil woman, Eve, and the wild exotic Indian, Sandeep. They would tell of how he acted with Sofia when they were at John King's house. They would also tell of the hours they spent talking to Mary C. and how they witnessed the most bizarre confrontation ever and how Mary C. shot a man and Jason's new son was declared an oak baby. It would be a story others would find hard to believe and they were glad they could back up each other's exciting and unbelievable tale.

It was Jason's favorite time of the day. That time when day and night cross over and there is a brief moment that is not day or night. Margie and Sofia both kissed Billy and made sure he was safe and comfortable lying on the front seat of the truck. They both wanted to kiss Jason too, but they didn't. They said thank you and good night and ran into the house. They were both excited and ready to tell their wild, but true, tales. The house was empty of family members. No one was home except them.

Jason was headed back home, but for some strange reason he turned the truck around. He decided to take Billy for a ride. He didn't know where or why he was going, he just knew he wasn't going home. He thought of the Giant's Motel and of Jessie as he turned onto the main road and passed Miss Margaret's store and John King's house. Jason looked toward the store, then toward Mr. King's. His eyes fell upon the sight he did not need to see. Eve was standing alone on the front porch with her hands on the railing. She was looking out toward the river, but she did look at the truck as Jason drove past. She didn't recognize Jason, but he knew her. He had a burning in his stomach as he drove on down the road.

Mary C. was an absolute wild animal in bed with Hawk. It was a good thing Jason didn't go back home, because it would have been impossible not to hear her noises of pleasure and sexual activity. When Jason was younger he hated being in the house when she was with a man in that way. Jason was happy his mother had a man like Hawk in her life, but he didn't need to hear her sexual outbursts.

Mary C. wanted to do everything and she wanted it rough. She got like that sometimes. Hawk knew he would do whatever she wanted because it was most pleasurable for him, too. He was like most men who wanted their women to be a lady on the outside and a whore in bed. At least Mary C. was one of the two. Hawk also knew it was going to take all his manliness to stay in the same dimension as the woman he had with him in that bed. Mary C. had a way of closing her eyes and leaving her partner behind sexually. It was as if she really didn't need anybody else.

It didn't take Hawk long to realize he would have to endure sexual pain, inflicted on him by Mary C., as she took her frustrations out on him sexually. He tried not to show any discomfort but he had to stop her a few times as her oral talents became abusive. She was literally eating him alive. After Hawk had survived her oral attack, she made it perfectly clear it was his turn to use his talents in the same way. He knew what she wanted when she was in that type of mood and he wanted to please her in every way. Even with Hawk doing the pleasuring she found a way to be the attacker. She almost suffocated him when she wrapped her legs around his head during his oral turn. Hawk had to actually break a scissor hold death grip she had around his head with her powerful and muscular thighs. They would both be sore and bruised after the Mary C. "Let's get my frustrations out," animalistic sexual encounter. Hawk fell asleep. Mary C. cooked some french fries.

Beth, The Werewolf Girl, pulled Big Bob's truck up next to Bill's Hideaway. She saw the jetty rocks fifty yards ahead. She knew she was in Jason's territory. The smell of the hush puppies cooking was almost intoxicating to her keen canine sense of smell. She lay her head back on the seat and closed her eyes remembering Jason's talk about the wild honky tonk on the beach. She drove to the rocks and turned the truck back around, headed south. Beth wanted to go up those stairs at Bill's Hideaway and have a cool one and a sack of hush puppies. She knew her appearance would ignite the curiosity she did not need and she also knew she had to be disciplined if she was to complete her most important life and death mission. Beth had come that far and she knew she would find Jason if she kept being smart and making the right decisions. She tried to think of the things Jason had said and remembered one place he had mentioned when he was talking about fishing with Big Bob. She would look for the little jetties.

Beth got out of the truck to stretch her legs. It didn't seem too risky at the time. There were no people on the rocks that she could see and the people driving up were parking at Bill's Hideaway. They were far enough away and should not cause her any problems. She had to hold her scarf or the wind off the ocean would have blown it off her head and down the beach or up into the rocks above her. It was easy to be curious about what it looked like if you stood on the rocks. She stepped up on one of the lower rocks to see how they felt underfoot. Beth held her scarf in place and stepped up on the second rock. Then the third. Then another and another. She found herself only two steps away from the very top layer of the huge pile of rocks, that separated the Atlantic Ocean and the St. John's River. One more little jump and two steps and she was there. Beth stood up and faced the river side of the rocks. The river was full of boats headed home and she was surprised at the number of people fishing off the rocks on the river side closer to the water. It made her a little nervous, but none of them seemed to pay any attention to the woman standing tall and holding her scarf, keeping it from blowing away.

Beth turned to the open ocean and saw two large oil tankers offshore. One was already headed north and the other was just turning south. She wished she had seen them both when they were floating down the river. She turned to see Bill's Hideaway again and then turned in the one direction she had not faced yet. It was west and in the direction of the little town of Mayport.

Beth slowly lowered her sunglasses as she focused her unique yellow eyes on a strange object in the distance beyond the last rocks. It stood high above and Beth's body quivered when she realized she was looking at Jason's oak tree. She was frozen with an overwhelming feeling of caution and curiosity. She was looking at a great centerpiece and she felt it was looking at her in return. She was pleased to finally see what had influenced Jason and Jessie. She was also glad to think they had the courage to complete the breeding. She hoped she would be brave enough to do the same. She wasn't sure why, during the happy moment, she had a flicker of fear in her body. She didn't like that feeling at all. It didn't fit and was not suppose to be there.

She climbed down slowly from the rocks and got back into the truck. She started the engine and hit the gas peddle. She knew what direction she was headed.

The Barnum and Bailey Circus Tour bus was crossing the Fuller Warren Bridge on the West side of Jacksonville. They had only stopped two times for bathroom breaks and one time to gas up and keep the tank full. They brought food with them and ate as they rolled. They were making great time.

Miss Margaret, and her two other daughters, Susan and Peggy, were working at the store. Miss Margaret was taking her shift and the two girls were staying to help restock the can goods shelf. Their mother had not requested they stay at work any later; they were just good girls. All three of them turned to the door when the bell rang to see who the next customer would be. Miss Margaret had no idea that the beautiful woman dressed in black, who had just entered her store, was about to bring bitter feeling and memories back into her blessed life.

Eve Klim was the new customer at Miss Margaret's general store. They all knew they were looking at a stranger in town. Or, at least she was a stranger to the two girls. Susan made the patented greeting.

"Good evening. May I help you with something?" Eve lifted her head from under her black wide rimmed hat.

"I needed some personal things. I have used most of my soaps, creams and powders while I was traveling and I need to refill my stock before we move on." Susan directed the beautiful stranger to a glass case near the register where a number of feminine items were located.

"I'm not sure if we have what you need, but maybe some of these things will help until you can get to a real lady's store." Eve moved to the counter.

"You're right. The selection is very limited, but we are not at May Cohens, now are we?" Susan smiled at the lady's comparison.

"No ma'am. Not even close." Susan was surprised when Eve touched her face with a gloved hand.

"You are the sweetest thing." She turned away from Susan and nodded to Peggy. "And you must be the fourth sister. How can all four of you be so beautiful? That just doesn't seem possible. There is always an ugly sister somewhere. Are you sure there's not a fifth one you keep locked in the attic at home?" Miss Margaret took notice of the stranger's comment. She smiled at first, thinking they had a real dramatic and theatrical individual in the store. Her smile would not remain on her face very long. Eve decided to make her identity known. It was no fun if Miss Margaret didn't know who she was.

"Now Margaret, where have you hidden that ugly daughter?" Eve looked directly into Miss Margaret's eyes. Miss Margaret knew the eyes but did not put the eyes and face together. It had been many years and Eve had many changes. The amount of make-up added to Miss Margaret's inability to know her at first. Eve knew she was struggling so she made sure she would not struggle any longer.

"Don't you worry at all little Miss Margaret. You can rest assured I have not come home to try and steal your husband again." Margaret's stomach went sour and her mouth went dry instantly. She knew the eyes, voice and the face. She knew Eve Klim stood in her store. She tried to keep her composure, but it was difficult. She would do the best she could for the girls. She was afraid, because she didn't know what Eve would say next; she had already said too much.

"Why Eve, I didn't recognize you at first. I should have recognized the sharp tongue. It must have been the hat." Eve smiled.

"And other things. I know I've changed. I see it myself. You are even more beautiful as an older woman. Some women are lucky that way sometimes. And these girls. The men must be driving you girls and your mother crazy. I know one of your beauties has already turned the head of my man." Miss Margaret wanted Eve to explain that comment, but she allowed the evil one to continue. Peggy and

Susan were nothing but ears as they both stood there with their mouths dropped open. Eve couldn't wait to tell of the encounter.

"The one called Sofia, that's her. What a rare beauty in this fish stink town. You need to get that one away from here. You need to get them all away from here. But you won't."

"What is it you want, Eve?" Eve walked over to the glass counter.

"Soap. Lots of soap."

The two girls watched in unsure silence, as their mother took the soap the woman requested from the case. The sisters noticed the eery stare between their mother and the strange woman. Eve bathed in the discomfort of the moment. Miss Margaret moved toward the cash register to bag the items and be paid for her services. Eve was ready to add more to the uneasy and awkward situation she had willingly and purposely created. She was true evil; head to toe.

"I don't carry money on me, just a minute please." Eve walked to the door. The bell rang when she pushed it open. Peggy and Susan looked at their mother. Miss Margaret was watching Eve at the door. The ringing door opened and Eve walked back into the store followed by her more than strange companion, Sandeep Singh.

Miss Margaret and her two daughters were given the shock of the month when the soldier-saint walked to the register and handed Miss Margaret the money she needed. He bowed to her as she gave him his change. Eve was waiting for the shock of Sandeep's appearance to settle. Sandeep bowed to the two girls as he walked to the door. Eve had no intention of allowing her next moment of shock to get away.

"Sandeep, this is the mother and the other sisters of the young woman, Sofia." Sandeep stopped and turned to Miss Margaret. He walked back to where she was standing. Miss Margaret wasn't sure what to expect and she did step back from the counter when he approached her.

"Please do not be afraid. I would feel very sad if I scared you. It is not my intent." Miss Margaret gave a cautious half smile and stayed back from the counter. The strange man continued.

"I am Sandeep Singh, and it is a great honor to meet you and your two other daughters." Sandeep turned and bowed to the two girls again. "I know you are most proud of the one called, Sofia. I have seen her, spoken to her, and touched her. She walks with God." Miss Margaret didn't mind him seeing Sofia or talking to her, she even liked the part about her walking with God, but the touched her statement didn't sit too well with her. Peggy and Susan zeroed in on the touched her comment, too and they had the dropped mouth syndrome. Miss Margaret found the courage to speak. "When exactly did you do all these things?" Miss Margaret gave Eve her cue, she just didn't know it.

"We met your other daughters at John's house this morning. That Margie, the oldest, she's a real spitfire, that one. She doesn't seem to fit as one of yours. Too head strong. I was surprised and pleased. Of course, I've only seen Sofia to compare. The other two here might be just as aggressive as Margie. That girl really defends her mother, like a good daughter should." Miss Margaret's head was swimming and her stomach burned.

"What did you say to Margie?" Eve smiled.

"Nothing she believed, but I thought you could tell her what was true when she asked you. Good night Margaret. Good night girls." Eve left the store with Sandeep, leaving Miss Margaret and the two sisters to talk about the strange new customers.

Margie and Sofia watched Sandeep and Eve walk up the porch steps at Mr. King's house. They had no idea the two visitors had been in their mother's store. The two sisters could not wait to tell their mother and sisters about the day they spent full of adventure. They had decided to walk to the store to find the rest of the family. Miss Margaret, Peggy and Susan turned to the door again when Sofia pushed it open and the bell rang. Margie followed Sofia, but Margie would talk first. It was understood.

"Mother, you will not believe what has happened to us today. I don't know where to start." Margie's hesitation gave Peggy the moment she needed.

"Why don't you start with when Sandeep touched Sofia?" Sofia's eyes lit up as she turned to her sister Peggy. Miss Margaret looked at Peggy, too.

"You stop talking like that. I'm surprised at you, Peggy. You stop right now." Peggy looked away and mumbled, "Yes ma'am." Margie and Sofia looked at Miss Margaret.

"Margie, slow down. We just met Eve and her friend and we aren't sure what's going on around here. I do know that if Eve Klim is part of it, we must be careful. She has a way to bring hardship to the folks who cross her path. It's a sad day now that she has returned." The room was silent as the four sisters listened to their mother. Mother had more.

"Sofia are you alright? That man said he met you this morning and he said something about touching you. It made me nervous." Sofia was about to ease her mother's mind, but of course Margie took the floor.

"He's crazy about her. He got on his knees to her." Peggy and Susan were all ears once again as their older sister continued. "He kissed her." All eyes widened to their fullest. Sofia jumped in.

"On the hand, Mama, on the hand." Margie was rolling.

"He thanked Sofia for allowing him to see her. It was crazy. He said his people would give her gold and jewels. Then we saw Jason's new son. He's an oak baby. We were having coffee with Miss Mary C. Then she shot a black man named Truck with a shotgun right before a voodoo woman put her thumb on the baby's belly-button." Miss Margaret couldn't take any more.

"Stop! You hold on a minute. You're talking a hundred miles an hour and your not making any sense at all. Have you been drinking? Sofia, has your sister been drinking?" Sofia and Margie shook their heads.

"No Mama, I haven't been drinking."

There was a strange noise coming from outside the store that interrupted the wild family discussion inside the store. The Barnum and Bailey Circus Tour bus drove up to the front of Miss Margaret's store. The day filled with adventure had one more chapter remaining before full darkness fell on the little town of Mayport, Florida, U.S.A.

Peggy was the nearest to the door when the bus rolled in. She looked out the screen as the door of the colorful circus bus opened.

The first sight she saw was Big Bob's eight feet, six inch frame step off the bus.

"Mama, I think you need to see this." Miss Margaret moved from behind the counter and joined Peggy at the door. Big Bob actually blocked any vision they had of the bus as he walked toward the front door. The bell sounded again when Big Bob pulled the door open and stepped into the front of the store, ducking his head low as he entered. It was a necessary habit.

"Evenin' ladies. Is this Miss Margaret's general store in Mayport, Florida? Home of the four prettiest sisters on God's good earth? Friends of Jason, Jessie and now Billy? Where you can get an iced cold Nehi and a honey bun anytime of day or night? How is everyone tonight? I'm Big Bob, from Gibsonton, Florida. My family and I are looking for a handsome young man named, Jason." Miss Margaret and her four daughters were spellbound and speechless. Big Bob's size was too intimidating for words to be spoken. Sofia surprised everyone with her courage and knowledge.

"You must be the Giant from the motel. Jason told me about you." Margie looked at Sofia as if to say, "What the hell?" Miss Margaret and the other two sisters didn't think what the hell? but they did wonder how Sofia had the information she seemed to have accumulated.

"Yes ma'am, I am that Giant, if you please." Sofia stepped forward and offered her hand to Big Bob.

"I'm so pleased to meet you. Jason told me all about you and how you helped him. He thinks the world of you." Margie continued staring at Sofia with that what the hell question burning inside her.

"And I feel the same about him." The bell on the door sounded again, causing all in the store to look to see who or what was entering. Black Beulla, the Fat Lady, was the next new customer. She had to turn sideways to enter the store. Miss Margaret and the four girls had mouth dropped open syndrome, as Beulla's southern belle voice filled the air.

"My, my, look at all these beautiful young ladies. We are definitely in the true South. Only in the South do you find this many beautiful women in one place. I'm about to bust, can y'all point my big butt in the direction of the lady's room, please?" She smiled and looked at Margie. Margie's mouth was still open and her eyes were as wide open as they could possibly be.

"I don't need ya to say nothin' sweetie, just point." Margie pointed to the back of the store where there was a small closet type room with a toilet and a sink. As Beulla turned to walk to the room, Margie found a bit of courage.

"Excuse me ma'am." Beulla looked back at Margie. "I don't mean to be rude, but I don't think you'll be able to get in the room back there. I don't think the door is wide enough." Margie's three sisters couldn't believe she said that to the fat stranger. Beulla understood perfectly.

"Come on honey, show me the back yard and some bushes and you stand guard for me." Margie looked at her sisters, her mother and the Giant. They all seemed to say, "she asked you not me" with their eyes. Peggy almost laughed out loud but she was able to control herself. Margie accompanied Beulla to the woods and bushes behind the store. She knew they would have to find a pretty big bush.

The bell on the door sounded and everyone looked in that direction once more. This time it was Norman Bates, the Skeleton Man, and the dropped mouth syndrome struck again. He was skin and bone.

"Well....hello....ladies. Is this Mayport or perhaps Heaven on Earth?" The girls and their mother could only stare as the bell sounded again and Helga, the Amazon Warrior, walked her six feet, six inch, muscular body into the store. She wore black boots and skin tight black pants with holes down the sides of each leg, showing circles of skin. Her midriff was showing under a half shirt, tied at her waist . Her huge breasts were evident and they were pushed together, forming a seven inch line of cleavage. She had a steel and leather collar type necklace around her throat with the same look on her wrists. She was an awesome sight for the three remaining sisters and their mother.

"I am so thirsty. Norman, find something cold to drink for me.

Please find something." Norman walked close to the three sisters. Peggy and Susan could say nothing, but Sofia was different.

"You must be Norman and you are Helga. I can't believe you are really here in our store. Jason told me all about you. He loves you all so much." The door opened again.

"And we all love him." All eyes turned to see Ana Kara, the only normal looking one on the bus. The girls and Miss Margaret thought she was beautiful. Ana almost floated across the wooden floor as she moved to where Miss Margaret was standing.

"Don't let these folks shock you too much. They are wonderful people and they are excited to be here." Miss Margaret and the girls had a moment of mental relief with Ana Kara standing there with them.

Margie led Beulla back through the back door and into the store where the crowd was gathering. Sofia directed Norman to the cold drink box where he opened the lid and reached into the icy water. The first dripping bottle of Nehi orange was for Helga. She was pleased.

"Now, that looks cold and refreshing. Thank you kind sir." She took the bottle of drink from Norman, as he reached into the box for another. He gave the grape Nehi to Ana, then another orange Nehi to Beulla, then a bottle of Royal Crown Cola to Big Bob and then a red strawberry Nehi for himself. Norman looked at Miss Margaret.

"Keep count on us. We just might drink every Nehi in the box. I'll lose count, so ya better keep an eye on us." Miss Margaret smiled and took out a tablet to keep track of the drinks the strange group was drinking. The bell on the door sounded and, as before, all eyes turned to see who was coming into the store. At first it didn't look to Miss Margaret and the girls like anyone had entered, but the visitors knew different. A mousy and irritating voice cut into the air around them all.

"Y'all were gonna just let me sleep, huh? You didn't care if I was thirsty or hungry, did ya?"

The four sisters and Miss Margaret looked in the direction of the voice and could not believe their ten eyes when they saw Tom

Thumb, the World's Smallest Man, walk into the middle of the room. There was no way anyone could speak at that moment, not even the comfortable Sofia.

"Don't stop talkin' on my account. The little pigmy don't matter anyhow. Just leave his little butt on the bus and you won't be bothered by him." Helga had heard enough.

"Tom, you stop right now. I told the others to be quiet and let you sleep. I didn't think you were feeling well and I thought you needed to rest. You always think we are doing things to you to be mean. We just wanted you to rest. Now you stop." Tom knew he couldn't continue after Helga's stand and direction. He turned his roving eyes and attention to the four young and beautiful sisters. He strolled to where they were standing.

Tom looked at Margie first. She was afraid and he sensed it. Peggy was next and he knew she was uncomfortable, too. He loved it. It was strange, but the room was silent as the little man made his inspection of the local beauties. He made a noise when he saw the beautiful Sofia and took a deep breath as he stared at Susan.

"Where are we? I know this can't be the fishing village we've been hunting. Are we in the real Shangri-la, where beautiful women outnumber the men and all they do all day is pleasure the few men around them? Is this a dream? Am I still sleepin' on the bus? Talk to me, Big Bob, where the hell are we?"

"You're not dreaming and, yes, this is Mayport. And, yes, you are surrounded by beautiful women." Tom flicked his tongue toward Margie. He scared her and made her jump.

"Even if we don't find Beth, the trip has already been worth the effort. Ladies, I am Tom and I am at your service, day or night. I prefer the nights." Norman moved past Tom and went to the door. The bell sounded when he pushed it open and stepped outside of the store and back to the bus. Helga handed Tom a grape Nehi she had pulled from the ice cold box.

"Stop fooling with those nice young girls. They don't need to have a bad first impression of us. We are the visitors, remember? Don't embarrass us, you hear me?" Tom smiled at the four sisters as he took the drink and walked to the other side of the room with Helga. His harassment of the sisters was over for the moment. He would bother them again later, if he was given the chance. He always looked for those chances.

Miss Margaret and her four daughters had their heads on swivels, turning and looking in all directions. They were surrounded by a group of the most strange and bizarre characters ever to set foot into Miss Margaret's store. Margie kept her eyes on the little pigmy pervert while the other girls scanned the room. Miss Margaret continued keeping a written record of the food and drink items being consumed by the outrageous group of customers. Each one of them was eating or drinking something.

The bell on the door rang once more as Norman pushed it open and held it for the most bizarre customers of all. Ming and Ling, the Siamese Twins, walked into the store. Actually, Ming walked in, with Ling hanging on behind. Miss Margaret and the girls had been mesmerized at what they had seen up until that moment, but nothing could have prepared them for the sight of the Twins. Norman held the screen door open, allowing Ming to enter first, facing everyone in the room. Even after the long ride, Ming looked beautiful, like a porcelain China doll. Miss Margaret and the girls thought Ming was carrying something on her back, but it never occurred to them it was another person. Big Bob made the introductions.

"Miss Margaret, these are our dear friends and family members, Ming ....Ming bowed to Miss Margaret....and this is her sister Ling." Ming turned her body around, swinging her sister, Ling, into Miss Margaret's view. The strange movement and introduction startled Miss Margaret and she stepped back, making a noise of surprise as Ling bowed her head with respect and a greeting. From where the girls were standing they could see both Twins. No one knew what to say. Big Bob understood. They all understood.

"I know we are not your everyday group of customers, but we're a pretty good group once you get to know us." Sofia stepped forward.

"We would like to welcome all of you to Mayport and our store. This is so exciting."

Little Tom moved toward Sofia quickly and his speed from where he was to where she was standing scared her. Big Bob wasn't having any of Tom's foolish tactics.

"Stop! And I mean now." Tom didn't like it, but he knew Big Bob was serious, so he retreated back to stand with Helga.

"I told you to behave yourself. Now, Big Bob's mad at you. This is why he doesn't want to take us places." Tom walked away from Helga. He didn't want to hear any type of reprimand at all. Big Bob turned back to Miss Margaret.

"We came to visit Jason and we are looking for our friend, Beth." Beulla wanted to say something.

"We're on vacation. I just love bein'round pretty people. It makes me feel pretty, too." Beulla looked at all four sisters. Their heads still looked like they were on swivels, turning and watching all the strange characters who had entered their store and their lives. Big Bob had a question.

"Do you have any motels or lodging houses near by? We do need to find a place to stay a few days. It's been a long day and riding always wears me out. I don't set too comfortable in any type vehicle. We'll go see Jason tomorrow, but for now we need lodging. Sleeping on that bus doesn't appeal to any of us." Miss Margaret responded.

"There's not much here in Mayport anymore. Used to be a few places, but one burned down years ago and the other has been empty and condemned for two years. It's all boarded up and probably full of rats and fleas." The bell on the door sounded again, alerting all in the store to a new arrival. Mr. John King entered the store and joined the crowd.

"Forgive me for eavesdropping, but I have a solution for your lodging needs." Every eye in the room, normal or strange, was on Mr. King. "I'm John King." He extended his hand to Big Bob.

Big Bob excepted the friendly gesture and returned the hand shake. "I saw you arrive and was intrigued by your mode of travel and unique appearance. You are either with the circus or you are running away from the circus. Whichever is true doesn't matter to me. I'm just glad you have chosen to stop here and I would like to welcome you to Mayport and offer you all lodging for the night, or as long as you need, for that matter."

Big Bob was also intrigued.

"You have a place for all of us?"

"My house is across the street. It used to be an active and popular boarding house at one time. The commercial aspect has long gone, but I still have twelve separate bedrooms with a bath between every two rooms. I do have two other guests, but they are using only one of the rooms. Please consider my offer. It would be an honor to have all of you in my house." The room was silent. The circus family waited for Big Bob to respond.

"This is awful kind of you Mr. King, taking in a group of strangers like us. My name is Big Bob. This is Beulla, Helga, Ana, Ming, Ling, Norman and Tom. And yes, sir, we did run away from the circus." Each member of the family smiled and gestured a greeting to Mr. King.

"It is a true pleasure to meet all of you. When you complete your business here, please feel free to come to the house and I will be there to direct you to your rooms. I am so excited you are here and I do hope you will join me and be my guests." Everyone looked at Big Bob again.

"You're a very kind man, Mr. King, and yes, sir, we would be honored to stay at your home tonight." The circus family was excited, too. John King walked toward the door and pushed it open, ringing the bell as he looked back at the strangers.

"Oh, by the way. I'm sure this won't make a difference to y'all, but my house is extremely haunted. I thought I should tell you that." Everyone looked at everyone after Mr. King's exiting decree. Tom looked at Norman.

"Well, you should fit right in." Helga looked at Big Bob.

"I don't like ghosts in my room, never have. Tom doesn't like 'em either." Sofia looked at Ana Kara.

"It is really haunted. It's a famous haunted house." Beulla looked at Margie.

"I just might need you to hold my hand again, sugah." Bob saw the looks on their faces after John King had made his informational statement.

"Well, I never really believed in such things, but we've all seen some strange things in our time, so nothing should surprise us. I'm tired, and if Mr. King can stay there with the ghosts so can we. He doesn't look like he's very scared. In fact he seemed rather proud of the fact his house is haunted. I liked him. I'm going to find my room for the night." Big Bob turned to Miss Margaret.

"It was a true pleasure to meet you and your daughters. We will see you all again I am quite sure. You have a good evening. Norman, pay the lady please and park the bus at Mr. King's house. Big Bob left the store and headed to the haunted house. Ana Kara and the Twins were the first to follow him, while Norman was settling the tab with Miss Margaret. Beulla kissed all four sisters on the cheek before she followed the group. The girls all smiled a half smile as the huge woman gave each one her turn for a kiss. Helga walked toward the door, too and had to go back and pull Tom away from the four sisters. He was walking slowly and drinking in their beauty with his perverted eyes and serpentine tongue. Norman was the last to leave.

"You have been very nice to us. I can see why Jason talked so much about you ladies. Until tomorrow." Norman tipped his chauffeur's hat and made a gentleman's bow as he made the bell ring on the door. He climbed aboard the bus and fired up her engine, pulling the bus away from the front of the store and in the direction of the haunted house.

CHAPTER FIVE

Jason had driven out to the Little Jetties with Billy next to him on the seat of Uncle Bobby's truck. He parked near the rocks and looked out over the St. John's River as it moved north in front of him. Jason knew not many other rivers flowed north. He heard the ferry horn blast as the Buccaneer left the Fort George side of the river and headed toward Mayport. How he still loved that sound. Billy filled the silent air with the noises babies make, as his young father thought of Jessie first, then Sofia, then Billy, then his mother, Mary C. Jason would enjoy his thoughts, memories and fantasies until he decided to go home. He knew he had to go shrimping later that night, but he would sit with Billy at the rocks for a while longer.

Mr. King was the perfect host as he directed each one of his guests to his or her own private room. It was easy to see his excitement and the genuine respect he had for the interesting and unusual characters in his home. Each room was a showcase of antique furniture, paintings and expert woodwork and carvings. Ana Kara had to express herself as she walked with Mr. King through the upstairs hallway.

"Mr. King, this is an exquisite home you have here. I would love to hear all the stories behind some of the beautiful antiques and paintings. The art and carvings are so unique and intriguing. You know there are always great stories behind great works of art." The pictures on the walls were not of ghouls and goblins. They were pictures of the King family members, children playing and scenery of the Mayport of the past. There was no look of the typical haunted house in the movies. It was just a beautiful old house with great memories and character and enough ghosts to start a softball team. Mr. King appreciated Ana's observation.

"Thank you very much. You're right. There are many wonderful stories about many of the possessions in this house. It took more than my lifetime to collect them and it would take just that long to tell all the stories. I suppose that's how things are forgotten, it just becomes too much to tell." Ana liked the way Mr. King talked.

"Perhaps while we're here you would take a moment and tell us at least about your favorite item. Everyone has a favorite." Ana Kara, the belly dancer, sure made Mr. John King smile.

"I'll be sure to tell you about my favorite. Please don't let me forget that."

"I'll remind you and I'm looking forward to knowing more about this wonderful house."

"Sometimes I forget the fine history behind some of these things. I thank you for reminding me of the beauty I have surrounding me each day. We tend to take things for granted until someone reminds us. We have a tendency to do people the same way." Mr. King actually wanted to continue their conversation, but he knew he had to tend to his other guests. Ana Kara smiled at her host and moved past him into the bedroom. Big Bob was already settled in the room next to Ana's and the Twins had been the first guests to be given a room. Helga was next, as Mr . King moved the others through the hallway. He opened the next door.

"I do hope this room is to your satisfaction." Helga stood at the entrance and did not enter the room.

"Where do the ghosts usually stay?" She peeked into the room. "Is this one of the rooms?" Mr. King smiled.

"They really don't have a specific room. They show up in different places, at different times. They seem to choose certain individuals and leave others alone. They are peculiar ghosts." Helga's eyes opened wider. Mr. King added to her concern. He was the master.

"I think they can sense the people who are afraid. They seem to gravitate to the more nervous guests. The possible believers, if you will. But, that's just my theory. Is this suitable?" Helga had not moved into the doorway at all. Tom Thumb's mousy voice cracked in the haunted air.

"It's fine. Come on my dear, I'm tired. If the ghosts come callin' we'll ask 'em to join us." Mr. King was surprised when he realized Helga, the Amazon Warrior, and Tom Thumb, the World's Smallest Man, were going to stay in the same room together. He would never have thought they were a couple. But, who would? He was surprised, but didn't show it. Beulla's room was next.

"I just want to get off my feet. These puppies of mine are killin' me. I've got a corn the size of a bummie marble on my pinky toe and my foot feels like it's on fire. I can't wait to get these hot doggies soakin' in some hot salt water." She opened the door to the room and moved her huge body past Mr. King and into the bedroom, closing the door behind her. Mr. King turned to his last guest. Norman was standing by the door of the next bedroom. Mr. King had to give him directions.

"That room's occupied by my other guests. I'm not sure if they're here or not, I don't think they are, but they could be sleeping. Your room is down here." Mr. King lead Norman to the last bedroom on the right of the hallway. Norman stepped into the room.

"I hope you like this room. It is my favorite of them all. It has a great history. I will share it with you at another time. I know you're tired and need to rest. Welcome to my home." Norman turned his skin and bones to Mr. King.

"I knew I would get the best room. I love the feeling, smell and atmosphere of this place. There is much here to marvel at and I feel that I belong here. Perhaps I'll return when my time comes." Mr. King smiled.

"Now or later, it makes no difference, you will always be welcome." Norman Bates, the Skeleton Man, walked into the best bedroom and closed the door. Mr. King felt great about his guests as he walked down the staircase. They were all safe and comfortable in their rooms. He walked out onto his porch and sat in one of his wicker chairs.

As Mr. King took a deep breath of the Mayport night air he saw Eve and Sandeep walking toward the front porch. He watched them as they approached the house from the direction of the ferry slip.

"Well, I wasn't sure if you were here or not." Eve responded as she reached the front steps to the porch.

"I took Sandeep to see the ferry. Then he wanted to ride it to the other side. He is like a child, now and then, when he sees something new to him. He wants to know about everything." Mr. King nodded.

"It's a beautiful evening for a ferry ride. I haven't taken one in years. I need to do that one night. But I couldn't do it tonight. I've been real busy." Sandeep followed Eve up the steps and they sat down with Mr. King. He told them about his other guests. He thought they needed to be prepared in case they ran into one of the circus family in the hallway upstairs.

Miss Margaret and her four daughters were still talking about the circus people, Sandeep and Eve, and the voodoo meeting with the oak baby. The girls wanted to know about their mother's past relationship with the devil woman, Eve, and the topic of Sandeep touching and kissing Sofia came up a few times. The voodoo gathering at Jason's house and the actual shooting of the man called Truck was also discussed. The only secret was the existence of the magic carousel.

Sofia told the others she was too excited to relax so she didn't mind working the next shift and someone could relieve her later. Miss Margaret was concerned.

"Are you sure you're alright? One of your sisters could stay." Margie was first.

"Mother, she's fine. I'll replace her later. We all know that man didn't do anything to her except give her the compliment of the century. He wanted to give her gold and stuff. He likes her and he's just a foreign man. He seems nice enough, he just doesn't know anything. She probably couldn't rest anyway with all the crazy things going on.

We don't all need to stay here." Miss Margaret nodded her head and smiled at Sofia.

"I guess you're right. We spend too much time here now. Thank you, Sofia. Margie will be back at ten o'clock." Margie smiled at Sofia. Sofia had her doubts about seeing her older sister at ten o'clock, but at the moment she really didn't care. Peggy and Susan had both worked an earlier shift and they knew they deserved to go home. Actually, Sofia was working Margie's shift because Sofia had worked her own shift that morning. They all said good-bye to Sofia and left the store.

Jason drove his Uncle Bobby's truck past Mr. King's house headed home. Jason touched Billy as he looked in the direction of Mr. King's porch. His eyes fell on the sight of Eve again, like before. He also got a quick glance at the Indian man he had seen earlier. Jason turned the truck onto the road leading to his house. He knew he would be leaving with Hawk in a few hours for their first shrimping trip together with Chichemo and Bosco.

Beulla was nodding off to sleep in a big soft chair with her big fat feet in a basin full of warm water. Ana Kara could hear Big Bob snoring in the room next to her. She stood in front of a wall mirror and admired her full and curvy real woman's naked body. She liked her naked profile and stared at her reflection for a few seconds, then moved to the bed. She liked the feel of the clean sheets on her bare skin. If a male ghost decided to visit Ana Kara, the Belly Dancer, that night he was in for a real alive visual treat. She always slept in the nude; haunted house or not.

Norman was the physically weakest of the family and the long day driving the bus had fatigued him to his limits. Norman, like Big Bob, was fast asleep. Tom was teasing Helga with the flicking of his pointed tongue on her big dark nipples.

"I do want to have sex with you in this haunted house, but we cannot be too wild and make noises. Do you hear me?" Little Tom nodded his head and crawled his little pigmy body under the bed covers to continue his pointed tongue assault elsewhere. Ming and Ling were also already sleeping. They were lying in the middle of the bed, facing in opposite directions.

Mr. King and his two original guests were still sitting together on the front porch. Sandeep was intrigued about the strange circus people Mr. King had just told them about. Eve wasn't so excited.

"John, you have always liked all the oddities and freaks of the world. You like living in a haunted house and you love to scare folks. You take in strangers like they're long lost cousins. You let any of the town drunks sleep it off out back. You are the original good samaritan." Mr. King smiled.

"Now, I'm not old enough to be the original one, I just look that old." Eve smiled at her old friend.

"I'm going to bed. I hope I don't trip over the midget somewhere in the hallway up there. Good night, John. Sandeep."

"I will join you later."

"I will wait for you." Eve touched Sandeep's shoulder as she moved past him and into the house. Her walk up the stairs and in the hall was uneventful. She would meet none of the other house guests until morning. Sandeep stood up from the wicker chair and walked down the steps of the porch.

"Good night, John King." Sandeep's sudden movement and exit surprised Mr. King, but he was not only a master storyteller, he was also a master of minding his own business.

"Good night, young man."

Jason stopped the truck in his front yard. Hawk was sitting on the front porch swing. Jason knew they would leave within the hour. The wild and rough sex had calmed Mary C. and taken its toll on Hawk. Jason took Billy into his arms and walked up onto the porch.

"You alright, Jason?"

"Yes suh, I'm fine. We're both fine." Jason looked through the screen door when he heard music coming from the living room; strange music. It was different and he was surprised to see his mother dancing alone in the room. He had a memory flash of Jessie and her friend, Ruby, dancing in Ruby's kitchen. He shook away the pleasant flashback and opened the door and walked into the room with Billy in his arms. Mary C. looked toward the door when they entered and danced over to Jason, taking Billy away from him. She

held the baby against her breasts and talked as she continued dancing to the strange music.

"This is my favorite new song, or it ain't a song, it's just music,
but ain't it neat? It reminds me of the baby. It's kinda spooky, don't
ya think?" Jason actually liked the sound he was hearing, but he did-
n't like his mother saying she liked it because it was spooky, like Billy.

Mary C. did have a strange way with words. She kept dancing.

"It's called "Green Onions" by somebody named Booker T. and
the MGs. Green Onions, ain't that neat? You know they must be
black, but so is Fats Domino." The song ended, Mary C. stopped
dancing and turned the radio off.

"I'm gonna go buy that record tomorrow. I could listen to that
thing all day. They've been playin' it a bunch today. I like it. Let me
give this boy a bath and get him into bed. He's had a little too much
excitement today for one little baby." She left the room with her
grandchild.

The bell rang on the door to the store and Sofia turned to greet
the next customer of the evening. Her heart raced when she saw the
Indian Sandeep walk into the store. Miss Margaret's official greeting
froze in Sofia's beautiful throat. She was nervous, even though his
voice was calm and pleasant.

"I was hoping you were still here. I thought I felt your presence
in my heart, but I wasn't sure. I was hoping we could talk again."
Sofia looked down.

"Of course, how may I help you?" Sofia's heart raced as she gave
a new version of the official greeting. Sandeep stepped close to her.
Sofia tried not to step away, but she wanted to talk to him from the
other side of the room, if she could. Sandeep knew she was uneasy.

"Please don't be afraid or nervous at all. You, for one, have nothing to fear from me. I am your servant and I am here to tell you the
things that should be said to you; if you will allow me to do so."
Nervous or not, Sofia, like anyone else in her position, was intrigued
and made curious by his strange words.

"I would like to hear what you have to say, I think." Sandeep
smiled and bowed his head.

"Then I will speak now. I have already waited too long." Sofia felt more at ease as Sandeep's soft voice began to fill the room.

"When there is one like you, they must know what they are. You are a chosen one. You are here to make the lives of others better, more fulfilling. You are a teacher, an example of what man should be. You have been misplaced in some way. You are surrounded with the strengths and forces of evil. This evil was here long before you. You cannot be complete or follow your true destiny here. You must find the courage to leave this place. Your reason for being cannot be fulfilled here." Sofia had to speak her thoughts.

"I can't leave. My family's here. Everyone I love is here. I'm not this person you say. You have made a mistake."

"There is no mistake. You are more than family and loved ones. You have been picked from all the others. You belong to the world. You have been given a duty. It is your calling."

"The only duty I have is in this store right now. That's all I know."

"Ah, but now you know more. Sandeep has told you more. I have the gift to see such things and it is my duty to bring the truth to light. We all have our duties. After a chosen one knows the truth, it will be their decision as to how they precede in life. I can do no more." Sofia had no answer or response, but she didn't need one. Sandeep took his prediction and prophecy even further.

"When I saw your friend, Jason, and John told me about him, I knew he was also chosen." I also knew he was already lost. This evil place has taken his true self away and he will not move on as a true chosen one. It is very unusual to find two such people in one place. One is rare. Two is another thing altogether. You have lost nothing as of this moment, but there are forces trying to take what you are from you. You may be seeing such forces in your dreams. Jason's dreams have taken his true self from him. This, too, will be your true fate if you allow it. I pray you are stronger than he." Sofia's eyes lit up.

"No one is stronger than Jason. He is good and, if he was one of these chosen ones, he still is."

"I can see you love him. It is deep in your eyes. It is only right for you two to be drawn to one another. You have no other match and he is the closest one to you, even though he has lost much. He has had no guidance and no knowledge of who he is and what he can do. He has been directed toward the wrong things and you must believe me, he is lost." Sofia dropped her head as Sandeep went on. "You are different. You are not lost. I praise God that He has guided me here to guide you, if you chose to be directed." Sofia had a strange idea and a vision popped into her head when Sandeep stopped talking.

"If you can see such things in people, can you tell if a baby is special or perhaps a chosen one?" Sandeep smiled.

"You are referring to Jason's new son. The one they call the oak baby." Sofia's beautiful big eyes were at their biggest.

"Yes, that's right. You know about him?"

"I've heard the stories of the oak tree and the breeding legend. Yes, I would know if the child was chosen, but I have no knowledge of the tree. To think there would be three chosen ones in this place is inconceivable. I do feel the obligation to see such a child." Sofia's eyes lit up even more than before.

"I can take you to see him. Or Jason could bring him to you. I know he would do that. He wants to know about his son. And you could tell Jason about what he is, too. Oh, this is so wonderful! They live at the end of the road next to the store. The one that goes between us and Mr. King's house. It's the last house on the road. I could take you there." Sandeep took Sofia's snow white little hand into his big brown hand as he had done earlier that morning when he first saw her. He felt her tremble at his touch.

"Thank you again for talking to me. If I am to see the child I will go alone." Sofia didn't think that was such a good idea and she had to share her thoughts with the Indian.

"I don't think Miss Mary C.'s going to allow you to see the baby. In fact, I don't think she's going to let you get anywhere near the baby. She's already shot one man tonight who wanted to see the child. She's really protective and you being a stranger and all, I don't think she'll like you just showing up and knocking on her door. I don't want you to get hurt. She can be real mean sometimes." Sandeep smiled at Sofia's word of warning and concern.

"She will never know Sandeep has been there. Good night, Sofia."

Mary C. was rocking Billy to sleep, when Hawk kissed her on the cheek.

"We gotta get goin'. We don't want to be late for our first run together , ya know. Bosco would be mad if we were late." Mary C. smiled at the tender moment with her man, as Jason walked into the room.

"I'm so happy we're all together and you two are going to run the boat. Please be careful and listen to Chichemo. He might be an old hard ass, but he knows his stuff. Please do what he says." Hawk smiled.

"I'll listen to Chichemo, but I ain't doin' nothin' the monkey tells me to do. I think he'd steer me wrong, don't you Jason?" They all smiled together as Jason nodded his head in agreement with Hawk's little Bosco joke.

Mary C. was left alone with her grandson. When he fell asleep from the rocking, she put Billy in her bed and turned on the radio again, hoping to hear her favorite new song, "Green Onions," again on the late night request show. If she didn't hear it soon, she would call the request in herself. She felt like dancing.

Mr. Leek met Jason and Hawk at the boat to see them off on their maiden voyage together. It would only be for one or two nights, but it was a beginning.

"Don't be too disappointed if you don't kill'em tonight. There haven't been any big catches lately. The boats have been catchin' enough to stay in the black, but no big single catches. Be patient, it will come. The boat looks great. And who knows, with a man like Chichemo on board you might just kill'em. He's found 'em when nobody else could." Chichemo tipped his hat to Mr. Leek's compliment. Mr. Leek had an idea. "Jason, you need to take this new thing called Dramamine so you don't get too seasick. I've got some in the office." Jason had not thought about taking something for his seasickness. He thought his good friend, Mr. Leek, had a great idea. Chichemo didn't have any sympathy at all.

"After three days of throwin' his guts out, he'll be fine. It'll only take three days, then he'll be like an ol' sea dog. Three days, I tell ya." Jason liked the idea of medication rather than the three days of vomiting suggested by the original "sea dog".

After Jason took the Dramamine and after ten more minutes of last minute preparations, the Mary C. left Mr. Leek's dock and headed down the St. John's River, past the oak tree, past the big jetty rocks, and out into the open ocean. Jason didn't look at the tree when the boat passed by it. His stomach was churning enough without the thoughts of the tree adding to his discomfort and delicate condition.

Truck and three other young black men stood in the wooded area behind Mary C.'s house. They wore pants cut off at the calf line of their legs. They were barefoot and wore no shirts. They had painted big white circles around their eyes. They were the other Calypsos Luther had left alive in the woods. The four bush machete knives, sheathed and strapped to their sides, gave them the final look of warriors. They were preparing to take the oak baby. Truck was preparing to kill Mary C.

They had been smart, as Voo Swar had suggested. They waited for Hawk and Jason to be gone and they knew there would be little resistance from one woman. The stage was set for the abduction and murder. Truck nodded to the other three Calypsos and all four men walked out of the woods toward Mary C.'s house. They could see that two lights were on in the house as they entered the back yard.

Beth sat under the oak tree for the first time. Her body was hot with anticipation and a desire to learn more about the tree. She was confused and didn't have the feeling she wanted. She sat down in the soft sand and leaned her back against the huge trunk of the tree. Sleep took her fatigued body.

Mary C. had just stepped out of the shower and walked to her bedroom. She dropped the towel she had wrapped around her and took her usual look into her oval shaped full length mirror. She was pleased with herself and turned from side-to-side admiring what she saw.

Mary C. and Ana Kara were cut from the same cloth. Her heart jumped and she couldn't believe it when the sound of "Green Onions" came from the radio. She jumped up, put on her white terry cloth bath robe and started her sexy dance. She didn't tie the rope of the robe at her waist as she jumped around.

The Calypso warriors had gathered together at the backyard of her house. Truck motioned for them to go in different directions. They all knew the plan. Mary C. continued her dance, a dance that was even more provocative than before, due to the fact she was alone and totally uninhibited. One of the Calypsos stepped up to one of the windows of the house and found himself watching Mary C. move her body to the "Green Onions" melody. He was distracted from his mission as he watched the loose white robe open and close and flop around her naked body, exposing her female attributes as she danced. He would enjoy the exotic dance show and then carry out his assignment.

Another of the warriors moved to the front of the house and stepped up onto the front porch. He was already at the front door when the "Green Onion" instrumental ended and Mary C.'s dance was over.

As her new favorite song ended Mary C. stepped to the mirror for one more look at herself as another song, the smooth sounding "Mack the Knife" by Bobby Darin came out of the radio. "Oh, the shark, babe, has such teeth dear," Mary C.'s heart screamed in her chest when she saw the reflection of the peeping tom Calypso's painted face in the looking glass. He had watched her too long and revealed himself. She was incredible when it came to surviving. She danced away from the mirror and the sight of the watcher as Bobby Darin sang to her, "And he keeps it, ah, out of sight." She ducked down flat on the floor and reached under her bed for the shotgun she had placed earlier that day. It was not the old heavy doubled barreled cannon she had used earlier that day. After the encounter with the voodoo crowd Mary C. had loaded Hawk's light weight Remington

The Remington Pump Action

pump action shot gun with double ought buckshot loads that had pellets the size of ball-bearings and placed it under the bed. Mary C. was always prepared. Bobby Darin told her, "Someone's sneakin' 'round the corner," but she already knew that.

She reached up and pulled Billy off the bed, placing him under the bed. He was asleep.

Mary C. lay down on the floor, shotgun at ready. The watcher was still at the window, but she could not see him. He could not see her either and he stayed there hoping she would return to his view. Mary C. could see through to the living room and the front door, from where she laid. She was afraid, but she couldn't think about that at the moment. She heard the man at the front door and her throat filled with a hot liquid that had risen from her burning stomach. She thought about the night she stepped out of her car to face the evil James Thorn, and how she knew what it meant to dig down deep and find something you didn't know you had. Mary C. jumped up off the floor as the front door came crashing open and the first Calypso entered her house with bad intentions and uninvited. The warrior's machete was drawn, but he never expected what he saw, for only a brief moment before Mary C. pulled the trigger of the pump action shotgun. The explosion and projectiles blasted him back out the broken door he had entered only seconds before. He was dead before he hit the ground. Mary C. wasn't listening when Bobby Darin sang, "Could it be our boy's done something rash." The watcher at the window was still watching in shock at the vision the sexy dancer had given him. Mary C. pulled the pump handle under the barrel of the gun. As the spent shell was ejected, another twelve gauge shell slid into the chamber, preparing the gun to fire again at her will.

The watcher at the window turned to run and tell the others what he had seen and that she had a gun. The explosion had alerted the other three to the fact she was armed, but the watcher wasn't thinking clearly after the sight he had just witnessed. As he turned from the window he saw the flash of an object coming through the air in his direction. The object hit him in the middle of his chest, followed by a burning sensation. He looked down at his final shock of the night. A strange big knife was buried deep into his chest. He saw a shadow in front of him as the Indian, Sandeep, stepped out of the darkness. Like the flash of the knife, Sandeep moved quickly and pulled the huge handle and blade out of his first victim and moved back into the darkness. The watcher was hoping it was all a dream as he fell to his knees, then to his face. He smelled the dirt of Mary C.'s yard with his last breath. Mary C. moved back into the bedroom with Billy. She knew they were after the baby and they would have to come there to get him. She heard movement outside near the bedroom and she was still afraid.

The third Calypso had heard the gun shot, but he had no idea their forces had been cut in half. Truck wasn't sure what had happened either until he looked around the edge of the front of the house and saw the lifeless body of the first warrior who entered Mary C.'s "Green Onion" house of pain. The third warrior drew his machete when he saw the body of the watcher, face down by the bedroom window. He saw movement, as a shadow passed in front of him and he took a defensive stance in the direction of the movement. He was scared.

"Truck, is that you!" He looked down at his fallen companion. "Truck, Sammy's hurt. I think she shot him through the window." A voice cut into the night air.

"No, I shot you through the window." The third warrior turned slowly to see Mary C. standing at the bedroom window with the shotgun pointed at his face. He had no chance to even blink before she pulled the trigger again, blasting the glass and window frame, as well as the shell full of pellets into his face. He landed on the watcher, but he had no nose for a last breath.

Truck knew it was a desperate situation but he had no idea he was the last one left. That was the farthest thought from his mind. He knew they had been there too long and the sound of the two shotgun blasts could bring others to see what was happening. His desperate thoughts created desperate action. He decided he would gather the others and actually storm the house. The numbers alone should overpower Mary C. He would circle the house until he found the others.

Truck had taken only a few steps when he saw movement to his left in the dark. He stopped and listened.

"Sammy, Jeep, who is that?" There was a flash in front of him and he felt the presence of someone. He had a burning sensation under his chin like someone had poured hot wax on him. He touched where he felt the burning and felt his own blood and the huge gash the blade of Sandeep's Kirpan sword had made in his throat. His warm blood poured out of the death wound like water coming out of a big lipped pump. Sandeep stood in front of his second victim. Truck wanted to ask who he was, but he could make no sounds. Sandeep understood.

"I am Sandeep Singh. I protect the golden ones." Truck fell to his knees and began to crawl toward the steps of the front porch. Sandeep knew the big man was no threat to Mary C. or the child, so he moved into the darkness, waiting for his next victim. Mary C. could still see the front porch from where she sat in the bedroom. Bobby Darin was introducing her to Jenny Diver, and Sukey Tawdry and telling her to "look out for Miss Lotte Lenya and old Lucy Brown." She wasn't sure what she was seeing when she focused her eyes on another painted warrior as he actually crawled up the front steps and over the body of the first fallen Calypso. She could see how badly wounded the man was, but she was still cautious and would not be tricked. For some reason she stood up and walked to the front door.

The fatally injured man lifted his painted face as Mary C. stepped up to him with the shotgun pumped and aimed at his head. She knew instantly it was the young black man Truck, she had shot earlier that day. He could not speak and it was obvious he was dying. Mary C. wanted him to know something before she pulled the trigger and put him out of his misery.

"I knew you were coming back for the baby, I just didn't think it would be this soon. Big mistake." She pulled the trigger as Bobby Darin sang, "Look out, old Macky's back!"

The first catch of the night hit the deck of the Mary C. It was always a good sign when you saw that the shrimp falling from the net out numbered the other sea creatures. Jason, Hawk, Chichemo and Bosco all began picking the shrimp out of the pile of live and moving sea creatures. Bosco left the others after two big Florida blue crabs went after him. It must have been his animal instincts that made him know the claws on the crabs could snap his little monkey fingers off with one snip. The spider monkey jumped and played on the riggings above the three men as they continued picking out the shrimp and the saleable fish. Thanks to the old sea dog, Chichemo, Jason and Hawk would become shrimpers.

A cold chill came over Jason. He didn't like the way he felt. He thought perhaps he was getting ready to have another bout with the seasick bug. His mother's face flashed in his head. She was holding Billy in the rocking chair and the new song, "Green Onions," was coming from the radio. He enjoyed the mental flash and tried to keep it in his head as he picked through the first catch.

Jason's vision of his mother sitting in the rocking chair was true at that very moment, but she was not holding Billy in her lap. Billy remained in her bed and she sat in the chair with the pump action shotgun across her lap. Mary C. never experienced the feeling of shock. She gave that feeling to others. She was alert and calm and prepared for anything. She also knew it wasn't over, but she didn't know what was next. It was only a matter of minutes before she would face her final challenge of that awful night. She would never know Sandeep had defused her last test.

There was movement on the porch again. Mary C. turned the

pumped and loaded gun in the direction of the noise. She was not afraid at all when Voo Swar, the skinny voodoo woman stood near the two dead bodies of the fallen Calypsos. The front of Voo Swar's dress was covered with blood; her blood. Mary C. could see the little woman could hardly stand as she swayed to keep her balance and the scarf head piece on her head. Mary C. knew there were no others with Voo Swar, she had come to see the results of the invasion. Voo Swar put her trembling hand on the broken door facing to keep herself from falling. Her voice was low and full of pain.

"He said his name was Sandeep Singh. But, I know he was Lucifer, wasn't he? He said he was here to protect the child, but I know he was here for you. You have always walked with the demons. I couldn't die before I told you I knew who he really was."

Mary C. had no idea what the crazy voodoo woman meant and she didn't care, as she pulled the trigger again, blowing the top of Voo Swar's head and scarf covering off. The blast caused the leaves and roots from under the scarf covering to fly all over the front porch and some even into the house. Mary C.'s house, front porch and yard looked like a battle field. When the leaves and dust settled from the last blast, Mary C. knew it was over. She also knew that not one of the invaders even saw the child, much less got close to stealing him. In a few minutes, Mary C. had redefined what the perfect grandmother should be.

CHAPTER SIX

BETH WOKE UP FACE DOWN IN THE SOFT SAND UNDER THE OAK TREE. HER clothes were scattered around on the ground and she realized she was naked. She could see her body prints in the sand as if she had rolled around when she was sleeping. There was a warm tingling between her legs. She touched herself and she was wet. Her thigh and stomach muscles were sore. She felt dizzy and there was a quivering inside her. Beth gathered her clothes, dressed and walked back down the sand hill to Big Bob's truck. She wasn't sure what had happened, but she knew she didn't like how she felt. She didn't like being unsure and feeling like something was done to her without her knowing. She thought perhaps she removed her clothes while she was sleeping. Beth hated to wear clothes and it would be like her to cast them off if she got too hot or uncomfortable. She didn't like the light headed feeling she was experiencing. Beth started the truck and drove away into the dark night.

Eve was waiting for Sandeep's return. She sat up in the bed and watched him pull off his turban and release his braided hair. She watched him wash himself from a basin of water on the dresser. She knew he was naked, but his hair covered most of his body. She also knew she would indulge in his body when he came to bed.

"I've been waiting for you; wanting you. I've wanted you all day." Sandeep continued washing himself.

"Did you see your dear Sofia?"

"Yes, but only for a moment. She had to know what she is. Now, it is up to her what she will do with what she knows."

"You want to take care of her and protect her, don't you?"

"I would defend her and keep her from harm, if needed, but I am dedicated to you. That has not changed."

"Are you sorry you are pledged to me?"

"Yes, I am."

"Why?"

"You already know why."

"Tell me again."

"You have evil in your blood. It was hidden from me in some way."

"Your desire for me made you blind. Even now, knowing my blood, you still are blinded by your desire for me. Once I did this for you..." Eve threw the sheet back that covered her, exposing her body that was covered from neck to toe in tattoos. Every inch of her body was covered with scenes similar to the animals and symbols of the world that covered Sandeep's body. He turned to face her. His hair fell behind him exposing his tattoo covered body, as well. Eve knelt on the bed.

"This was my gift to you. This was your dream and your request. This is my part of the bargain."

"I know what I asked of you for my pledge. You gave me the greatest tribute one has ever made to Sandeep. I will never forget it. I belong to you until you release me of your own free will or you are dead." His desire for her tattooed body was as Eve had said, it was blinding for the soldier saint. He joined her in the bed. They embraced and fell onto the bed. Sandeep's hair covered them both like a raven black blanket.

"Where have you been so long?"

Mary C. still sat in her rocking chair with the shotgun on her lap. She was physically and mentally drained and wasn't thinking about what to do next. She looked up at the hole where the front door used to be when she heard another noise coming from outside the house.

Like before, she pointed the shotgun in the direction of the noise. Mary C. smiled and lowered the gun when she saw Margie, the oldest sister, standing at the bottom of the porch steps. Margie looked at the signs of the massacre all around her. She took a deep breath and stepped over the bloody bodies on the porch and in the doorway. Mary C. didn't move from the rocking chair.

"Well, well, you come to see me twice in one day. I'm gonna start thinkin' you like me." Margie stepped closer to the chair.

"I do like you Miss Mary C. Are you alright?"

"I'm fine. You probably need to ask them that question." Margie could see Mary C. was trying to recover from a horrible ordeal and fight for her life.

"Miss Mary C., where's the baby; where's Billy?" Mary C. looked toward her bedroom.

"He's in there but don't wake him. The little fella's tired as hell."

"Is it O.K. if I take a look at him, if I don't wake him?" Mary C. nodded her head. Margie wanted to see if the baby was safe and uninjured. Margie didn't see Billy under the bed at first and she heard him make a noise. She looked under the bed and he was awake and she knew he was not hurt. She reached under the bed and held him in her arms. Margie could see that the window in the bedroom had been torn out. She stepped to the damaged area and looked outside. She saw the two other dead Calypso warriors. Margie pulled her head back and moved back to the living room where Mary C. still sat on guard. Margie knelt down on one knee next to Mary C. and touched her hand.

"Miss Mary C., he was awake and I hope you don't mind me holding him. We have to call the police and get some help out here." Mary C. smiled.

"I really don't need no help now. Coulda used some an hour ago, but not now. I took care of it myself, but thanks for askin'. If ya know somebody who'll fix my door and window, that would sure help me out. I don't think I know no late night carpenters." Margie knew she was not going to get anywhere with Mary C. in her present state of mind.

The Keyhole

"Miss Mary C., I'm going to go now, but I'd like to come back in a little while if that's alright with you?"

"Give me the child. You're always welcome here, Margie. Good night." Margie handed Billy to his grandmother, stepped over the dead bodies and ran toward the store.

Tom Thumb, the World's Smallest Man and sexually perverted pigmy, walked out of the bathroom at John King's house. He couldn't help but hear the muffled noises of pleasure coming from one of the bedrooms. Without hesitation he moved in the direction of the sounds and stood outside the door of Eve's and Sandeep's room. The keyhole was in perfect position for his eye. In fact, every keyhole in the known world was perfect for him. Again he didn't hesitate to see what was going on behind that door. He liked it when others watched him and he thought everyone else probably liked to be watched, too. He saw movement in the room and as he focused he knew the movement was in the bed. It didn't take the peeping Tom but a few seconds to realize nothing he had ever done before prepared him for what he was seeing through the keyhole of a haunted house.

The movement on the bed had no individual dimensions. It looked like one huge pile of color and animals and faces. The tattoos on their bodies seemed to melt together and become liquid in form. The colors and faces ran together and even seemed to change bodies. Tom could not see where Sandeep's body ended and Eve's body began. His eye was frozen in the keyhole and even though he was scared, he could not turn away. Tom was able to see Eve's female frame for a moment when she sat up on top of Sandeep. Tom could see her back and the huge tattoo of a black panther that almost covered her entire back. It was drawn to give the impression the huge cat had jumped on Eve's back and the cat was sticking it's sharp claws into Eve's shoulders and sides. The cat's eyes were closed, but it's mouth was wide open, showing its sharp teeth. Eve began moving her naked painted body above her mate. She pumped her hips and threw her head back. Sandeep's hair covered both sides of the bed and the floor. Sandeep reached up and grabbed Eve's butt cheeks with both his hands to assist her in her forceful pounding motion. Every time she would push her hips downward, Sandeep would push his hips upward to actually collide with her lower body. Tom was almost scared to death by the next vision he saw through the little keyhole. The wild sexual frenzy was at its breaking point. Tom recognized the look and sounds of a biblical proportioned climax to a true animalistic sexual encounter, but he was not prepared for something like he was getting ready to witness.

Sandeep pushed his hips upward, driving his manhood to it's deepest level inside Eve's body, lifting her into the air. Eve made a noise that was more like an animal than a human. As the noise bounced off the walls in the room, the brilliant eyes of the panther opened and flashed as if they were alive. The big cat's claws dug deep into Eve's shoulders and sides. Crimson blood dripped from the marks the claws made. Every animal, person's face and strange creature on her body opened their eyes as the panther did when Eve's hot body fluids exploded from her painted body. Sandeep exploded at the same moment and at one time it looked like the tattoo pictures on his body changed places with the pictures on Eve's body. The two lovers and all the painted pictures came alive. Tom remained frozen in fear and a strange need to see more. More came.

As Eve's climax ended and Sandeep had emptied his fluids deep within her, Eve fell forward in complete exhaustion. When her breast fell against his chest all the tattoos returned to their original places and all eyes closed. It was too much for the little pigmy pervert. He pulled away from the keyhole and moved back to his room and Helga's side. As Tom lay in the bed with Helga sleeping next to him he thought perhaps he had been dreaming. He also thought that if the tattoos did seem to move, perhaps they had been drawn and created to cause the optical illusion of the movement he had witnessed. He had seen pictures before that the eyes in the drawing would open and close because of movement. He tried to think of the reason he had seen what he had seen. The truth of the matter was that he had been humbled and had never been so scared in his little life. Tom even thought maybe they were ghosts. He would not sleep that night.

Eve's Panther

Officer Jimmy Johnston's patrol car drove into Mary C.'s front yard. Margie was in the car with him. He drove his car as close to the front porch as he could. He saw the three dead bodies on the porch and in the doorway. Officer Johnston called to the station before he even got out of his car.

"This is Jimmy. I need anybody who's available to get out to Mayport, right now. Is Mr. Butler there?"

"Right here, Jimmy. What's goin' on? You alright?"

"Yes sir, but you need to get out here to Mary C.'s house right away. I don't know what happened yet, but there's a lot of dead people here."

"We're on our way." Margie had already left the car and was back inside the house. Mary C. had put the shotgun down and she was rocking Billy in the rocking chair.

"You did come back. I'm glad. And you brought Officer Johnston back with you to help. You are the sweetest thing. All you girls are so sweet all the time." Officer Johnston looked at the three bodies at the front door. A chill ran through his body when he saw the painted faces and clam digger pants. He hadn't thought about the Calypsos in about a year. He thought they were all gone or they had decided to stop their rituals in the nearby woods. It was obvious they had returned to visit Mary C. He didn't recognize the skinny woman with part of her head gone. Mary C. greeted the young police officer. She had talked to him many times before.

"Well Jimmy Johnston, I've heard the police are always late and now I guess it's true. I sure could have used you about an hour ago. That big one over there, his name is Truck. He's the leader. I already shot him once today. I knew I shoulda killed him then. The other painted one was the one who broke my door down. I killed him first. He had a big machete knife in his hand. I knew they was here to steal the baby, so I knew the machete was for me. I think the big one over there was mad 'cause I shot him this mornin'. He acted like it didn't matter, but I could see it in his eyes. I can't believe they thought they could come into my house, take my grandson and chop my head off, too. You know I just couldn't let that happen, don't ya?" Mary C. didn't care if her question was answered, she never did. "The skinny woman with the sticks and leaves all over her is a voodoo woman, called Voo Swar. She was here this morning and Jason let her touch the baby. I shoulda killed her this morning. I knew when I saw her this mornin' she was comin' back. I knew it all the time." Jimmy knew Mary C. had just survived an incredible fight for survival.

"Are you hurt at all."

"They never even got close to me or the baby. There's another one on the side of the house under my bedroom window. Margie looked at Jimmy and corrected Mary C.'s dead body count.

"Miss Mary C. there's two men under the window, I saw two men there." Mary C. smiled.

"Hell, I musta got two with one shot, damn." Jimmy left the room and went to see the other two bodies. When he found them he couldn't see very much in the dark. Jimmy could see there were two of them and one had no face at all, his paint was gone. He noticed the chunks of wood window framing and pieces of glass on the ground and on the bodies. He knew Mary C. had fired the fatal shots through the bedroom window. He thought out loud. "Two for one shot, damn." He walked back to his car.

"This is Jimmy again. I need an ambulance for Mary C. and five body bags. Four male and one female, I think. Y'all please hurry."

Margie knelt down on the floor next to Mary C. and Billy, like she had done earlier that evening. "Miss Mary C., please come stay at my house for the night. You and Billy can be comfortable there and you can be away from all this. Please don't say no. You don't need to stay here. Jimmy can take care of things here. Please." Mary C. had her strange moments and she was always unpredictable. Her head was actually clearing. She was mentally strong when she needed to be, even though she had her weak and simple moments. Officer Johnston walked back onto the front porch and stepped over the bodies again. Margie wanted his support.

"Jimmy, I asked Miss Mary C. to come and stay at my house tonight. She and the baby don't need to stay here. They will be safe and comfortable with us. They need to be away from here, don't you think?"

"I think that's a fine idea, but I'll have to be sure if she can leave when Mr. Butler gets here. She can wait that long. He's on his way. I think it will be alright under the circumstances and I'll take y'all over there." Mary C. surprised them both.

"I'll need a few things. We can't stay here tonight with that door and window broken. The mosquitoes would eat us alive." Mary C. stood up from the rocking chair, handed Billy to Margie and went to her bedroom to pack for an overnight stay at Miss Margaret's house. Officer Jimmy Johnston had to talk to Margie. "I'm gonna take her to your house, but you can't let her leave, you know that?" Margie was put out with his remark.

"She's not leaving and you know it. She knows she did the right thing here and you know that, too. She's not leaving Mayport and you know she's not going to jail either. I don't know much about the law, but I'm willing to bet this is that little thing called, self defense. Look at all those machetes. They didn't come to visit, they came to kill her and did they make a mistake. Isn't she the most incredible woman you've ever seen?" Jimmy was impressed with Margie's little, "I'm willing to bet self defense" speech.

"Well, you're probably right, but Mr. Butler's gonna want to know everything and he's gonna want to hear it from her."

The second drag of the night poured out of the dripping net onto the deck of the Mary C. It was a similar catch to the first one and the shrimp clearly outnumbered the other sea creatures. Their first night out would be respectable. Jason was excited about the shrimp they were catching and he was even more excited that the Dramamine had kept him from getting seasick. Chichemo said they would drop the nets and drag one more time and then head for Mayport. They would unload at Mr. Leek's dock in the morning.

Three unmarked police cars drove into Mary C.'s front yard and stopped near Officer Johnston's car. Jimmy met them in the yard. Mr. Butler could see the bodies on the porch. The other officers moved to the porch and began examining the bodies.

"Holy shit, Jimmy. What the hell happened here?" Jimmy took a deep breath.

"It seems that four of the old Calypso boys tried to steal Mary C.'s new grandson. They brought their machetes with them in case they got any resistance. Mary C. seems to have been more resistance than they expected." Mr. Butler looked at Officer Jimmy Johnston.

"And that's it?" Officer Johnston took another deep breath.

"Well, not exactly, sir. These dead people were here this morning and wanted to see the baby. Mary C. was trying to make them leave her property when her son, Jason, came home and let them see the baby." Mr. Butler interrupted Jimmy.

"Her son's back? I thought he was gone for good."

"Not only is he back, but I guess he brought a baby back with him." Mr. Butler was amazed at what he was hearing. Jimmy continued.

"They came back tonight when she was alone to take the child. The woman over there, covered with leaves, is the voodoo woman called Voo Swar." Mr. Butler had to stop Jimmy again.

"Hold it! Stop! I gotta get my bearings here. First, tell me why they wanted the baby?" Margie's voice cut into the conversation.

"Because he's an oak baby." Mr. Butler and Officer Johnston turned in the direction of the voice, as Margie walked up to them. Jimmy wasn't sure he wanted Margie to be part of the conversation. Mr. Butler made her just that.

"'Cause he's a what?"

"He's an oak baby. From the oak tree. He may very well be the most perfect one of them all." Jimmy interrupted again.

"Mr. Butler, you remember the stories about the oak tree and the oak babies, don't ya sir?"

"Oh, of course, the oak babies of Mayport. Sure it's my favorite story." Mr. Butler's comment had a large amount of sarcasm in its tone and delivery.

"And you are Margie, Jimmy's friend?"

"Yes sir. I was here this morning when all that stuff happened. I came by tonight to see how Miss Mary C. was doing and found all this." Officer Johnston jumped in.

"Margie called me and told me what had happened. She knows

a lot about it." Mr. Butler turned his attention back to the talkative Margie.

"I didn't think your mother would let you girls believe in such a thing. I've never met her, but I've heard you have a wonderful family. You seem to think this baby is the real thing."

"I do, because he is. That voodoo woman wanted him for what he is and what he will be able to do as he grows. This whole thing's pretty scary. People stealing someone else's baby."

"It's scary alright. Anytime I'm near Miss Mary C. I'm scared." Margie looked at Officer Johnston after Mr. Butler's admission of fear. Jimmy made the request he knew she wanted from him.

"Mr. Butler, Margie wanted to know if Mary C. and the baby could go wait at her house for the night until we were finished here. With the house torn up like it is and the amount of work we have to do, perhaps it would be better if they were not here." Mr. Butler was a reasonable man.

"Yes, that is a good idea. I don't see why not. I don't think Mary C. will go anywhere. She's never left during a killing before. Why would she start now." His sarcastic tone remained. Margie was a little surprised he agreed so quickly. He wasn't finished.

"I do need to talk to her before she leaves. Jimmy, when she gets to your car I'll talk to her then." Jimmy nodded his head and motioned for Margie to go help Mary C. get ready to go.

"Yes sir. Oh, and by the way, there is one more thing." Mr. Butler cut his eyes at Officer Johnston.

"And what exactly is that?" Jimmy took this third real deep breath of the night so far.

"There are two more dead bodies on the side of the house under the bedroom window. Calypsos, I think. One is for sure, but the other one doesn't have a face so I couldn't see if he was painted or not. I'm assuming he was." Mr. Butler gave Jimmy a blank stare. His sarcasm remained.

"Just two more, that's all."

"Yes sir, just two, as far as I could see in the dark."

"And Miss Mary C. killed them all?"

"Yes sir, it sure looks that way." Mr. Butler leaned against Jimmy's patrol car.

"Four men with weapons and a voodoo woman, and Mary C. killed them all. She killed five people. Is she hurt?"

"No sir. She seems shaken, but I don't think she's hurt at all."

"Four men with machetes and a voodoo woman with her magic leaves invade this house and Mary C. kills them all and she doesn't have a scratch on her. She's just shaken. Is that the word you used to describe her condition at this time." Jimmy nodded his head again.

"Yes sir, that's about the size of it." Mr. Butler took his own deep breath.

"Take her and the child with you and your friend. I'll talk to her later. I need to take a good look at these poor dead devils. Boy, this woman is something else, my friend. I'm not sure exactly what that is, but she is definitely something else. I need to help the others." Mr. Butler called one of the other policeman over to him and they walked to the side of the house where the other two bodies were located.

Jimmy saw Margie standing at the door with Mary C. and the baby. He motioned for them to come to his car. When they got to the car and the three were in the back seat, Margie reminded Jimmy of what she had heard Mr. Butler say when they were talking.

"Don't forget to tell Mr. Butler we're leaving." Jimmy started the car.

"He said he'd talk to her later. She needs to get away from here and get some rest. I called an ambulance in case Mary C. was hurt. When it gets here they can take a look at her at your house." Mary C. looked at Margie, smiled and shrugged her shoulders. Officer Jimmy Johnston drove his patrol car out of Mary C.'s front yard and in the direction of Miss Margaret's house. They would be there in a matter of minutes.

Mr. Butler turned the two dead bodies under the bedroom window so the were both on there backs. He could hardly look at the faceless victim. One jungle machete lay on the ground next to them. The faceless man still had his machete sheathed at his waist. He talked out loud to the other officer and to himself as well, as he looked up at the hole where the bedroom window used to be.

"This thing is probably the wildest I've ever seen. And I've seen some crazy things in my years on the force. I should have known that sooner or later this woman would be the one who topped it all. It was her and my destiny. There's no telling how many people have died with her involved. Me and Jimmy talked about it last year. I knew things had been too quiet around her lately. And now that her son's back, all hell breaks loose. He shows up with a baby, how the hell does that happen. And this ain't no regular baby. It's a baby voodoo and Calypso people want to steal and they'll kill to do it. And why was this woman so prepared for them. This is something else, just like her, she's something else, I tell ya." The other officer just listened, he knew his boss was pressed and frustrated at the bloody carnage around them. The other two officers joined them at the side of the house and they moved the two bodies to the porch area with the others.

Officer Jimmy Johnston's police car pulled up to the front of Miss Margaret's house. He picked up his radio hand mike.

"This is Officer Johnston. I need that ambulance headed to Mayport to come to 2072 Palmer Street. I'll meet them there." Margie assisted Mary C. with Billy as they got out of the back seat of Jimmy's car. Miss Margaret came out of the house, followed by her daughters, Peggy and Susan.

"Margie, what's wrong. Are you alright?" Margie walked toward her mother, holding Billy to her chest, with Mary C. following her, carrying a small suit case.

"I'm fine Mama. I asked Miss Mary C. to stay with us tonight. She needs a place to stay and I knew she could stay here for the night." Peggy and Susan were both wide-eyed and curious to know what was going on. Miss Margaret stepped to assist Margie with the baby.

"Of course she can stay with us. Please, Mary C. come in out of the night air." All the women walked into the house. Jimmy waited outside for the ambulance to arrive, so he could inform them of the situation. The head lights of the ambulance flashed as it turned onto the road leading to Miss Margaret's house. Jimmy stepped away from his car so the driver could see him. The ambulance stopped in front of the house and the driver got out. Jimmy had gone to school with the driver, Chris Hoye and they knew each other well.

"What's goin' on, Jimmy?" Jimmy took his fourth deep breath.

"I'm not sure what to do, Chris. I'm glad it's you, maybe you can help me."

"I'll do my best. What do you need?"

"I got a woman in here and she just killed five people who were trying to break into her house and steal her grandbaby." Chris had to stop Jimmy for a second.

"She killed five people? Tonight? Five?" Jimmy nodded as an answer to all three questions.

"The thing is, when I called for an ambulance I thought she was hurt physically, or at least mentally, from being in shock. Now, that I've talked to her and seen her she seems fine, almost calm and unaffected by the whole thing. I thought you could talk to her and see what you think."

"You know sometimes shock won't hit a person 'til later. They seem fine and normal and then it hits 'em like a brick to the head. Or maybe she's just a cool cookie and it has had no affect on her. There are some people who can handle these things." Jimmy nodded again.

"She could be one of those people, I'm sure. Her entire life has been filled with death and tragedy. She could be just that used to such things. Besides, I don't think she'll go with you anyway. At least we can say we tried to assist her. Come on in the house and talk to her." Officer Jimmy Johnston and his friend, Chris Hoye, walked up the steps of Miss Margaret's house and knocked on the door. Peggy opened the door.

"Hey, Peggy. This is Chris, he's one of our paramedics. He needs to talk to Mary C. and find out if her or the baby needs any medical attention." Peggy turned and led them into the living room where all the others were sitting. Jimmy could tell Margie had not told the gruesome tale yet. They were all catering to Mary C. and the baby and making them as comfortable as they could. Miss Margaret had not asked any questions. She knew she would be given information later if she needed it. Mary C. was the first to notice when Jimmy and Chris walked in the room behind Peggy.

"Well, Officer Johnston." All eyes in the room turned toward Jimmy. "Have you come to take me away?" All eyes turned to Mary C. and then back to Jimmy. "I see the man in the white coat has arrived." All eyes turned to Chris, then to Mary C., then back to Jimmy. Officer Johnston stepped closer to Mary C.

"He's just here to see if you or the baby need any medical attention. You have gone through an awful thing tonight and we want to be sure you're alright. We really haven't had a chance to ask you very much about your condition. Chris is here to help you if you need it. If you don't need help he'll leave." All eyes were on Mary C. when she motioned for the young ambulance driver to come closer to her. Chris stepped up and stood by her.

"Can you put a bedroom window in?" The room was quiet and all, but Margie and Jimmy were surprised at her strange request.

"Yes ma'am I sure can. My daddy taught me how. He taught me a lot of handy things. How are you feeling?" The young man knew how to handle the situation.

"I feel good. In fact, every time I look at Billy, over there, I feel real good." Chris knelt down on one knee on the floor next to her.

"Did you get hurt tonight? Sometimes people don't realize they have been hurt. The adrenalin keeps them from feeling anything until later. Do you have any pains. Are you hurting anywhere?" Mary C. touched the young man's face with her hand.

"You are the nicest young man. I think the young people around here are the nicest things. I believe I am hurt."

"Can you tell me where it hurts."

"They hurt my feelings. Everybody hurt my feelings. I usually don't care if my feelings get hurt, but this time it was different. Billy made it different. You see it doesn't matter what happens to me, but Billy is a different story. He matters. No one listened to me and that really hurt my feelings." Chris looked at the silent faces around him when

Mary C. stopped talking. "Well, I'm sorry to say I don't have anything in my little satchel to fix that. If you need anything tonight or anytime later please call the service and I'll come back out to help. It doesn't matter when, please call." Chris turned to Jimmy. "Not much for me to do here, she's not physically injured. Call me if you need me. Good night ladies." Jimmy walked his friend, Chris, out to the ambulance.

"It's hard to say how stable she is, but at least she's safe here and they will take care of her and the baby. I'm sure they'll call if they need me."

"Thanks for comin' out. I know it's a long way."

"Hey, I'd rather not be needed when I get to a call, that means everything's alright. It's better to be safe than sorry, you know that. Good night my friend."

"Good night."

Mr. Butler had all five bodies laid out on the ground in front of Mary C.'s front porch. They were all on their backs and face up, for the one's that had faces. Mr. Butler stepped to the first body and knelt down on the ground for a closer look. It was Truck's body.

"Now this was a big boy here. She had to blast him at pretty close range to do this sort of damage. I don't understand, if you're trying to sneak up on someone and you've planned your attack, how in the hell did he let her get so close to him. It was like she just walked up to him, put the gun in his face and said good night. I just don't understand it."

Officer Jimmy Johnston's patrol car lights flashed as he pulled up into Mary C.'s front yard. He jumped out of the car and hurried to join the other officers and Mr. Butler. Mr. Butler greeted him.

"I'm glad you're back. I need you to work with me here. You got them settled over there?"

"Yes sir. Chris Hoye met us and talked to Mary C., but with no physical injuries he couldn't do much. He said to call him if we needed him."

"Come look at these poor devils over here." Jimmy walked to where the five bodies were stretched out. Mr. Butler was still near Truck's body.

"Look at the size of this one. And she was able to shoot him in the face at close range, like he let her just walk up to him for a kiss." Jimmy recognized the body that Mary C. had pointed out to him.

"Mary C. said this big one's called Truck. He was the leader of the group that came here this morning to see the baby. She had already shot him once this morning. She said she should have killed him the first time." Mr. Butler shook his head.

"And he was dumb enough to come back and let her just walk up and finish the job. Nobody's that stupid. He came here because he knew he could kill her and get the baby. He didn't come here to die, none of them did. Even the old voodoo girl over there, she came here to watch it happen. They didn't expect to be blown to pieces." Jimmy bent down next to Truck's body. His head was torn away from under his nose to the top of his forehead.

"You're right, she had to have the gun touching his face when she pulled the trigger. Look at the way the force opened this gash on his throat. It had to be a direct barrel blast to bend his head back with such force." Mr. Butler moved to Jimmy's side and looked at the neck area of the dead man. He concentrated on the gashed area Jimmy was talking about.

"My goodness, Officer Johnston. Isn't this the cleanest cut you've ever seen from a shotgun blast. It actually looks like she slit his throat first and then stuck the shotgun in his face." One of the other officers added his thought.

"Or somebody else slit his throat first and then she put the gun in his face." Jimmy looked at Mr. Butler.

"Let's look at the rest of 'em." They both stepped to the next body. Jimmy remembered what Mary C. had said.

"This was the first one she shot. He broke the front door down and when he ran in with his machete drawn, she was waiting to blast him. The force of the blast threw him back out the door. I don't know how she was so prepared." Mr. Butler had an observation.

"We'll check him again, but it looks like the shotgun blast was the thing that killed him."

"Now this one here is a different story. He was under the window with this no face bastard over here. She did them through the bedroom window. This poor devil here must have had his face against the window glass when she pulled the trigger. His peepin' tom days are over. But, this one here has me puzzled. He's got blood all over him, some I'm sure it belongs to no nose, but he has not been shot. He has a huge wound in the middle of his chest. I don't think the glass could have made such a cut. I even thought he had fallen on one of the machetes, but it doesn't look that way." Jimmy remembered more of his first conversation with Mary C.

"Mary C. thought she had only killed one at the window. When Margie told her there was two she thought it was great that she had got two of them with one shot." Mr. Butler's brain wheels were turning.

"And this one here." He stepped to Voo Swar's little body. The top of her head was gone like she had been scalped by Apaches. Even though they had moved her, she still had some leaves and branches from under her scarf headdress, on her body. "She was shot in the head from a little distance, but she's got a cut in the middle of her breast bone that you can put your hand into. I even thought one of the Calypsos might have cut her with a machete by mistake. It being so dark and all. Once the shooting started these painted warriors could have very well went into a panic gear and the old girl just walked up at the wrong time. Hell, with all these damn machetes being waved around they could have killed each other trying to get away from Mary C. I do know one thing. Two of these individuals got cut and shot, one just got cut and the other two were shot. I don't think Mary C. did any cutting, but she did all the shooting. And I can't wait to talk to her in the morning. Call the wagon out and get these bodies out of here. Get somebody to bring out some plywood to close the house up for the night. They might have some out back of the house. I really should talk to Mary C. tonight. I've got a mind to go over there and get this over with. She's the only one who can tell us what happened here. I need to know now." He turned to Officer Johnston. "We can't wait on this one. You need to take me where she is." Jimmy nodded. Mr. Butler had another interesting thought. "Seeing these painted faces laid out here made me think that maybe your boy Luther was back from the dead and he was the other shooter or should I say, cutter. And I have to tell ya, nothing would surprise me when it comes to these people out here."

Margie put Billy on her bed. He was sleeping again and she had given up her room for the overnight guests. Her sisters were still waiting to hear what had happened and why Mary C. was their house guest for the night. Margie surrounded Billy with pillows so he would not move around and fall off the bed. Then she returned to the living room where all the others were sitting with Mary C.

"He's sleeping again. New babies sure sleep a lot, don't they? He is so beautiful." Mary C. smiled at Margie's compliment. Miss Margaret had a comment.

"That's when babies grow. The sleep and rest makes them grow." Peggy looked at her mother.

"I've never heard that Mama, is that true?"

"I've always believed that and it does seem logical. We all know how good and strong we feel when we get the right amount of sleep. It makes us stronger, more alert and able to cope with life. Sleep is good medicine." Mary C. wanted the other women to know why she had to stay with them that night. She knew they had to be curious and fully understood their curiosity. Margie sat down next to her sister Susan. Mary C. had a new topic for the conversation.

"I know you are all wondering why I'm staying here and what has happened tonight." Miss Margaret had to interrupt her. "Mary C., you don't have to say anything at all. If Margie wanted to help you tonight, that's good enough for all of us. You are most welcome here and you don't have to explain a thing to any of us. Your business is your business and we're just happy you're here." Mary C. wanted them to know.

"I really do appreciate that and I know you mean what you say. Y'all are the nicest family I've ever seen, but you have a right to know what has happened." Peggy and Susan were all ears and they both sat up on the edge of their seats, as Mary C. began retracing the events of her wild day, starting with the visit from Sofia and Margie,

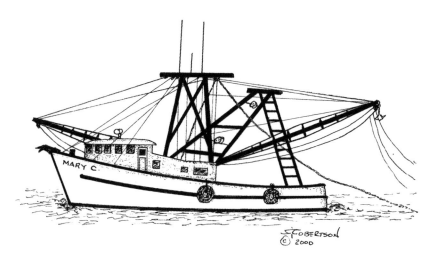

Nets Down

to the moment she blew the top of Voo Swar's head off. She would talk for about an hour, giving details of what happened and her thoughts while it was happening. No one even considered leaving the room or interrupting her incredible words. They were all spellbound, including Miss Margaret. Mary C. was an unusual, but special and brave, woman and all in that room recognized it that night.

Jason, Hawk, Chichemo and Bosco were picking out the shrimp and fish from the third drag of the night. The three catches had been very substantial and they had all agreed to drop the nets for a fourth and final drag. Jason had still not gotten seasick. It was a great night for shrimping.

Mr. Leek pulled his truck into Mary C.'s front yard. He had picked up some strange police talk on his citizen band police radio when he was at his house on Mayport Road. He heard one officer mention Mary C.'s address and that they needed assistance there. He knew something was seriously wrong and he had decided to make the drive and check up on his friends. He stopped and stepped out of the truck. He could see the police activities on the porch. He also saw men carrying bodies on plank boards to the morgue wagon. A young police officer met him before he could move toward the house.

"Excuse me sir, you can't go up there."

"I'm a close friend of the family. Are they alright?"

"Yes sir, the people who live here are fine. They're not here." Officer Jimmy Johnston walked up behind the other officer.

"I'll talk to this gentleman, Dave. You go on home now and thanks for all your help."

"No problem, Jimmy. I wouldn't have missed this one for anything. It was a classic." The young officer nodded his head to Mr. Leek and walked to his patrol car.

"Jimmy, what has happened here. Who are all those people being carried off. They all look dead. And where is Mary C.?" Jimmy tried to answer the questions as they were asked.

"Well, first of all, these people tried to kill Mary C. and steal Jason's son. And, yes, they are all dead and Mary C. killed them. Mary C.'s stayin' at Miss Margaret's house tonight. Her and the baby are both fine." Mr. Leek's head was spinning as he tried to absorb Jimmy's incredible answers. Before Mr. Leek could ask anymore questions, Mr Butler joined them.

"Hey, Al, what brings you out this way?"

"Actually, I picked up some strange talk on the C-band and I thought I should come out here and see if Mary C. needed my help. I just got a feeling something was wrong."

"That's one woman that doesn't need much help, but that was awful nice of you. Me and Jimmy have to go talk to her, whereever he left her. You can come along with us if you want. She might respond to a friendly face and someone she trusts, if you don't mind hearing all the gruesome details when I question her."

"Not at all. You have a job to do and I would just like to help her anyway I can."

"Then, let's go."

The clock over the fireplace mantle in Miss Margaret's living room chimed eleven times. Mary C. had just finished her complete incredible story of her life and death struggle. Margie looked at the clock and remembered she was suppose to relieve her sister Sofia at the store at ten o'clock. Miss Margaret remembered, too.

"Margie we plum forgot about Sofia. You start the car and I'll call and tell her we're coming. I'll drive her back and come relieve you later. I'm the late shift tonight. Are you able to work?"

Peggy and Susan were all ears again, but this time they were waiting for Margie's reply to their mother's question. They knew Margie was the best at getting out of work and Sofia had already worked the shift that was originally Margie's. They also knew if she used the trauma of the evening as an excuse, Miss Margaret would either tell one of them to work or go work herself. They both stared at their older sister.

"No ma'am, I'm fine. I'm too keyed up to sleep or relax anyway. Let's hurry over there and give Sofia a break." Susan and Peggy couldn't believe their ears. They were happy, but surprised. They had thought Margie would milk the current situation for all it was worth. There was a knock at the front door as Margie walked toward it to leave. Mary C. made a request.

"If they're wearin' white coats, tell 'em I ain't here." Margie opened the door when she saw it was Officer Jimmy Johnston doing the knocking.

"Hey Margie. Mary C. alright?"

"Yes Jimmy, she's fine and she's still here." Mr. Butler spoke from behind Jimmy.

"We know it's late, but I have to talk to her." Margie turned her body, allowing the three men to enter the front of the house. Miss Margaret was the next to greet them.

"Jimmy, Al, come in." Miss Margaret smiled at Mr. Butler. Jimmy made the introduction.

"Miss Margaret, this is my boss, Mr. Butler, he needs to talk to Mary C." Mr. Butler shook hands with Miss Margaret.

"I'm sorry for the late hour visit, but you do understand the reason, I'm sure."

"Yes, I do. Please come in, all of you. She's in the living room. I have to leave you for a moment and take Margie to the store and pick up Sofia. I'll be right back. Make yourselves at home." Miss Margaret and Margie left as the visitors walked into the front of the house. As the three men entered the living room Mary C. was her usual interesting self.

"Hey Officer Jimmy Johnston, you fix my door yet? You did want to help me, didn't ya? Hey, Al, you're out too late. And Mr. Butler, isn't it? You come to help me, too? Tooooo late!"

Mr. Leek stepped forward from the others. "You alright Mary C.?"

"My dear friend, Al. I wonder how many times in our lives you have wanted to know if I was alright? You are a dear and I know you're really concerned about how I am. And I can honestly say I'm mad as hell, Al. Folks always want to know how I am 'after the fact'. That's what they say , Al, after the fact. I do have a lot of after the facts, don't I ? I'm just real mad after the fact." Mr. Leek didn't know what to say and he was glad when Mr Butler took over.

"I need to know about tonight from you. I'm trying to figure it all out, but only you are the key. I know it's late, we're all tired and you have gone through something we can only imagine. But, will you talk to me now?" The room was silent in anticipation of Mary C.'s refusal to talk or a strange remark. As usual, she was full of surprises.

"I'd be more than happy to talk about what happened. I want y'all to tell everybody you see. So the rest of those painted voodoo devils will understand what they will face if they try to take that baby again. Hell yes, I been waitin' here to tell ya." The room was silent; almost too quiet.

Mr. Butler didn't know where to start. Her willing reply had mentally thrown him back a few feet and he was getting his legs back. Peggy and Susan were both hoping they would be able to stay and hear the story again. Mr. Butler moved a small chair so he could sit next to Mary C. Mr. Leek and Officer Jimmy Johnston sat on a couch on the other side of the room. No one said anything to the two sisters. Mr. Butler had collected his thoughts.

"Mary C., we've got five dead people at your house. Do you know how they died?" She gave a half grin.

"Of course I do. I killed 'em."

"Was anyone else there with you when it happened?"

"I don't think so. One time I felt like there was somebody else outside, but they didn't come in the house. Then later I realized it was that voodoo woman. She was the last one. When she came to the door I figured she was the one outside I felt was watching me."

"You told Jimmy you shot one through the bedroom window."

"That's right, he was talking to someone and he said I had shot Sammy through the window. I hadn't shot through the window yet. But, while he was talkin' and his head was at the window, I took the shot. That was the first and only one at the window."

"You know there were two dead under the window, don't you?"

"Yes, Margie saw them and told me. I figured I got the talker and the one he was talkin' to, all with one shot. That scatter gun does scatter, ya know?"

"You did shoot the talker, as you call him, but the one he called Sammy was not shot at all. He had been gutted like a sea bass, by something real sharp."

"Maybe he fell on his own machete. Wouldn't that be a hoot?"

"We don't think so, but maybe." Mr. Butler looked at the other two men before he returned to his questioning. "What about the big one."

"What about him?"

"When did you shot him?"

"That was strange, like when I shot Voo Swar."

"What do you mean, strange?"

"They both were hurt already. I wasn't scared at all because I could tell they couldn't hurt me. Even the one they call Truck. I wasn't scared at all when I put that barrel in his face. He was crawling on his belly and I just walked over there and pulled the trigger. I did say a few words to him, 'cause I wanted him to know it was me pulling the trigger. I thought he needed to know that."

"So the big one was hurt before you shot him?"

"He was bleedin' like a stuck pig. He was probably goin' to bleed to death in a few minutes. I just put him out of his misery."

"And the woman, she was hurt, too.?"

"She couldn't hardly stand up. She was bleedin'bad. It was just a matter of time for her too. I just made it quicker."

"You didn't think it was funny that they were both hurt before you shot them?"

"I really didn't think about it at first, but later I wondered if they had hurt each other in the dark when it was all goin' so crazy. Maybe they was swingin' them damn jungle blades at any thing that moved in the dark. It was wild for a few minutes. Hell, anything could have happened out there in the dark. They were pretty stupid, if ya ask me."

"We thought about that same thing. And how in the middle of panic, folks can do crazy things to each other. Fear changes everything. And that just might be what happened. There just seems to be something missing. Maybe I'm wrong. But, thank you for talking to me, I do appreciate it."

CHAPTER SEVEN

Miss Margaret dropped Margie off at the front of the store and she pushed the door open, ringing the bell. Sofia was standing at the cash register counter with a disgusted look on her face.

"I can't believe you did it to me again. I must be the dumbest human being on the face of the earth. I knew when you left earlier you would do this to me. How stupid can I continue to be?"

Margie smiled and shook her head at her younger sister's dramatic ability. She was like everyone else, she really did love Sofia. "Well, Mr. Sandeep doesn't think you're stupid. He wants to give you gifts." Sofia didn't think Margie's remark was very funny. Margie continued.

"I know it looks like I took advantage of your good nature, but I really do have a good excuse this time. I promise you will understand and you won't be as mad when you hear what happened."

"Don't bet on it. You've got to come up with a real winner for me not to be mad at you forever." Margie smiled again.

"Mama's waiting for you outside and she needs to get back home. We have company."

"What company this time of night?" Miss Margaret blew the car horn to alert the girls she needed to go. "What company?"

"Just go on with Mama and she'll tell you all about it. You've been here much too long and you need to get some rest." Sofia wasn't sure what to think of Margie's suggestions. The horn on the car sounded again.

"You better get out there so Mama can get back to the house." Sofia wanted Margie to talk to her right then, but she also knew she would not keep her mother waiting.

"I'm not sure what's going on, but I don't like the way you do me." Margie looked at her little sister.

"I know you don't. Mother's waiting." She looked toward the door. Sofia left the store and joined Miss Margaret in the family wagon.

"Sofia, you didn't hear the horn? I've got to get back to the house." Miss Margaret hit the gas.

"Mama, what's going on?"

"I'm sorry we were late, the time just got away from us and we just got caught up in all the excitement."

"Mama. What excitement?" Miss Margaret had her eyes on the road.

"Margie didn't tell you?" Sofia shook her head.

"She said you'd tell me. I was so mad I didn't let her talk anyway."

"Well, you'll have to forgive your sister this time. She has a good excuse."

Ana Kara, the Belly Dancer, stepped out of the back bedroom door and onto the upstairs balcony of John King's haunted house. She had wrapped her naked body Roman style in the white sheet off the bed. The air of the summer night was cooler than what she expected with the breeze coming off the river. From her vantage spot she could see the lights of the houses on the other side of the river. Her heart jumped when the ferry horn blew and the Buccaneer left the Fort George side of the river and headed back to the Mayport side where she would dock and remain for the rest of the night. The far end of the top porch was pitch black and she stared in that direction for a moment. She wasn't sure why, she just did. She turned her head back toward the river and sat on the top of the railing with her back against one of the large wooden posts that held the roof up over the top balcony porch. The sheet fell down to her arms, exposing the tops of her breasts and her round shoulders. The air touching her bare skin felt pleasant so she left the sheet where it had fallen. The wood on the porch made a cracking sound causing Ana to turn back toward the dark area of the top porch. She wasn't sure, but she thought someone was there.

Ana was about to ask if anyone was there, when she saw something that stopped the words from coming out of her mouth. It was a small red circle of light or fire and it was floating at eye level about five feet in the air at the pitch dark end of the balcony. The red circle seemed to be hovering in one place and it would go dim and then bright again. The light did not move toward her and she felt no threat from the red circle. Ana stayed in her position on the railing and did not take her eyes off the light. The light moved, but slightly, only an inch or so to the left or right. It basically remained in the same place.

Ana slid her sheet half covered body off the railing and stood facing the small light. When her bare feet hit the wood slate floor she was sorry she had made the move. The light began to move toward her slowly. For the first time she was uncomfortable with her vision. The light came closer, but it was still in the dark section of the balcony. She found her voice.

"I don't scare too easy, but I think this is doing the trick. If you are one of the ghosts here I didn't mean to disturb you out here. I'll be happy to go back in the room." Even though Ana was trying to be brave and even reasonable with the spirit at hand, fear took her as a big cloud of smoke bellowed from around the small red light. Ana's heart bounded harder as her mouth dropped open and she dropped the loose fitting sheet onto the floor of the balcony porch. She was standing there scared and completely naked when a man's face came from the middle of the smoke.

"Pretty neat effect, don't ya think?" Ana Kara's heart continued to pound as Mr. John King stepped out of the darkness and through the smoke. He had been puffing on a big cigar and the ashen tip had been glowing fire red each time he sucked hard on the other end. The end of the cigar had been the fire red circle that appeared to be hovering

in the air. Stepping through the cloud of smoke was just an added special effect. Ana had to get her bearings and calm her heart.

"I did not intend to scare you. I am sorry. When I first saw you
come out I got lost in watching you. Then, when I realized you had
seen the light of the cigar I went on with my silly little joke. I should
have said I was there. I have no excuse, but that I enjoyed watching
you. I wouldn't blame you if you didn't forgive me." Mr. King bent
down and picked up the white sheet that had fallen off her naked
body. "I can't say I'm sorry about this, because I'd be lying to you."
He handed Ana the sheet as she looked into his eyes. "I wouldn't
blame you if you don't speak to me. A host and gentleman should not
have conducted himself in such a manner. I am ashamed of myself."
She continued her stare as she took the sheet from Mr. King's hand.

"I have to tell you that I have never seen a woman like you ever
in my life. I have heard of such women and have read or seen pictures of such women, but never in the true flesh. Seeing that women
like you do exist with my own eyes makes me a little more complete.
Men are always looking for ways to be more complete. Some have
experiences that make them more complete than others. You have
given me something wonderful and you don't even know it. But, I
know it. And even though I have behaved poorly I thank you for the
opportunity to have this vision. I will not bother you again. Good
night, Ana Kara. I hope I dream of you." Mr. King bowed to Ana and
turned toward the dark end of the porch. In a few steps he disappeared. Ana Kara was hypnotized by the words of praise. Her heart
was still pounding and she quivered inside. There was passion, real
women know and understand passion. Her body was on fire as she
took the first step and followed Mr. King into the darkness, dragging
the white sheet on the floor behind her naked body.

Miss Margaret pulled the family wagon up to the front of her
house. Sofia was quiet and in a mild state of shock after her mother
had given her a fast and condensed version of the Mary C. saga. Mr.
Butler, Mr. Leek and Officer Jimmy Johnston were leaving her house.
Miss Margaret stepped out of the wagon. "Everything alright gentlemen?" Officer Johnston was first.

"Yes ma'am, Miss Margaret. Things are fine. Mary C. was a great help and she cooperated to the fullest. Thank you for letting us come so late and thank you for taking her in tonight. You have always been willing to help when ever you were asked." Mr. Butler was next.

"It went real well ma'am. I think being here helped her to be calm and the support you gave her was what she needed." Mr. Leek had to be third.

"I'll see y'all tomorrow Margaret. If you need me I'll be at the dock early. Good night and God bless ya." Now, it was Miss Margaret's turn.

"Good night gentlemen. Please be careful as you're driving home." Sofia and Miss Margaret entered the house as the three men drove off in their three separate vehicles. Mr. Leek would check on the dock and then head home out on Mayport Road. Mr. Butler headed back to Mary C.'s house to see if all his requests and orders had been followed. And Officer Jimmy Johnston headed for Miss Margaret's store. He was hungry, but not for a honey bun, unless Margie was sitting on it.

Miss Margaret was preparing Margie's room for their overnight guests. Peggy, Susan and Sofia were sitting with Mary C. in the living room. Peggy and Susan had not left Mary C. the entire time she had been there. They were afraid if they did they would miss something. It was an exciting night for the, most of the time, sheltered sisters. Sofia had been given that fast condensed version of Mary C.'s battle by her mother on the ride home, so she knew some of the story. Sofia was concerned.

"Miss Mary C., is there something I can do for you? Are you hungry?" Mary C. surprised the three sisters with a quick answer.

"Y'all are the sweetest girls. I'm not hungry, but I would really like to take a shower and go to bed. Can one of y'all check on Billy while I take that shower?" All three girls lit up and said, "yes" at the same time in triple stereo. Mary C. smiled at their willingness.

"Well, I know he'll be fine with you three around. Can one of y'all show me to the bathroom?" Sofia stood up.

"Follow me please, ma'am." Mary C. stood up and shook her head.

"You are just too cute, Sofia. All of you girls are just too cute." She followed Sofia while Susan and Peggy went to check on the baby.

Officer Jimmy Johnston's police car stopped in front of Miss Margaret's store. Margie saw the car when it pulled up at the door. Her heart raced and she was excited Jimmy was there. He was excited, too, but he wasn't sure how she was going to react to him after the way she acted the last time he was there. Jimmy was also concerned about her mood after the awful things she had witnessed at Mary C.'s house. He would be careful and cautious with his words and actions. The bell on the door sounded as he pushed it open, announcing his arrival. Margie was standing at the door as he entered.

"Don't talk. Just kiss me." Margie wrapped her arms around Jimmy and shoved her young hard body through him. The kiss was as passionate as he had ever experienced in her arms. He could feel the heat coming off her body as she sucked his tongue as far as she could into her mouth. Margie reached down and touched her excited partner. She unzipped his pants so she could feel skin and his body heat. She held him in her hand as all the blood in his veins seemed to flow to the very spot she was holding. Jimmy was surprised when she stopped sucking his tongue and the kiss ended, but he was more surprised when Margie dropped to her knees and began sucking again. At first the heat of her mouth took his breath away. He actually thought he was dreaming as he looked down at the top of her head. Jimmy looked at the door and thought about the bell ringing and a late night customer coming in to find him in this wonderful, but compromising situation. She was eating him alive. It was exactly what he wanted to happen, but didn't think there was a possibility at all. Margie was full of surprises and he loved being the recipient of her passionate moment. He was nervous as she continued her oral attack, yet he would do nothing to interfere with or discourage her activity. He watched out the door and window for any movement or car lights. Jimmy felt the heat from her lips leave his skin. Margie stood up and they were face-to-face again.

"Don't talk." Margie took Jimmy's hand and directed him to the little back room of the store.

He followed her and did not say a word or zip his pants. He knew they had not finished.

Margie unbuttoned her blouse, exposing her braless breasts, but leaving the blouse on. Then she pulled her pants down stepping out of only one leg and leaving the other leg on. She broke the silence she had requested.

"Just pull your pants down. Don't take anything off. This has got to be a quickie, but I need it now. Don't talk, just do it, please." Jimmy didn't hesitate to pull his pants down. Margie pulled a chair close to them and moved Jimmy to the chair. When he sat down she straddled him and sat down across him, as he directed his manliness in the right direction. He knew when she started to move, all he had to do was hang on and let her go. It was going to be a wild ride for them both. Jimmy buried his head between her exposed breasts and let his oak tree lover have her way.

Sofia knocked on the door of their downstairs's bathroom. "Miss Mary C., I have you an extra towel and a new bar of soap."

"It's alright, come in." Sofia had no idea she would see Mary C. completely naked when she opened the door. Mary C. was standing in front of the small wall mirror and Sofia had a side view at first. Sofia looked down when she realized Mary C. was naked. She was shocked and embarrassed and wasn't sure what to do or say.

"Excuse me, I didn't mean to walk in on you. Here's the towel and soap." Sofia kept her head down as she handed the items to Mary C. Sofia was turning to end her embarrassment when Mary C. was just Mary C.

"Can you help me a second, Sofia?" Sofia stopped but didn't turn toward Mary C.

"Yes ma'am, what do you need?" Mary C. turned toward her nervous and embarrassed young friend, changing her body to a naked frontal view.

"Can you feel a knot under the skin here. I think I have a knot under the skin here, or maybe a broken bone. See if you can feel it."

Sofia couldn't believe what she was asked to do. She hadn't looked up yet so she didn't know where she was suppose to touch. Mary C. added to the awkward moment for Sofia when she stepped closer and made her request again.

"It's right here where these bruises are. I really think I broke somethin'. I guess I shoulda let that nice young man check me out. Can you feel it?" Sofia took a deep breath and lifted her head. She saw Mary C.'s muscular legs, black hair, flat stomach, full breasts and face, as her head moved upward. Mary C.'s naked body was inches away from hers. Mary C. had her hand near her shoulder rubbing back and forth on her collar bone.

"It's right here. I think something's wrong." Sofia forgot about the embarrassment of being with a naked woman that wasn't family, when she saw the awful bruises on Mary C.'s shoulders and arms.

"Miss Mary C. how did this happen. We should get you to a doctor. I need to tell Mama."

"Wait a minute, I think I'm fine. I'm just a little worried about this spot right here." Mary C. touched her collar bone again. Sofia raised her hand and barely touched the same spot with the end of her fingers.

"You can put some pressure on it. I want to see if you think there's a knot under the skin."

Sofia pushed her fingers harder on the bruised area. Mary C. flinched her naked body and Sofia moved her hand away quickly.

"Oh, I'm so sorry! I hurt you! I'm so sorry!"

"It's fine. That was the spot. Did you feel a knot or something strange?"

"I don't know, but I think you're hurt and you need to see a doctor. That must hurt something awful."

"I've been bruised before. Bruises won't kill ya. I've always been a fast healer. These things won't kill me. Thanks for the soap." Sofia had her chance to leave the little bathroom and the awkward situation as Mary C. turned away from her and stepped into the bath water she had drawn before Sofia entered the room. Sofia stood there and watched Mary C. lower her bruised and battered body into the hot water until she was sitting. Mary C. looked at her young new friend.

"Nothin' like a pipin' hot bath to heal bruises. Take it from someone who knows." Sofia was frozen in place as she watched the strange woman who had entered their lives.

"Did those people you killed do that to you?" Mary C. looked at Sofia.

"You could say it was their fault, but it was the shotgun that beat me like a drum. That pump action of Hawk's kicks like a mule. I almost dropped it one time it hurt so bad when it went off. I knew if I did drop it, they might have gotten to us so I just held on and tried not to think about the pain. Holdin' on was too important at the time." Sofia was amazed at the strength and philosophy of the naked woman sitting in her bathtub. None of them had ever seen anything like Mary C.

Officer Jimmy Johnston pulled up his pants and tucked his shirt in before he buckled his belt. He watched Margie button her shirt and pull the one leg of her pants back up to her waist. They were both breathing heavily and they had not said a word to each other during the wild sexual encounter in the chair. Jimmy was glad and relieved that the bell on the door did not ring during their so called quickie. He wondered where Margie heard that term. She had never said that before, but she was always coming up with something new. Jimmy thought maybe she read too many women's magazines. He had to admit the quickie was just what the doctor ordered. He felt great and he could tell she was satisfied with their encounter. They both walked out of the little room and back into the main store. Jimmy would not break the silence until Margie did. She did.

"That's was so exciting, wasn't it?" Jimmy smiled and was going to answer, but as usual she really didn't care about an answer. "I don't know what happened to me. It was Mary C. and the way she is, and the way she acts, and her strength. How does a person get like that? It made me want to be wild. And those dead people, I wasn't afraid. I just wanted to help Mary C." Jimmy listened and let Margie talk. The way she was praising Mary C. was strange to him but he knew he should not comment on what he thought. She went on.

"And I thought about you. I wanted you when we were in the yard at Mary C.'s. If your Mr. Butler hadn't been there I would have screwed your brains out right there on the ground, in the car or in the house, with all the dead people. It didn't matter." Jimmy thought to himself, "Who the hell is this?", as she kept talking.

"Oh, and I knew you were coming here. I could feel you wanting me. I was sorry I treated you so ugly before. I wanted to make up for it. I hope I did." Jimmy thought to himself again.

"Now you're talkin'." He smiled and finally joined the one sided conversation.

"You didn't have to make up for anything, but thank you. It was great and you know it. And I know you like Mary C., but her life and the things she's been through have made her what she is. Maybe that's a good thing when she faces something like she did tonight, but it's a hard way for anybody to be, man or woman." Margie surprised Jimmy again when she put her arms around his neck and kissed him gently, with substance and care. He responded to the strange but welcome kiss. The kiss ended.

"Would you like to stay here with me and keep me company until my shift is over?"

Beth drove Big Bob's truck off the main road and onto a side dirt road that looked deserted. She was tired and confused. Her first encounter with the oak tree had caused an unwanted uncertainty as to what she should do next. Her keen senses had given her a strange feeling about the tree. It had been a long day and she needed to rest so she could collect her thoughts and plan the next step in her venture. She wasn't afraid to sleep in the truck in the woods; she never had been very afraid of things. It came from knowing she would be the one who did the scaring if she encountered others. She also knew it was better for her to stay hidden until she could find Jason and ask him to breed with her and guarantee the continuation of her species. It didn't matter how uncomfortable she had to be, her quest was the most important matter at hand. Beth knew she should do her activities at night, but she was too tired. She would sleep all night and make plans in the morning.

Mr. Butler sat in his office at the Atlantic Beach Police Station. He was going over the events of the night in his mind and he was actually trying to count the number of people who had been killed as the result of knowing Mary C. and Jason. He thought he had counted them all when he hit nineteen, but he could have missed a few. Human nature made him count again trying to hit the incredible and even number of twenty.

Chichemo had the Mary C. headed to Mayport. The four net drags had been a great success and all four members of the crew were excited and pleased with the effort, including Bosco, the spider monkey. Mr. Leek's voice came over the ship-to-shore radio.

"If anyone aboard the shrimp boat Mary C. is listening, please respond." The only crew member in the wheel house was Bosco and he didn't respond. He was too busy steering the Mary C. toward Mayport with help from the automatic pilot.

Even though Mr. John King was older than Ana Kara, she enjoyed the spontaneous passion he had ignited in her and she had given into. When real women allow passion to direct them they become daring and take chances they would not normally take. It makes them more than what they were before. Like their male counterpart they become more complete. There is always something strong about burning a secret deep in one's belly. Ana Kara moved her sheet wrapped naked body back out onto the top porch and floated on her tiptoes to the outside entrance to her bedroom. For some reason she knew her hypnotic moment with Mr. John King was a one time encounter of passion. She also knew he was a man who knew how to belly burn a secret. She smiled in the darkness of her bedroom as she climbed back into the bed. She unwrapped the sheet from her naked body because of the heat that she had generated with Mr. King. Ana lay spread eagle on the bed as a way to cool her hot spots. If the ghost of the house wanted to see her naked, it would be an easy task.

Miss Margaret's house had calmed down. Peggy and Susan were in their beds staring at the ceiling and going over the events of the night. Mary C. loved the feeling of the cool clean sheets against her tired and bruised body. She smiled when she touched Billy's little head as the baby lay next to her. "No one will ever hurt you as long as I'm alive. I love you, you handsome little green-eyed rascal."

Sofia was standing in her bedroom with a towel wrapped around her young body. She felt good after her bath and was ready to get some sleep. Sofia thought about standing in the bathroom with Mary C. She dropped the towel from her body onto the floor and stood tall and naked in front of her mirror. Sofia had never done such a thing for the purpose of looking at herself and actually admiring what she saw. She turned from side-to-side and liked what she saw. Mary C., Ana Kara and Sofia were all cut from the same cloth.

Miss Margaret was rising from her knees. She had just finished her prayers and had thanked God for her family and the blessings He had given her. She also asked him to bless Mary C. and give her the strength she would need to get through the awful thing that had happened. She also asked God to soften Eve's evil heart. Miss Margaret walked down the hall and said good night to the closed doors of her three daughters and Mary C.'s room. All three daughters and their overnight guest responded with a good night. Miss Margaret was going to relieve Margie at the store and take the after midnight shift in her open twenty-four hours a day store.

Officer Jimmy Johnston and Margie had just ended another quickie and were adjusting their clothes. What a wild night it had been for Officer Jimmy Johnston. Margie knew what they had to do.

"I'd like to do this all night, but Mama will be here any minute. She doesn't need to get the vision of you being here with me like this. I love screwin' here. I don't really know why, but I just love it. It's so daring and the suspense makes it even better." Jimmy looked at Margie and wanted to say, "Stop sayin' that word. Who the hell are you?", but it had all been just what he wanted and there was no way he was going to make her think otherwise.

"You need to go. Let's not be too crazy tonight." Jimmy smiled and moved toward the door.

"Next time you're in town, Big Boy, don't forget to look me up again." Jimmy didn't look back at Margie. He shook his head and got into his patrol car. Miss Margaret would not know he was ever there.

Chichemo stepped into the wheel house as Mr. Leek made another call. "If anyone on the Mary C.'s listenin', pick up please.

"This is the Mary C., come back."

"Al Leek here, that you Chichemo?"

"That's a roger, talk to me. Come back."

"There's a serious problem here and Jason needs to get here as soon as possible. I don't think I should give any details over the air. You'll have to trust me on this one. Tell him everybody's alright and no one is hurt, but he really needs to come back in. Come back."

"I read ya loud and clear. We're headed home now and we'll be there in the morning. Most likely between six and seven. Since we're on our way in anyway, I'm gonna keep this to myself. No reason to worry the boy. You just be sure somebody meets us when we arrive and tells him what he needs to know. Come back."

"That's a good thought. See y'all in the mornin'. Over and out."

The bell on the door of the store rang as Miss Margaret walked in. Margie was cleaning off one of the counters with a dust cloth.

"Oh, Mama, is it time already?"

"Yes it is. And you need to go home and rest. Take the wagon and then Susan can come back for me at six, she has the morning shift. Everyone's in bed and settled at the house. Boy, what a night. You did the right thing in bringing Mary C. home with you. I'm very proud of your decision and your willingness to help a friend in need. I have tried to keep you girls from the ugly and evils of this world, but no matter what I do, those things just keep jumping up in front of us. I suppose it becomes part of growing up and seeing the other side of things. I just want to protect you girls so much." Margie knew her mother was troubled.

"Mama, maybe you are trying to protect us too much. We need to know what to do when these things do jump up in our faces. I understand you wanting us to feel no pain or have no contact with the wrongs of the world, but that isn't very realistic, now is it?" Miss Margaret smiled at her oldest daughter as Margie continued. "All four of us are becoming women and there will be many things we will have to face without you. We will have to know how to handle everything that comes our way. And even though I hope I never have to face what Mary C. faced tonight, I still would like to think I would be able to do the same thing if I had to protect someone I loved and was responsible for. I think she is the bravest and strongest woman on this earth. And in spite of what people think about her personal life, she is a real woman in every sense of the word. And by the way, Mama, I love you very much even though you have never taught me to shoot a pump action shotgun." Miss Margaret had to show a big smile after Margie's little moment of adult humor.

"I love you too, Margie. I've always been so proud you were my first born." Margie shivered with the chill that ran through her body when her mother made such a loving and profound statement. She had never said such a wonderful thing to her oldest daughter before that moment. Margie couldn't help herself as she threw her arms around Miss Margaret's neck with the most love filled contact she had ever made with her mother. Miss Margaret returned the hug.

"Stop this right now, you're going to make me cry." Miss Margaret's request was too late. They were both crying. "Now, get that butt of yours home and get some rest. Go on now."

Sofia sat in the middle of her bed again with the magic carousel sitting on the bed in front of her. There was a soft knock at her bedroom door, then the door opened slowly, as Margie walked into the room. "Sofia, you still awake?" Margie saw the magic box. "What are you doing? Are you going to turn it on?" Sofia knew she had made another mistake. It seemed to be a habit she was forming when it came to the beautiful carousel Jason had asked her to keep safe for him. Margie didn't give Sofia time to respond to her questions. "I guess you forgot we're bed partners tonight. I gave up my room to our guests. So it looks like it's me, you and this little music box. Now, my little sister dear, what does it do?" Sofia looked at Margie and knew she had to tell her what she knew, or what she thought. Margie climbed into the bed and sat on the other side of the carousel across from Sofia. The youngest and the oldest were about to share a secret and embark on a strange, but delightful journey. Sofia knew Margie was waiting on her and started to tell what she knew.

"It has something to do with your dreams. When it's on, and the lights are moving and flashing, and the music plays, it makes your dreams better, more real. The colors of the carousel are in your dream. You have no fear. It's true I felt it." Margie's eyes widened. She had no moment of doubt. She wanted it to be magic. She believed in the magic of the box the moment she first saw it.

"What do we have to do to make it happen?" It was easy for Sofia to see how serious her sister Margie was about making the box create the dream state Sofia had told her about.

"Do we turn it on and go to sleep? Is that it?" Margie seemed to want it to be more complicated than Sofia had said. Sofia could see the excitement and anticipation in Margie's face. Sofia joined her sister's magical wants.

"I think all we have to do is turn it on, watch the lights, listen to the music and relax. I think it does the rest." Margie didn't say another word. She moved to Sofia's side and they both faced the carousel.

"Do we leave it on the bed or on the floor, or what?"

"I had it on the bed when I did it. I fell asleep watching the lights and it going around." Sofia was excited when she had a vision of exactly what she had done that first time. "Oh, I know! I turned it on and laid down next to it like this." Sofia positioned herself on the bed next to the carousel as she had done before. "You do the same on the other side." Margie did not hesitate to follow her younger sister's directions. She was a more than willing participant. Both girls were lying on the bed with their faces close to the box. Their big, beautiful, young eyes were opened as far as they could be opened. They stared at each other for a moment in a silent and serious mental preparation. Margie broke the silence of the moment.

"Go ahead, turn it on." Sofia took a deep breath and reached for the small switch that would begin their colorful journey. It took Margie's breath away when the carousel began to turn and the lights began bouncing all over the dark room. Sofia smiled at her sister's reaction to the beauty that was surrounding them. The circus music began and only added to the soothing and thrill of the moment. Margie laughed out loud as the lights touched her body and flashed in her eyes. Her reaction made Sofia laugh, too. It was a great moment for the two sisters to share. They both lay their heads on the soft bed and allowed themselves to get lost in the lights and music. The lights began flashing to the extent that either sister could see the other only a few feet away. Within seconds they stopped thinking about each other and they actually felt alone with the spinning object. Sleep and the magical carousel took them both.

Sofia found herself exactly where she wanted to be; under the oak tree, naked on her back in the sand. She pushed her back against the soft sand as a willing offering to the hands that pleasured her before. It was her dream, so she didn't have to wait for the magical hands and probing digits to make their appearance. Sofia was even more relaxed this time as the hands went to work on every part of the young sex starved body. She even opened her legs wider when that one single hand appeared between them. She felt her stomach muscles tighten as her body fluids came from as deep as her toes, when two of the probing digits entered her body. Sofia was lost in the dream she wanted and she did not want to be found or it to end. She realized her calm and relaxed state would prolong her stay under the tree. She was not afraid. The warm comfort she felt made sure of that.

It was strange that Margie's colorful dream took her to the tree, as well. She was also naked and sitting straddle style on her favorite limb. There was heat between her legs as she moved her pelvic area back and forth against the limb. She had always worn clothes during her sexual encounters with the limb so the rough limb would not injure her tender skin, but this was her dream and there was no pain when she pushed and slid her tender areas against the rough bark of the oak tree. The same was true when she fell forward and rubbed her bare breasts and nipples on the hard tree. Margie sat up and put both her hands on each side of the limb. Then she began to hump and slide her lower body with all the force she could muster. She had never rubbed the tree with such force and aggressiveness. Margie knew the feelings that accompanied sexual encounters with humans and with the oak tree, but she had never felt the raw reckless and savage feeling that was raging in her body at that moment. Not even the daring moment in the store with Jimmy came close to what was happening to her during the dream. Margie screamed with pain, fear and delight when she felt the tree enter her body. She pushed her hands down on the limb to break the hold of the tree. She heard a scream that wasn't hers. Margie looked down at movement below her in the sand. She saw Sofia with the hands of pleasure holding her in the sand. Sofia screamed as the hands pulled her harder, trying to cover her with the sand. Sofia looked up and saw Margie on the limb above her. Their eyes met as they had met when they were preparing for their journey, but this time there were no smiles of anticipation. Their eyes were full of fear and shock that they had entered the same dream and now they were fighting for their way back to the reality and safety of Sofia's bedroom. Margie pushed away from the limb again and fell to the sand where Sofia's naked body was almost entirely submerged in the sand.

Margie grabbed her sister's hand as the sand sucked Sofia down. The carousel stopped spinning. The lights stopped bouncing. Margie and Sofia both sat up in the bed at the same time. They were once again staring at each other with fear and disbelief in their big eyes. They couldn't say a word. They only wanted to hold each other and be sure it was all over. They both cried in each others arms and even though Margie had made a commitment about not being afraid, she was afraid again. They would not fall asleep again that night, but they would not talk either. They didn't know what to say. There was nothing that could be brought to Mayport that was more magic than the oak tree.

CHAPTER EIGHT

MISS MARGARET'S FOUR DAUGHTERS WOKE UP TO THE SMELL OF FRENCH toast cooking in their kitchen. Susan was the first to be up and dressed because she was to relieve her mother at the store. She walked into their kitchen and was greeted by their house guest, Mary C.

"Good morning, Susan. I hope you like french toast, it's one of my specialties. As a matter of fact it might just be my only cooking specialty." Susan stepped to the stove where Mary C. was standing.

"It smells great. You can smell it all over the house. I 've never had french toast before." Mary C. was pleased to be the one who introduced Susan to the bread, egg, sugar and cinnamon combination. Mary C. would sprinkle the cinnamon and sugar on the toast and egg while it was hot and stack the pieces of toast on top of each other, causing the cinnamon and sugar to melt and form a sweet syrup covering each slice of bread. She handed Susan a plate with four slices of the toast and then a glass of cold milk.

"You can't eat french toast like this without milk. I don't know why the two go together so well, but they do and that's a fact." At first Susan thought the four slices stacked on the plate were going to be too much for her, but she didn't say anything to her cooking guest.

"Thank you, Miss Mary C., it looks great." Susan sat down and began eating the new breakfast food from their new friend. Mary C. knew the look on Susan's face could only mean it was delicious.

"Good huh?" Susan swallowed.

"It's great. It really is. And you're right about the milk. It's the perfect combination."

"This is Jason's favorite. I save it for special days, like birthdays, him comin' home, him comin' back from that awful hospital, that kinda stuff. And days like today. I didn't know how to thank y'all for what y'all did for me last night. I thought this could be a start."

"You don't have to do anything. We like having you and Billy stay here with us. You're our friend and you were having a bad time. You needed to get away and be here." Mary C. smiled at Susan's kind words.

"You want some more?" Susan looked down at her plate. She had eaten all four slices and emptied the glass of milk.

"Oh, my! I never eat much breakfast. I have made a pig of myself." Mary C. was having a great time.

"You didn't do it, honey. It was the french toast. It'll make pigs of us all." They both laughed at Mary C.'s pig comment as Peggy joined them in the kitchen.

"What smells so good. I thought I was dreaming and I was in a bakery or somewhere. What is that?" Mary C. handed Peggy her first plate of the sweet tasty squares and a glass of milk. Mary C. was in heaven.

The shrimp boat, Mary C., pulled in to Mr. Leek's dock. Mr. Leek was waiting as the boat moved closer and Jason threw one of the ropes at the bow of the boat. Mr. Leek tied the rope off on one of the black creosote pylons that held up the dock. Then Mr. Leek moved down the dock so he was at the stern of the boat, where Hawk threw him another rope that he tied to another pylon at that end of the dock. Chichemo and Bosco were both at the wheel making sure she came in easy and with as little contact with the dock as possible. As always the docking was perfect with Chichemo at the wheel. Mr. Leek knew they would want to unload their catch, but he would stop them until he could tell them about the night before. Jason jumped off the boat and onto the dock right where Mr. Leek was standing. He was excited.

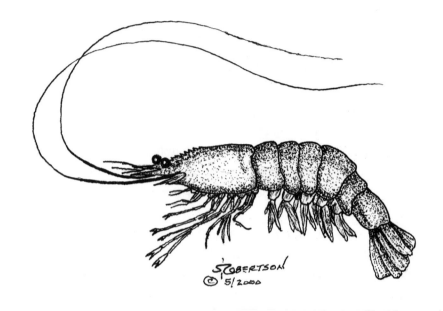

Mayport Shrimp

"Mornin' Mr. Leek. I think you're gonna be real happy with the Mary C. this mornin'."

Mr. Leek gave Jason a smile and turned to Hawk, who was still at the stern of the boat.

"Before you start unloadin', come inside and talk to me." Hawk didn't like the way Mr. Leek had requested their attention. Jason felt funny, too, as he looked at Hawk, who jumped up onto the dock to be with Jason and Mr. Leek. Chichemo turned the boat's engine off and remained on the boat with Bosco. He didn't know what was happening and he thought that if Mr. Leek wanted him to know he would tell him. He was like Mr. John King and he also knew how to mind his own business. He watched Mr. Leek talking to Hawk and Jason inside the fish house. The looks on their faces were hard to read but he knew something big had happened. Then Jason and Hawk left in a hurry and didn't even look back toward the boat. Chichemo knew they would unload their catch later. After Jason and Hawk left the dock to find Mary C., Mr. Leek walked out onto the dock and stepped down on the Mary C. He would share the entire bizarre story with his friend, Chichemo.

Margie and Sofia were wide awake. They did not sleep after the joint dream. They spent the night silently comforting each other just by being together. The carousel was quiet and still at the end of the bed. Sofia stood up on the floor.

"I'm putting it back in the closet to stay. I'm telling Jason to take it back today if I see him."

She picked the colorful dream maker up off the bed and placed it back in the closet under the blanket, like she had it before. Margie tried to make normal conversation.

"Somebody's cooking something that smells great. Let's go see what's going on." Sofia knew Margie was trying to act normal in an abnormal situation. She would follow her older sister's lead and wait until they both wanted to talk about what had happened during the night. Or perhaps they would never mention it again.

Margie and Sofia walked into the kitchen to see Susan leaving the table. She had to go relieve her mother. Susan passed them at the

kitchen door. "Good morning Margie, Sofia, the french toast is unbelievable. Save some for mother, she'll be home in a few minutes."
Mary C. joined the sisterly greeting.

"There's plenty and I'll make more if I have to. Tell your mama
to take her time." Susan left the kitchen. Sofia and Margie sat down
at the table. Mary C. served them as she had done the other two girls
with french toast and milk. The three remaining sisters had never
tasted such a sweet and satisfying breakfast treat. Margie did like
Mary C.

There was a different aroma at Mr. John King's haunted house. It
was bacon cooking, and like Mary C.'s french toast, the aroma filled
the house. The combination of the bacon sizzling and the Maxwell
House coffee brewing, made all the overnight guests take pleasant
deep breaths as they opened their sleep filled eyes. Big Bob thought
he was the first one of the circus family to dress and walk downstairs
to see who was cooking breakfast. When he entered the kitchen area
he realized he was the second member of the family to wake up.

Ana Kara, the Belly Dancer and Mr. King's special new friend,
was standing at the kitchen stove stirring a huge pan of scrambled
eggs. Mr. King was turning the bacon strips. They were the breakfast
cooks who had caused the pleasant aroma to tantalize the sleepers.
Ana turned to Big Bob when his huge shadow covered the wall next
to her.

"Good morning. You're just in time to make those perfect pancakes you are always bragging about. The mix and additions are over
there on that table." Big Bob smiled.

"Good mornin' to you, too. Mornin' John." Mr. King looked up
and smiled at the Giant standing in his kitchen.

"Mornin' to you. We were hopin' you'd come down. I'm lookin'
forward to your pancakes. I've always had a weakness for a good
flap jack." Big Bob looked at Ana and then at Mr. King.

"Nothin' like a little pancake pressure first thing in the mornin'.
I hope I can live up to Ana's build up." Ana smiled, too.

"You'll do just fine, you always do." Big Bob took the compliment and stepped to the table where the pancake mix waited for his

culinary expertise. Ana poured the scrambled eggs into a big bowl.

"We're gonna put everything on that counter over there and let everyone serve themselves buffet style. We're gonna give them lots of choices. Isn't this fun?" Mr. King looked at Big Bob and they both rolled their eyes at the same time. They both laughed at having the same thought at the same time. Ana noticed the male moment.

"Now boys, you know you love cookin', so stop actin' like you're miserable and don't want to be here. There's aprons over there in that drawer if you need one. I have a feelin' John's in one of those aprons now and then." Beulla was the next one to enter the kitchen.

"Good mornin' y'all. I woke up when I thought I heard a piece of that bacon callin' out my name. What can I do to help? You know you can't have a big breakfast like this without my cheese grits so hand me that big pot and point me to the grits bag. I know a real southern gentleman like Mr. King here has grits somewhere in this kitchen." Beulla smiled a big smile when Mr. King opened the bottom cabinet next to him and pulled out a new bag of Dixie Lily. Beulla could not help her southern self.

"Hot damn, boy! You are after my big ass heart, ain't ya?" Mr. King had to laugh again. He knew it was going to be the most exciting breakfast in the history of his haunted house and he was loving every minute of the morning. Ana Kara being there with him didn't hurt matters either. He loved the secret they had burned deep in their bellies. He placed a torn paper bag on top of an empty plate and then put the crispy bacon slices on top of the paper. The paper absorbed some of the excess grease off the hot bacon strips.

Ana Kara opened the oven door and took out a tray of buttermilk biscuits she had prepared earlier. They were perfect. Helga and Tom were the next two standing at the kitchen door. Helga wanted to join the cooks.

"I want to cook something, too. What can I cook?" Beulla needed help.

"Cut up that block of cheese over there into little pieces and drop them into the grits while I stir it." Helga went right to work; no other questions asked. Tom wanted to be part of the action.

"What can I eat first and when can I eat it?" All the cooks turned to the little pigmy. Mr. King was the first one to burst into laughter, followed by the others. Tom smiled and felt good about the reaction to his comment, but Ana wanted everyone working. She was, no doubt, in charge of the breakfast buffet.

"Tom, how' bout puttin' the plates and silverware at the end of that counter over there; you know buffet style. That's what we're goin' to do. Serve ourselves and fill our own plates, buffet style." Tom nodded his little head, followed Ana's instructions and wondered how many more times she was going to say buffet style. Norman Bates was the next circus family member to enter the now crowded kitchen.

"I'd like to help, but I don't think there is any room in there for me." Tom couldn't resist.

"There's always room for you, just get in the broom closet." Even Norman had to smile at Tom's morning humor. Norman looked at his tiny friend-enemy.

"I'll have to admit that was a good one, Tom. I hope this vacation doesn't sharpen your wit too much. I couldn't take it." All the cooks laughed again and appreciated Norman's early morning sense of humor. Ana made another suggestion.

"Norman, why don't you go help the Twins come down. We'll be ready to feast by the time they get down here." Every member of the family knew Ana had made a great suggestion. Norman didn't hesitate to go back up the stairs to see if the Twins were awake. The only guests not accounted for were Eve and Sandeep. Only Mr. King and Tom Thumb had seen them.

Miss Margaret stepped out of her family wagon in front of her house. Susan had relieved her at the store and told her about Mary C.'s french toast. Jason and Hawk pulled up behind the family wagon in Uncle Bobby's truck. Miss Margaret could tell they knew something had happened. She waited for Jason to come close to her.

"My dear boy, I'm so glad you're here."

"Is my Mama still here?" Hawk stepped up behind Jason.

"Yes and the baby's here with her. They're both just fine. Please come in." Jason and Hawk followed Miss Margaret up the front steps. She used her key to open the front door. Margie heard the door open and knew it had to be her mother.

"We're in the kitchen, Mama." The three sisters were still sitting at the kitchen table when Miss Margaret walked in with Jason and Hawk. None of the young women wanted to be seen by two men that early in the morning. They were still in their revealing bed time attire and did not consider themselves presentable for male visitors.

Sofia was wearing a cut off t-shirt with short-short pajama bottoms. Peggy was wearing a sheer, see through negligee top with panties. And Margie wore a red halter type top with the same type panties as Peggy. None of the girls wore any underwear. The morning sunlight hitting them as they moved exposed their shapely profiles and their female attributes. All three girls left the table quickly and went into hiding. Both men saw plenty as the three embarrassed sisters moved out of the kitchen, but they couldn't enjoy the show because Mary C. was the center of their attention at the moment. Miss Margaret wasn't worried about the girls' modesty.

"Look who I found outside my door." Jason stepped to his mother.

"Mama, are you alright?" Mary C. smiled and had to be Mary C.

"Yes, I'm fine. Would y'all like some french toast? I'm makin' some more for Miss Margaret and I know how much y'all like it. Sit down both of you and eat. How was the trip?" Mary C. looked at Hawk. He didn't like the way the early morning meeting with her was going. He felt strange when she looked at him. Jason thought her tone was strange, too. She turned to Miss Margaret.

"Please sit with me and let me fix you some breakfast. I want to thank you for all your kindness. And it seems the men ran all my good company off. Your girls have been so nice to me. They have made me feel like family. I love them all. I hope you like french toast." Miss Margaret nodded her head and sat down at the table. Mary C. turned to the stove and the pan she was using for the toast. With her back to the others, she had questions for her men as she cooked the egg soaked bread slices.

"You didn't say how the trip was. Did y'all catch anything?" Jason looked at Hawk.

"Yes Mama, we did good." She turned a slice of the bread over in the pan.

"How many boxes?"

"We didn't unload yet. Mr. Leek told us what happened and we came here first. We were worried about you and Billy." Mary C. gave a half smile, but they did not see it.

"It's called after the fact." Jason looked at Hawk again. Mary C. turned holding the handle of the frying pan in her gloved cooking hand. She put the hot slices of french toast on Miss Margaret's plate. Then she sprinkled the sugar and cinnamon mixture on the toast. Miss Margaret smiled.

"Thank you, my dear. It looks and smells wonderful." Mary C. smiled and turned back to the stove.

"After the fact. You know. People worry about people after the fact." Hawk had to join in.

"Mary C., what are you talkin' 'bout. We're both worried about you and we hurried here as soon as we heard about it." She turned to face them.

"You're right. You are worried about me. You're worried now that it has happened. I think people should worry about their loved ones before something happens. I think people should listen to other people when they feel so strongly about something. How many pieces of toast y'all want?" With the change of subject matter there was a knock on Miss Margaret's front door.

A fully dressed Margie was passing the door on her way back to the kitchen when she heard the knock. Margie had dressed quickly. She wasn't going to pass up a opportunity to be around Jason and Mary C. Margie looked through the glass window of the door and recognized Mr. Butler; another early morning caller. She opened the door.

"Mornin' Margie."

"They're all in the kitchen. I was just headed that way myself." Mr. Butler followed Margie to the gathering place with the great aroma.

The kitchen crowd turned to the doorway when Margie and Mr. Butler walked in. Mary C. was the first to greet them. "Margie, I'm so glad you came back. Mr. Butler, good mornin'. You didn't sleep here did ya? Can I fix you some french toast?" Mr. Butler looked around the small room.

"Good morning, everyone." He looked at Hawk, then Jason. "I'm glad you two are back." Mary C. turned back to the stove and her self-appointed duty. Miss Margaret's pleasant voice cut through the uneasy air around them all.

"You gentlemen should have some of Mary C.'s french toast. I don't think I've ever had such a tasty breakfast in all my days, and that's a lot of days. Please sit down and at least have some coffee. It has been a rough night for us all, especially Mary C. I think it is extremely gracious of her to cook for us this morning. Mary C. I commend you on your ability to be stronger than others during the hardest of times and conditions. I wish I had your strength and courage. The girls and I were talking about how much we respect your courage." Mary C. was emotionally lifted at that moment to a place she had never been before. The word respect, coming from Miss Margaret and directed at her was almost overwhelming. Mary C.'s heart raced in her chest and she could not respond to the praise and honor bestowed upon her.

Margie loved what her mother said and she was all smiles as she looked at Mary C. The attack of the Calypsos could not bring a tear to Mary C.'s eyes, but Miss Margaret's declaration of respect was a different story. No one in the room, including Jason, had ever seen Mary C. cry until that moment. Mary C. turned her back to the others and continued making the toast. The room was silent. Even Mr. Butler knew they had all witnessed a touching moment with the two women. Miss Margaret, once again, cleared the air.

"Margie, will you get these gentlemen coffee if they are interested?"

"Yes ma'am. Who wants coffee?"

The haunted house buffet breakfast was in full swing. Norman helped Ming and Ling position themselves so they could eat and see the others at the table. All the others were in the buffet line, filling their plates with many selections of breakfast foods. Mr. King stood to the side and watched his unusual guests as they fixed their plates and found a seat at his big dining room table. Ana Kara's buffet idea was a great success. Norman prepared plates for the Twins and took it to them before he ate. He considered it a true honor to assist the Oriental beauties.

Ana Kara didn't miss anything.

"John, please fix your plate. You don't have to wait on us. We're all family here." It was funny to Mr. King when each of his guests nodded their heads up and down at the same time in agreement with Ana's statement. Mr. King smiled and followed Norman in the buffet line as the others took a seat in one of the twelve chairs. Mr. King was excited. It had been a long time since he had nine living people sitting at his table. It was a great morning.

No one had started eating, not even the hungry Little Tom. The family knew they would wait for Big Bob to give thanks for the food. Mr. John King was a practicing Catholic and he always blessed his food. He could tell his guests were believers as well. Mr. King had even allowed the local Catholic priest, Father Kelly, to hold Mass in his house before the St. John's Catholic Church was built. Big Bob's voice silenced the individual conversations that were going on at the table.

"Well, well. Here we are." All eyes were on Big Bob. "First I know we are all thinking the same thing and we all want to thank Mr. King for his most gracious and unbelievable kindness." They all looked at Mr. King again. "John, in all our time together, no one has ever opened their heart and home to us as you have. Without hesitation you have allowed us to become part of your life with no questions or signs of reservation. I didn't know people like you existed. You have given us a new look and way of thinking. We ventured out to help a friend, but we also did it to see if we could do it. We have traveled the world as attractions, freaks if you will. We have been accepted only because we could entertain, either by sight or some small talent. We are seldom accepted as actual people. You are a rare breed of mankind and we will never forget you. Meeting you has made the trip a success no matter what follows today. Please pray with us John." Everyone bowed their heads and waited for Big Bob to continue. Mr. King's head was spinning with Big Bob's words.

"Dear Lord, thank you for a safe trip or with Norman driving should I say safe landing. Thank you for this food and, please Lord, bless those pancakes, it'll take a little pressure off me. Be with Beth and protect her during this hard time. Thank you for John King. Amen." They all said "Amen". John did too, out of habit, but he felt funny about his name ending the prayer. The praying, talking and cooking was over and the eating began. It was the greatest breakfast ever to be enjoyed in Mr. John King's haunted house.

Margie had served coffee to Hawk and Mr. Butler. Jason didn't drink coffee unless he had something to dunk into it. Mary C. had placed a big platter of french toast in the middle of the table for anyone to enjoy.

"That's the last of the toast. Miss Margaret, I used all your bread, but I'm gonna buy you some more when I get over to the store later today." Miss Margaret smiled and looked at Mary C.

"Oh, don't worry about that. This was the nicest treat for us all and I do appreciate your hard work. Gentlemen, please eat the rest of this delicious french toast. Jason, your mother tells me this is your favorite breakfast, please don't be shy." Mr. Butler looked at the cinnamon brown toast.

"It smells so good. I'd like to try some." Mary C. was surprised and delighted when Mr. Butler asked to try the toast. She gave him a plate and a clean fork. Mr. Butler stabbed two slices and put them on his plate. Mary C. gave him the usual suggestion.

"Can't eat french toast without milk. I know you've got your coffee, but I promise ya it ain't the same." She poured Mr. Butler his milk and looked at Hawk. "Now, I know you're hungry and we ain't talkin' bout none of that other stuff until later. I thought you two would have understood that by now. I am a guest in this house and we are not going to ruin this beautiful mornin' with talk about things that don't matter right now. So both of y'all stop lookin' at me like I'm crazy and sit down and eat some of my french toast." There was another knock at the front door as Jason and Hawk sat down from the not so subtle urging from Mary C. Margie was on the move.

"I'll get it." She hurried to the door. They had never had so much company in the morning.

Margie's heart skipped a little beat when she saw her friend and wild sex partner, Officer Jimmy Johnston, standing at the front door. She pushed her face against the window, flattening her nose.

Jimmy smiled at her early morning silliness as she opened the door. She still wanted to act a fool.

"Well, good mornin' big boy. I didn't think you'd be back in town so quick. You must have really missed me." She pushed the front of her body against his as he stepped into the house.

"Stop, your mama might see us." Jimmy's words of caution only ignited her daring. Margie really pushed against him now. She reached down and touched him between his legs.

"It feels loaded." Jimmy moved her hand.

"Stop I said. You're gonna get us both killed."

"You're the one with the loaded gun." Jimmy wanted to yell, "Who the hell are you!," but he didn't. She wanted to worry him even more.

"Let's go screw in my room while everybody's in the kitchen. We can do a quickie and they will never know." Jimmy couldn't believe his ears.

"Are you crazy. I know you're just playin' with me. Now stop." Margie shook her pretty head.

"Try me. We can walk up those stairs right now and be back down before they know you're here. Do something crazy with me." Jimmy actually looked up the stairs and considered her dangerous proposal. She was a true temptress.

"I want to do it standing up with you behind me. I saw this great picture and I want to try it like that. Come on." Margie took Officer Jimmy Johnston's hand and started up the stairs. He felt he was in a dream for a moment. Miss Margaret's voice stopped their advance up the stairs.

"Oh, Jimmy, that was you at the door?" Officer Johnston turned with his heart in his throat to face Margie's mother. Margie was too quick and smart for them.

"Mama, I need to tell Jimmy something about last night and I don't want that Mr. Butler to be with us. I don't like talking to him. I don't like the way he talks to people. And I really don't like the way he looks at me. He gives me the creeps. I thought we could talk privately and then Jimmy can go in there." Miss Margaret always understood.

"That's fine, but what do I tell Mr. Butler?" Margie had the answer.

"You don't have to tell him anything. We'll be right down in a few minutes. We're going to be quick. If you have to tell him something, tell him Jimmy will be in there in a moment. But, I don't think you have to tell him anything. All this talking we're doing, we could have been done." Miss Margie nodded and turned to return to the kitchen. Margie pulled Jimmy up the stairs and into her bedroom. She closed the door and pulled down her pants, turning her backside to him.

"Hurry! Just undo your pants, but leave them on." Margie turned to the wall with her bare butt aimed in Jimmy's direction. She leaned over and put both of her hands on the wall, inviting him to enter her when he was ready. Jimmy fumbled with his nervous hands until he exposed his manhood behind her.

"Hurry, please, I'm so excited I can't stand it. Do you believe they're all right down there eating french toast and we're up here doing this. Hurry!" Jimmy stepped toward her butt cheeks and maneuvered his manliness into position. Margie had told the truth about her degree of excitement; she was wet and Jimmy was able to move with no resistance. Her body fluids were as hot as Jimmy had ever felt. She pushed back toward him and invited him to push in return. Jimmy grabbed both sides of her butt cheeks and pulled her even harder back toward him. Margie made a noise as Jimmy began pumping harder. They were deep in the clutches of Margie's want for dangerous sex when the door of the bedroom opened and Mary C. walked into the room. They both turned and actually froze for a second when they saw Mary C. standing in the room with them. Jimmy pulled away and Margie stood up. They fumbled with their clothes as Mary C. closed the door and walked over to the bed.

"I came to check on Billy and take him downstairs to Jason. I'm sorry I interrupted your fun." Margie and Jimmy couldn't believe they had been in the room with the baby in the bed. Mary C. picked Billy up in her arms and looked at the two embarrassed lovers as she moved to the door.

"Y'all got me excited. That was one of my favorite positions." She left the room with Billy and closed the door as she left.

Ana Kara's haunted house buffet breakfast was a great success. Everyone was talking, eating and enjoying the fellowship. Norman Bates, the Skeleton Man, had a question for Mr. King.

"John tell us about this wonderful house." Ana Kara wanted to know, too.

"Yes, John, tell us please and don't forget to tell us about your favorite object or artwork." John looked around the table. All of the strange circus eyes seemed to be genuinely interested.

"I don't want to bore anyone." Big Bob assured Mr. King.

"John, we would love to hear about this place. How did you come to live here. When did it become haunted. What ghosts are here. Why are you not afraid. There are many questions to be answered. We know that we are strange and unusual, but John you were born normal and you have chosen to be strange and unusual. Yes, we would like to know why, how, when and all the other questions. We are always telling our story. It is time for us to listen to yours. We loved hearing Jason's stories. Please, tell us yours." Mr. John King was a master storyteller, but he was nervous with the circus family waiting for his story. Little Tom had been too quiet too long.

"It started on a stormy night in Mayport." Everyone at the table burst into laughter. Mr. King joined them. Tom's little joke put Mr. King at ease and when the laughter subsided he was ready to use his knowledge and skills to entertain the world's greatest entertainers.

"The original house was a boarding room house for the sailors, travelers and even pirates of the time. The first house was built over an old Spanish grave yard that had been flooded and filled in some time at the end of the 1700's. My Daddy told me folks thought the first ghosts came from the grave yard, but I feel those ghosts have moved since then. Maybe to another house or to the other side. Sometime around 1850 or so, that boarding house burned down along with three other big houses on this street. That could have been when the Spanish ghosts left. My Daddy said those ghosts had set the tone and atmosphere for others to follow. My great grandfather rebuilt an exact replica of the first house, the one we're in today. It became a boarding house once more and many sailors, travelers and even pirates began stopping in and staying over night. There was no ghostly activity for about fifty years and then all hell broke loose." The room was silent and only Mr. King's voice could be heard, until his all hell broke loose statement. Helga didn't mean to interrupt, but she had to.

"You gonna start tellin' scary ghost stories now?" She had a concerned look on her face. "I thought you were just gonna tell us about this beautiful house. I didn't know we might get scared." Everyone smiled, but no one made fun of her question. Ana Kara wanted to ease Helga's mind.

"If you think you are going to be scared, we can do this at another time." They all shook their heads in agreement. As a family they would always protect the feelings of the others. Helga didn't want to end the pleasant moment, but before she could say anything, Little Tom had an idea. "We want to hear the stories, so just give her a signal when you're gonna scare the hell out of us and she can cover her ears." Helga nodded her head.

"You don't have to stop in the middle of the story and signal me. I'll try not to be a baby, but I might cover my ears when I think it's coming." Mr. King smiled and continued.

"It all seemed to have started because of a strange love affair. My Great Aunt Viola was in charge of the house and the boarders. Her picture's in the living room on the far wall. Why don't we go into the sitting room and we will be more comfortable on the couches and soft chairs. I would like you to see her picture." Ana was first to rise.

"Let's do. The atmosphere with the art and carvings will add to our interest. We'll all do a family clean up after John has finished." The circus family and Mr. King moved into the living room.

Jason, Hawk and Mr. Butler were finishing the last slices of Mary C.'s french toast when she walked back into the kitchen with Billy in her arms. All eyes in the kitchen turned to see them. Miss Margaret was first.

"There's that pretty boy. He sure slept a long time. He was tired from all the excitement." Mary C. knew Jason was wanting to hold his son. She really didn't want anyone else to hold him, but she would speak her mind when her family was together alone. She handed the baby to his father.

"Here he is, Jason. In perfect condition, just like you left him." Jason detected a small amount of sarcasm in his mother's comment, but he too knew they would talk later. He ignored her tone and took the child. Margie and Officer Jimmy Johnston joined the kitchen dwellers.

Mr. Butler was waiting for Officer Johnston.

"Jimmy, I'm glad you're here. We have a lot of work to do. You missed out on the french toast. You're always late and miss out on the good stuff." Mary C. looked at Jimmy as to say, not this time, but she didn't. Jimmy knew what Mary C. was thinking and that she would keep her thoughts to herself. That was Mary C.

Margie looked at Mary C. with the smile of a woman who had just shared a secret with her best friend. Mary C. returned the smile of sexual sisterhood as Mr. Butler interrupted the moment of bonding for the two ruthless women.

"I came over to tell y'all that you can't go to the house today. We still have a lot to do and we were hampered in the dark last night. No matter how hard you try, flashlights just don't do the trick. We need to see things in the daylight. My crew's on the way out there and I told them to go ahead and we'd be there soon. I feel bad about having such a great breakfast before I meet them, but that's the perks of being the boss." Mary C. wanted to go home.

"I need to go home. The door and the window need to be fixed.

The clean up is gonna take all day." Mr. Butler had the answer, but not the one she wanted.

"I can't let anyone down there now. It is a crime scene and it is officially mine until the investigation is over. I'm sorry, but that's the way it is." Miss Margaret wanted to ease Mary C.'s tense feelings.

"We have all you need right here and we have plenty of room for Jason and Hawk, too." Margie's eyes lit up at the prospect of Jason staying under the same roof with her. Jimmy didn't see Margie's reaction. Miss Margaret continued. "The faster Mr. Butler gets going, the faster it will be over and you can go back home. But for now, you are all more than welcome to stay here." Mr. Butler wanted to help with Mary C.'s worries, too.

"We're going to fix the window and door just like new, paint and all." Then he surprised everyone in the room. "Jason, I'd like you and Hawk to come with us to the house. We could use all the manpower we can get and I think you could really help us in this investigation." Jason and Hawk were both pleased with the idea of going to the house. They both knew very little about the night before and they needed to know what they were dealing with when they talked to Mary C. They were more than happy to go.

Hawk remembered the boat. "We have to help Chichemo unload the boat. At least one of us has to do that first." Jason nodded his head in agreement.

"I'll go help Chichemo and you go on to the house with Mr. Butler and Jimmy. I'll be there as soon as we're finished. No sense in both of us goin' to the dock. I'll meet y'all later." Jason handed Billy to Margie, kissed Mary C. on the cheek, thanked Miss Margaret, said good-bye to the others and was out the door.

Mr. John King's huge living room was full of his circus guests. They were all comfortable in soft chairs and couches. Helga was sitting in a beautiful green rocking chair next to the massive brick fireplace.

"The picture at the end of the room is my Great Aunt Viola King. As you can see she was a rare beauty to behold. All the men who passed through Mayport back then fell deeply in love with her just by seeing her. Her kind mannerism and soft voice made everyone feel as if they were the most important thing on earth. The young sister Sofia you met last night reminds me of Aunt Viola." They all looked at the picture in a large oval frame at the end of the room.

The beautiful young woman in the picture was wearing a half sleeved, turtle neck collared, snow white ruffled blouse, tucked into the small waist of a dark full body length skirt. It was easy to see her skin was pure white with not a blemish to be seen. Her hair was pulled up high on the top of her head. There were no teeth showing in her demure smile, but you could see confidence and contentment. Mr. King continued.

"Viola didn't toy with the affections of the men who wanted her attention. She was a true lady and treated them all the same, showing favoritism to none. Any of them would have taken her for their own if she had shown an interest. She would only treat their advances with kindness, but never committed herself to them in any way. Until 'He' came to Mayport." Helga couldn't help it.

"Who came to Mayport?" Tom couldn't help it either.

"Shhhh, Helga listen." Mr King had an interesting feeling inside. It was an honor for him to have the attention of such a unique and special group of people. He loved being with them.

"His name was Yankee Williams. He was a hardened man from New Bedford, Massachusetts. He talked about being a whaler as a younger man. He didn't say much about his past and didn't stay long when he began staying here at first. He was tall and had a rugged look. It was that rugged look that some women call handsome. He was no pretty boy, like Tom over there, but you could tell the women liked the way he looked. I'm sorry to say my Aunt Viola had her innocent head turned for the first time." Beulla had a thought.

"He sounds yummy to me." The group laughed at Beulla's little moment of humor. Mr. King smiled and went on.

"It has always puzzled me how the beautiful women of substance seem to be drawn to the rebels or renegades of the world. They seem to want to take on the forbidden. The bad boys, if you will. What is it ladies, about the bad boys? They seem to be able to take the heart of a good Christian woman and make her do things she would dare not consider or dream of, until the bad boy appeared. Do you have an answer?" The room was silent after Mr. King's question to the ladies. Little Tom looked at Helga as if he wanted her to say something about him being a bad boy. Ana was first again.

"I can't speak for anyone else, but the real men of the world are never the pretty boys. And as for women being attracted to the bad boys, I think the so called bad boys are more aggressive and women like that sometimes. Some men take charge with a certain strength that women like. The word you used a while ago was forbidden. It's the excitement of the unknown and doing something out of character. We all need that." Mr. King knew exactly what Ana Kara meant and he also knew he had shared a forbidden moment with the exotic beauty. Beulla had her own bad boy philosophy.

"Bad boys, good boys, I like 'em all. Sometimes you want the good boy Rhett Butler to carry you over that mud puddle and sometimes you want that bad boy Rhett Butler to jump on your big ass when you're layin' in the mud puddle." Little Tom couldn't resist.

"It would take both Rhett Butlers and then some to carry you over a mud puddle."

"Don't you start with me. You ain't that funny, ya know?" Big Bob had to remind them.

"Alright now, remember where you are and the truce you made on the bus. John, please tell us about this Yankee Williams character." The group settled down and looked toward Mr. King.

"Aunt Viola was completely taken by his rough mannerisms. She had never seen a man display the confidence he walked around with. He didn't fall all over her like the others. In fact he even ignored her at times. It made her think he had known other beautiful women and for some strange reason the thought of him being experienced in the world made her want him more. He never flirted with her or told her she was pretty like the many other suitors she saw each day. At times he would not even look her way if she passed him in the room or outside. Before long she was going out of her way to be near him and having mood changes if he was gone for days at a time.

Some of the men who came to know him said Yankee knew a lot about boats, but he didn't go out on any of the Mayport boats. It was rumored he worked for the railroad as a special security agent and he traveled all over Florida doing dangerous undercover assignments for the company. Viola loved all the talk about his mysterious life and asked people questions about him all the time. She was in love for the first time in her life and the man she loved seldom gave her the time of day. Aunt Viola King hardly knew what to do with him or herself. It was a situation she had never faced before." Beulla had to stop Mr. King.

"I'm so sorry to stop ya sugah, but I got to take a personal break and I don't want to miss a word. I just love a good love story." Ana took control.

"Let's all take a break and start cleanin' that table off. Get some more coffee and when Beulla gets back John will continue his wonderful story."

Beth, the Werewolf Girl, stepped out of Big Bob's truck and into the woods around her. An early morning call of nature had her squatting behind a palmetto fan plant to relieve herself. As she finished and started to stand up she heard voices coming from somewhere near in the woods. She looked toward the voices and could see movement through the trees about fifty yards away. Beth ducked down low on the ground and crawled back to the truck, climbed in as quietly as she could and started the engine. The sound of a gun blast startled her and she hit the gas peddle, spinning the truck wheels in the dirt and leaves as the truck jumped into gear and was rolling once again. She didn't want to be a hunting casualty in the Mayport woods.

Mr. Butler, Officer Jimmy Johnston and Hawk walked out of Miss Margaret's house together. Mr. Butler and Officer Johnston had separate cars. Jason had taken Hawk's mode of transportation so he would have to ride with one of the others. Jimmy offered first.

"Hawk, you ride with me and we'll meet Mr. Butler there."

Hawk nodded and moved to the driver's side of the car and got in. As Officer Johnston moved toward the driver's side of the patrol car, Mr. Butler stopped him.

"Jimmy, could you talk to me for a minute?" Officer Johnston stepped away from his car and walked to where Mr. Butler was standing. "Yes sir?" Mr. Butler spoke in a low tone. It was obvious to Jimmy he didn't want Hawk to hear their conversation.

"I just have to say this, so bear with me. This Mary C. is something else, I tell ya. I have never seen anything like her in all my days. What kind of woman kills five people during the night and then the next morning cooks french toast for everybody in the neighborhood? And good french toast, too. I'm not sure what we're dealing with here, but like I said last year, 'Too many people die around her and that boy.' The sooner we get this thing over with the sooner I'll feel safe myself. Hell, I was scared to eat the toast, but it smelled so damn good I couldn't help myself. Even though she talks against that voodoo stuff, I think she could have some in her, or witchcraft, or somethin'. Hell, it might be that damn tree. Are you listening to how crazy I sound?" Jimmy didn't say anything after Mr. Butler's question. He knew his boss really didn't want an answer, Mr. Butler already knew how crazy he sounded.

"These Mayport people might just send me into retirement." Mr. Butler took a deep breath. Alright, let's get out there and get this over with." He turned and got into his unmarked police car and Officer Johnston joined Hawk in the other car. Hawk was interested.

"Your boss looks troubled. This thing with Mary C. is pretty bad, ain't it?" Jimmy nodded his head as he started the car engine.

"Wait 'til we get out there and explain what we know and some of the things we think."

The circus family were all back in their seats in Mr. John King's living room. They were all ready for the rest of the story he had started. Ana was the spokesperson this time.

"John, sorry 'bout the interruption, but we're back now and ready to go."

"There was another man in Aunt Viola's life. His name was

Ralph Cason. Ralph was one of the long time suitors who was so madly in love with Aunt Viola that he usually made a complete fool of himself when she was around. He was the worst of the lot. He worked at the old Pogy Plant and smelled of fish all the time. Ralph hated it when Yankee was around because it was easy to see how Aunt Viola was taken with the man. As I'm sure you can gather, Ralph Cason was not close to the man Yankee Williams was and he knew it.

It all began when Yankee was staying one night and it was the second day of a bad Northeaster. The weather had everyone inside and the dreary darkness had a strange hold over this house. Yankee had gone to his room and was reading his favorite book, Moby Dick, him havin' a whalin' background ya know? I still have the copy of the book. Folks said it was the devil or maybe the ghosts that gave Aunt Viola the immoral courage to go to his room. You see, it could not be the fault of a woman with her moral stature, there had to be other forces that compelled her to throw herself at a man. She wore a long white gown over a naked body; a twenty-five year old woman's body that was untouched by human hands. She went to his bed and gave herself to him freely, as if she was hypnotized by the fact he showed her no interest.

Yankee was no gentleman when it came to women. He didn't abuse or beat them, he just liked to be rough when it came to sexual relations. It was the first time she had been with a man and she was bruised and sore when the wild night was over. But, she was also madly in love with the first man who touched her. Aunt Viola was physically spent from her first sexual encounter and she lay naked on her stomach, face down in Yankee's bed. He was standing at the dresser and washing his face with water from a basin. There was a knock at the door of his room. The unfeeling Yankee opened the door to see Ralph Cason standing in front of him. Ralph had come to the room to ask Yankee for a ride to work at the Pogy Plant. It seems he was late and his old car wouldn't start. As he requested Yankee's help, he looked past him and saw the naked body of his true love, Viola. He had dreamed about seeing her naked and being with her for years, but he didn't think he would see her in another man's bed. I'm sure Ralph's heart broke into a million pieces at that very moment. They say he ran from the house and into the storm. He didn't go to the Pogy Plant that day.

They say, Yankee left her in the bed and went out into that storm. No one knew where he went or why, he just left. Late that night, Aunt Viola was sitting in her favorite rocker in this very room. She was by the fireplace and she was thinking about the physical contact she had with the man she loved. Viola heard the front door open and the first thing that entered her mind was that Yankee had returned and she was more than ready to lay with him again. Viola tried to stay calm and not run foolishly into his arms, so she remained seated and waited for him to come to her. Her heart was racing with the anticipation he would appear at the door of this room, that door right there." Everyone in the room turned and they could imagine Yankee Williams, as he stepped to the door. Mr. King changed their vision.

"She knew by the shape of the shadow that was moving toward the room that the visitor was not her beloved. She asked, 'who's there' and a voice she knew very well answered. It was Ralph Cason and he was carrying the strangest thing over his shoulder. Viola said, 'Well, Ralph Cason, where have you been all day?' Viola had no idea he had seen her after her most immoral deed. Ralph didn't answer her question as he moved closer to her. She remained in the rocking chair. Viola noticed the strange object Ralph had against his shoulder. The sight of it prompted another question from her. 'What are you doing with that. It's raining too hard for late night yard work.' Ralph was still silent as he came even closer to her. 'Are you alright, Ralph? You look like you're sick. Put that heavy thing out on the porch and come sit by the warm fire with me. I don't know why you would carry a pitchfork in the house, anyway. Are you returning it?' Without a word Ralph took the pitchfork off his shoulder and held it high in the air. Aunt Viola had no idea why she was being pitchforked to death that night of the Northeaster. The first thrust of the sharp tool sent three metal prongs through her beautiful face and pinned her to the chair. She screamed as he pulled the handle back and pushed it again, sticking her throat and her shoulders. Her second scream ended when the third thrust pierced her heart and lungs. It was the death blow. Ralph Cason's body was found the next morning floating face down in the water next to the Pogy Plant. He had left the pitchfork sticking in Aunt Viola. After that awful night and Yankee Williams' total disappearance, folks said that Yankee's style of ignoring a woman until she came to him was his way of seducing women. Folks say he was the devil and came to take Viola's goodness. Others said Ralph Cason killed Yankee before he killed Viola. I have to tell you that Aunt Viola is definitely one of the ghosts who remain here with me. In fact that's the chair she was killed in and she rocks there now and then." Mr. King looked at the green rocking chair where Helga was sitting. Her eyes opened wide as the others looked at the chair, too. Ana was the first again.

"John, are you saying that this rocking chair, right here, is the actual chair Viola was sitting in the night that happened?" They all waited for his answer, especially Helga.

"Yes, we just had it recovered." Helga exploded from her comfortable position in the rocking chair.

"Oh my God! Why didn't you tell me. Oh my God!" Helga was on her feet and moving toward the door. Norman Bates stared at Mr. King in disbelief. Beulla was trying to calm Helga down. Little Tom was roaring with laughter. Ana Kara had open mouth syndrome. And Big Bob knew they were in the presence of the greatest storyteller of them all. He stood up and bowed in respect to his host and new friend.

"One should always be prepared to be scared if they choose to stay in a haunted house. I think we all should go out onto the porch and get some of that morning air in our lungs. Mr. John King, you are a rare find, sir. I, for one, am very thrilled that we found you." Big Bob bowed again like an English gentleman. Mr. King returned the gesture as the others all walked out onto the downstairs porch. Beulla was fanning Helga and trying to calm her. Ana Kara remained in the living room with Mr. King. They were alone.

"John, that was a wonderful story. And the way you used Helga was masterful. With her being the one easiest to scare, how did you know she would sit in the rocking chair?" Mr. King smiled.

"You know I can't give away my secrets. I might have to use them on you sometime."

"You won't ever have to trick me John, just ask and I will do it." John looked at what he considered a real woman.

"What a wonderful thing for you to say to me. Thank you. I will never trick you."

CHAPTER NINE

OFFICER JOHNSTON AND MR. BUTLER KNEW WHAT TO EXPECT WHEN THEY arrived at Mary C.'s house. Hawk didn't. At first he saw the piece of plywood where the front door used to be. One of the other officers was prying the sheet of wood off the door facing so they could enter the house. Hawk stepped up onto the porch and saw blood stains from the first Calypso Mary C. killed, Truck and Voo Swar. He followed the policeman into the house where he saw broken glass, pieces of wood, empty shotgun shells and leaves all over the floor, as well as more blood stains.

Hawk stepped to the bedroom and saw the hole where the bedroom window used to be. Officer Johnston stepped up behind him.

"We should have put a piece of plywood in that window last night, but we forgot. I don't think anyone climbed through there in the night. I hope not." Mr. Butler joined them as they all took a look at the destruction around them. Mr. Butler wanted Hawk to know the entire story.

"As you can see, your woman went to war here last night. I don't know how she did it. I wanted you to come here so we could talk. You have to understand what I'm up against. Five people died here last night. Mary C. says she killed two of them for sure, but the third one was by luck and the other two were both dying when she finished the job. I need to know if you came back here last night and helped her defend this place?" Mr. Butler knew right away from Hawk's expression that he knew nothing about the killings. Hawk had his own question.

"What do you mean? I was out in the ocean all night. No, I wasn't here." Mr. Butler admitted his feelings.

"I just had to ask. I guess I knew it wasn't you when you walked in the house." Mr. Butler looked at Officer Johnston. "Tell him Jimmy what we think." Hawk looked at Jimmy.

"We're pretty sure someone was with Mary C. last night."

After Mr. King's story the circus family had settled on the front porch of the haunted house. Ana Kara was in the living room with Mr. King.

"John, I still can't get over the way that story unfolded and the way Helga played a part in the ending. You are very good. I just wonder how much of the tale was true." Mr. King smiled.

"I'm sure it has changed a great deal through the years of it being told, but the basic love story premise is true and the part about being killed with a pitchfork." Ana squinted her eyes at the thought of such a brutal way to die.

"It is so sad that she had to die the same day she made love for the first time and she was so beautiful. She had been so good all her life. It's as if she was punished almost instantly, because she went to his room. Was Yankee Williams the devil himself?"

"Who can really know. Not us mortal men that's for sure. I do believe she is still here. And she walks these halls nightly and she rocks in that chair." Ana smiled.

"John, you do have a way of saying things. You just gave me chills when you said that." Mr. King did like the way his beautiful house guest and so far, one night stand, talked.

"By the way John, which one of your collection is your favorite item?" Mr. King walked near the rocking chair and the fireplace.

"I have always loved the chair. Visitors have seen it rock with no one sitting in it. It has always been a great conversation piece, especially when I tell the Aunt Viola story. But, to tell the truth I have a new favorite." Mr. King looked up at the mantle over his fireplace and pointed his new favorite addition to his collection of oddities. Ana Kara looked up to see a white human skull in the middle of the wooden mantle.

"This is my new pride and joy." Ana stepped closer to the scary face.

"John, don't tell me this thing is real."

"It's not only real, it's someone that I knew." Ana's eyes opened wide.

"A family member?"

"No, a local young man. Mean as a snake. Somebody tied him to a tree deep in the woods and he was most likely eaten by the creatures in the woods."

"John, that's awful. Is that true or another way to scare me? Why would you want such a thing and how did you get it?"

"It's true alright. I want it because it adds something real to this house of the unreal and unknown. This skull is the real thing. I can't say how I got it."

"You are an interesting man, John King, and I like you." She could make John King smile.

"You spend your life with a group of the most unusual and interesting people on the face of the earth and you think, I'm interesting? Isn't life strange? Shall we join the others?"

"I really would rather stay in here with you, but I guess we had better see how Helga is." John King did like the way she talked.

Mr. Butler had told Hawk his theory about the night before and how he was pretty sure someone had assisted her in defeating the warrior-like attackers. He had also told Hawk that he didn't think they would charge Mary C. with any type of crime because it was obvious the intruders were trespassing and they were there to do harm to Mary C. and possibly steal the baby. It was a clear case of self-defense and defending one's property. He was concerned about the reaction of the small black community in Mayport, but he would have to deal with that situation if need be. Mr. Butler wanted Hawk to see the five victims of Mary C.'s wrath. He thought Hawk needed to see exactly how wild and unbelievable it really was during the battle. They left the house and drove to the Beaches Hospital where the bodies had been taken. Officer Jimmy Johnston stayed with the other officers at the house looking for signs of an accomplice.

The ferry horn sounded as John King and Ana Kara joined the other haunted house guests. Each member of the family had found a comfortable place to sit, drink another cup coffee and enjoy the morning air. Big Bob had to compliment Mr. King one more time.

"John that was a classic in there. It was excellent." The others clapped their hands in respect for Mr. King's gift.

"Thank you all. I enjoy it very much and you were a captive audience. That always makes it easier. Helga, are you alright?" She nodded her head. Her partner, Tom Thumb, was sitting next to her and Mr. King saw a strange look come over the little pigmy's face. If Mr. King didn't know better he would have thought the ghosts were appearing to Tom during the day. All the color left Tom's little face. Tom couldn't help expressing himself out loud.

"Oh my God! It's you. I wasn't dreaming." All eyes on the porch looked at Tom and then in the direction he was looking. There was a collective gasp of surprise and caution from the entire group except Mr. King, as the warrior-priest, Sandeep Singh, stepped though the door and onto the porch with his hair touching the floor behind him. Sandeep's physical stature and physique was an awesome sight, especially to the women. The group of unusual characters all had the open mouth syndrome, a condition they usually inflicted on others. Mr. King was the first to break the visual trance they had all fallen under.

"Ladies and gentleman, now that the initial shock has passed, may I introduce another of my guests. This is Sandeep Singh. He ain't from around here." Big Bob spoke quickly.

"I don't believe this. What an honor for us all. I never thought I would see a Punjab priest in this part of the world, much less Mayport, Florida. This is becoming a wonderful adventure for us all." Everyone was quiet and all eyes were still on the new addition to the already strange group. Sandeep was curious about the giant of a man who was knowledgeable of his origin.

"How do you come to know of the Punjab?" All eyes turned to Big Bob.

"I spent time in your country when I was a young man. I have been to the land of five rivers. We were on our way to India and then Pakistan. When I was there I read about your ancient King Porus and his dealings with Alexander the Great." Big Bob looked at his family members. "He comes from a land of great saints and great warriors, it is an interesting combination and culture. We are honored to share this time with you." Sandeep stepped forward and shook the Giant's huge hand. He then stepped to each family member individually to touch each one.

Helga wanted to be the next one touched by the priest. Her heart raced behind her massive breasts and she could not hide the excitement created by his presence. Little Tom nodded but there was no way Tom was going to allow the long haired warrior to touch him. He didn't like Helga touching him either. Tom was afraid Helga would be more than happy to bring those tattoos to life if she had the chance. Ana was speechless for the first time that morning when he touched her hand and bowed to her beauty. Sandeep said nothing to her, yet she felt complimented by his touch. When Sandeep touched Beulla's hand it was obvious she could swallow him whole if given the opportunity. Norman Bates waved to Sandeep, as if to say, "Hello, but you don't have to touch me". Sandeep bowed in his direction.

Sandeep moved to the Twins, Ming and Ling. The porch was quiet as he knelt down next to the beautiful Siamese sisters. He took one of each girl's hand in his hands, kissing one hand and then the other. "Thank you for being with me today. You are a true gift to the world. I love you both with all my heart." The girls smiled and in stereo responded to the handsome mysterious stranger.

"We love you, too." Every member of the family understood how the Punjab felt. Sandeep turned toward the others and looked directly at Mr. King.

"I did not understand the substance of your guests when we spoke last night. You bring great honor to us all with your open heart and kindness. God will bless you many times over for these days."

The group remained quiet as Sandeep had more to say. "I am not sure what powers have brought such gifts to this place. There is a strange and wonderful gathering here, as if the powers of good and evil are coming together for the one and final battle. There are many gifts from God here including the golden children. There is also a strong presence of pure evil and it has already reared it's head as the night passed us by." Little Tom looked at the Punjab as if to say, "You're telling me it reared its head, I saw it through the key hole." Sandeep had more for the mesmerized audience. "It is good that we are all here together. There is a reason for all that is taking place. We may find our true destiny in this place called Mayport." Beulla ended Sandeep's hypnotizing words.

"Would you like some cheese grits?"

Jason was down in the hold of the Mary C. and he was filling the metal baskets with ice and shrimp. When the basket was full he would attach the hooks at the end of two chains onto the handles of the basket. When he whistled and gave a yell, Chichemo would turn on the winch of the boat and hoist the full basket out of the ice packed hold. He would then swing the boom over to the dock, where two of Mr. Leek's dock workers would unhook the baskets and carry them into the fish house, where they dumped the contents of the basket onto the heading table. The group of headers would begin popping the heads off of the shrimp and keeping tally on the poundage they were heading. There was money to be made at the tables that morning. Jason would stay in the hold and Chichemo would stay at the winch until the hold was empty of the cargo. Before the work was over there would be fifteen boxes of shrimp unloaded and headed. At one hundred pounds a box it was a great catch for their first time out. When the last basket was pulled from the hold, Chichemo told Jason to go on home to his mother and he would settle up with Mr. Leek. He would meet them later.

Mary C. sat on Miss Margaret's back porch. Sofia was with her, holding Billy on her lap. Peggy was painting her own toe nails and Margie was trying to talk Peggy into painting hers next.

"I'm not doing your toe nails. The last time I did them, you complained and said you didn't like them. I told you then I wasn't doing it anymore." Margie turned to Sofia.

"I hate doing my own toe nails don't you?" If you do mine I'll do yours." Peggy had a warning to share with her little sister.

"Sofia, make her do yours first. If you don't she'll find some reason to do yours later and then never get to them. Don't be a fool, little sister, you know I'm right." Mary C. absolutely adored being with Miss Margaret's daughters and they loved being with Mary C.

"I'll settle this nail thing. I'll do all y'all toes." The three sisters liked Mary C.'s offer. She would soon find herself up to her neck in pretty little toes.

Sandeep sat at John King's dining room table with Ana Kara, Helga and Beulla. Beulla had reheated her cheese grits and a number of the other buffet breakfast items. He had a full plate of food and a full table of admirers. His long black hair ran down his back covering the back of the chair and the floor around him. The other men and the Twins were still on the porch. Once the Twins got settled they didn't move around very much.

Without any prompting or request the talented Twins began to whistle in incredible harmony. It was a natural thing for them to do when they felt happy and loved. Their wonderful and unique sounds would bring joy to all who heard them. They whistled a Big Band tune by Perez Prado called, "Cherry Pink and Apple Blossom White." They sounded like a hundred silver throated birds all singing at once. The sound from their red puckered lips carried on the morning breeze and touched many more ears in Mayport than just the guests at John King's haunted house. It was true magic how the sounds they were making could he heard in every corner of Mayport.

Sandeep left his plate of food to stand near the Twins again. Susan stepped outside of the store when she heard the wonderful tune carry past her. The people waiting in their cars for the ferry rolled down their car windows to enjoy the pleasant sounds. It was as if the Twins were standing next to their cars. The morning patrons at the Blue Moon Tavern left the juke box and went outside to hear the melody that was carried on the wind. The headers at the tables stopped as the bird like sounds seemed to bounce off the walls of the fish house. Mary C. and the three girls stopped talking and painting, as the sound moved across Miss Margaret's back yard. Even people fishing on the little jetties heard the pleasant sounds as they were carried across the water and to the rocks.

The group at John King's haunted house knew they were the most privileged individuals on the Earth at that very moment. Anyone who heard the beautiful sounds would think about it during the day and crave more. Sandeep loved them even more. Another new magic had come to Mayport. When the Twins ended their magical whistling, Eve was standing at the door of John King's haunted house.

"What have you found now, John? Are these the circus people or have the ghosts decided to come out during the day?" Tom Thumb's heart raced in his tiny chest when he saw the female half of the tattooed sexual display he had watched through that key hole. "My dear John, how do you get yourself into these things. That good Samaritan heart of yours will be your undoing." Eve stepped out onto the porch to get a better look at the other guests. Mr. King was worried about what Eve would say next. He knew her nature was to make fun of or belittle others. He thought perhaps if he made a proper introduction, all would be fine.

"My good new friends, this is an old good friend, Eve. Her father and I were in the shrimping business years ago and we were best friends from our childhood. Eve is visiting her old home town and she is my guest. Eve, these are my new friends." Big Bob stepped to Eve. She looked up at the Giant and her expression did not change as he took her hand.

"My pleasure ma'am." Eve smiled and shook his hand. Big Bob felt no warmth from her smile or her touch. Norman nodded to her as he had done to Sandeep. He didn't want to touch anyone.

Eve turned to Little Tom. His heart pounded like a jungle drum.

"I was afraid I would trip over you last night in the dark. But, that was rather foolish of me don't you think?" Tom wasn't sure what to say. He looked at Eve and her eyes became the eyes of the black panther tattoo he had seen. Tom jumped off the wooden stool he was sitting on and ran into the house. Helga, Ana and Beulla watched Eve through the living room window. Eve stepped to the Twins.

"My goodness, you are two of the sweetest things. Sandeep, are they not the most unusual sisters you have ever seen?" Sandeep looked at his companion.

"They are gifts from God and there are none like them anywhere else. They are one of a kind."

"You mean two of a kind, don't you? Is everyone you meet a gift from God. Mayport used to not have any gifts from God. I wonder why there are so many, now that we came to town." Mr. King thought about what Sandeep had said earlier when he first saw the Twins.

"Sandeep was sayin' the same thing. He seems to think something big is gonna happen here. Some kind of battle between good and evil. He seems to be glad he's here for it. I ain't so sure I'm too happy about his theory." Big Bob smiled. He did like John King's way of saying things.

Mr. King had been thinking about something ever since Eve arrived at his doorstep and he thought it was a good time to talk to her about his thoughts. It would also get her away from the other guests. Mr. King changed the subject at hand.

"Eve, I need to speak to you privately, please. Would you give me a moment?"

"Of course John, let's go inside. I've been wanting to talk to you, too." She took Mr. King's arm and they walked toward the front door. "Please excuse us for a moment." Big Bob nodded, but the others did nothing.

Mr. King escorted Eve into his big living room as Ana, Beulla, Helga and Tom left the window and joined the others on the porch. Tom wasn't staying in the house with Eve nearby.

Big Bob brought something to their attention.

"I was thinking how we are having such a wonderful time here with John, but we have forgotten about the real reasons we came here; Beth and Jason." Norman lit up.

"That's true. We need to see Jason and Billy and find dear Beth." Ana added to the thought.

"When John comes back we'll get him to tell us where Jason lives and we'll go there first."

Eve and John King sat across from each other in the living room.

"What is it John. You think I'm going to be mean to your collection of freaks out there?"

"You're being mean to me right now and, yes, it did cross my mind that you would hurt their feelings."

"John, I'm sure their feelings are like leather after the torment they have endured throughout their pitiful lives. But, for old times sake, I won't say anything else to them. Except the little one. I like him being afraid of me. I might have to use that on him. You know, John, like the way you like to scare people. Isn't it funny how you can do that to people." Mr. King changed the subject again, because he had another serious concern.

"Eve, no more games and cute remarks. You have to tell me the truth about something."

"You sound like my daddy when he was mad at me, John. Are you mad at me, John?"

"The truth, Eve." Eve smiled and nodded her head. "Why are you really here? It can't be to say these petty things to Margaret's daughters. It can't be that you came all this way to insult whoever you meet and make a few more enemies. What is the real reason you have come home?" Eve looked into the eyes of her father's best friend.

"I'm here to punish the ones who have hurt me. I am here to punish the ones who have taken two of my loved ones away from me. I know how Charlie died. I need to know how James died." Mr. King had to think for a second. They were silent as he collected his thoughts.

"Eve, are you talking about Charlie Klim?" Eve's eyes opened wide.

"Yes, he was my friend." Mr. King's eyes opened wide.

"Eve, he was an awful person. He killed Bobby Merritt and a young woman. He was no good and you know that."

"He changed after that boy of Mary C.'s cut him up so bad. He wasn't the same after that. He went crazy after that. Now folks say that boy finished the job in those rocks. Charlie was wild and reckless, but he wasn't crazy until that boy chopped him up." John knew the story.

"Charlie was beatin' Mary C. and the boy came home and defended her." John could tell Eve didn't like what he said. She seemed to grit her teeth for a second.

"It sure is funny how somebody has to save her from men all the time. Men seem to pay for being seduced by her. She is always the victim. That boy has to pay for what he did to Charlie. He's just like her, he seems to get away with everything. I'm a little late, but he won't get away this time." A cold chill ran through Mr. King's body when Eve made her threat. He could tell it was not an idle one. He thought he knew the right answer but he still asked his next question.

"And who is James?" Eve had a mean glare in her eyes.

"Little James Thorn. His mother, Mildred, was my best friend. I used to rock James to sleep when he was sick. He was a sickly little boy. Mildred called it the croup. It got better when they took his tonsils and adenoids out. I ate ice cream with him when he was in the hospital. He was eight years old and the sweetest little thing." Mr. King brought Eve back from her trip down memory lane.

"He was a thief and sold stolen property for his own profit. He even sold guns to children. He was not the sweet little eight year old you remember." Eve had the same glare.

"They say somebody took him out into the woods, tied him to a tree, and let the animals eat him alive. I get crazy when I think about it, John, absolutely crazy." Mr. King's heart raced in his chest when he looked at James Thorn's smiling skull on his mantle, directly behind Eve. He gained a little composure and had the answer to one of her questions.

"They have already found James' killer. That fella they called Skinny who lived near the beach was the one they say did it."

"I heard that, too. Maybe it's true, but I also heard he did it for

Mary C. The old fool was in love with her and he did it for her. Hell, she probably was there and watched the whole thing. She was mad at James for something and she used that Skinny to do her dirty work. I plan to ask her in person and I'll know as soon as I see her eyes when I ask the question. She's always been the victim of something. She wants men to want her and take her and when they do she becomes the victim. I hate her. I always have. And ain't it strange how her and that boy seem to have a hand in killing two people I cared for? That doesn't seem strange to you, John? Just a little?"

"You're going on what you think is true with no proof but your feelings. You've got it in your head they're responsible and that's the way it is as far as you're concerned. I think you just want to hurt somebody."

"Not just anybody, John. These two have hurt more people than you can count. You just don't know about certain things, but I do and it's time somebody put a stop to them."

"And that should be your job?"

"John, I have brought the instrument of revenge, an avenging angel, if you will. The perfect tool to rid the world of evil. The warrior-saint will stop them." Mr. King had his own thoughts about Sandeep.

"I don't see that young fella hurtin' a fly. I've seen how he acts and his philosophy of life. It would take a lot to make him hurt somebody, much less kill 'em."

"You said 'kill', not me. I said revenge. I want Mary C. to hurt and know who hurt her. I want her to look into my eyes one more time and know I have taken something she loves from her."

"That still means killin' somebody and you know it. Just 'cause you don't say it, don't mean nothin'. You gonna kill that boy, ain't ya.?"

"John, I'm not talking about killing anyone. I just want Mary C. to suffer. You asked me why I was here and I told you the truth. Now, you don't like what you heard. And now I expect you to mind your own business, like you always have. And to be truthful again, John, I don't give a rat's ass what you think." She left the room and passed

Ana Kara as she turned to go up the stairs. The two women were eye-to-eye. Ana smiled, Eve glared and went up the stairs. Mr. King looked at James Thorn's skull and thought what Eve would do if she knew it was his. Ana Kara walked into the living room to see Mr. King after her look from Eve.

"John, I don't think your lady friend likes any of us very much." Mr. King looked at his new sex partner.

"I'm sorry about that. She's never been very friendly. Well, I'm sorry."

"John, you don't have to be sorry for someone else and what they do. Oh, let's not talk about her. We need your help. Norman's getting the bus started and we're going to find Jason's house. Would you like to join us in the bus and maybe give us a tour of this wonderful town of yours?" Mr. King knew he wouldn't miss that bus ride for anything.

The circus family was on the porch. Norman was in the driver's seat of the purple and yellow bus. A truck pulled up to the front of John King's house and stopped behind the bus. Mr. Leek stepped out of the truck and walked slowly to the porch. His eyes were as big as coffee cup saucers when he saw the interesting characters who were sitting or standing on the porch above him. He was relieved when he saw Mr. King standing with them and he looked safe. Mr. King knew Mr. Leek was a bit cautious as he approached the steps.

"Al, come on up. I want you to meet my new friends. They're spending a few days here with me." Mr. Leek stepped up on the first step. Mr. King continued. "This is Big Bob, Norman over there, Beulla and Helga there, Tom and Ana. The two ladies over there are Ming and Ling." Everyone said hello to Mr. Leek. Big Bob did the handshake for them all. Mr. King continued. "We were all gonna take a ride in this great bus and see what's happening out at Jason's and take a little tour of Mayport. These are the folks that helped Jason when he left home. He stayed with them over in West Florida." Mr. Leek's head was on a swivel as he took in the strange sights at the haunted house. He remembered why he had stopped to talk to Mr. King and he could give them some information and save them a ride to Jason's.

The Cadillac Gothic Hearse

"John, I can see you haven't heard what happened last night. I don't know where to start. This is gonna be very hard to believe." Mr. King was interested and the porch went silent. Before Mr. Leek could tell his tale, the sight of Sandeep and Eve walking through the front door stopped him. He saw Sandeep first. His hair was still not braided and was hanging to the floor. Eve stepped in front of Sandeep. "I don't believe it. Al Leek, you haven't changed a bit. You handsome devil." Mr. Leek stared at Eve for only a second.

"Eve, look at you. If it's possible, you are even more beautiful than the last time I saw you. Time has been very good to you. You must tell me your secret. We all need to know." Eve moved to Mr. Leek and hugged him affectionately. He returned the squeeze. She turned to Sandeep. "Al, this my companion and protector, Sandeep Singh. He is a Punjab priest."

Mr. King couldn't resist.

"Al here is a Deacon at the Oak Harbor Baptist Church. He don't carry no Kirpan Sword, but I'll bet ya a dollar he's got a two blade pocket knife on him right now." Nobody understood Mr. King's little joke except Eve, Sandeep and Big Bob. Eve didn't think it was funny. Sandeep didn't pay any attention to the remark. Mr. King and Big Bob thought it was really funny. They smiled at each other and enjoyed the joke themselves. Mr. Leek was in the dark and he just wanted them to know what had happened. Mr. King took the conversation back to the original topic. "Al, what were you going to tell us before the reunion with Eve?"

"Last night while Jason and Hawk were shrimpin' four black men and a black woman, a voodoo woman they say, went out to Mary C.'s house and tried to kill her and steal the new baby." Every face on the porch had a different reaction to what Mr. Leek had just said. The concern on all the faces of Big Bob's family was obvious. Eve wanted to know about the possibility someone killed Mary C. and Mr. King wanted to hear more.

"My God, Al, are they alright. Why would they want the baby?" The porch was quiet in anticipation of Mr. Leek's next words.

They're both fine. They were not hurt at all. In fact the crazy thing is that Mary C. killed them all. She killed all five of them, even the woman." The porch was silent and full of looks of pure shock. Eve stared at Mr. King as he had the first response to what he had just heard from his good friend.

"Al, I know what I heard you say. But, I need to hear it again just in case I misunderstood it."

"Five blacks attacked Mary C.'s house last night carrying machetes and the woman with the four men was of the voodoo craft. Mary C. defended the baby, herself and the house. She killed them all with a shotgun. I don't think anyone can go out there. The police have it blocked off while they do an investigation." Eve stopped Mr. Leek as she continued to stare at Mr. King.

"Add five more to her death count." Eve left the porch and went into the house. Mr. Leek had more. "Mary C. and the baby are at Miss Margaret's. They stayed there last night. The front door of Mary C.'s house was destroyed and I think a window or two was also blown out by the shotgun blasts. The police wouldn't let them stay there last night. Jason and Hawk came in this mornin'. I guess they're over there now." The information Mr. Leek was sharing was an incredible story. Sandeep listened like the others. He could have given much better details than Mr. Leek, but he said nothing. Big Bob was concerned.

"This Mary C. he's talking about is Jason's mother?" Mr. Leek responded.

"Yes, it seems those people had gone there during the day and seen the baby. They call him an oak baby from the oak tree here in Mayport. There are folks who believe in this tree and they think the child has some special powers. I'm not sure what an oak baby is suppose to do, so I can't say why they wanted to steal him. One thing I do know is that they made a huge mistake when they went to face Mary C." Big Bob wanted to do something.

"Is there anything we can do to help Jason. He could probably use some support at this time." Sandeep surprised the group when he joined the conversation.

"The child is golden. If he learns his purpose early he will touch many lives and make them better. If he stays here he will be lost like his father. The woman is of great strength. She has faced many hardships. She walks a thin line between good and evil. She is not protected, but she will survive." The group was silent, especially Mr. Leek and Mr. King. They both knew what Sandeep was saying was true, but they wondered how he knew so much about Mary C. Ana Kara joined in.

"I don't think we all need to go to see Jason under these circumstances. Big Bob, you and Norman go over there and tell Jason we're all here for him and maybe he will come here to see us. We shouldn't just show up at this Miss Margaret's house full force. We do cause a great deal of confusion as a group." The family all nodded in agreement and support of Ana's idea. Big Bob knew she was right.

"John, will you go with us to see Jason?"

"Of course I will. Al, you want to go too?"

"No, John, I need to get back to the dock. There's a few more boats comin' in and they'll need me there. I just wanted to tell you about Mary C. It was nice to meet y'all." Everyone said good-bye to Mr. Leek.

"Tell Eve, welcome home." Mr. Leek got into his truck and drove toward the dock.

Mr. King had an idea. "I'll get my car. No sense in us three takin' that big bus." Eve walked back out onto the front porch.

"Sandeep, we need to braid your hair. It's getting late." Sandeep stood up and walked into the house with Eve and they went up the stairs to their room. Before Norman left he helped the Twins to their room so they could rest. Ana, Beulla and Helga cleaned the kitchen of the breakfast buffet aftermath. Little Tom stayed near Helga and helped in the kitchen. He didn't want to leave Helga alone in the same house with Sandeep. He knew the women were attracted to the warrior-priest and he was jealous.

A car horn sounded in front of the house. It was John King driving up in his newly acquired 1941 silver Cadillac Gothic carved panel hearse. He had traded in his black Mercury traditional hearse for the Cadillac Gothic model. It was equipped with wide gangster white wall tires, chrome globe shaped wheel covers, winged side wheel skirts over the two back tires, and blue stained glass on both sides of the main casket area. No one at the house had ever seen such a chariot for the dead. Mr. King had truly outdone himself and taken his role as the master of the haunted house to a new level with his most appropriate mode of transportation. Big Bob and Norman stepped out of the house and couldn't believe they would be riding in the ultimate hearse. Mr. King was excited.

"Ain't it great? You can't have a real haunted house without a car like this. Don't y'all love it?" Big Bob and Norman did like Mr. King's style. He was a sport. They climbed in and they were off to find Jason.

Hawk and Mr. Butler returned to Mary C.'s house. Jason had gone there, too, and was waiting with Officer Johnston and the other policemen. Mr. Butler and Hawk stepped out of the car. Officer Johnston and Jason walked out of the house and met them in the yard. Officer Johnston spoke first.

"We're 'bout finished here with what we can do. We haven't found any evidence at all that anyone else was here with her. There's so many different footprints outside from all the people here that day and that night, nothing unusual at all." Mr. Butler responded.

"We know somebody sliced those three open before Mary C. finished them off. And she could be right about them going crazy in the dark and cutting each other up by mistake. They might have even got in fights themselves as the night went on. At this point that's the only theory we have to go on." Mr. Butler looked at Hawk. "We'll get someone out here and help y'all fix the door and window tomorrow." Hawk didn't need any help.

"We'll get 'em fixed. Thanks anyway. We'll put the plywood back in the door and some in the window. Mary C. and the baby can stay at Miss Margaret's again tonight 'til we get this mess cleaned up." Mr. Butler had to tell them one more thing.

"I'm going back over there to see Mary C. one more time. She may have to make a statement in front of the judge, but I don't know for sure. They may just close it. It looks pretty cut and dry. Self-defense all the way. I would like to know if anyone really helped her or not. If she was alone, she is an amazing woman." Hawk and Jason both smiled. Hawk spoke up.

"That might be the case here, ya know?" Mr. Butler smiled, too.

"I don't know how you feel about it, but that's a scary thought to me. Jimmy, I'm going home after I talk to Mary C. and get some sleep. You need to do the same."

"Yes sir, I think I will." Mr. Butler left. Officer Johnston talked to the other officers and then they left. Hawk and Jason sat on the front porch.

Mary C. and the three sisters were sitting at the kitchen table. Peggy was leaving to relieve Susan at the store. She opened the front door as Mr. King's big, long, silver hearse pulled up in front of their house.

"Mama! Get out here!" Miss Margaret, Mary C., Sofia and Margie, all ran to the door when Peggy gave her cry for Mama. Peggy stepped to the side when Miss Margaret pushed the door open. Mr. King emerged from the hearse, first.

"Hey Margaret, didn't mean to frighten the girl. I've got some friends of Jason's with me. You met them last night at the store. We were hoping Jason might be here."

"He's not here, John, but we do expect him later."

"Al told us about what happened last night. Is there anything we can do?"

"Everything's pretty calm now, John, and we hope it stays that way. Mary C. and the baby are here and doing just fine." When Big Bob and Norman heard Billy was there, they both got out of the hearse. Miss Margaret remembered them and so did the girls. Mary C. had no idea who they were. She was amazed at the size of Big Bob. He had to speak up.

"Miss Margaret, Norman and I are concerned about Jason. In fact, the others are all waiting to here how Billy and Jason are doing. We were all there when Billy was born and we love him as if he was ours. He has a place in our hearts forever. The little rascal brought new life to our lives and we love him and Jason for that. They are part of our family. We would love to see Billy, but we do understand that we are strangers to you. When Jason returns perhaps you could tell him we are at Mr. King's house and we would love to see him and Billy, and meet his mother if she would like to meet us." Miss Margaret started to respond to Big Bob's heartfelt request when Mary C. walked past her at the door carrying Billy in her arms. She walked down the steps and took Billy to where Big Bob and Norman were standing near the hearse.

"I'm Mary C., Jason's mother. I want to thank you for taking care of my son and grandson when they were with you." Mary C. pulled the blanket back so they could see Billy's face. Big Bob smiled a huge smile when Billy's green eyes seemed to flash in the sunlight.

"I will be sure Jason and Billy come see you at John's house." Big Bob felt the warmth from Mary C.'s voice. It didn't fit the cold heart-ed survivor he had heard about. Sofia joined them at the hearse.

"Are you enjoying your stay in Mayport? Were you scared to sleep at Mr. King's house? Did you see any ghosts?" Sofia was a three question woman and she liked being near the strange circus friends Jason had told her about. Miss Margaret joined them.

"Sofia, stop asking all those questions. Would you like to come in and wait for Jason?" Mr. King had the answer to one question.

"No, Margaret, I have to get back to my other guests. I haven't had this much fun since the Little Man in Red came to haunt the house." Big Bob was curious.

"Another story for us later, John?"

"If you wish, sir." John had an idea for them all. "When Jason returns, why don't you all come to the house and visit this evening. I would love for you to hear the Twins sing. They're going to sing later tonight. You should have heard them whistle today. I can't even explain what it was like listening to them." Sofia was excited.

"We heard them! We were in the backyard. We didn't know what it was, but I'm sure it was them." Big Bob understood.

"I'm sure it was them. They have a way of projecting their sounds into the air and nature does the rest." Mr. King was intrigued.

"You mean they are able to throw their voices that distance? They are gifts from God." The three visitors said good-bye and climbed back into the silver hearse. Mr. King didn't think about Mary C. and Eve crossing paths if Mary C. came to his house later with the others.

For some strange reason Tom Thumb found himself with his eye pressed against the key hole to Sandeep's and Eve's bedroom. The Twins were sleeping and the three women were finishing their clean-up downstairs. Even though he was still afraid his sexual perverted curiosity was stronger than his fear. If their was a chance for him to see the tattooed lovers in action again, he would take that chance. Eve was braiding Sandeep's hair as the little man watched from his position in the hallway. Eve was doing the talking.

"You keep speaking of God's gifts being here in Mayport. I'm not sure if you're right. It has become too easy for you to say. It doesn't seem real."

"I know what you are saying. And this has never happened before. That's why I feel something is going to happen. All elements are meeting here. Why? I don't know. I wish I did so I could prepare myself, but I don't know how."

"You speak of a battle between good and evil. Is it not your duty to fight evil?"

"You say these things to me because you will request an evil deed of me. It has been your plan for many days now. You will offer me my freedom and release me of my obligation if I will do this thing for you. You also know that one sin on my soul is worth the freedom to protect the golden ones. You have known all along I would have to do as you say."

"But, you would be fighting the evil of this place. Mary C. and her son have taken many lives on their path of destruction. The evil they have created must be stopped."

"You are wrong. Jason was golden, but he is now lost. He has had no direction. The woman is just a woman, who has learned to survive at all cost. She does not cry from pain. There is a hardness, but it is not from evil. She is able to remove all deeds from her mind. It is a talent she has learned from necessity. She is no gift to the world and she is not evil." Eve didn't like what she was hearing about Mary C.

but she did like Sandeep saying he would sin to be free. Little Tom heard voices downstairs and he left his keyhole. He hurried down stairs.

Mr. Butler drove up to Miss Margaret's house. Sofia saw him walking up the walkway to the front door.

"Mama, more company's here." Miss Margaret met Mr. Butler at the front door.

"Mr. Butler, how are you?"

"I'm fine Miss Margaret. I'm tired though and headed home to sleep. I was hoping to talk to Mary C. one last time before I called it a day. Would you ask her if she would come out and talk to me?"

"It would probably be more comfortable inside. Come on in and I'll call her down." Miss Margaret stepped back into the house and called up the stairs for Mary C. Sofia had already told her Mr. Butler was there and Mary C. was headed down the stairs.

"I'll step outside and talk to him, Miss Margaret."

"Whatever you wish, child." Mary C. walked down Miss Margaret's front steps and met Mr. Butler near his car.

"Jason and Hawk are fixing the door and window at the house, they'll be here later. Will you talk to me for a minute?"

"Sure, I like talkin' to you. You'll be able to tell the others what to expect when they come callin' for Billy again."

"Why do you think I'll talk to anyone?"

"They'll come to you because you're the law. And when they see that I'm free, after killin' five of them, and one was a voodoo queen, they will want what they think is justice. Me being free will not be justice to them. You see, you have to let me go. I've done nothin' wrong in the eyes of the "law". The law you have to uphold. That law means nothin' to Macadoo and the others. Those five dead people are someone's sons, cousins, uncles, aunt, friends, queen. They will be looking for their own justice. When you tell them why I am free they will be angry and want their own justice. You will be able to see it in their eyes. That's when you will tell them what they will face if they try to take anything from me." Mr. Butler was always amazed when he was with Mary C. He remembered how his good friend, Sheriff

McIntosh fell in love with her during an investigation of a murder case. He also remembered how he told Officer Jimmy Johnston that people who get involved with her didn't live very long. Mr. Butler didn't want to be the next one. He thought about Hawk and the fact he was still around, but he also knew Hawk was different when it came to being a man. He liked Hawk, but knew he was flirting with danger if he stayed with Mary C. Mr. Butler needed to get a few questions off his mind before he went home and went to bed.

"Mary C., is there anything you can think of that might have been strange during your battle with those painted devils? I know the whole thing was strange, but did any of them say anything to you before they died? Did you hear them talking? Did you say anything to them? You might be right about them going crazy and cutting each other up in the dark. It is possible and maybe that's what happened. Something keeps me doubting it did. Think about it and if anything comes to mind call me right away. And you're right, you are free." Mr. Butler turned to go to his unmarked police car. Mary C. had her own question.

"What did you call them?" Mr. Butler stopped and turned back to her. "The black men who attacked me. What did you call them?"

"I'm not sure what you mean. When?"

"Just now. You called them something." Mr. Butler had to think for a second.

"Painted devils."

"That's it, devils. The voodoo woman said that to me at the front door." Mr. Butler stepped to Mary C. as she went on. "I just thought it was voodoo talk or talkin' out of her head with pain. She said she knew he was the devil. She said the name Lucifer. I think that means the devil." Mr. Butler was intrigued.

"I wonder who she meant?"

"She said something before that, but I wasn't really listening with those shotgun blasts still ringing in my ears."

"Can you think of any of the words?" Mr. Butler could tell Mary C. was really trying to help him.

He was impressed with her honesty and effort. "She said something like, 'He told me his name, but I know it was Lucifer.' She said I walked with the devil." Mr. Butler felt they were getting somewhere and he wanted it to continue.

"So you're saying the old woman acted like she had talked to someone before you saw her?"

"Yes, I didn't think of it before, or I would have told you."

"I believe you would have. Can you remember if she said what he said his name was?"

Mary C. smiled. "This is gonna sound crazy."

"Nothing sounds crazy to me anymore. Now, please say what you think." Mary C. kept her smile and took a deep breath.

"She said something like, 'He said his name was Singin' Sandy, but I know it was Lucifer.' I told you it would sound crazy. That's what it sounded like to me. Like I said the blasts were ringing in my ears." Mr. Butler smiled.

"Singin' Sandy, with a big butcher knife. You're right it does sound funny, but at least it's something. If you think of anything please let me know. I'll keep in touch." Mr. Butler left Mary C. at Miss Margaret's house. It was hard for him not to like and respect the woman he had named the Black Widow a year ago.

CHAPTER TEN

TOM THUMB WATCHED FROM MR. KING'S FRONT PORCH AS ANA, HELGA and Beulla walked across the street to Miss Margaret's store. He had climbed up on the porch railing and sat there with his short legs hanging down. His back was against one of the posts that held the upper balcony up over the porch. Sandeep walked out onto the porch. He was dressed in black with a matching black turban wrapped around his head. He was an impressive sight as Tom turned to see him. Tom couldn't get down off his perch on the railing quick enough. Sandeep surprised him by speaking first.

"I know you are a curious man and a man of the flesh. It is in your eyes when you look at the women. It is not your fault. It is in your nature. The curiosity and the flesh. I have nothing to hide from you. If you want to know about me, ask me. Don't watch me and think of things that are not true." Tom was speechless and very afraid. He had no idea why he said what he said, but it just came out.

"What is the Kirpan Mr. King spoke of ?" Tom wanted to take his question back, but it was too late. Sandeep knew the question was from fear and nervousness. The warrior saint gave a rare half smile. Sandeep reached under his clothing and unsheathed the Kirpan sword of his ancestors. Tom's heart screamed in his tiny chest when he saw the gleam of the blade and golden handle. It was a short sword with a wide blade like the jungle machetes of the Calypsos,

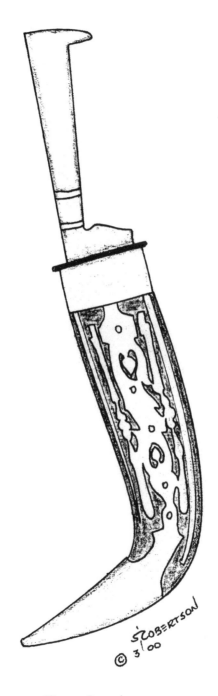

Kirpan Sword

but the blade was curved wickedly toward the end. Sandeep saw the awe and fear in the pigmy's dark eyes.

"The Kirpan reminds me that I am a Sikh warrior. It is our duty to always remember that first. It is used to defend our way of life and protect the weak and helpless." Tom listened intently and never took his scared eyes off the Kirpan blade. Sandeep was not holding the sword to intimidate the little man, that was not his way. He was answering Tom's question. The intimidation was in Tom's interpretation of the moment. Tom had a thought to ask Sandeep about the tattoos, but it remained only a thought.

Jason and Hawk drove up to Miss Margaret's house in Uncle Bobby's truck. Mary C. and Miss Margaret were sitting in the front yard in white lawn chairs enjoying the afternoon. Billy was lying on a blanket next to them on the ground. Mary C. was fanning his little body with a flat wooden handle that had an oval shaped piece of cardbord attached to it. The cardboard had an Oriental scene on both sides. Mary C. spoke first.

"Well, we thought y'all had gone back shrimpin'." Jason sat next to Billy on the ground.

"We've been workin' on the house. Some mess over there."

"Ain't it though?" Jason touched Billy's little head.

"How's he doin'?"

"He's fine and he's gonna stay fine." Hawk was next.

"How 'bout you Mary C.?" She smiled and liked her man being concerned, but she had to remind them both what she had said before.

"I'm better than fine, if that's possible. I'm still not sure how to say what I feel about all this. My mind has different thoughts. We'll talk later when we're settled at home. For now let's just be happy about us all being safe and together." Jason and Hawk knew they could not ask her about that night and how she felt until she was ready to talk to them. They would not ask her again. Miss Margaret made her earlier suggestion again.

"I would still like you two to stay here tonight. Then you can decide what to do tomorrow."

Hawk was a good man. "I'm gonna stay at the house tonight and keep workin' on the damage. Jason's gonna stay here with Billy and Mary C." Mary C. did love Hawk. Miss Margaret had another thought to share.

"It will be nice to have a man around the house at night. Hawk, if you change your mind there is room for you both. My husband won't be back until next week. He's gone more these days than he's here." Margie walked out of the house as Miss Margaret was talking. Her heart raced in her chest at the thought of Jason spending the night in the same house with her.

Sandeep was sheathing the Kirpan sword as Ana, Helga and Beulla approached the front steps of the porch. They were carrying bags of items they had bought from the store. Beulla spoke up first.

"Hey Mr. Sandeep, hey Tom. We just had the best time over at the store with Peggy. They all are the nicest girls. What are you two boys doin'?" Tom gave a nervous half smile.

"Just talkin'." Ana was next.

"We've got a bunch of goodies. We've got honey buns, Nehi drinks, moon pies, and penny candy. We've got Squirrel Nut Zippers, Mary Janes, Tootsie Rolls, Bazooka gum, Fire Balls, and those caramel circles with the white stuff in the middle. We've gone sweet tooth crazy." Tom jumped off his perch on the railing and started looking in the bags for the penny candy. Helga had the right bag.

"Back off, now. We're sharin' and takin' turns. You know the penny candy rules." Tom knew he would have to wait and he knew not to challenge Helga in front of the others. She moved to one of the chairs and turned the bag she was holding upside down, dumping the contents into the chair. Helga was in control of the candy. She had penny candy etiquette and she knew the proper thing to do. "Mr. Sandeep, you get first pick of the candy pile and we won't take no for an answer. You must pick." Sandeep was surprised at her offer, refusal and command all in the same breath. He stepped to the chair and scanned the pile of colorful treats. He had never been given such a choice or been a participant in sharing penny candy. He chose a Squirrel Nut Zipper, to the three women's delight. Helga knew Tom was about to go into candy convulsions so she let him be next.

"Your turn Tom, one piece at a pick." Tom grabbed a Squirrel Nut and looked at Sandeep as to say, "It takes a real man to chew one of these babies." Then Beulla picked, followed by Ana and Helga. When Helga had picked she reminded the others of the penny candy rules.

"We'll each get four picks and then leave the rest for the others. Mr. Sandeep, your turn."

Sandeep was first in the rotation and the others followed in the same order as before. After four picks per person, Helga bagged up the remaining candy and set the bag aside. They all began enjoying their sweet selections. Even Sandeep had a mouth full. He chewed his way through the Squirrel Nut and wished he had chosen more of the chewy item. They were all chomping away when Eve walked through the door and out onto the porch. She did not even glance at the others as she looked directly at Sandeep with his jaw looking puffed and swollen. Eve's eyes opened wide at the sight of his red lips.

"What has happened to your mouth?" Sandeep smiled revealing his red teeth and tongue.

"I think it's called a Fire Ball." The four members of the family all smiled, but turned away so Eve couldn't see their reaction. Eve had a disgusted look on her face as the silver hearse pulled up in front of Mr. King's house and stopped next to her Mercedes Benz. Mr. King, Big Bob and Norman got out of the death wagon and joined the others on the porch. Ana greeted them first.

"Did you see Jason and Billy?" The others were quiet and interested in the answer. Big Bob had the information.

"We saw Billy and he's fine. We met Jason's mother. She was very nice to us and let us see Billy. She thanked us all for helping Jason." Norman jumped in.

"Billy's beautiful and he's gettin' big." All the faces of the family members lit up like flood lights and the ladies all made a loving noise as they thought about the vision Norman had given them. Norman went on.

"Miss Mary C.'s gonna tell Jason to come see us with Billy, when he gets back; they all might come." The family was excited. Mr. King looked at Eve to see her reaction to what Norman had said. Her expression didn't change. Mr. King looked at Sandeep and realized the soldier-priest was sucking on something. Mr. King didn't dream it was a Fire Ball. Helga was in charge of the candy. She picked up the bag.

"A little something for you three and the Twins to share. We've had our turns." Helga looked at Eve and remembered her penny candy manners. "Would you like to pick penny candy first?" The entire porch went silent waiting to see Eve's reaction to Helga's question and offer. Sandeep surprised them all.

"Get one of those Squirrel Nuts, they are very good." Eve shook her head and walked back into the house. Sandeep was hoping they would offer him Eve's turn, but they didn't. Helga shrugged her shoulders and handed the bag to Norman.

Hawk was leaving in Uncle Bobby's truck to go back to Mary C.'s house. Jason was going to stay with Billy and Mary C. He needed to spend time with them. Hawk understood, in fact he was the one who suggested it. He would finish the work at the house and they would return tomorrow as a family. Miss Margaret had a request for Margie.

"Margie, take Sofia to the store and pick up Peggy." Margie wanted to add to her mother's suggestion.

"Jason, come ride with us and we'll take Billy for a ride, too." Mary C. joined in the plan.

"You girls are the sweetest things. I'll help Miss Margaret with dinner and y'all take a ride." Jason had no choice at all. It was clear the women were in charge.

Sandeep knocked on their locked bedroom door. In a few seconds Eve opened the door and stepped back as he walked in to the room. She was still upset.

"You're letting those freaks of the world make a fool of you. They like people to look as foolish as they do."

"I think you're wrong about them. They are full of life and I think they mean no harm to anyone. I like them all. They have been mistreated throughout their lives, but they have chosen not to mistreat others. I think the Giant one has created this way of being."

"Is he a another gift from God?" Sandeep did not respond to her sarcasm. "I don't care if you talk to me or not. I want to be with you now. If I don't release the boiling in me, I will surely burst into flames." Eve took her shirt off exposing her colorful and tattooed bare upper body. Then she took off her pants exposing the rest of her womanly features. Eve lay down on the bed and used her body movements to beckon the soldier-saint. She was right about Sandeep, he could not resist her when she desired sexual contact with him. He was naked in a few seconds and next to her. Their physical ritual began as each tattoo was in its proper place. There would be no spectator during this afternoon delight. Their two bodies would run together and fuse as one mass of swirling colors and creatures. For Sandeep it was a duty he craved. For Eve it was a cleansing of her need to inflict pain on others. She was the aggressor and they both enjoyed the pain.

For some reason, Mr. King, Big Bob, Norman and Tom Thumb found themselves together in Mr. King's living room. The ladies had gone to their rooms to rest or get ready in case Jason did come with the others and the Twins were still upstairs in their room. After meeting Mary C, Big Bob had a few questions for Mr. King.

"John, tell me about Mary C. and Jason. When I met her I didn't see the ruthless woman she is suppose to be. Can you tell us about them?" Mr. King knew the full story would be too long, but he could give them a condensed version.

"I'll try to tell you without taking hours. Maybe the high points."

"Yes, that's good. We are all so very interested. We would like to know." Mr. King decided he would start at the beginning.

"Mary C. has always been rough as a woman goes. They say she was free and wild as a young woman and the encounters with men have hardened her in many ways. She was married to Jason's father at a young age. He was killed in a hunting accident that Jason witnessed as a five year old. Jason was lost in the woods alone for days. When his grandfather found him he was alive, but different. His grandfather, Daddy Bob, was killed when Jason was seven. He saw the killing but has never talked about it. Some say the man Jason cut up with a Bowie knife when he was sixteen was the man he saw kill his grandfather. The man, called Charlie Klim, was attacking Mary C. and Jason protected her by using the big knife." The three guests were completely enthralled with Mr. King's story about their friend.

"Charlie Klim was a mean man and he survived the attack from Jason. He was not the same after that. He was even meaner than he was before. Then Jason played in a game they used to play here called Duckin'. It was full of superstition and stupidity. There's strange superstitions about this big oak tree here in Mayport. It makes for fun conversation and sure helps the ghost business, but I don't know if it's true or not. It is exciting when you think about it.

This tree is suppose to have powers and when you get hooked on believing it pretty well takes you over. It's suppose to give you an oak baby if you keep the secret that you did the breeding under the tree. Jason and Jessie are suppose to have done the breeding and Billy is the result: a special child with powers given by the tree. There's five dead people who thought that was true. Jason played in this Duckin' game and it became extremely violent because the devil came to play in the form of a boy." Bob looked at the others when Mr. King made that statement.

"Folks say one of the young boys had to prove his bravery to his father and he allowed the devil to direct his actions. It was a bloody day in Mayport. Some say as many as eight boys died. Some say five. Either number, it was too many. Here's the clincher. Jason was the only one left standing and alive at the tree. That marked him as one protected by the tree. During the year following the blood slaughter at the tree, Jason went into a darkness in his mind and did not speak to anyone for over a year. No one knows what ended his silence, but when he did talk he never talked about that day of the game. He was the only one who knew what happened but it was lost inside him.

Then four or five years later it looked as if Jason was going to be fine and have a normal life, compared to what he had been through. He went to work on the jetty rocks, was highly thought of as a worker, saved a man's life who had been hurt and fell into the water, and was well liked by all who knew him. Then something happened to Mary C. She became a suspect in the murder of a sailor she had been with. Folks said she was raped and beaten and she got her revenge. Then all hell broke loose in Mayport. People started dyin' and gettin' killed on a daily basis. The man Jason had cut up five years earlier returned to Mayport for his revenge on Jason and Mary C. Now, you talk about crazy, he was the craziest of them all. This Charlie Klim killed Jason's uncle, Mary C.'s brother and Jason's best friend. Everyone loved Bobby Merritt. His killin' was a crushing blow to the whole town. It was from pure meanness and nothin' else. Charlie Klim had warned Mary C. he was going to do something to make her pay for what the boy had done to him. He killed Bobby as their punishment. He also killed an innocent girl because she was with Bobby. She was in the wrong place at the wrong time.

Jason knew Charlie would kill Mary C. next so he went after him, before Charlie could get to Mary C. They fought near the rocks on the beach and once again folks were amazed when Jason defeated the much stronger and insane man. Jason was hurt but alive. Folks said he could have never defeated a man like Charlie alone. The tree protected him again. The only problem was that Jason was physically injured and he was mentally injured and lost in the darkness of his mind again. He was placed in the Chattahoochee Mental Hospital.

A few weeks later the bones of a man named James Thorn were found in the woods. He had been tied to a tree and the animals ate him alive. Or that's what they say." Mr. King's audience was completely spellbound by what they were hearing. He went on because he knew they had nothing to say.

"Mary C.'s name came up during the investigation of the man tied to the tree. Later they found out that a friend of Mary C.'s had done that awful deed. He did it because he thought that James Thorn had been the one who hurt Mary C. The Sheriff was killed during that time while investigating the crime against the sailor. The man who left James Thorn in the woods died of natural causes in his home. Three black men were killed in the woods by a boy named

Luther. The boy shot them all with his huntin' bow and then went home and stuck an arrow in his daddy. We actually lost count of how many died during that five years around here. Folks say how strange it is that Mary C. and Jason always face these life or death situations and they seem to be the last ones standing." Norman was the first one to break the silence of the audience.

"Could the tree be real?" Mr. King smiled.

"You know how I feel about such things. I don't doubt anything, anymore. It's all possible if you ask me." Big Bob was completely exhausted from Mr. King's condensed version of Jason's and Mary C.'s tales of woe. Mr. King could not resist telling his captive audience about the skull on his mantle over the fireplace.

"I would like to share a secret with you three if you don't mind." Big Bob spoke for the three of them.

"Of course John, please." Mr. King looked at the skull. The other three noticed the direction of his eye contact and they looked where he looked. They all saw the skull. Mr. King didn't say anything as they stared at his prize possession. Big Bob wasn't sure what to think.

"What is it, John. Tell us. Your secret is safe with us." Mr. King looked back at the skull.

"Gentleman, may I introduce you to Mr. James Thorn." The three men looked at the skull then at Mr. King. Tom had the first verbal outburst.

"Are you crazy? This is the head of the man who was killed in the woods last year? How in the hell did you get his head?" Tom was a three question pigmy. Norman was quiet and shocked by what he realized was true. Big Bob shook his head and knew Mr. King took his role as the master of a haunted house to the most serious limits.

"John, is it legal to have such a thing? Shouldn't it be buried with the rest of the man?" Mr. King loved the questions and controversy ignited by James Thorn's skull. He tried to answer the questions in the order they were asked.

"Yes, I'm sure I'm crazy. Yes, that's his head. I can't tell you how I got it. It's probably not legal, but I don't think anyone will bother me with that problem. Maybe morally it should be with the rest of the man in the grave, who knows?" Ana Kara walked into the room and she could see the seriousness of the conversation.

"You fellas look like you've seen a ghost. Did I miss something? I hope I'm not interrupting some men talk. I hate when that happens, don't you? Now, was it a ghost or were y'all talking nasty?" The men didn't know what to say to any of her questions. She didn't wait for an answer. And she surprised them all with her next question.

"Did John introduce y'all to his friend James Thorn? Ain't that a hoot?" The three men looked directly at John King, as if to say, "Big secret, huh?" John smiled because he knew what they were thinking. He was the first to burst into laughter, followed by the others. All four men were roaring with laughter. When they would calm down, one of the others would start laughing again causing a chain reaction. It was loud enough to keep the regular ghosts away. It was the ultimate belly laugh. Ana got caught up in the contagious laughter, but had no idea what was so funny.

Eve and Sandeep had finished their ritual of animalistic and sometimes sadomasochistic sex. The love of giving and receiving pain. The liquid type movement of the tattoos had ended and each one was in their original position. The laughter downstairs had erupted at the same time Eve had screamed during her climax. Only the Twins, Beulla and Helga heard the noises. Helga recognized the noises of pain and pleasure and she had been aroused. She knew it was Sandeep and Eve. She fantasized about the warrior-priest. Helga knew she would be a good match for the sexual abilities of the Squirrel Nut eating, Fire Ball sucking, Mr. Sandeep. It reminded her of a song she liked. Helga sang a few bars of the song as she looked in the mirror at her muscular female body. She changed one of the lyrics of the song from "Mr. Sandman" to "Mr. Sandeep" but the tune and the other lyrics remained the same. She sang her newly created version as she moved her body in front of the mirror. Little Tom was in for the night of his life if she could fantasize that he was Sandeep Singh. The ghosts were in for another real treat if they came calling that night.

· Margie drove the family wagon up to the front of the store. Sofia was holding Billy in her lap in the back seat. Jason was sitting in the front seat with Margie. Margie blew the car horn to let Peggy know they were there. Sofia handed Billy to Jason and got out of the back-seat. Peggy was at the screen door.

"Well, look here. Everybody came to pick me up." Sofia stopped at the door.

"Jason, I'll see you and Billy later. Maybe I'll go over to Mr. King's when I get off if y'all are still there. Thanks for letting me hold Billy. He's so beautiful." Jason smiled. He did love the way Sofia talked. He always had.

"You're welcome and I'm sure we'll see ya later." Margie rolled her jealous eyes as Sofia went into the store, but no one noticed. Peggy jumped into the back seat of the wagon.

"Get me home. I want a hot shower and I'm hungry. It was boring today in there. Well, except when those three circus ladies came in. They were funny and crazy acting. I wish they would have stayed longer. I wouldn't have been so bored. They spent about twenty dollars on candy and some other junk. But after they left I was bored to death. Hey Jason, hey Margie, hey Billy. Can I hold him?" Margie waited for Jason to hand Billy to Peggy. When Peggy and Billy were settled she hit the gas peddle and they were headed home. Margie had to tell Peggy the interesting possibilities for the evening.

"Peggy, we might all go over to Mr. King's house tonight and visit the circus people. Two of them came to the house and they want to see Jason and Billy later tonight. Mr. King invited us all." Peggy had her doubts about going.

"I don't know if I want to go. I'd like to see those ladies again, but night time at Mr. King's, I'm not too sure about that. I can't believe you want to go back after your last time over there. I know you haven't forgotten that night." Margie had the solution.

"Mama's going too."

Sandeep and Eve lay on their backs recovering from their physical encounter. The bed was wet from sweat, body fluids and there were a few spots of blood. With Sandeep in a position to listen, Eve's black heart took hold of her thoughts.

"I want Mary C. to suffer the pain of losing someone she loves." Sandeep was calm with his reply.

"Has she not felt such pain already in her life?"

"I want to be the cause of the pain. Whatever has happened to her up to this point means nothing to me. I want to be the cause and I want her to know it. You will be the instrument of this revenge."

"I will not hurt the child. That cannot be the pain you wish."

"I want to talk to John about James Thorn and find out what the police found out about his death. Perhaps the information will direct me. You need to stay away from those freaks John has allowed to contaminate his home. They will make fools of us all and move on like gypsies to infect others."

"The hardness of your heart makes me sad. It does not fit your beauty. You are a true contradiction of human nature." Eve smiled and touched his chest.

"You are a silver tongued devil, aren't you? Was that a compliment or an insult. You did say beautiful somewhere in there, so I'm calling it a compliment. You didn't say gift from God and that hurts." Sandeep knew she was being mean and sarcastic.

"You have chosen your path of hate and destruction. It did not and does not have to be that way. You are not the gift I speak of , but you have been given gifts, you chose to use them against others instead of using them to help others."

"Please stop, you're giving me a headache and I was feeling pretty good, 'til you became my father. There is nothing you can say that will change what I am. You speak of your destiny and what you must do. Am I not allowed to have my own destiny? I know mine crosses Mary C.'s path. I've known it for many years. If there are forces gathering in this place as you say, it has nothing to do with your golden ones. It has to do with the punishment that I will inflict on that awful woman." Sandeep had to speak his thoughts.

"If you are right and she is the evil one, I do hope your evil is stronger than hers, for your sake."

Eve sat up in the bed and slapped Sandeep's face.

"You will be the strength I need. I will be the one who tells her of the deed."

The group in John King's living room had settled down from the laughter and Ana had left the room to make coffee for everyone. The four men sat together. Tom had something on his mind. "If I was to say something, would you listen and take me seriously?" The three others looked at Tom, but Big Bob responded.

"What a strange question, Tom. Of course we would. What do you wish to say?"

"I know I act foolish at times and I make everyone mad with my remarks and teasing. I've always been like that and I'm sure I will remain that way. I do want to talk to John and I hope the information I have will help in some way." Mr. King was next to respond.

"Please Tom, I promise I will listen to you and consider what you say." Tom took a deep breath and slid down off the couch so he could walk over and be in the middle of the other three men. He stood there and lowered his voice. The three others knew he was serious and perhaps even scared. Even Norman knew he would respect what Tom was to tell.

"I know this Eve woman is an old friend of your's, Mr. King and I would not say this unless it was pressing me. I am afraid she is here, with that sword toting soldier, to hurt Jason and his mother. They are enemies from years ago and now she has the means to do something to them. He is not what he appears to be. All that kindness and hand kissing means nothing. He is here to do her bidding and I really think he is a killer for hire, or better yet a killer for sex." Tom's killer for sex comment raised the eyebrows on the three listeners. Tom added more as their eyebrows went down. "I'm ashamed to tell you, but I watched them last night." Mr. King interrupted.

"What do you mean you watched them?" Tom put his head down.

"Like I said, I'm ashamed, but I did it and because of my desire to see them, I am now scared that they will kill me as well as my friends. I want to tell you what I saw, but at the same time I am afraid of what may happen if I do tell you." The three listeners were too intrigued to stop now. Tom had whet their appetite. John King knew he wanted to know everything. Big Bob made an attempt to ease Tom's fears.

"We're not going to let anyone hurt any of us or our friends. Perhaps what you know will save us all. All we can do is listen and decide what to do when we know what you know."

Tom smiled a rare smile and nodded to his friend. "This is going to sound crazy and you're gonna think I was dreamin' or drunk, or stupid, but I can't keep it inside anymore. Whatever you think will have to be." Before Tom could continue, there was movement at the entrance to the living room. They turned expecting Ana to bring the coffee. Tom's blood ran cold in his little veins when he saw Eve standing in the doorway. He felt it was too much of a coincidence that she would show up at the moment he was going to tell about her. Tom was sick to his stomach. Mr. King greeted her.

"Eve come in. We've got coffee on the way." She remained at the door.

"When you have a moment, I would like to discuss the matter we talked about earlier today. I would like the name of the person who investigated James' murder." Everyone in the room looked at the skull on the mantle except Mr. King and Eve. Mr. King knew what the other's were thinking and he made sure he did not look at the skull.

"Do you need to speak to me now?"

"No, we're going out for awhile, I'm not sure if we'll be back tonight or not. Tomorrow I would like to contact the investigator if that's possible." Mr. King could give her the information she requested at that moment.

"His name is Butler. Mr. Butler. He's the head man at the Atlantic Beach Station when it comes to investigating the crimes committed around here. I don't think I've ever heard his first name. I just know him as Mr. Butler." Eve nodded.

"Thank you, John. I guess we don't have to talk later."

"We can always talk, Eve. Y'all be careful." Eve gave an interesting smile.

"You don't have to be careful if Sandeep is with you." She turned from the doorway as Sandeep joined her on the way to the front door. In a few seconds the silent group in the living room heard the Mercedes Benz's engine start and then the sound moved away. They all looked at Tom in anticipation that he would continue his revelation. There was another interruption when Ana walked in with a tray filled with coffee cups.

"I'll bet you guys thought I had forgotten 'bout y'all. Sorry it took so long. I just couldn't get my act together for some reason. If I was a believer, I'd say a few of John's deceased guests played with me in the kitchen. I couldn't do anything right. One time something just seemed to jump off the shelf and hit the floor. I don't think I dropped it, but maybe I did." Mr. King smiled.

"It was them. Or I should say it was the Lady in White if you were in the kitchen. She does most of her haunting in there. She was killed on her wedding night when their car ran off the road at the little jetties and flipped over. She settled here. It was the closest place for haunting and she loved the big kitchen. Her dream was to be a great housewife and cook for the man she loved. She became rather territorial when she got here. She's one of the most active we have. Many people have seen her, including me. She wears the wedding gown she died in and she is usually sighted at the kitchen sink or at the table. The two nights I saw her she had this sad and pitiful look on her lifeless face. It was like she wanted to say something, but couldn't. I felt sorry for her." Big Bob had to comment.

"John, I don't know what to think of you or this house, but these are wonderful stories and true or not, real or unreal, I for one, like being here and hearing them." Mr. King smiled and turned to Tom.

"Are you alright to talk to us now?" Tom looked at Ana Kara.

"Oh, I am sorry. Did I come in on something private. I won't stay." Tom surprised her.

"No, Ana you should know this. It's too important to not share it with everyone. I was really scared when she was standing over there. I'm glad I hadn't started talking yet. She could have heard me and then I would have been worried." Big Bob wanted to reassure his little friend one more time.

"Tom, we're not going to let anyone hurt any of us. You need to tell us what you have seen and heard." Tom looked at each face in the room and then began.

"I don't believe much in magic, or at least I didn't until last night. I actually thought they were two of John's ghosts at first. I'd rather think the ghosts were real than it being magic. I was coming back from the bathroom and I heard those noises. You know what kind I mean. Man and woman noises." They all knew what Tom was referring to and he could tell in their faces they understood. "Well, like I said, I ain't too proud of it but I looked through the key hole. Not a difficult chore for me." Norman smiled at Tom's new found honesty.

"There they were, you know, naked, but not naked." They were all giving their undivided attention as Tom told his interesting tale.

The white Mercedes Benz rolled up near the steps at Bill's Hideaway. Sandeep got out of the car and opened the door for Eve. "Oh, Sandeep! I forgot my gift for my friend back at the house. You must go back and get it or I will be so embarrassed. I'll go on up and surprise him. You go get my gift. It is on the bed. I can't believe I left it." Eve turned away from Sandeep and walked up the outside steps to the honky tonk.

At Mr. King's, Tom was telling what he had seen. "Both their bodies are completely covered with tattoos, even hers. At first, when they were next to each other it looked like they were one big mound of tattoos. Then it began to happen and I was scared." Tom looked around the room at his captivated audience. Big Bob was, as usual, the one to encourage.

"What scared ya, Tom? It's fine, tell us." Everyone was all ears.

"When they really got to goin', it looked like the tattoos came alive and moved all over. The eyes on the animals opened and flashed like they were real. Blood dripped from Eve's shoulders where the big cat on her back had its claws stuck in her. I know this sounds crazy or that it was a dream, but I really don't think it was. Either it's magic or of the devil." Mr. King had to respond.

"I have found that anything is possible. And I must say Eve and her friend are as strange as I have seen. If such a thing was true I would think they could do it, especially if evil was involved." Tom liked the fact Mr. King did not scoff at his story. The little pigmy wanted them to know his other thoughts.

"I'm also afraid they will hurt Jason and his mother. I heard them talking about an evil deed she wants him to do and that scared me, too." Mr. King knew in his heart that part of the little man's story was true. He added to the thought.

"I think you're right, even though I don't want to think that's true. I do think you're right." Big Bob was concerned.

"If this is true and we know our friends are in danger, we have no choice but to keep this evil deed from happening." Tom remembered more of what he heard.

"Now that I think about it, she said she wanted Jason's mother to suffer from losing a loved one. She wanted her to know who caused her the pain and misery. I thought she might be talkin''bout killin' Jason. We can't let that happen. She has some kind of hold on Sandeep. He owes her big time for something. I think it has something to do with the tattoos, but maybe not. I just know what I saw and heard and they're here to hurt somebody." Ana had to speak her mind.

"Do we call the police and tell them what we think? At least get the thought in their heads until we find out more." Big Bob wasn't sure.

"What do we tell them? We can't tell them Tom's full story, that's for sure. They really haven't done anything. I'm not sure what to tell them. I do know one thing. If this Punjab warrior, priest or not, wants somebody dead it will take a miracle to keep them alive." All eyes in the room opened wide at Big Bob's statement. Mr. King responded.

"I feel like we need to warn Mary C. and Jason about what we think, but after what she just went through I hate to add to the situation. Maybe we can take care of it ourselves. Get them out of town and away from here. Ana's idea about the police might be the answer. One of the policemen is a young man who knows everybody around here. He might just help. He's sweet on one of Miss Margaret's girls and he knows Jason and Mary C. He might be the answer." Mr. King had another thought.

"I'm worried about Mary C. comin' over here and Eve comin' back. That would be a bad situation for us all to face." There was a knock at the front door that ended their conversation for the moment. Beulla heard the knock as she was walking down the stairs.

"I'll get it y'all." She moved her six hundred pound body to the door and opened it. She let out a holy southern holler. "Oh my dear sweet Jesus! You are the best lookin' thing I know. Hurry everybody, Jason and Billy are here!" It didn't take but a second for the living room to empty and the front door way to fill up. Jason had not even stepped into the house yet. Beulla changed that.

"Don't just stand out there handsome, get in here where I can give you the hug we both deserve to enjoy." Jason stepped into the front of the house as the family crowded around, smiling, touching him and looking at the baby. Jason hugged the two ladies and after shaking the men's hands; he hugged them, too. Mr. King stood off to the side.

"Jason, you come alone, son?" Jason looked up from the others.

"Hey, Mr. King. Yes sir. We just walked up here. I wanted to see everybody. I couldn't wait. Mama's helpin' Miss Margaret cook dinner. Miss Margaret sent Margie and Susan off somewhere and Peggy's sleepin'. Me and Billy hightailed it out of there." The group moved Jason toward the living room. Beulla started crying when Jason handed Billy to her.

"Oh my goodness. You trust me to be the first one to hold him. I do love you for that, but I'm too nervous and my hands are too fat. I don't trust myself. Here." She handed Billy to Ana Kara. Ana held the child and made sure Beulla walked with them into the living room. Ana sat down and made sure Beulla sat with her so she could be close to Billy. Beulla cried every time she looked at the baby. Jason sat down on the other couch facing Beulla and Ana. Tom Thumb climbed up on the couch next to Jason and stood up next to him. As Mr. King and Big Bob sat in the other chairs, Helga walked into the room. Beulla saw her first.

"Helga, look who's here. He let me hold the baby first." Helga smiled at Beulla's proud moment and stepped to Jason.

"Give me a hug Jason. I know Beulla's already squeezed you

first." Jason stood up and hugged the Amazon Warrior. "Look at Billy. He's a wonderful combination of you and his mother. We have missed you." Jason sat down after the hug and Helga sat down next to Tom.

It was easy for Mr. King to see how excited everyone was and how much they loved Jason and he loved them. Jason knew there were family members missing.

"How is Beth and the Twins?" Big Bob was the spokesman.

"Ming and Ling are upstairs resting. And as for Beth, we don't know where she is. We were hoping she was with you." Jason looked puzzled, but so did Mr. King. He couldn't wait to hear who Beth was. Jason had to ask the only question he could ask.

"Why would she be with me?" Big Bob hesitated and Tom took over.

"That same clock of hers is still runnin' and she lookin' for you to be the stop watch." Norman smiled, but didn't laugh. Big Bob ignored Tom's attempt at a humorous remark. Mr. King was even more curious now. Jason was concerned.

"I hope she's alright. I don't think she's here. Are you sure she would come all this way?"

"You know Beth, pretty head strong and she thinks it will preserve her kind." Mr. King was beside himself with interest. He wanted to ask who Beth was, but he waited. Big Bob added to Mr. King's interest.

"She made sure to respect Jessie's relationship with you and she was going to ask Jessie's permission. She was rather confident Jessie was going to give her blessing and then ask you to help her. It all fell apart when Jessie died and then you left. She still thinks you are the answer to the survival of her species." The survival of her species statement was too much for Mr. King.

"I'm sorry to jump in here, but please tell me who this Beth is and what does she want with Jason?" Tom was ready for such a question.

"Beth is the Werewolf Girl. This is the real thing. Hair, pointed ears, fang dog teeth, flat nose and she howls every now and then. I think it has something to do with the moon." Big Bob stopped Tom.

"That's enough Tom, I'm sure John has got the picture." Mr. King may have had some of the picture, but not all of it.

"What does she want Jason to do?" The family looked at one another. Big Bob looked at Tom.

"I know you can't wait to say it, but you don't have to be too graphic if you don't mind."

Tom couldn't believe Big Bob had given him the go ahead. He was lost for a few seconds and realized he was on the spot to speak properly. He would not be a fool this time.

"Beth feels she is the last of her kind; the last Werewolf Girl. Beth has a sixth sense about things and when she heard about Jason's tie with this tree here in Mayport, she knew Jason was special. The way Jason treated her also made her feel comfortable with asking him and Jessie for permission to breed with her hoping she would conceive a son to continue the species. Pretty wild stuff, huh?" Mr. King was dumbfounded and had nothing to say. The others were even more dumbfounded at the way Tom presented the information. The little sarcastic and usually rude pigmy was full of surprises that night. His fear of Sandeep and Eve had made him dependent on the group and he did not want to distract from their desire to stand with him.

Ana had been quiet, but joined in after the others finished. "I hope we do find Beth. We've gotten away from thinking about her with all the other things going on. I hope she's alright and not somewhere hurt or scared." Big Bob added his feelings.

"We all want her to be alright, but until she shows up we'll have to wait and pray for the best." Helga looked toward the entrance to the room.

"Come in Mr. Sandeep, join us." Every head in the room turned quickly to the entrance. Sandeep was standing in the opening. Helga did not know about the earlier conversation about Eve and Sandeep and the possible evil deed they were planning against Jason and his mother.

"Come sit down with us and meet our good friend, Jason and his son Billy." The group was quiet as Sandeep stood at the door. He surprised everyone when he responded to Helga's invitation.

"I only returned to get something Eve left in the room. She is visiting a friend and she had left her gift. I came back to get it. I would like to sit with you, but I must return with the gift. You must be Jason. I am Sandeep Singh. I have heard a great deal about you and your son. I told Sofia the child is golden, you should be proud. I wish I could stay and spend time with you and the child, I would be a better man if I did so. Perhaps another time." Sandeep looked directly at Helga.

"Miss Helga, if you have time tomorrow, I would like you to show me where I can get more of the Squirrel Nuts. I have been wanting another one since the first one." Norman reached in his pocket and pulled out one of the chewy little rectangles and tossed it to Sandeep. Sandeep plucked it out of the air like he was catching a speedy fly.

"Thank you, Norman. I will supply them tomorrow. I'm sorry I interrupted your conversation. Good night." Sandeep turned and went up the stairs to his room. There was a strange feeling from the group in the living room. Jason noticed how quiet they were after Sandeep left.

"I saw that man when he first came here. I thought I saw evil in his eyes, but he's very nice and I'm sorry I judged him." Tom was quick to break the family silence.

"Don't be too sorry too quick. I think he's evil, too. That smooth talkin', turban headed, Kirpan totin', so called priest has something up his sleeve." Helga still didn't understand the thoughts against Sandeep.

"Let's not talk about all that stuff. Let's enjoy being with Jason and Billy."

Eve sat at a corner table in Bill's Hideaway, with her old friend Bill, the owner of the honky tonk on pylon stilts. Sandeep had not returned from Mr. King's house with the gift she had intended to give to her dear friend. She had forgotten the gift on purpose and it was her plan to talk to Bill alone. She was looking for information and she knew he would be able to supply what she wanted.

"Eve, Eve, Eve, where the hell you been all my life, you beautiful woman? I didn't think I would ever set these poor eyes on that face again and here you are sitting with me. Where the hell you been?"

"Bill, look at you. Your still good lookin', you're successful, and your restaurant's famous, ya know? You've done pretty good without me, don't ya think?"

"Yeah, I guess so. Damn, it's really good to see ya. Are ya here to stay? Say you're home for good."

"Bill, I'm sorry, but I can't say that. I'm just a visitor. I have to take care of some important business and then I'm off again. Actually, I hope to be finished early tomorrow and be gone before dark."

"Where ya been all this time?"

"Bill, I've been all over the world. It would take a full year to tell you about my travels, but thank you for asking about me. I know you care about me and I do you too." She reached across the table and touched his hand.

"Bill, I need to ask you a few questions if you don't mind." Bill held her hand.

"Not at all, Eve. You know you can ask me anything. We never had no secrets." Eve smiled and kept contact with her hand.

"Tell me what you know about the awful way James Thorn died in those woods. I know there had to be talk about it. Please tell me what you know or what you heard." Eve could tell Bill was surprised with the nature of her question. She gave him time to prepare his answer.

"I was a good friend of his mother, Mildred, and I used to take care of him when he was a baby. How could such a thing happen?" Bill was ready to answer the question for his old flame.

"First, you need to know James had gone pretty bad. He was mean and a thief. He was alone after Mildred died and he got pure mean. They even found evidence, after his death, that he killed the local sheriff. They found all kinds of stolen goods at his place."

"Tell me about his death. What was said about it?"

"Everyone admitted it was a horrible way for anyone to die. It took a while but they finally found out a man named Skinny Shimp did that awful thing. I knew about the man called Skinny, but never did see him. He was suppose to be an old friend of Mary C.'s, maybe a lover, and he killed James for something James had done to her."

Eve's heart raced in her chest as her friend, Bill continued. "Some folks say James raped and beat Mary C. and that's why he killed him. They even said he stuffed a pair of Mary C.'s panties in James' mouth before he left him to the critters." Eve was sick to her stomach. She looked past Bill to see Sandeep enter the main door of the restaurant carrying Bill's gift of a beautiful pearl handle Afghanistan hunting knife. Eve's conversation about James Thorn was over, she had heard enough.

CHAPTER ELEVEN

OFFICER JIMMY JOHNSTON HAD RETURNED TO THE ATLANTIC BEACH POLICE Station after he left Mayport. He stopped by the coroner's lab. All five of Mary C.'s victims were stretched out on separate tables completely naked. He remembered last year when another group of Calypsos were laid out on those tables and he also remembered the lone Calypso laid along side of Little Zeke Shackleford. He stepped to the first table where the only female victim, and voodoo queen, Voo Swar, lay on her back. The coroner walked out of a small closet type room.

"Hey Jimmy, you need me?"

"I don't know, Doc. I'm tired and I should have gone on home. Butler told me to go on home, but I headed here instead and here I am. Don't ask why. I got no idea." They both looked down at Voo Swar's naked body. The coroner had a few observations to share with anyone who came into the lab. He always had plenty of information.

"This 'ol girl was put together pretty good for her age. I'll bet she was sought after in her younger days. She's still built up pretty good, don't ya think? I mean, she must be seventy or more." Officer Johnston was always amazed at the insensitive attitude of the coroner, but he attributed it the difficult job he had to do. He thought perhaps you become calloused and unfeeling after dealing with the dead for a long length of time. Maybe you have to laugh or make remarks to keep from crying. He stepped closer to Voo Swar's table and continued. "This is the strangest one we've had in here in quite awhile. That thing she wore on her head was to cover the roots and plants that had started to actually penetrate her skull. They had rooted in her skin. They were there for a good long time, to take root like they did. They had become part of her head. Of course, the shotgun pellets tore some of them out, but some were still attached. I'm sure it was some kind of voodoo ritual of passage. They tell me she was the local voodoo queen. Did you know that?" Jimmy nodded and stepped to the next table where he recognized the Calypso lying there.

"This is the one we found by the bedroom window. He wasn't shot. He was gutted by something with a big and sharp blade. The doctor had another observation.

"That cut's interesting, too. It looks like the blade was stuck deep into his chest, then the long cut was made when somebody pulled down on the handle when they were pulling the blade out of his body. It just laid him open." Jimmy looked at the huge wide cut on the corpse, that went from his chest right below his neck, all the way down to his navel. The doctor had even more information. "And I found the strangest thing on this one." He indicated the one with the huge cut. "It's right over here." Jimmy followed the doctor to a long counter and pointed to the top of the counter. "Look at that." At first Jimmy couldn't focus in on what he was suppose to see.

"I guess I'm not lookin' in the right place." The doctor pointed again and moved his finger in a straight line. "Right there." Jimmy moved his face closer to the counter top. Then he saw it.

"It's a hair ain't it?"

"It ain't just a hair, my boy. It's an eight feet long hair. It was on that one right there. I picked it off him to check it out. I knew it wasn't from any of the dead folks. I thought it was from the shooter, Mary C. When I picked it up, it just kept on comin' and comin' and comin'. When I realized it was that long and it was real, I knew it could have some strong bearin' on the case. I ain't never seen the likes of it. It really is almost eight feet long and it's real. It is a human hair. Whoever lost this hair is the one who pulled that razor blade out of that one."

"Does Mr. Butler know about this?"

"Not yet. I only found it an hour ago. He'll be back in the mornin' I'll show him then."

The bell on the door of Miss Margaret's store sounded and Sofia turned to greet her next customer. Her beautiful blue eyes lit up and her heart jumped when she saw Jason walking into the store.

"What are you doing here?" Jason moved toward Sofia.

"Now, that's not Miss Margaret's greeting I used to hear. Has it changed since I've been gone?" Sofia smiled and bowed her head.

"No, silly. You surprised me, I didn't expect you to come here tonight. I must tell you it is a very nice surprise. Now, let me correct my mistake. Good evening, may I help you with something?" They both smiled as Sofia moved to Jason and hugged him for a few seconds and then kissed him with one of the Sofia specials he had felt before. As before, their lips melted together as if her face went through his. There had never been a kiss between them that wasn't a wonderful experience for them both. They were soul mates and nothing would ever change that. The kiss ended and Sofia still wanted the answer to her first question.

"Well, what are you doing here? You should be with your friends. They came so far to see you. I just think they are so much fun. I'm a little scared of that little man. He gives me the creeps when he looks at me. He looks nasty, you know?" Jason smiled and nodded his head.

"Tom's strange, but he has some good points. They're just hard to find." Sofia nodded too, but didn't really think the little pigmy had any good points. Jason answered her question.

"I was over at Mr. King's with my friends. I knew you were still working and I wanted to see you without all the others around. I asked them to take care of Billy for awhile and here I am. I needed to see you." Sofia was thrilled with his words and the conversation, but that changed quickly when Jason had a question she didn't want to hear.

"Do you like the carousel?" A different chill ran through Sofia's beautiful body. Jason sensed her uncomfortable reaction.

"What is it? Something wrong?" Sofia put hear head down again.

"I used it. I turned it on. You trusted me to protect it and I used it." Jason smiled.

"That's O.K. You can't help but want to turn it on. That's what it's for."

"It made me dream." He smiled again.

"I know. That's what it does. That's the magic." Sofia looked at Jason.

"The dreams were wonderful at first and I wanted more. Then, when Margie turned it on." Sofia stopped talking when she realized she had said too much. Jason knew it.

"Margie used it, too?" Sofia's head went down again. Jason smiled, but she didn't see him.

"It's fine. Tell me what happened." She didn't lift her head.

"I feel that I have betrayed you and let you down in the worst way. I have disappointed you and you will never trust me again." Jason kept his smile and touched under her chin with two of his fingers, lifting her head so he could see her beautiful ice blue eyes.

"You will never let me down, disappoint me, or betray me. I will always trust you. Now, tell me what happened." She looked into Jason's eyes.

"Jason, you are so good to me. Why do so many things keep us apart? Why can't we be together? We both have known we belong together since that first day we had coffee right here in the store. Why are we still so far apart?"

"We're together right now and all the past things are just that, in the past. Whatever has gone before is now gone. Tell me what happened." A thought flashed in Sofia's head.

"Is Billy O.K. at Mr. King's house?" Jason knew Sofia was nervous about her dreams and was looking for the way she would share the personal fantasies.

"Billy's fine. They love him as much as I do. He's safe with them and you should have seen them when I asked them to keep him.

They were all so happy. Now, they might be fighting over who gets to hold him, but he's very safe." Sofia smiled. Jason knew it was a nervous one.

"I used it by myself one night. It was beautiful and made me feel wonderful." She hesitated and found the nerve to say what she was feeling. "It made me feel like a woman. I wanted you there to see me and be with me. I wanted you to see the woman inside me. It was wonderful. And now I think about being with you and making the dream come true. I think about it all the time." Jason knew Sofia had never talked that way before. He was honored she was sharing her intimate desires with him. He knew there was something else that troubled her.

"What else is bothering you? You need to tell me." She wanted to feel comfortable with Jason and be the woman she so wanted to be.

"Then I told Margie about the magic. I couldn't keep her away from it. We turned it on together and the dreams came. It was wonderful again, at first. It took me to the oak tree, you know?" Jason was surprised when Sofia mentioned the tree. He didn't say anything, as she continued. "I was also at the tree in the first dream. This time it was the same for me. Almost the exact same dream. I was pleased and wanted it to be the same. Then something happened and the dream became mean and painful. I was scared and I screamed. When I screamed I heard another scream that wasn't me. I looked up into the tree above me and saw Margie sitting on a big limb. She made the other scream I heard. The limb held her so she couldn't get free. The sand held me and I was sinking." The thought of an old dream from Jason's past flashed in Jason's head. He had met Jessie at the tree. Her strong naked body beckoned him to her. When they embraced the sand at their feet softened and they were sucked into the roots beneath the tree, where they heard babies crying and saw oak babies inside the big roots, in different stages of embryo development. Jason shook the old dream away from his head and returned to Sofia. She always knew when he had left her.

"What were you just thinking about? Are you alright? Are you still having those day dreams. Or should I say, evening dreams." Jason returned from his trip to the past.

"I'm sorry." Sofia wanted to tell him more.

"Margie was screaming above me on the limb. She was scared and hurt. The limb was holding her and she couldn't get free. The sand held me and I was sinking. We both screamed when we realized we were in the same dream. It was awful. Then I think the carousel stopped spinning and we woke up." She hesitated again. Jason was trying to absorb all that she had said.

Sofia had another profound thought to share.

"Jason, I think the carousel has wonderful magic, but I think the oak tree has more. The tree will not allow other magic to be here. That's what I think. I'm sorry about the carousel."

Sofia had given Jason interesting food for thought. He was sad the carousel dreams became painful and frightful for the two sisters. He wanted Sofia to know he was listening to her.

"I hadn't thought about the tree in all this. You may be right. The carousel has never been anything but beautiful and kind. You saw that the first time."

"But, I was at the tree. Like the tree wanted to see what the carousel did. I think it was the evil side of the tree that did all that stuff to us. I think Billy is of the good side, don't you?" Jason hadn't heard Sofia speak as if she believed in the tree. Margie had always been the one who was talking about the tree, never Sofia.

"You're talking like you think the tree is real and has powers. I don't think I've heard you talk like this before." Sofia's eyes lit up again.

"What about Billy and those people saying he's of the tree? And you're of the tree. Doesn't that make you feel good?" Sofia was rolling and had been wanting to say those things to Jason.

"And Sandeep said you were a golden one, but you had lost something. I don't believe that. I know you are still golden." Jason had to stop her and see if what he thought he heard was what she said.

"Sandeep is that man at Mr. King's? You talked to him?" Sofia was excited and Jason could see it in her ice blue eyes.

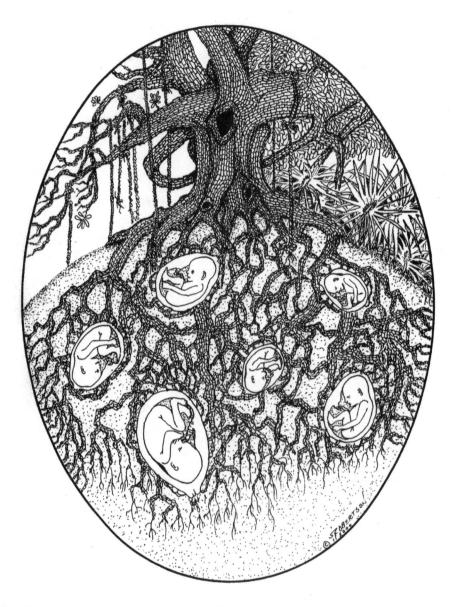

Jason's Dream

"He told me I was special and golden, also. He said he knew we had to be attracted to each other because we were the same. No one else was like us. Doesn't that sound dreamy? It's what we have known and felt all along. I just feel he's right about us, but he's wrong about you."

Jason didn't know how to respond to her surprising enthusiasm about the man with the evil in his eyes. "I'm not sure about this Sandeep. He's here with a woman named Eve and she is pure evil. Why would a good man be with her?"

"I don't know the answer to that. Maybe he's trying to help her be better. I know he feels like Billy is special like us. He went to see Billy." Jason's heart jumped in his chest.

"When did he do that!" Sofia could tell Jason was disturbed by what she said.

"I told him Mary C. wouldn't let a stranger see Billy, but he did-n't care. He said he would see the child and she would never know he was there. I don't know if he went down there or not."

Jason knew at that moment Sandeep was the person who helped Mary C. when the Calypsos came calling. He didn't mean to, but he thought out loud.

"He went down there." Sofia was too excited to notice the deep thought look on Jason's face. She was wrapped up in her own womanly thoughts and was ready to share it all with the golden one; the oak baby she had been waiting for. Her next statement would put Jason deeper in the state of shock.

"I want to make my wonderful dream come true with no carousel spinning. I don't want hands in a dream touching me and making me feel like a woman. I want your real hands to do that to me. And I want it to happen under the oak tree. I don't think we should be afraid anymore. I want to make the dream come true soon. How many people can make their dreams come true? I have an opportunity to do that and I want to do it. You have to be part of it. You are part of it. You always have been. Whatever happened to you with Jessie was part of this destiny that has been set for us. There was a reason for Billy to come to you. Maybe both of us are the ones to take care of him and make him what he is suppose to be." Jason's head was spinning like the carousel. He had never heard such talk from Sofia and never thought he ever would. He was still speechless and she wasn't.

"I think we should do it tonight. It's the perfect time. I'll get off late. If we can't meet then, we'll meet in the early morning. You'll be at the house tonight and we'll be able to get away sometime during the night. Please Jason, we have been so close before and now it is time for us to be together. I knew that after the first dream. The carousel made me know that." The bell on the door of the store ended Sofia's plan for the moment. Jason and Sofia's hearts screamed like Margie and Sofia did in the dream, when they both saw Sandeep and Eve walk into the store.

Sofia was silent at first, then she remembered her duty.

"Good evening. May I help you with something?" Eve stared at Jason as she walked past him on her way to the cold drink box. Sandeep stood at the door. Eve needed help.

"Miss Sofia, could you get me one of the red drinks? I'm so thirsty for some reason and I really don't want to put my hand in that cold water."

"Yes ma'am, of course." Sofia walked toward the ice box. Sandeep moved toward the box, also. Eve saw Sandeep.

"She can get it for me." Sofia and Sandeep reached the drink box at the same time. He put his hand on Sofia's shoulder to stop her forward motion.

"No lady has to have a wet, cold hand when Sandeep is near." Sandeep put his hand into the cold water and pulled the strawberry Nehi from the box and looked at his companion, Eve.

"This is the one you desire?" Eve's eyes had as much evil in them as eyes could hold. She turned and walked toward the door.

"I'm not thirsty anymore." The bell on the door rang as she left. Sofia looked at Sandeep.

"Thank you for doing that, but I really didn't mind getting it for her. I do it all the time. Nobody likes to reach in there, especially the ladies. But, thank you anyway. I think your friend is pretty mad at you right now. I don't think she likes me very much. Have you met my friend, Jason?" Sandeep looked at Jason.

"Yes, at Mr. King's house. Hello again, Jason."

"Good evening, Mr. Sandeep." Sofia took advantage of the opportunity to have them together.

"Sandeep, please talk to Jason and tell him he has a gift and how he should use it." The two men looked at each other again.

"Perhaps we will talk another time." Sandeep put the red drink back into the box. Jason found a strange courage.

"Thank you for helping my mother and Billy. I know you were there." Sofia's eyes lit up again. She couldn't believe what Jason had said. She looked at Sandeep for his reply. Sandeep turned from the drink box and faced Jason.

"I am a Punjab priest and soldier. I protect the weak, the helpless and the golden. There was no weakness there that night, only the golden." Sofia's mouth dropped open as Sandeep made his profound statement and walked out of the store. She looked at Jason with a million questions running through her head.

Mr. John King sat in his living room with Big Bob, Norman and Tom. Ana, Helga and Beulla had taken Billy upstairs so Ming and Ling would not have to go downstairs to see the child. Big Bob had been thinking about the things Tom had heard at the door of Eve and Sandeep's bedroom. "I will not allow anyone to hurt that boy or that child, not if I can do something about it. Tom has given us this information and I think we can do something with it. Even if it doesn't happen, we can still be cautious and prepared. If we're wrong and they go about their normal business, that's great, but if they are here to hurt that family, we need to stop it." Norman had his concerns.

"Big Bob, this Sandeep character, this priest or whatever he is; what do you know about him?" Big Bob knew a great deal.

"He is first and foremost a warrior; a true fighter, if you will. He fights for causes and the weaker individuals of the world, but he will always find a reason to fight. It is in his nature. He is a master of Gatka. It's a form of the martial arts from the regions of India using meditation and different weapons, but he mainly uses the sword." Tom knew about the sword.

"It's that thing he pulled out on me, the Kirpan. I think he was trying to scare me and he did."

Big Bob nodded.

"They always carry one of the ten weapons on them, so they are always ready to defend themselves and others. I'm sure that Kirpan is his choice of weapon. He is a Punjab and his religion is called Sikhism. He believes that protecting the weak at any personal cost makes him invincible. That's what makes them such fierce fighters. He believes dying for a noble cause is the privilege of heroes. I'm sure Sandeep is willing to give the ultimate sacrifice for what he believes or for another's safety. I'm troubled by the thought that this great defender of the weak, and man of integrity and faith, would team up with an evil force like this Eve woman. It doesn't fit the man who fights for truth." Mr. King had a thought on the matter at hand.

"Many men of Faith fall to something; anger, lust, greed, or another of the seven great sins. We see it happen all the time. Great men lose their morals and beliefs because of one of these sins." Big Bob was in agreement and he nodded again.

"That's true, but when I hear Sandeep talk it makes me sad he may have deserted his truth for a woman like Eve." Tom joined the conversation again.

"If you had seen what I saw you'd know he is truly addicted to her painted flesh. It was pure black magic I saw through that little hole. Black magic, I tell ya and he's under the spell of that tattooed body." The room was silent for a few seconds as they contemplated Tom's words. Norman was next to speak up with his idea of ending the dilemma that had them all so worried.

"Let's kill'em both while they're sleeping and say the lady in white did it because she wanted her bed back." The other three men looked at Norman. He didn't smile. Tom nodded his head.

"That's a thought." Big Bob shook his head and took over the conversation.

"I don't think talking to him would make a difference. If he is addicted to her he will do anything for her, I'm sure." Tom remembered something else.

"She said that she honored him by tattooing her entire body. He said it was the greatest tribute anyone could give another and he belonged to her until she set him free or she was dead."

Norman had another idea.

"Let's kill her when they're sleeping and wake him up to tell him he's free."

Sofia wanted to know what Jason meant when he thanked Sandeep for helping his mother. She had heard Mr. Butler talk about the possibility that someone else was at the house when the Calypsos and Voo Swar came calling. Her eyes were as wide open as Jason had ever seen. He knew she was excited and she wanted to know more.

"Why did you thank him for helping your mother?" Jason knew Sofia was serious and concerned.

"When you told me what he had said and that he was going to see Billy, I knew then he was the one who helped Mama. I don't think she knows he was there, I really don't. But, after what he said to me, I know he was the one."

"Are you going to tell the police?"

"I don't know what to do. They may do something to him, him not bein' from around here. They might blame him for the killin's. I would hate it if he got in trouble over something I told. He helped save Mama and Billy. No, I won't say anything about it. Please don't tell anyone." Sofia was looking for another chance to prove her trustworthiness and it had been dropped into her lap.

"You can trust me Jason, I won't say a word about it. I promise." The bell on the door rang and they both turned to see Susan entering the store. She had come to relieve Sofia of her duty.

"Well, hey Jason. Didn't expect to find you here. Sorry I'm on foot, Sofia, but Mama sent Margie to Winn-Dixie for a few things we need for dinner and I had to walk over. We had already been to the store once, but Mama forgot to list a few things, so Margie's on the road again. You'll have to walk home." Even though Susan was not as close to Jason as Sofia, she still remembered their intimate moment every time she saw him. She would always be willing to relive their wild sexual encounter. In her heart she knew they would one day. She was good at not showing her emotions as openly as the others, but she still wanted to be with Jason when she got the chance. She knew he had strong feelings for her younger sister, Sofia, yet she would take her turn with him if it was offered.

"Jason, I thought you probably went over to Mr. King's to see those wild friends of yours." Jason smiled. "I did go over there. Billy's there now. I need to go check on him. You're right, they're a wild group." Susan walked behind the counter.

"Go on home little sister I know you're tired of being here." Sofia moved to the door and looked back at Susan.

"Do you think Mama's going over to Mr. King's house tonight?"

"I don't know. Her and Mary C. are cooking up a storm and somebody better be there to eat all that food. Margie wants to go over there after they eat and she said when she did, she would bring me a plate. I don't care about being over there with those ghosts. There are enough strange characters around this place now. We don't have to go looking for them. They seem to find us."

"I think I'll go over there with Jason and see those circus people again." She turned to Jason. "If that's alright with you?" Susan rolled her eyes at Sofia's question?

"Of course it's alright with him. What else could he say to you after you invite yourself to go with him." Sofia didn't notice or care about her sister Susan's little reprimand. She was out of the store and walking with Jason to Mr. King's house.

As Jason and Sofia approached Mr. King's front porch the white, black tinted windows Mercedes Benz drove up to the front of the house. Sandeep got out of the car and opened the car door for Eve. She stepped out onto the ground and walked up the steps to the house. Sandeep saw Sofia and Jason as they came closer to where he was standing. Sandeep bowed to them as they passed him and followed Eve up the steps. Sofia was the first to speak.

"Hey Sandeep." He bowed again.

"Miss Sofia, we say hello again. Jason." Jason nodded but did not speak. Eve entered the house ahead of them and went directly up the stairs to her room. Jason and Sofia entered the house and walked to the living room where they found the foursome still engaged in serious conversation. No one but the foursome knew they had devised a plan if they had to defend Jason and Billy from the warlike talents of the Punjab priest. They all knew their roles if it came to a confrontational showdown and they had all vowed to keep the plan a secret. Jason and Sofia walked into the room. Mr. King greeted them.

"Jason, Sofia, come in, come in." Big Bob knew Jason would be wondering about Billy.

"Billy's upstairs with the ladies. Ming and Ling wanted to see him. Good evening, Sofia."

"Hey Big Bob, Norman, Tom, Mr. King. You gentlemen looked so engaged in conversation when we came in I'm sorry to interrupt you." She did know how to talk to folks. Jason stared at her as did the other men in the room. "I'm sure you don't need me here while you're talking men talk. I just wanted to say hey again. I really need to get on back home. Mama and Mary C. are cooking and they'll be looking for me to help I'm sure." Ana Kara stepped to the living room entrance.

"Jason, why don't you go on home with Sofia and have a nice dinner. You can leave Billy here with us. We are having so much fun with him. Go enjoy dinner and y'all come on back later. Maybe Miss Margaret and your mother will come back and visit with you." Sofia looked at Jason with please say yes, in her eyes. Jason knew what Sofia wanted him to say.

"If you're sure they don't mind having Billy longer."

"Trust me, they don't mind at all. We are all happy to spend time with him and you if you'll go eat and get on back here." Sofia took Jason's hand and they were out of the room and out of the door. Sandeep was sitting on the porch as Jason and Sofia stepped out onto the porch and down the steps. They didn't see him as he watched them leave and disappear into the dark. When he could not see them any longer, he went inside and upstairs to Eve.

Sofia was too excited to maintain herself. It was her opportunity and she would not pass it up.

"Jason, take me to the tree, please. I meant what I said about the dream. I want it to come true with you." Jason loved the way her eyes burned into him. Jessie's eyes had the same look to them. He would not pass up the opportunity they had been given, either. He took Sofia's hand and they walked in the direction of the oak tree.

Miss Margaret and Mary C. had prepared a feast. They had truly gotten carried away with the fun they were having and had cooked way too much food. When they realized what had happened they sat down on the kitchen floor together and roared with laughter at the many wonderful dishes they had prepared. The family wagon pulled up into the front yard and Margie jumped out of the car carrying a Winn-Dixie bag in her arms. When Margie entered the kitchen and the two cooks saw another bag of food to prepare, they burst into laughter again and sat back down on the floor. Every time they would look at the bag Margie was holding they would start laughing again. Margie found herself laughing at them, not with them, because they looked foolish and she had no idea what was so funny. She put the bag on the kitchen counter and started to leave the room. Miss Margaret stopped laughing long enough to talk to Margie.

"Margie, hold on a minute. I'm sorry dear, we are just being so silly. I need you to do one more errand for me, please." Margie had already left the house twice and she didn't like the thought of doing it again. Out of respect she listened to her mother.

"I need you to go over to Mr. King's and invite them all over here for dinner." She looked at Mary C. "We definitely have enough food and I'm sure they are ready to eat if they have not already done so. I would rather you invite them in person if you don't mind. And tell Jason to come on, too. We think he took Billy over there and he's visiting his friends. He and Billy went out and I'm sure that's where they are." Margie's attitude about leaving again had been adjusted and she was more than happy to go make the invitation. She was out the door and back into the family wagon.

Sofia told Jason she wished they had a blanket so they would not have to lie in the sand. Sand all over them would be hard to explain once they went home for dinner. Jason took a white sheet off Miss

Wilma Pack's clothes line as they walked through her yard. Sofia was surprised.

"What are you doing?" Jason rolled the sheet up in his arms.

"We'll bring it back." Sofia smiled and they increased the speed of their steps. She was so excited that she was going to make the carousel dream come true. It was the only thing on her mind. She had waited for Jason to return to her and it had happened. She wanted to make the dream come true and now that would happen. She wanted him to see the woman she had become, and the opportunity was now. The sand hill and the oak tree came into their vision as they moved forward.

Margie drove the family wagon up to Mr. King's front porch and stopped next to the white Mercedes Benz and behind the hearse. The porch was empty and she got out of the wagon and went to the front door. Before she could knock, the door opened and at first she saw no one in the door way. A cold chill ran through her young healthy body when she heard a mousy voice she recognized as belonging to the pigmy pervert who had stared at her at the store the night before. She looked down to see Tom Thumb lick his lips with his pointed serpentine tongue in a sexual gesture.

"Well, what are you doing here, Margie?" Margie could feel the blood run to her face and she knew he could see her reaction also. "I was hoping you would come to see me. I knew we had a brief meeting of the minds last night and I knew you would come eventually."

Margie had no idea what to say to the midget's advances. She was in a state of mild shock and was trying to find her bearings. Another voice saved her from her embarrassing moment. It was Ana Kara.

"Margie, come in. Don't stand out there, come on in. Oh, hey Tom, I didn't see ya down there. I didn't know you were lettin' her in. Sorry. Come on with me sweetie, all the girls are upstairs with Billy." Margie moved past Tom so she could get close to Ana. As she passed by him he flicked his long tongue out and licked her on the arm. Margie kept moving and didn't look back as she and Ana Kara went up the stairs. She did take the sleeve of her blouse and pull it down to wipe off her wet arm.

When Margie walked into the bedroom, Billy was lying in the middle of the bed surrounded by all the circus women. They all turned to see who was joining them. Ana Kara reminded them who she was. "You girls remember Margie from the store last night. She's Miss Margaret's oldest daughter, and the prettiest, if you ask me." Margie smiled at the compliment. Beulla added her thoughts about the four sisters.

"They're all pretty in their own way. They are so different to be sisters. You like Margie's features because she could be your sister, y'all do favor, and, yes, she is a beauty. She looks strong and the way a woman is suppose to look, just the way you do Ana. I can see why she's your favorite." Ana smiled at her huge friend.

"You are always so smart when it comes to beauty." Beulla could not have had a bigger smile.

"Ain't I, though?" Margie had been so distracted by Tom at the door and now the compliments she had forgotten why she was there. With the moment of silence she could tell them.

"Ladies, my mother would like to invite all of you and the gentlemen to dinner at our house in an hour. Come as you are and enjoy the evening. She has made enough food for an army and you must come help us eat it." The circus ladies all looked at each other. Beulla was first and actually said it for them all.

"Sounds good to me." Ana took Margie's hand.

"Let's go downstairs and tell the men folk about the dinner invitation. They're gonna be thrilled. They'll be ready to go right now. Beulla, y'all make sure Billy has a bath before his daddy comes back to get him. We'll go tell the others about dinner." Margie had a question for Ana as they left the bedroom.

"Jason's not here?" They kept moving down the stairs.

"No, he was here, but he and Sofia went to your house to eat. They were gonna come back later and get Billy, but now I guess we can just take Billy to him when we go. Margie stepped up her pace to the living room with Ana. The foursome were still intact.

"Gentlemen, Miss Margaret has sent this lovely young lady messenger to ask you something."

Ana turned to Margie. Margie did not look at Tom.

"My mother would like all of you to join us for dinner at our house within the hour. Come as you are and be comfortable. She has more food than you can imagine. Please do us the honor of coming." All four men smiled at each other and then at Margie. Big Bob knew what they were all thinking.

"What do you say, John? Dinner away from the house tonight?"

"I do believe so my good friend. We would be total fools to refuse this young lady. And I see no fools in this room. Margie, tell Miss Margaret the bus will arrive within the hour." Margie nodded.

"See you in a little while." She was out the door and into the family wagon. She knew she had not seen Jason nor Sofia at the house and she had not passed them on the road when she drove to Mr. King's.

Sofia and Jason stood next to the great oak tree. Jason had stood there many times before. Sofia had only been there in her carousel dreams. Her heart was pounding and she was as nervous as she had ever been. She was determined to prove her womanhood to Jason, once and for all. Jason wanted her to be sure and positive about her decision to be there.

"Sofia, we can go back you know? You don't have to do this."

"No, I'm just nervous that's all. It's just the way I am, you know that. I know what I want and it's time for me to grow up and have it. I have been planning and waiting for a long time. There is a reason we were pushed together tonight. I will not stop now." Jason smiled and kissed her. She returned the kiss with a typical Sofia, unbelievable kiss. The heat of their lips and their bodies were noticeable to them both. Jason was surprised when Sofia took the sheet from him and spread it on the sand next to the tree. He then got the biggest surprise so far that night when Sofia began taking her own clothes off in somewhat of a hurry.

"Please hurry a little. We can't be gone too long with all the things going on tonight. They'll be worried about us. I was completely naked in the dream and I laid right here." She pointed where she had already spread the sheet. Jason started taking his clothes off, but he never took his eyes off Sofia as she stripped.

Her body was snow white and perfect. Her skin was like smooth porcelain. Her bare legs were toned and slender; perfectly proportioned. Her butt cheeks were round and solid and as smooth as the rest of her. She had a deep crease down her back where her back muscles ran down the edge of her spine and backbone. Sofia's breasts were bigger and rounder than the year before and Jason knew he was standing in the presence of a woman of the highest physical quality. Her feet were even perfect.

Jason took his last piece of clothing off as Sofia laid herself down on the sheet. She was on her back like in the dream and she lifted one knee. Sofia was the most beautiful woman Jason had ever seen. And he had seen many beauties in the last few years. Jason moved down on the sheet with her and she wrapped her arms and legs around him to hold him as close as she could to her body. He reached down and touched Sofia between her legs. She was prepared for his touch because she knew it was part of the dream. She was glad the sheet was under her just in case the hands of the dream were real, they could not get to her. She only wanted Jason's hands touching her. At one moment she thought she was in another dream, but Jason's eyes told her it was real and she was becoming the woman she wanted to be. His eyes left hers as he moved his head to her breast. She saw the top of Jason's head and felt his mouth and tongue on her breast and wanted him to suck and kiss her breast harder. She pushed her breast toward his face to let him know she approved and wanted more. His hand touched her and she felt his probing fingers, just like the dream. Sofia closed her eyes and didn't want to look up into the tree. She was afraid Margie would be stuck to the limb above her. She felt Jason's mouth and tongue move down her stomach and she felt his tongue in her navel. He kissed her thighs one at a time. Then there was a new feeling of wet heat between her legs. It wasn't like before and had an all new sensation to it. It was Jason's mouth and tongue again. She had never felt such pleasure, not even in the dream. She opened her eyes and looked down her body to see Jason's face buried against her lower body. He pushed her legs open and the heat increased as his tongue went deeper inside her. Sofia was in absolute sexual ecstasy and she lay her head back to enjoy what was happening to her body.

Sofia felt what she thought was Jason's hot breath on her face. She smiled but did not open her eyes, waiting for another kiss. The breath was heavy on her face, but she could still feel Jason's mouth and tongue giving her pleasure elsewhere. Sofia opened her eyes to see an upside down hideous face with yellow eyes and huge long sharp teeth directly over her face. She was frozen with blood curdling fear as she looked deep into the yellow eyes above her. She even hoped it was an awful dream. To Sofia, it seemed she was looking into those eyes for a long time when it had actually been only seconds. A sharp pain went through Sofia's fragile heart when the ugly nightmare creature spoke to her.

"When he's finished with you, can I be next?" Sofia screamed and jumped up off the sheet. Jason looked up to see Sofia screaming and jumping up and down naked. He looked next to the tree and saw Beth, the Werewolf Girl, standing near Sofia. Beth held her hairy hands over her sensitive canine ears as Sofia kept screaming. Beth smiled her ugly teeth filled smile and shrugged her hairy shoulders at Jason.

"I didn't mean to scare her. I thought since you were breeding, I could join in. I should have stayed hidden, but I got a little carried away once that head of yours ended up between her legs." Sofia didn't hear anything but her own screaming. Jason picked up the sheet and covered Sofia's naked and now trembling body. Jason looked at Beth.

"What are you doing here? The family's worried about you. They're all here at Mr. King's house. This is crazy." Beth held her head down in shame. Sofia was still hysterical and could not control herself. Jason didn't expect it, when Sofia pulled away from him and began running, crying and screaming down the sand hill, with Miss Wilma Pack's white sheet wrapped around her naked body. Jason knew he had to go after Sofia. He put on his pants as he talked to Beth.

"Beth, come with me. I've got to catch her. She can't take this.

She's too weak to handle it alone. Come with me." Beth added to Jason's plight when she took off running down the sand hill too, following Sofia. She was ashamed and embarrassed. Jason grabbed up Sofia's clothes and the rest of his and started after the two fleeing women.

There were car lights at the bottom of the hill as Margie drove up in the family wagon. Margie looked up the hill to see a white sheet headed in her direction. A second look made her see it was her little sister, Sofia running toward her. Margie jumped out of the car and met Sofia at the bottom of the hill. Jason could see Beth in front of him running toward Margie and Sofia. Sofia ran into her older sister's arms and hugged her. Jason could hear Sofia crying and screaming. Margie looked up to see Beth running down the hill in their direction. Sofia jumped into the wagon on the front passenger seat as Beth ran by the wagon.

Margie focused her eyes on the yellow eyed creature and watched in disbelief as Beth ran back into the woods. Margie looked at Sofia through the wagon window.

"What the hell was that?" Sofia had no words for her sister. Margie heard a noise coming out of the woods as a truck went speeding onto the road and was moving away. Margie looked at Sofia again.

"Oh my God, it drives a truck." Jason's voice scared Margie when he came up behind her.

"Sofia you alright?" Margie turned quickly to the voice.

"Damn, Jason, you scared me, too. No, she's not alright. Look at her. What the hell's going on here? What was that thing?" Jason handed Sofia her clothes through the wagon window. Sofia didn't look at him.

"I'm so sorry." He turned to Margie. "Can we get Sofia out of here and I'll explain it all when we make sure she's alright." Margie got into the driver's seat as Jason climbed into the back seat. The family wagon was on the move again.

CHAPTER TWELVE

The circus bus pulled up to the front of Miss Margaret's house. The dinner feast, fit for a king and an army, was going to be tested by Beulla and the rest of the group. Peggy had gotten up from her nap and saw the bus from her bedroom window.

"They're here Mama." Miss Margaret was at her huge dining room table, setting out the plates.

"You don't have to holler, Peggy. Go open the door and greet our guests." Peggy wasn't too keen on doing what her mother said, but she knew it was not a suggestion, it was a command. Peggy headed to the front door. Mary C. was in the kitchen cleaning up some of the mess from all the cooking so there wouldn't be so much to clean up later. She had not seen the entire circus family yet, only Big Bob and Norman.

Margie stopped the family wagon in front of the store. She knew Susan was working and they could calm Sofia down and get her dressed if they could isolate her in the back room of the store. The back of the store was the prefect place for them to go. Susan's eyes opened wide when the bell on the door sounded and she saw Margie walk into the store, followed by Sofia, wrapped in a sheet and Jason following them with, what looked to be, Sofia's clothes. Margie was the first to speak to Susan.

"We need to use the back room. Sofia's not hurt, she's just scared.

I'll tell you about it when she gets dressed." Susan knew her older sister was serious and she did not question her at all. Margie escorted Sofia to the small back room. When the two of them got to the door, Margie turned and took Sofia's clothes from Jason and closed the door behind them.

"Get that thing off and put your clothes on, and hurry. Margie pulled the sheet off Sofia and her little sister stood there completely naked and still shivering.

"I don't think you're hurt, but I know you got real scared up there. I was scared, too. Help me with these things so we can get you home. It will be much easier if you help me. I can't dress you like a child." Sofia began dressing herself while Margie assisted her and kept talking.

"Sofia, you of all people don't need to be an oak baby mama. You are not cut out for all this foolishness. Men are going to be madly in love with you all your life. I know how you feel about Jason, but this whole thing is not right for you. You must be able to see that." Margie began fastening the buttons on Sofia's blouse. "And as for tonight, you have got to snap out of it right now and get back to normal. We have to go home and have dinner like nothing has happened. We'll tell Mama I picked you up and we helped Susan with some stock before we left her. And stop crying. You want to be a woman so badly, then be one right now and snap out of this." Sofia was dressed and she stopped crying. Margie had more directions for her little sister.

"Now, we're going out front and talk to Jason. I'm sure I know what was suppose to happen, but I'm more interested in what did happen. And what or who was that thing we saw?" A chill ran through Sofia's body again when she visualized the yellow eyed creature that stood over her at the tree. Margie opened the door of the little room and she and Sofia joined Jason and Susan at the front of the store.

Mary C. watched the circus family find seats at Miss Margaret's dining room table. Miss Margaret could see that Mary C. was captivated by the array of unusual characters who were filling the room. There was a buzz of conversations, but no specific person was talking and there was no set topic of discussion, other than who was sitting where and how wonderful the food looked. Mary C. liked what she saw when her man, Lester "Hawk" Hawkins, walked into the dining room and joined the other guests.

Margie, Sofia, Susan and Jason stood at the front of the store. Margie had the floor first.

She looked at Susan and attempted to bring her up to speed on the bizarre encounter at the tree.

"Our dear little sister was up at the oak tree with our mutual friend here. I'm sure it was her choice and idea. Her desire to be a woman has taken away her reasoning ability, but we all can identify with that, can't we?" She looked at Susan, but got no comment or reaction. Margie wanted Jason to talk. "Jason, you have to tell us what we saw up there. I know you know. There's no doubt whatever it was, it interfered with Sofia's plan and ended up scaring her senseless. What was that thing we saw that looked like an animal but drove away in a truck?" Susan's eyes widened again, waiting to hear more. Jason had been ready for the question.

"First of all, it was as much my fault as it was Sofia's. I could have said no and not gone up there, but you know I'm not too strong when the answer should be no." Margie and Susan both smiled at Jason's admission to his weakness. A thought came to Margie's mind and with all the honesty floating around the room, she interrupted Jason. Margie had a number of motives for her next forward and surprising question.

"Is there a possibility my little sister's going to carry an oak baby for the next nine months?" Sofia looked at Margie with her big eyes more than wide open. She answered before Jason could react to Margie's abruptness.

"No! Nothing happened!"

"Good! Now, that worry's out of the way." Margie was definitely in charge. She looked at Jason and he knew he was to continue.

"What you saw at the sand hill was, Beth. She's the Werewolf Girl, from the circus family. That's why they came here. They're looking for Beth." Sofia's eyes remained wide open.

She had another question for Jason.

"You mean, you know that thing?" Jason took a deep breath.

"The way Big Bob explains it, she's really a person with wolf-like characteristics. Her eyes are yellow, her nose is flat, her body is covered with hair and she has those big long sharp dog-like teeth. She's really a nice person, she just looks so scary. She stays hidden most of the time and only comes out in the evening." Margie couldn't help herself.

"Like when the moon is full?" Margie was surprised but pleased when Sofia asked another question. It meant she was coming out of her frightened state and getting back to as normal as she could, under the circumstances.

"What was she doing at the tree?" Jason knew he would add more to their present state of shock if he answered Sofia's question. The three sisters waited for the answer. Jason took another deep breath and the next version of "To Tell the Truth" began.

"Beth thinks she is the last of her kind; the last Werewolf Girl. She wants to breed before it's too late for her to have children." Margie read between the lines and had to interrupt Jason again.

"And she wants to breed with you under the tree you told her about. What a surprise." If sarcasm has an appropriate time, Margie had chosen the right moment. Jason told the rest of what he knew.

"Beth ran away from Gibsonton and they followed her here, hoping to take her back before she got hurt or she hurt somebody." Margie still couldn't help herself.

"Jason, no one else has things like this happen to them, but you. Your life is beyond abnormal, it is outrageously bizarre and there seems to be no relief for you or your mother." Margie changed her sarcasm to a small gleam of pity for Jason and Mary C. Margie turned to Susan.

"Susan, we will not talk about this again unless it is to each other. Sofia, you seem fine now and when we get home we will all enjoy a great meal with our company. Jason, I'm not sure how you plan to tell the others about seeing Beth, but I'm sure you will find a way without Sofia being part of the sighting. Susan, I'll bring you a big plate of food back as soon as I get home, before I eat, as a matter of fact." Susan smiled at her older sister.

"Just eat with the rest and bring me something later."

Every seat at Miss Margaret's big table was full. Ming and Ling were sitting to the side at a small card table. Hawk had gotten a bench from the back porch and put it at the little table, so the Twins could lean against the wall and eat in a little comfort. Norman sat at the card table with them so he could assist them if he was needed. He loved the Twins dearly and would always help them. He liked Hawk for the way he tried to make the Oriental beauties more comfortable.

The others sat at the main dining room table. The middle of the table was filled with plates, bowls and platters of the most wonderful food known to man. There was a regular roast and a pork roast. There was white rice, mashed potatoes, and yellow rice if you preferred color. Bowls of string beans, peas, and sliced cooked carrots dotted the table. There was Texas toast, buttermilk biscuits, and those little Merita, brown and serve rolls, that went with any meal. A platter of Mary C.'s country fried steaks was the center piece in the middle of the Mayport feast of the century. At one end of the table was a long pan filled to the edges with a shepherd's pie, topped with mashed potatoes and melted cheese. At the other end of the table was the same size pan filled with baked macaroni and cheese. The aroma of fried shrimp topped off the main courses. The iced tea was sweet enough to cause cavities. No one would leave Miss Margaret's house hungry that day.

Margie, Sofia and Jason walked into the dining room. Jason knew Margie had saved the day. He would never forget the way she took over and he liked it. Sofia had recovered the best she could from the ordeal at the tree and at least she was trying to act normal. She thought about running upstairs to her room and reading her white covered Bible, but she wanted Margie to see she was a woman and could handle what had happened. Miss Margaret greeted them first.

"Well, there they are. We didn't think y'all would make it. You'll have to sit over there at that table by the wall. Hawk had set up the small kitchen breakfast table to the other side of the main table. The three newcomers got their plates and filled them with food before they sat down. Mary C. had something to say to Jason.

"Billy had his first ride on a bus tonight. He seemed to like it." Ana Kara joined in as an effort to support Jason.

"Jason, thank you so much for letting us spend some time with Billy. We all love him so much. And you are so unselfish. We all thank you." All the circus family began clapping their hands in agreement with Ana's words of praise for Jason and their love for the child. Miss Margaret had to tell her feelings.

"My goodness, you are giving me goose bumps. What a nice way to say, thank you to a friend and show your feelings for them. I don't think anyone has ever clapped for me in my life. Jason, these are wonderful friends you have brought to Mayport." Beulla was next to join in.

"Miss Margaret and Miss Mary C., we would like to be the first to applaud this incredible meal you have created for us. And I must have the recipe for this country fried steak before I leave." They all clapped again for the two cooks and Mary C. was excited about someone else wanting one of her recipes. She bathed in the attention. No one had ever clapped for her either and she felt the same chill run through her body that Miss Margaret had mentioned earlier. Sandeep and Eve did not join the dinner party and no one spoke about their absence.

During the meal, Hawk tried not to stare at Ana Kara, but he did like her full woman's figure and cleavage line. He did steal a few glances when he was sure Mary C. wouldn't notice. However, Ana noticed each time the handsome Hawk stole a peek. Sofia was quiet as she recovered from another sexual fiasco with her soul mate. Margie made sure she didn't look at Tom Thumb, but she knew he was looking at her. Margie was glad she wasn't sitting at the main table. Billy was lying in a big soft chair, surrounded by pillows near Mary C.'s chair. She would tend to him if need be. There was no one single conversation with everybody listening to one person. There were five or six individual conversations going on at one time. It was a great dinner.

The two tattooed bodies of Sandeep and Eve were deep into the latter stages of a sexual frenzy. She had mounted him for the usual physically exhausting finale. Eve knew the house was empty of the living and she didn't care if the ghosts were on the prowl or not. They would have to run to a safe place when she screamed at the end of a full hour of movement and contact with Sandeep. It ended with the final release of her body fluids, that caused cramps in her stomach muscles, sending sharp pains through her entire body when the flow hit her. Eve adored the pain, but it carried her to another dimension and she mentally left Sandeep.

Her body lay on him, but her mind was elsewhere. Her sexual journeys never lasted more than a minute or so, but she always strived to reach that point during her sexual encounters. Sandeep would allow her to lay on him until she gained consciousness and returned to him mentally. He was addicted to her and she was addicted to him. The tattoos were all back in the right places.

Jason stood next to Big Bob at the dessert table. The choices of sweets were mind boggling. Jason stepped closer to Big Bob.

"When we get a chance, I need to talk to you. I saw Beth." Big Bob knew not to react to Jason's information. He could tell Jason wanted it to be private. They went back to the table. Margie turned to Miss Margaret.

"I need to fix Susan a nice big plate and take it over to her." Sofia spoke up.

"Here, I'll help you. You drive and I'll hold the plates."

Eve had returned from her sexual journey. She lay next to Sandeep as she recovered. It was time for their final discussion about the deed he was to perform for his freedom. She was her evil self.

"You know once you are free of me, you will even want me more than you do now. We are one person, not two. The pain we both went through to make our two bodies one will bond us forever. The Sofias and Mary C.s of the world will not satisfy or complete you as I do. I don't think you have considered your needs. You believe your freedom is essential for you to fulfill your destiny, when in reality I am your past, present, future and your destiny." Sandeep listened to her words and then had his own thoughts to share with her.

"I'm not sure what you will have me do, but you must remember I will not harm the woman, the child, or Jason. That will not happen, even if I do not get my freedom." Eve smiled at her lover, saint, priest, warrior and slave.

"You have made that very clear to me. We leave tomorrow night, after it is done."

"What is it that I must do?"

The great Mayport feast was over. Miss Margaret had told everyone to make themselves a care package so they could eat later that evening if they got hungry and needed a midnight snack. Ana and Beulla were wrapping some goodies to take to Mr. King's for later. Sofia and Margie had gone to give Susan her dinner. Jason was sitting on the couch, holding Billy and talking to Helga, who was sitting across from him. Hawk was sitting with Mary C. and he leaned toward her and whispered in her ear. "You can sleep at home tonight, if you want. I've fixed everything and cleaned everything up. If you want to, I'd like us all to be home together tonight. It's up to you." Mary C. liked Hawk telling her that she could go home when she wanted. She smiled and patted his thigh.

"I'd like to be home tonight." Jason stood up and handed Billy to Helga.

"I need to talk to Big Bob for a minute, be right back." Helga smiled. She loved holding the baby. Jason walked out onto the back porch where Norman, Big Bob and Mr. King were sitting, allowing the big meal to settle. Big Bob was the first one to acknowledge Jason.

"Hey young fella, I'm miserable. And it takes a lot of groceries to fill up this tank of mine, but I'm as full as I've ever been. The girls are packin' up more food to go. It was great wasn't it?"

Jason nodded and sat down next to his friends. Big Bob would not mention Beth in front of the others unless Jason did it first. He wasn't sure if Jason wanted the others to know. Big Bob would wait for Jason to say something about it. Jason trusted the three men he was sitting with.

"I don't want the others to know, but I saw Beth. She's here." Big

Bob was the only one not surprised by Jason's statement. Norman was first.

"Where was she? Is she alright?" Jason hesitated as he thought of Sofia and Margie.

"She seemed fine. She was in Big Bob's truck. I asked her to come back with me and that y'all were here looking for her. I told her everyone was worried about her." Mr. King was interested also.

"Where was she?" Jason knew he had to tell them, but he would not mention Sofia or Margie.

"I went to the tree." Mr King looked at Jason with curious eyes. "I don't know why, I just did. Beth must have been watching and waiting near the tree. She came out of the dark and she wanted to..." Jason hesitated again and looked at Big Bob. ..."you know, she wanted to breed with me. I told her the whole thing was crazy and she got mad and ran away." Big Bob took a deep breath.

"Well, she could be long gone if she's mad or embarrassed. She can't take too much embarrassment, you know? I don't think she'll go back to the tree now that she knows you won't do the deed." Norman smiled and added his two cents.

"She is crazy, you know? Even though we love her and wish no ill will on her, she is crazy.

It may be heredity or what she has to live with each day, but whatever the reason she is a real looney." Jason was waiting on Big Bob to say something to Norman about his comment about Beth, but it didn't come. Instead Big Bob looked at Jason and had his own observation about the Werewolf Girl.

"Norman's right, you know? She is quite nuts." Neither Jason nor Mr. King had a reply to the analysis of Beth's mental state.

Margie, Sofia and Susan were sitting at the small table in the store. Susan was eating her dinner as the other two sat with her.

"How was it with all those strange people at the house?" Margie had the answer for Susan.

"I'm tired of them. Actually, I'm tired of everybody. You get used to not having so many people around. I like it just being us. I hate that little man. He licked my arm when I was at Mr. King's house." Sofia and Susan both made faces. Susan had to reply.

"I am trying to eat here, if you don't mind."

"Sorry, but I hate the way he looks at all of us. I'd hate to be alone with him somewhere. Now, he's scary." Sofia had her thoughts about the circus people.

"I like them, but I do feel sorry for them. The little man is the least likeable, for sure. I don't like seeing the Twins. The way they're stuck together makes me want to throw up. I'm sorry I feel like that, but I do. How do they live like that?" Margie liked Sofia talking because it meant she was recovering from her ordeal at the sand hill.

"It's all they have ever known. They've been that way since birth. That's all they understand. I feel sorry for them, too, and they are hard to watch." Margie smiled about a thought she had and continued. "What about that Ana woman? She's a belly dancer. Is she built or what? It wouldn't take Mary C. very long to hate that one. She'd be stealing all the men around here if she stayed around very long. She just looks wild to me. I wonder if she screws the Giant Man?" Sofia and Susan were shocked at Margie's question. Their eyes popped open from surprise. Susan added to the girl talk moment.

"I'll bet his thing is huge." Sofia couldn't believe her ears. Margie had more.

"You'd like to see that big thing wouldn't ya?" Sofia looked at Margie then at Susan. Susan had more.

"And you wouldn't like to see it?" Sofia was outraged.

"You two stop right now. We don't talk like this. Please stop." Margie smiled at her little sister.

"Sofia, will you please stop being Mama. I have already asked you that before. We do talk like that sometimes and this is one of the times. Two hours ago you were butt naked under the oak tree, waiting for Jason to stick his thing inside you and now you don't want us to talk about the Giant's giant pecker." Sofia's mouth flew open as her two sisters burst into laughter.

"You two are just being nasty and making fun of me. I love Jason and I thought it was meant for me to go there with him. And you were right, it was my idea. He did try to stop me at first, but I insisted. Maybe you're right about me not being cut out for this sex stuff and being suited for Jason." Margie looked at Susan and then at Sofia.

"No one may be suited for Jason. Somehow he has done something to us all. Maybe it's our fault because we have all wanted adventure and we hate our little nothing lives. Everything about him and his mother is wild and untamed, and we all think that is exciting. But, there is a price to pay for such a life. Are any of us really ready to pay the price to be part of it. I keep talking about not being afraid, but every time something happens, I'm still afraid. Mary C. and Jason are never afraid. I don't think any of us will ever be able to match up. They have even killed people. I don't want to kill anyone, but if you're with them it may just come to that." Susan and Sofia were both looking at Margie as she shared her well thought out philosophy.

"Remember, we are all attracted to Jason, like it or not. And we all know we would open our legs for him if we had the chance. We have all already proven that fact of life." Sofia was shocked by Margie's comments, but she didn't react in any way. She actually wanted to hear more. Susan just nodded her head in agreement with the truth Margie was telling. The oldest and wisest sister had more. "All of us but Peggy, would open our legs. She would open her mouth."

"Oh Margie, I don't believe you said that about our sister. But, that was too funny. You should be ashamed of yourself."

"I am."

The circus family had thanked Miss Margaret and Mary C. a hundred times for the wonderful dinner and company. The circus bus had all the passengers aboard and Norman closed the door. They were headed to the haunted house. Mary C. walked into the living room where Miss Margaret was relaxing in her favorite chair.

"Miss Margaret, I will never be able to thank you for all your kindness. You are the most wonderful woman I have ever known. I will clap for you anytime." Mary C. moved to where Miss Margaret was sitting and hugged her neck. Both women had tears well up in their eyes.

"You're very welcome, my dear. I have enjoyed every minute you have been here. I haven't had so much fun cooking in years. It reminded me of when my sister Margie and I would try to out cook each other and ended up with way too much food. It was sure fun, wasn't it?"

"Yes ma'am it was." Miss Margaret was a wise woman.

"But, now, Hawk is taking you home, isn't he?" Mary C. smiled at Miss Margaret's intuition.

"Yes ma'am, he is. I need to go home and put all the sad stuff behind me. Being with you and the girls has helped me do just that. I love you and the girls."

"We love you and your family, as well." Hawk walked into the room. Mary C. looked up at her man and had a good idea.

"On the way home, let's take Chichemo and Bosco a big care package."

Beth ducked down onto the front seat of Big Bob's truck when she saw a set of car lights coming toward her on Seminole Road. The truck was out of gas and she had pulled off to the side of the road before it stopped completely. She was mad at herself for not checking the gas and she was frustrated about the impossible situation she had created for herself and the people who cared about her. Beth decided to walk back to Mayport and find her family. She knew she had to stay off the road and walk near the woods in case cars went by. She could hide until they had gone by. She knew it was a long walk, but she was happy with her decision and there was another thing to be happy about.

The moon came up at its fullest out of the ocean. It was as big and round as it ever had been. Beth loved that full moon and it always put a little bounce to her step. It would lead the way back to Mayport and give her the strength she needed to end her self-inflicted misadventure. Her family had come a long distance to find and protect her and she wanted to give them the same respect they had given her. Beth locked up the truck, looked up at that full moon and started her journey to Mayport on foot, or paw.

It was Margie's turn for the late shift at the store. Susan's shift was over and Sofia would be back for the early morning shift. The family wagon was rolling again, but Margie was not at the wheel. Susan was driving and she and Sofia were headed home. She blew the horn of the wagon at the big purple and yellow circus bus as it pulled up into Mr. King's front yard. Norman blew the bus horn back at them and it played "Dixie". The family wagon disappeared down the road as Officer Jimmy Johnston's patrol car passed the circus bus as its passengers were getting off. Officer Johnston slowed the patrol car down when he saw Norman assisting the Twins up the stairs and into Mr. King's house. He stopped his patrol car in front of Miss Margaret's store.

Margie saw his car pull up and she was glad she would have some company. She was also excited from the talk about Jason and the male anatomy with her sisters; especially, the Giant's giant pecker. Officer Jimmy Johnston would benefit from the earlier evening activities and conversations, he just didn't know it yet.

The family wagon stopped in front of their house. Susan and Sofia got out of the wagon and walked up to the house as Jason, Mary C., Billy and Hawk were all walking out of the house. It was easy to see they were leaving. Miss Margaret followed the four of them into the front yard.

"Come back any time, you are always welcome here. Don't be strangers. Bring Billy over when you need a babysitter." Mary C. walked over and hugged Sofia and Susan as Hawk started Uncle Bobby's truck. Jason's eyes met Sofia's eyes and they both knew they had a great deal to say to each other, but it would have to be said at another time. Uncle Bobby's truck was rolling to the dock to feed Chichemo and then Mary C. was headed home. The four of them squeezed into the cab of the truck and they were down the road.

Norman helped Ming and Ling get settled in their room. They were exhausted from all the moving around they had done. Helga and Tom were lying in their bed. He had unbuttoned her blouse and exposed her huge breasts. He would play with her for a little while.

Big Bob and Mr. King were sitting on the front porch and they were both sucking on big cigars from Mr. King's Havana collection.

Beulla had her bummie marble sized corns soaking in warm Epsom Salt water and Ana Kara was taking a bubble bath. She had plans to sit on the upper deck porch with her naked body wrapped in a sheet, waiting for Mr. King to scare her again. She wanted to be sure she smelled extra good.

Before Officer Jimmy Johnston had the chance to tell Margie how he missed her and he couldn't sleep because he was thinking about her, she requested another quickie. Margie pulled her pants and panties down to her ankles and bent over the little table next to the cash register counter. Her butt cheeks were requesting his contact. Jimmy unbuckled his belt, unsnapped and unzipped his pants. He stepped up close behind her. Margie was always full of surprises.

"I want you to do it real hard. As hard as you can. If it hurts I'll tell you to stop, but I want it to hurt some. But, don't stop unless I say so." Margie was so excited Jimmy's entry was smooth and easy. He followed her instructions and honored her request. Jimmy pumped her as hard as he could. She made noises, but didn't say stop. Margie pushed toward him each time he pushed toward her. She surprised him again when the sexual encounter was at its peak and she told him to "come on, harder" and challenged him for more. Margie had never said such a thing during the other times they were together. He found himself wondering, "Who the hell are you?" A mousy voice that Margie recognized instantly joined the noises she was making.

"She said harder man, don't let her down." Jimmy pulled away from his contact and Margie stood up. They both turned toward the voice to see Tom Thumb the perverted pigmy standing outside the store at the screen door. Margie pulled up her pants and panties and Jimmy fixed his pants as the bell on the front door rang. The nasty little man walked into the store while they dressed.

"I'm sure glad I was thirsty for one of those cold Nehi drinks. I would have missed the show and I do like that kind of show." Jimmy didn't like the little man walking toward the cold drink box, but he really couldn't say anything to him. Margie was red faced and hated the fact the little man had seen her. Jimmy found a little courage.

Beth's Hunters

"Do you always sneak around on people." Tom looked at Jimmy with a disappointed look.

"Actually, I do. But, coming to the store isn't exactly sneaking around, is it? And you two really like to live dangerously. I have to hand it to y'all. Right out here in the front. You have my respect, I must tell you that. I like people to watch me, too, but you two live on the edge and I feel fortunate to have seen you in action." He bowed his head in sexual respect. "How much is the drink?"

Jason jumped out of the truck and took the food to Chichemo. He gave Jason the money Mr. Leek had paid for the shrimp and fish they had unloaded. With all that had happened Jason had forgotten about the shrimp. Chichemo reminded Jason they needed to make another trip in the morning. Chichemo knew of their troubles and he told Jason if they didn't show by six, he would go without them.

"We need to go when the shrimp are running." Chichemo didn't mind going alone, but it was always better with a crew. Jason told him at least one of them would be there in the morning.

"It depends on how Mama's feelin'." Chichemo nodded his head because he did understand, but he would be leaving at six in the morning; crew or not. They were all happy when Jason returned to the truck with the money. They headed home at last.

Beth stepped into the woods when she saw another set of car lights coming in her direction. She realized she was standing on a side dirt road that led up into the woods, probably a hunter's trail or maybe someone's access to their home somewhere in the woods. As the light passed by her on the main road, another set of lights flashed behind her coming up the side dirt road. She left the dirt road and ducked down behind a group of Palmetto fans, to hide from whoever was approaching.

It was a truck loaded with young men. Two in the front cab and three standing in the back truck bed. Beth's heart went crazy in her hairy chest when the pickup truck stopped next to the Palmetto fans she was squatting behind. They were close enough for her to hear them talking.

One of the young men held up a flashlight in the direction of the woods opposite Beth's hiding place.

"I saw something, I tell ya. It looked like a bear." The other young men laughed and another voice spoke up above the laughter.

"You are always seein' a damn bear. And when we get there, it's gone. You need to get your eyes checked or better yet, check that imagination of yours." They all laughed again at the bear spotter.

"Well, it might not have been a bear, but it was something or somebody." He pointed his flashlight in Beth's direction and scanned the area behind her. She knew the light was bouncing off the trees and bushes around her, but she did not move. Beth knew she could not panic and she had to keep her wits about her. It was crucial for her to stay focused and still. She wanted to run, but she didn't.

Beth looked through the Palmetto fans and her yellow eyes fell on her most disturbing sight so far. The young men in the back of the truck all had hunting bows across their backs. They were night hunting with flashlights, bows and arrows. The young bear spotter was not finished.

"What ever it was couldn't have gone very far, even if it was a person. They have got to be around here somewhere."

"Maybe they went on out to the main road and got in their car. I hope no one's hiding out here in the dark because we came up on 'em and scared 'em. I'd hate to shoot at some poor devil makin' out with his girl 'cause you thought he was a bear." The young man shouted toward the woods. "If you're hidin' out there. Come on out before 'ol Daniel Boone here grins ya down."

The young men burst into laughter again, even the bear spotter laughed. Beth was scared and trembling from her fear.

"I ain't too sure I want to find a bear in the dark anyway. A flashlight and an arrow doesn't give me much confidence, especially with you guys doin' the shootin'."

"Very funny! You'll be glad we've got these bows if he comes runnin' out of these woods, with you as a meal on his mind." Another voice added to the conversation Beth was listening to.

"You know they have spotted bears out here before. There could be one out here." The young men got quiet for a moment. Beth lay her body flat on the ground. Her heart was racing to the extent of causing chest pains. She had to maintain herself. The cover of the tree limbs and leaves above her had blocked out the bright full moon light or they would have surely found her by now. Beth could see the three young men in the back of the truck as they all turned up a bottle to their mouths and took a swig of beer. She was close enough to see the Schlitz label on the brown bottles. When they would empty each bottle the young men would throw theirs into the woods. One hit a tree and shattered to their delight. One sailed over Beth's head and landed somewhere in the bushes behind her. The third bottle hit the palmetto fans next to her and ricochet down, hitting her on the leg. It was painful, but the Palmetto fan slowed the bottle's momentum before it hit her. She made no sound because she understood pain and the life and death situation she was facing.

For some reason, the truck moved backward and Beth thought they were leaving. The front headlights shined directly on Beth's hiding place. The young men in the back of the truck were not paying attention to the woods around them. Beth could see the young driver of the truck through the front windshield. He looked directly at her as the truck's headlights flashed in her yellow eyes. Beth knew, by the expression on his young handsome face, he saw her. She didn't move until he yelled.

"There it is! Right there!" In his excitement he stepped on the gas peddle with the truck still in reverse. The truck jumped backward again, throwing the three young men in the back all over the truck and each other. The truck stopped moving.

Beth was already on her feet and running away from her hiding place. She had no idea where she was going, but at the time and under the circumstances, it didn't matter. Beth saw lights from the flashlights flash and bounce off the woods around her. She knew the young hunters were trying to spot her in the dark. There was a strange quiet around her as she ran. She heard nothing, but her own panting. Beth felt good about the distance she had put between her and the young men. She knew not to stop running until the distance was even greater.

Beth thought she heard the wind whistle behind her as something pushed her in the back and knocked her off her feet. She fell face down into the dirt and leaves on the ground. Beth's back and chest felt like they were on fire. She stood up in an unnatural reaction to her fiery pain. She turned back to see the small lights coming toward her. Beth was in a dream world when she reached down in front of her body and touched the arrow head that had entered her back and came out of her chest. She looked at her own blood on her hand and fell to her knees, as another arrow flew past her head and hit a tree behind her. Beth fell forward, hitting her face and chest on the ground, driving the protruding arrow head back into her chest. She was disappointed in herself for not preserving her species. She heard talking around her and knew the young hunters were standing above her, but she could not lift her face out of the dirt. The last words Beth heard before she died were the same words she had heard throughout her entire life.

"What the hell is it?"

Ming and Ling sat up in their bed from a deep sleep. They held hands to comfort each other. They were not sure what had made them wake up so suddenly, but they new something was terribly wrong. Tom Thumb was back in the bed with Helga and his encounter at the store with the novice lovers had boiled his juices. Helga would be the beneficiary and the recipient of his lustful thoughts and needs. Ana Kara stood in a familiar place again. She was pleased with her naked reflection in the mirror in her room. She thought about how Hawk had watched her when he had the chance at the Mayport feast. Ana knew she would be happy to wear a sheet over her naked body for a man like him if she was given the opportunity. He was definitely the kind of man she would like to get to know. Ana Kara was a true free spirit and knew how to use her physical attributes for her pleasure and the pleasure of others. Ana loved men and they loved her.

The white Mercedes Benz rolled up in Mr. King's front yard and stopped next to Mr. King's hearse. Sandeep got out of the driver's side and opened the back door for Eve. She took her lover, priest, chauffeur's arm and walked up the steps to the porch. The cigar smokers and Norman were still sitting in the night air enjoying good company and fellowship.

"Those hog legs you're smoking sure do stink, John." Mr. King took a big drag on his hog leg and blew the smoke in Eve's direction.

"You know you love the smell of a good cigar, girl. Your daddy smoked this same brand his entire life."

"And I hated it every time he lit one up. I can't stay out here with all this smoke. Good night gentlemen. Sandeep and I will be leaving some time in the morning. John I'm sure you will be up before we go, so I will thank you and kiss you good-bye when we leave. I'm tired and have a few more things to do in the morning, so good night." The three men nodded as Eve walked into the house. Sandeep bowed to his host and the other two men and followed Eve to their room.

Big Bob had an observation.

"The priest is kind of quiet tonight. They're leaving in the morning. You don't think they still might do something to Jason before they go, do ya?" Mr. King wasn't sure what to say. Norman had a solution.

"I think I know how we can find out, so we'll be sure of what to do and if we should use our plan." He left the others smoking on the porch.

Officer Jimmy Johnston had agreed to stay with Margie at the store until Sofia relieved her at six in the morning. Margie didn't want to be there alone if the pigmy pervert got thirsty during the night and she did want a few more quickies. They would go to the back room and lock the door, but they would indulge a few more times during the morning hours. Jimmy would do it hard, too. The little man would not return to bother them, he had his own business to attend to.

Eve stood completely naked next to her bed. Sandeep was deep into a tattoo trance as she moved her body to entice him. He knew she was making her own music in her head as she danced around the bed. Even a Punjab priest appreciated a woman who danced for him. He took his turban off his head and his braided locks fell in one long braid to the floor. It was twisted together and tied at the end like a thick rope. Eve talked to him as she moved.

"With us leaving in the morning, is it alright to leave your hair braided and tied. I will not have time in the morning to fix it if we are to take care of the business at hand." He didn't answer her, but he did reach for her as she moved past the bed. She was too fast and danced away from him. She had her motives.

"You can have me tonight for the last time as an obligated man. Tomorrow you can have me as a free man if you choose to. We will not touch tonight until we go over what we are to do in the morning. I want no mistakes and timing is the key to us getting out of here. We'll be gone before anyone even knows we were there. Let's go over it one more time."

Mary C. and her family walked up to the front steps of the house. The new front door was beautiful and the screen door was also nice. Hawk had done a great job with the doors and the window and the general clean up. Jason took Billy to his room and lay him on the bed.

Mary C. hugged Hawk and whispered in his ear. "Thank you for getting me back home so quickly. I'd rather be home than anywhere. I can't wait to get you in the bed tonight. I've missed you, even if it was just one night. I didn't like waking up without you." Jason turned on the radio as Mary C.'s new theme song "Green Onions" filled the house. Mary C. stepped back away from Hawk and started to dance.

"That's it. That's my new favorite song. 'Green Onions' listen, Hawk." Hawk knew about good music. He was a great dancer in his honky tonk, jukin' days, and he and Mary C. had danced a few times at the Band Shell in Jacksonville Beach. He took Mary C. into his big strong arms and demonstrated a few of his old dance floor moves. They were doing a slow version of the beach bop to the strange "Green Onion" beat and melody. Jason stepped out of the bedroom to watch them. They were fluid and smooth with their steps and motion.

Mary C. absolutely loved moving with him across the living room floor. The dancing and contact started her juices flowing. When the song ended she kissed Hawk and left him standing there. She was in the shower and getting ready for bed. Hawk would be the one to benefit from Mary C.'s flowing juices before the morning came. Jason went into his room and lay next to Billy. Hawk joined Mary C. in the shower.

Midnight had come to Mayport. The moon was high above the Atlantic Ocean and at it's fullest. Sofia was in her bed reading her white covered Bible. She looked at the closet where the carousel was hidden, but didn't take it out. Officer Jimmy Johnston and Margie were enjoying their third quickie at the store. Ana Kara was still naked and had fallen asleep across her bed before she got the chance to be seduced or do the seducing. Only the ghosts of the house would enjoy her full woman's body that night. The Twins had fallen back to sleep after their abrupt awakening. Beulla was snoring like a freight train with one foot still in the basin of water. Helga was in her bed alone.

Mr. King, Big Bob and Norman were still sitting outside on the front porch. Eve and Sandeep were in their final sexual frenzy at John King's haunted house. They had gone over their evil plan for the morning and Eve had kept her promise to mingle tattoos. They were once again at the pinnacle of sexual ecstasy, when pleasure and pain become one and nothing else matters.

Tom Thumb stepped away from his favorite key hole. He had completed the mission he was given. He hurried to the front porch for his report. Mary C. knocked on Jason's bedroom door and opened it slowly.

"You sleepin'?" She stepped into the room.

"No ma'am, just relaxin' with Billy. I was waitin' on you to get out of the shower."

"Wait a little while. I used a lot of the hot water. Sorry."

"If I don't fall asleep."

"I want you and Hawk to go on shrimpin' in the mornin'. Don't let Chichemo go alone. Things are too good and the shrimp seem to be runnin' for us. I know your Uncle Bobby would have to go when they was runnin' and we're gonna do the same. That's a lot of money we got tonight and it can happen again, but not if y'all think y'all have to baby sit me. You go on and get some sleep. You can shower in the mornin'. Good night my two sons."

Beth's dead limp body lay in the back bed of a pick up truck. The three hunters were sitting around her in the back. The other two were in the front cab. They were on their way to the Atlantic Beach Police Station.

Little Tom stepped out onto the front porch to report to mission command. The cigars were gone and the midnight air was cooling the three men as they waited for the pigmy commando.

Tom motioned for them to follow him to the far dark section of the porch. He was worried about Sandeep coming to the front door and hearing him. The three men followed Tom as he turned the corner of the house. They all stopped when he stopped. All three men bent over to be close to Tom.

"It's Hawk. She wants him to kill Hawk. He's gonna do it in the morning before they go. She won't be there. She just wants Mary C. to lose someone she cares for. He won't kill Jason, Billy, or Mary C. She has told him about Hawk killing others and that he is as evil as Mary C. Sandeep wants his freedom and he will do this deed to gain it. He thinks it is worth one evil life to pay for his freedom. It's Hawk."

CHAPTER THIRTEEN

IT WAS STILL DARK WHEN HAWK OPENED HIS EYES AND LOOKED AT THE clock next to the bed. He could feel the effects of his sexual relations with the woman lying next to him. The bed spread covered Mary C. to the waist, but her naked upper body was in full view and it was a most wonderful sight to meet Hawk's eyes before he left on his next shrimping trip. He was sore from her aggressive sexual activity, but it was worth any small amount of pain he may feel as the day went on. Hawk was always amazed at Mary C.'s sexual stamina and her unconditional acceptance of any sexual act. She was a physical and sexual marvel.

It was still dark when Eve opened her eyes to see her lover, slave, priest, Sandeep Singh, wrapping his black turban around his two day braided hair. Some of the braids had loosened, but the tie at the end of his eight foot mane of hair was still attached.

"Do you need me to help you?"

"No. Perhaps you will assist me later and braid it correctly when we are away from here."

"It will be my pleasure. What time is it?"

"It's five o'clock. I couldn't sleep. I didn't want to stare at the ceiling any longer."

"You're excited about being free of me." Sandeep did not respond to her statement. He turned to the small mirror and continued wrapping the turban cloth around his head. Eve sat up on the edge of the bed, exposing her tattooed naked body. Sandeep saw her reflection in the mirror. Eve rotated her head to ease a stiff neck and stretched her painted arms up over her head, lifting her breasts to attention. She knew Sandeep was watching her.

"You may not like being free of me like you think. This could be the last time you watch me dress. I'll do it slow so you will enjoy it more and later you will remember."

It was still dark when Chichemo opened his eyes. He had started sleeping on the boat after he decided he could save rent money if the boat became his home for a while. He knew he wouldn't work on the Mary C. but for a few months and he would be able to save a little cash if he called the boat home.

It was still dark when Sofia's alarm clock buzzed at 5:15 A.M. She opened her beautiful sleepy blue eyes. Sofia was good at jumping right up and not staying in bed. She knew Margie would be ready to get home and sleep after her long all night shift at the store. Margie was more than ready to get away from the store. There had been no late night customers after the pigmy man, and even though the sex with Officer Jimmy Johnston had pleased her, she was still tired and ready to get home.

Jimmy had fallen asleep in the back room about four o'clock and Margie let him sleep for two reasons: she knew he had to go to work early and she knew he had been sexually drained by her aggressive demands. Margie would wake him up in a few minutes because she didn't want him to be there when her little sister Sofia came to relieve her.

It was still dark outside when the five young bear hunters sat in the waiting room of the Atlantic Beach Police Station. They had brought Beth's body to the station and told what happened in the woods. The dispatcher had tried to get Officer Jimmy Johnston on his radio, but Jimmy had not answered. Mr. Butler was on his way to the station.

It was still dark outside when Eve knocked on Mr. King's bedroom door. He was up and dressed when he opened the door.

"Good morning, John. I knew you would be up. Men like you are always up before the sun. Y'all are so afraid you'll miss something."

"Good morning to you too, Eve. And you're right, I don't miss much. Time to go?"

"I told you I'd kiss you and thank you before we left for all your kindness and hospitality. I do appreciate you letting us stay here with you and your new friends. You should keep that Ana around. She looks like she could be a lot of fun, if you like that sort of thing." John was surprised at Eve's comment about Ana Kara. He thought perhaps Eve paid more attention to the other guests than he realized. He thought maybe some women just knew things. Eve kissed her father's best friend on his lips and touched his face with her gloved hand.

"John, you are such a dear. I know you don't approve of me or my life style, but no one ever has. I didn't get this way overnight and it would be far too painful to change now. As a matter of fact, I really do like myself quite a bit and they say you have to like yourself first. Well, no problem here." John gave her a little smile.

"Tell Sandeep I said good-bye. He is an interesting young man."

"Of course I will. He thinks you're pretty interesting, too. He's waiting in the car. John, I don't think I'll be getting back this way again, so keep all those ghosts in line. Good-bye, John."

It was still dark when Mary C. stood at her kitchen stove cooking breakfast for her two shrimpers. Jason was taking the shower he had missed the night before and Hawk joined Mary C. for a cup of coffee at the small kitchen table. Hawk knew Chichemo would be leaving without them in about thirty-five minutes, but Hawk thought they had plenty of time to have a little breakfast before they left.

Officer Jimmy Johnston kissed Margie in the store before he stepped outside to his patrol car. Margie was glad he was leaving.

"Go on now before Sofia drives up and sees you. I don't need a lecture from her this early in the morning. No thank you, sir." Margie always had a surprise for Jimmy. "If you're not too tired when you get off, let's go out to eat or something. Or we don't have to eat we can just, something." Jimmy was already tired, but he smiled and nodded his head. As he was leaving the front of the store Jimmy passed the white Mercedes Benz headed in the opposite direction.

It was still dark when Big Bob, Norman, Mr. King and Tom met in the downstairs living room. They knew what they had to do. Ana, Beulla, Helga, Ming and Ling were all asleep. As soon as Officer Jimmy Johnston drove past the little jetties on his way out of Mayport, Mr. Butler's voice came over the car radio.

"I know it's early, but are you out there, Jimmy?"

"It is early, but I'm here, sir."

"You need to meet me at the station. I'm not sure what we've got over there. Just meet me."

"On my way, sir."

It was still dark while Sandeep backed the white Mercedes Benz down a side dirt road near Mary C.'s house. The car lights went out. Eve and her soon to be free slave sat in the dark as the first part of their evil plan began to unfold.

Sofia was driving the family wagon when it rolled up in front of the store. Margie was ready to turn the keys and the store over to her little sister. Margie was so tired she was silly.

"Good morning, oak tree woman. May I help you with something?" Sofia didn't think her oldest sister was very funny. She handed Margie the car keys.

"Very funny. Very funny."

The sun would not show itself for another thirty minutes; it was still dark in every corner of Mayport. Chichemo was having a bit of breakfast himself and he was sharing his bowl of Cheerios with the spider monkey, Bosco. He would be leaving the dock with the arrival of the sun.

Mary C. walked out onto her front porch with Hawk and Jason. She kissed them both.

"Don't let that Chichemo leave y'all. And don't worry about me and Billy. Just fill them nets with money." Jason smiled. He did love his mother. Mary C. had another request.

"Leave me one of those trucks. Me and Billy might just go shoppin' today. In fact, leave Hawk's truck. I don't drive that stick of your

Uncle Bobby's too good. I'd rather have the automatic." Hawk took the keys to his truck out of his pocket and threw them to Jason, who then handed them to Mary C. Hawk climbed into the driver's side of Uncle Bobby's truck and Jason jumped into the passenger side. They had no idea they were being watched as they moved past the white Mercedes Benz parked off the road in the dark.

Margie had showered the long night and the sex off her young body and she stood in front of the bathroom mirror. In her mind she compared her naked body to Sofia's naked body and thought she matched up to her little sister rather nicely. She was cut from the same cloth that made Ana Kara and Mary C. She would start spending more time in front of the mirror. Women of sex do that.

Mary C. checked on Billy and, as usual, he was sleeping. She left the bedroom door open so she could hear him if he woke up or moved around. She liked being home.

Officer Jimmy Johnston walked into the coroner's lab again. Mr. Butler was standing next to one of the flat tables that were placed throughout the room. Jimmy knew there was a body under the sheet on the table next to Mr. Butler. Mr. Butler looked at Jimmy as he walked up.

"Prepare yourself for this one, Jimmy." Jimmy thought, "How bad can it be, I've seen everything?" He stepped closer to the table as Mr. Butler pulled the sheet off and exposed Beth's hairy and bloody body. Jimmy's heart jumped when he saw the ugly creature on the table. Beth's body shape and large breasts identified her as a female.

"Is it make-up or a great costume?"

"I don't think so. I'm afraid she's the real thing."

"What real thing is she?"

"She's half woman and half animal; wolf I think. The eyes, teeth, nose, hair...wolf I think. Hell, these boys might have found the damn missing link or Mayport's version of Sasquatch. Like I told you before, nothing surprises me out there anymore. I was waiting for someone to say Mary C. killed it or it was a relative of Mary C. and the oak tree. Maybe it's some kind of mutant inbred." For some reason, the sight of the circus bus parked in front of Mr. King's house popped in Officer Jimmy Johnston's head. He looked at Mr. Butler again.

"What is it Jimmy? What are you thinking?"

"She's from the circus." Mr. Butler didn't understand.

"What? What circus?" Jimmy took a deep breath.

"There's a group of strange circus people staying at Mr. King's house. I just feel she's one of them."

"Oh, my God! She's the Wolf Woman in the circus or something like that. And these huntin' fools have killed her. I wonder what she was doing out in those woods at that time of night, anyway?"

"Full moon."

Hawk stopped the truck on the road between Mr. King's house and Miss Margaret's store. Jason jumped out of the truck.

"I think Sofia's workin' this mornin'. I really need to talk to her. Don't let Chichemo leave without me." Hawk smiled and understood Jason wanting to meet with the blonde haired, blue-eyed, Mayport beauty.

Margie opened the closet door in Sofia's bedroom and took the blanket off the magic carousel. She picked up the musical antique and carried it to the bed. Margie wanted to have a magic carousel dream without Sofia's company. She lay across her sister's bed with her face close to the music box. Margie turned it on.

The white Mercedes pulled out of it's hiding place in the woods near Mary C.'s house. Sandeep was driving, but he was alone. Hawk pulled the truck up to Mr. Leek's fish house and parked away from the working ramps. He stepped out of the truck and went into the fish house and out to the main dock where the Mary C. was tied. He was greeted by an excited Chichemo as he approached the boat.

"I figured one of y'all would be here. If I know Mary C. she wants this boat movin'. I hope she's alright. I heard about all that stuff."

"She's fine and you're right, she wants us both out there with you. Draggin' our butts off."

"That's the way ya make it, though. She's right. We gotta get 'em while they're here. Hell, they could be gone tomorrow. Where's the boy, anyway?" Hawk had to smile at Chichemo's change of subject and his question.

"He's at the store with one of Miss Margaret's daughters and he told me not to let you leave him." Chichemo smiled a bigger smile than Hawk's.

"Hell, I'd like to be with a woman this early in the mornin' myself. I'm a mornin' man when it comes to the ladies. Damn right we'll wait. But not too long." Hawk stepped down to the boat railing and then onto the deck.

Mary C. could see Billy on the bed from the kitchen, as she cleaned up the breakfast dishes left by her workingmen. Her uncanny ability to compartmentalize the events of her life had enabled her to place that night in the recesses of her mind and she would not think about the five people she killed, unless she was reminded. It was her way of coping with the deeds and decisions she had been forced to make during her life. A knock at the door sent a cold chill through her body at first. She thought about getting the shotgun from under the bed, but for some reason she didn't. Mary C. didn't want to be scared every time someone came to the house.

Chichemo stepped off the railing of the boat and onto the dock. His sidekick, Bosco, rode on his shoulder. "I need to get my rubber boots. I left them in the back of the fish house so I wouldn't track up the floor in the office." Hawk lifted his hand and stepped into the wheelhouse of the boat. Hawk didn't know it, but Chichemo only saw a shadow as he was knocked unconscious and ended up lying under one of the heading tables. The spider monkey, Bosco, sat next to his unconscious partner, waiting for him to wake up.

Mary C. walked through the house and stopped at the front door. She could see a figure of a woman through the new screen door and the glass of the new main front door.

"Who is it?" A woman's voice answered right away.

"An old friend, come callin' early, Mary C. Come to talk about old times." Mary C. was immediately intrigued by the voice and the statement. "I didn't come all this way this early to be turned away. I promise I won't bite." Mary C.'s hesitation was over. She opened the main door and left the new screen door closed and latched. She tried to focus in on the woman standing in front of her.

"Who is that?" Eve stepped closer. Mary C. looked at her visitor and still had no idea who she was.

"I'm sorry, ma'am, but I really think you've got the wrong Mary C. I don't know you."

"Now, do you really think there is another Mary C. here in Mayport?"

"You have me at a big disadvantage, you know my name."

"You know mine, too. It's just been a long time. We've all change so much. All of us, but you. You have been blessed with the ability to age gracefully, if at all. You have always been that way. Always the prettiest with the best figure and the most men." Mary C. wasn't sure if she was being complimented or not. But one thing she did know and that was she didn't know who she was talking to. The strange visitor spoke again.

"You may not want me here when you do finally recognize me, but I was hoping you would give me a moment of your time. I'll be leaving Mayport in a few minutes and I wanted to tell you some things before I left. Our past together was very tainted, but that was a long time ago, and even though we will never be able to be friends, I still need to talk to you before I go."

Mary C. was still puzzled. She was uneasy and cautious, but intrigued to the hilt. She was also tired of the guessing game they were playing.

"I will be happy to talk to you about anything you want, but I do need to know who you are."

Hawk fired up the boat engine so it could warm up, then walked out of the wheel house to make sure the wench was going to run properly. He stopped dead in his tracks when he saw Sandeep Singh standing on the stern deck of the Mary C. Hawk's heart pumped his blood into all the right places. He knew the look and stance of a man with bad intentions. Hawk would begin the conversation.

"I had a feeling, when I first saw you, we would stand together like this. I was hoping it was my imagination, but now I know it wasn't. I'm not sure why this has to be, but I suppose you have your reasons, or someone else's reasons. Men like me and you always end up doin' something we really don't want to do for a woman. I have a feeling that's the case here too. We don't even know each other. What a shame. I have to tell you something. I won't talk to you anymore, but I will not die easy or maybe not at all."

Eve stepped back away from the screen door and continued the game.

"I'd love to sit out here on the porch with you and talk about old east Mayport times for a little while. The porch swing really takes me back. It reminds me of the Big House in east Mayport. Eve left Mary C. at the door and walked to the end of the porch. She sat down in the swing. Mary C. couldn't stand the mystery any more. She unhooked the latch, pushed the screen door open and walked out of the house onto her front porch. When Eve looked up at Mary C. from the swing, Mary C. knew what old friend had come calling. Mary C.'s body shivered when she realized who was sitting in her porch swing. Eve could tell Mary C. had realized who she was.

"It's been a long time Mary C."

"Yes, it has, Eve. I'm not sure what to say to you. In fact, I can't imagine what we would have to say to each other." Eve pushed off the porch floor with her feet and the swing began to more back and forth.

Sandeep stepped closer to Hawk, but Hawk did not move at all. His eyes were glued to the big Indian and he would not take his eyes off him for any reason.

"Today I am Sandeep Singh the warrior. Your blood will set me free to save many others. One life, to save many is not much to ask." Hawk wanted to say, "It's not much to ask, if it's not your life that's being taken", but he had said he would not talk again and he would not.

"I am Punjabi and you cannot defeat me. I will make it quick and you will feel very little pain. You have my word." Hawk smiled and shook his head at his ridiculous challenger, but he knew he was going to have to fight for his life.

The swing on Mary C.'s front porch moved back and forth.

"You really don't have to say anything at all, Mary C. I would like to share some things with you and then I'll be on my way. If you wish to say something that will be just fine, but your response is not necessary." Mary C. hated Eve being there, but her curiosity had the best of her.

"I don't think I have anything to say to you, but go ahead and say what you came here to say and then please leave my house. You're not welcome here."

"I know I'm not welcome, but I also knew you would want to hear what I have to say. You've always been that way. You have never wanted to miss anything." Mary C. didn't like the way she felt and she knew Eve could sense, and was loving, her discomfort.

"Eve, stop this foolish game and tell me why you're here, so you can go about your business and me mine." Eve was ready to do the talking.

Hawk was afraid when Sandeep reached under his shirt and unsheathed his Kirpan sword. It's curved blade was the first thing Hawk saw as Sandeep held it to his side.

"This is a holy blade and it will cleanse you of your sins and free me from mine." Sandeep slashed out toward Hawk as Hawk moved to the other side of the winch. Sandeep was only a few feet away. Hawk saw a strange movement behind the warrior, but he knew he could not take his eyes off the Kirpan. The movement was from above. It was Tom Thumb using his old acrobatic talents to swing down to the boat. He used a boom block and tackle line to sail past Sandeep and scooped the turban off his head, causing the warrior's two day braids to fall down to the deck of the boat. The aerial attack shocked Sandeep and he took his eyes off of Hawk. Hawk sent a thundering right fist to the side of Sandeep's head, directly on his ear. The warrior-saint had never been hit that hard before, but he was strong and slashed out with the Kirpan at Hawk once again, backing him to the winch again. As Sandeep turned his attention and ringing ear to Hawk, the pigmy dive bomber made his return trip on the rope. Sandeep did not see him coming again as Tom got right over

Sandeep's head and released the rope, jumping on Sandeep's back and grabbing his single, rope-like braid. As Tom slid down the rope of hair he pulled all the ties loose. Sandeep felt the little man pulling his hair so he twisted his head quickly, sending Tom on an unwanted ride through the air. Tom lost his grip on Sandeep's hair rope and the pigmy warrior was slammed into one of the wooden pylons that was holding up the dock. Tom bounced off the pylon and fell into the river. Norman ran to the edge of the dock where Tom had gone down a dove into the water after the brave warrior.

Tom's second attack had distracted Sandeep again and he took another crushing right hand from Hawk, as his hair fell down around his body, covering his feet and the deck of the boat.

Hawk's second blow to Sandeep's head had opened a huge cut under his eye. The warrior stepped away from Hawk to get his bearings. Hawk knew the look of a desperate man. He knew it was the worst kind.

"Mary C., first of all I do salute you. You are a true survivor. In time I have realized we are both cut from the same mold. You will never admit that, but in your heart you know it to be true. We are both much more evil, than good. I have learned to live with that and actually enjoy what that entails. You have yet to admit that fact to yourself." Mary C. surprised Eve when she interrupted her.

"You have no idea what I have admitted to myself through the years." Eve was delighted.

"Ah! You will talk to me. That's good. We need to have a dialog. Women like us should meet and compare deeds from time-to-time. If we hadn't hurt each other early in our lives we very well could have been allies at some time or another and probably ruled the world in our own way, or at least our own world. But, it is too late for an alliance between enemies like us. It's a shame but it's true." Eve made the swing move again before she continued.

"Mary C., you have taken many lives during your reign of evil terror. Hell, you took five this week." Mary C. stared at her nemesis from the past as she went on. "You have the ability to inflict pain, suffering and even death and never think about it again. I wish I could do that. It's your gift. I'm learning. We are both survivors in a world of men. We have both learned to use our womanly charms to the highest advantage possible. Hell, Mary C., we can make men kill for us. And as hard us we try to fade away from this life of turmoil it always finds us. We will never be free. I have resigned myself to that fact, and have made the choice to accept and welcome the evil that grows within me. You have not done so. You still think all will be fine one day. What a pity."

Sandeep's ability to move quickly and with force was greatly hampered by his long hair. Hawk knew the warrior was still a danger and could kill him with one slice of the Kirpan, but Hawk would not allow Sandeep to get close to him. Sandeep made another awkward lunge toward Hawk with the Kirpan and his hair fell all over his extended arm and hand, covering the sword. Sandeep pushed his hair back behind him as a huge shadow come over him. Big Bob the giant stood on the railing of the boat making him look even taller.

"I was told once by an old gentleman that the Punjab warriors were the most efficient fighting machines on the earth, unless their hair was out of the turban, then they were not so effective." Sandeep was angered by the Giant's words and turned away from Hawk. In his anger and frustration, Sandeep ran at Big Bob, jumped and sailed through the air, landing with both his feet in the middle of Big Bob's chest, blasting him off the boat railing and into the river. Norman was pulling Tom back up onto the dock when he saw Big Bob fall head first into the water. Norman left the wet and bleeding pigmy warrior on the dock and jumped back into the river after Big Bob.

When Sandeep knocked Big Bob into the water, Hawk had moved from the safety of the winch and moved up behind the priest. Sandeep turned to end the battle with his Kirpan and met one more lightning right hand from Lester "Hawk" Hawkins. It hit Sandeep on the point of his chin. The blow sent both sides of Sandeep's jaw bone backwards, breaking both sides of his jaw at ear level. The warrior saint knew his bones had broken. Sandeep staggered backwards from the blow and tripped over his hair one more time, sending him backwards into the gears of the winch. Sandeep did not realize he no longer held the holy Kirpan in his hand. He tried to lift himself off the winch when the motor next to him started and the wheels of the winch began to turn. In a matter of seconds the rotating discs were wrapped in Sandeep's eight feet of black hair. His body and head were pulled taut and he could not move at all. Sandeep heard the winch motor stop and the wheels stopped turning. He could not see Chichemo standing behind him, holding the lever that turned the winch on and off. Hawk held the Kirpan.

Mary C. wanted Eve gone, but her old enemy had a hold on her at the moment. Eve decided to get to the meat of her visit.

"I know you're wondering, what the hell does she want. I want you to feel the same pain you have inflicted on others. I want you to know who has caused you this pain. I want you to know who is the true evil one of the two of us." Mary C.'s head was aching from Eve's evil tactics. She had no words as Eve went on.

"As we speak, the blood in the veins of your new man flows freely onto the ground." Mary C.'s throat went dry and her stomach burned. "The instrument of death will only take one life or I would have had all who you love taken from you. I wanted you to know it was me who ripped your heart out. You need to feel such pain." Mary C. struggled in her mind to be able to respond to the evil one.

"I want you to leave my home and leave me and mine alone. I think you're trying to scare me, like always, and I don't want to talk to you anymore. You're just as crazy as you've ever been. Please leave, I need to check on my grandson." Eve smiled.

"I'd like to see the little golden breed. I've heard about him, but haven't had the pleasure. I promise not to try and steal him. I've heard that could be dangerous to one's health. I would really like to see him." Mary C. stepped to the door.

"Your visit's over. After I check on him I want you gone from here when I get back." Eve smiled again.

"We still have a few things to talk about."

"No we don't." Mary C. went into the house. Mary C. heard the swing move again as Eve pushed with her feet.

"Bring him out here, Mary C. Then I'll go. You know how I like

The Winch

little babies." Eve looked toward the screen door when it opened. Mary C. stepped out onto the front porch with the butt of the pump action shotgun pressed against her shoulder and the wooden stock against her cheek. She had it pointed directly at Eve like she was hunting quail in the woods. Eve had no time to react or speak. She knew Mary C. was the most evil of them all as the shotgun exploded, sending hundreds of double aught pellets into Eve's body. The force of the pellets and her body's reaction pushed Eve through the back wooden slats of the swing, breaking them into pieces. She fell to the porch floor behind the swing with blood gushing from her open wounds. Mary C. stepped quickly to her and pulled the pump handle down, loading the chamber of the shotgun with another shell. It was easy for Mary C. to see the pain and shock in Eve's, soon to be dead, eyes. Mary C. had seen that helpless and hopeless look many times before. Eve felt very little pain from the second blast of the shotgun. She was dying anyway and you could always count on Mary C. to put her victims out of their misery. She didn't like to see people suffer very long. It was one of her better traits.

Sandeep looked up from his winch and hair captivity. Hawk stood above him holding the Kirpan sword. As Sandeep focused his eyes on Hawk and the sword, preparing himself for death, his mind was covered with a darkness he had never felt before. At first he thought it was the way a man feels when his own death is near. When in reality it was the hand of death telling him he was free of the evil one. Hawk stepped closer and Sandeep made his request.

"Make the cut quick and clean. I will pray now." Sandeep closed his eyes and prayed while he waited for the fatal slash of the holy Kirpan.

Mary C. knew Eve was dead. She walked back into the house and placed the shotgun in the corner behind the bedroom door. She checked on Billy to be sure he had not been disturbed by the two blasts of the gun. He was safe, asleep and rather cozy between the pillows. She walked back onto the porch. Mary C. grabbed both of Eve's blood soaked ankles and pulled her body across the porch and

The Garbage Drum

down the steps. Mary C. liked the way the back of Eve's head bounced off the three steps as she pulled the evil one's body onto the ground. Mary C. continued pulling Eve until she had her at the side of the house out of the view of anyone who may come up to the house. She left Eve's body on the ground and walked to the back porch where she took hold of the two wooden handles of a wheel barrow, rolling it to where Eve's body lay.

Mary C. placed the side edge of the wheel barrow up against the side of the house so it would not tip over when she lifted Eve's body into the barrow container. With one strong lift, Eve was half way into the container. Then the second lift made it complete. Mary C. and Eve were rolling like children giving each other a ride. Mary C. pushed the wheel barrow to the wooded area behind her house and down the narrow path that led to the garbage hole and barrel.

Sandeep opened his eyes and saw the nets hanging above him. The sun had taken the darkness. He was dazed from his injuries and he knew others were standing near him. He turned his head and saw the winch that had held him captive. He also saw his hair still captive and twisted in the working discs of the machine. He couldn't lift his hands to touch his head but he knew his hair had been cut to free him from the winch. Mr. John King's face was close to him.

"He should have cut your head off, boy, and fed it to the toad fish. But he didn't. That's the Hawk."

Sandeep was pulled off the deck of the boat and he knew he was being carried off the boat and through the fish house. He could hear voices and he saw Big Bob's face as the one carrying him.

Sandeep saw the Mercedes Benz and then someone opened the door of the car. Sandeep knew he was sitting in the front seat of the car. Big Bob stepped away and Sandeep saw Hawk's face.

"This didn't have to happen. It was your choice. I'm keepin' the knife. I earned it."

Mary C. stopped the forward motion of the wheel barrow when she reached the garbage hole.

The large fifty-five gallon burning drum was only a few feet away. She put both of her arms under Eve's arms and lifted her dead weight out of the wheel barrow and into the drum. The bottom part of the drum was buried into the ground so she did not worry about it tipping over. Eve's limp and bloody body fell head first into the drum. With Eve's black clothes and blood stains, Mary C. would never know her old enemy had a body full of tattoos.

Sandeep started the engine of the Mercedes Benz and shifted the gear column into reverse so he could back away from the fish house. He saw Hawk and Mr. King standing to one side as the car moved away. Big Bob, Norman and Tom stood on the ramp to the fish house. They were all three soaking wet. Tom had a cut on his face from hitting the pylon, and Big Bob held his hand over a pair of broken ribs. Norman was just wet and fatigued from his two daring rescues. Chichemo walked up behind Hawk as the Mercedes turned and was out of sight.

"I hope he don't come back. Who the hell was he?" Big Bob had the answer.

"He was a priest. A Punjabi priest."

"What the hell kinda religion is that. Damn, that's a kick ass religion when the priest has a knife and shit." Chichemo turned to Hawk. "Tell Jason to stay over there with that little slit tail. We can't do no shrimpin' with all that hair stuck in the winch. What the hell was he, again?"

Mary C. rolled the wheel barrow back to the back porch and returned it where it belonged. She ran into the house and made sure Billy was still sleeping. He was. She bounced on her toes back to the screen door, when she heard a song by the Coasters, coming from the radio she had left on. "Take out the papers and trash. Or you get no spendin' cash". She thought the lyrics were perfect for the task at hand. On her way back to the garbage hole she reached up on a shelf on the back porch and took down a five gallon gas can. Mary C. shook the can to be sure it contained the gas she would need. She picked up two paper grocery bags filled with trash and placed a few pieces of the scrap plywood Hawk had left into two empty cardboard boxes. Mary C. hurried to the garbage hole and stuffed the bags of trash, wood scraps and the boxes into the burning drum, covering

Eve's body. She poured the gas from the can on top of the pile of trash. A lighted match did the rest.

Uncle Bobby's truck drove up to Miss Margaret's store. Hawk could see that Jason was standing near the doorway in a lip lock with the blonde haired beauty. Chichemo would have enjoyed the sight Hawk was seeing. He blew the truck horn and Jason looked his way and walked out of the store with Sofia hanging on to Jason.

"I wanted to tell you we're not goin' out. Winch trouble. I didn't mean to interrupt y'all. I'll tell you about the winch later. Go on back to doin' what ever you were doin'." Jason and Sofia smiled and walked back into the store. Hawk headed home to Mary C.

Mr. King was the first to walk up the steps to his haunted house. Ana Kara came through the front door and stepped out onto the front porch. She saw Mr. King first and then her eyes fell upon the three members of her family. They were still wet and she could see something had happened.

"What has happened to y'all?" She could see the pain on Big Bob's face and the cut on Tom's face. "Y'all have been hurt. Norman, what's goin' on?" Big Bob tried to ease her mind.

"We're fine. We're much better as a team. Let's sit down and we'll tell you all about it."

"Let me help y'all."

Lester "Hawk"Hawkins, drove Uncle Bobby's truck into Mary C.'s front yard. He could see Mary C. spraying the front porch down with the water hose. He stepped out of the truck and walked to the porch.

"What are you doin' here. Chichemo went and left y'all didn't he?" Hawk smiled at Mary C.'s assumption. Hawk saw the smoke from the trash dump.

"That's a hell of a fire you got goin' back there."

"There was a hell of a lot a trash to burn." He looked at the damaged porch swing and the blood she was washing off the porch.

"That's a hell of a lot of blood and a real broken swing you got there." Mary C. gave him a silly grin.

"It was a hell of a big racoon I had to shoot. It was actin' sick, like something was wrong with it. I was scared for the baby. You know rabies and stuff. When it climbed up in the swing I put it out of it's misery. It looked like it was sufferin'. It's in the fire, too. Sorry about the swing. I should have waited for it to climb down. I wasn't thinkin' when I pulled the trigger. But, with a handy man like you around, I'm sure that swing will be just like new before ya know it. Maybe we'll even get a new one." Mary C. squirted Hawk with the water hose and he chased her into the house.

Mr. King and his guests were all sitting on the front porch. The ladies had been told the story of Hawk and Sandeep. Helga had cleaned and bandaged her pigmy warrior's face. Ana Kara was wrapping a support bandage around Big Bob's rib cage.

"You probably have broken ribs, Bob. We need to get you checked out. And, Tom, that's a nasty cut. You could use a few stitches. I can't believe we slept through all this action. We were no help at all." Beulla had a thought.

"We were sleepin' beauties, and I for one am damned glad I wasn't there. My big ass heart couldn't take nothin' like that." Norman walked out of the house wearing dry clothes. Little Tom had to praise the "Skeleton Man".

"If it wasn't for Norman, me and Big Bob would have been goners. I was hurt bad and takin' my last breath. I was goin' down for the third time, and y'all know what that means. Then, when he saved me and got me out of the water he had to save Big Bob. He did go under for the third time and y'all know what that means. I don't know how Norman was able to keep Big Bob from drowning, he's sure stronger than he looks. " Everyone on the porch looked at Norman and clapped their hands for the hero.

As the clapping subsided, Office Jimmy Johnston's police car rolled up to Mr. King's front porch. Officer Jimmy Johnston and Mr. Butler stepped out of the car at the same time. Mr. King met them at the edge of the porch. Mr. Butler looked around at the battered warriors. He took a deep breath.

"Oh, boy. Jimmy, look at this." Jimmy looked at Mr. King.

"We came to talk to you about something. We didn't expect to see this. What's happened here?" The circus family let Mr. King talk to the young policeman.

"One of my guests tried to kill Hawk on the Mary C. and these good folks stopped it from happening, at great risk to their lives." Mr. Butler had to get involved.

"Where's Hawk now?" Mr. King was still the spokesman.

"He's fine. He went home. There was some damage to the boat and they won't be shrimpin' today." Helga was sitting next to little Tom. She had not said anything up to that point. She had only been concerned with Tom's injuries. She had something bothering her.

"I can't believe Sandeep would hurt anybody. He was suppose to protect people, not hurt them. I'm so disappointed in Sandeep. I'm just sick about it. It was that woman who made him do all those awful things. She's a witch. You can see that in those evil eyes of her's." The name Sandeep didn't mean anything to Mr. Butler the first time Helga said it. Mary C.'s words rang in his head when he heard the name the second time. He stepped toward Helga.

"Excuse me, ma'am." Helga looked up at Mr. Butler. "Who did you say disappointed you?"

"Sandeep. Sandeep Singh. He seemed to be so nice. He's a priest, ya know?" Mr. Butler turned to Mr. King.

"The man who attacked Hawk is named Sandeep Singh?"

"Yes, he came here with an old friend, Eve Klim. They were leaving today, after he killed Hawk." Mr. Butler's brain wheels were turning.

"This Eve Klim wouldn't happen to be related to Charlie Klim, now would she?" Mr. King nodded his head. Mr. Butler looked at Jimmy. "Why doesn't that surprise me?"

"Because nothing surprises you any more, sir."

"That's right, I forgot." Mr. Butler looked at Mr. King again. "Did this Sandeep fella have a nickname of any kind. Did anybody ever call him 'Singin' Sandy'?" The group on the porch looked at each other and Mr. Butler knew it was a stupid question. "Forget it. Where could I find this Sandeep Singh if I wanted to find him?" Tom Thumb had the information.

"You can't miss him. He's drivin' a top of the line white

Mercedes Benz and you'll find it parked at a local hospital or barber shop." No one laughed out loud, but Tom's information was a real hoot to the ones who understood his meaning. Mr. Butler turned to Officer Jimmy Johnston. "Get on the radio and tell them to find that white Mercedes and bring 'ol Singin' Sandy in to the station."

Sandeep was in too much pain and had to stop driving. He pulled the Mercedes off Mayport Road and into the parking lot of Tony's Seafood Shack. Sandeep leaned back against the leather car seat. He knew Eve no longer held him. A group of Tony's black customers walked out of the Shack to see the white Mercedes. Singin' Sandy would be easy for the police to find.

Mr. Butler stepped up to the middle of the porch. He wanted to tell the circus people about the reason he had come there. Officer Jimmy Johnston had made the call to pick up Sandeep and he was standing on the porch steps. He knew it was time for Mr. Butler to tell them about the death of their friend. Mr. Butler tried to direct his words to everyone on the porch.

"Jimmy and I came out here this morning to talk to all of you. Last night something happened and I think it will concern you." The porch was completely quiet for the first time that morning. They waited on Mr. Butler to continue. "There was an accident last night. A hunting accident."

A cold chill ran through the bodies of each one of the circus family. "A young woman was killed. We think she's one of your group. I don't want to offend anyone and believe me I am sorry." There was a silence as he paused for another deep breath. "She looked like a wolf." Beulla was the first not to contain her feeling.

"Oh, God! Sweet Beth! Oh my God!" She dropped her head and cried. Helga hugged Tom and she cried. Norman knelt down next to Beulla and held her hand as he cried. Ming and Ling sat up in their bed and held hands as they cried. Ana turned and looked away from the others. Big Bob was the only one who could talk.

"You said it was a hunting accident. Could you explain that, please?" Mr. Butler did not want to explain it at all, but he had no choice.

"Some young men were hunting in the woods. They saw her running and thought she was an animal of some kind. They killed her. I really do think it was an accident, because the young men brought her to the station to tell us what happened." Big Bob took his one deep breath.

"Isn't it sad when you can't talk to people because of how you look. I hate it that we were not there for her. I know she was scared without us. I don't like thinking about someone I love being scared and me not being there to keep them safe. It was no accident, it was everyone's fault."

The Barnum and Bailey Circus tour bus was ready to roll. The destination panel displayed: Gibsonton. Norman was at the wheel wearing his hat and driving gloves. His passengers for the return trip were Helga, Beulla, Ming and Ling. Big Bob was sitting in his fishing truck with Ana Kara to keep him company during the ride home to the Giant's Motel. The third vehicle in the South bound caravan was Mr. King's 1941 Cadillac Gothic carved-panel hearse. Beth's ride home would be in style. Tom would ride in the hearse with Mr. King. It was Mr. King's tribute to the member of the circus family he did not have the pleasure of meeting. The circus caravan drove away from the front of John King's haunted house and left Mayport, Florida, U.S.A.

Margie's second carousel dream had given her the urge to visit the oak tree for one of her sexual releases. She stopped the family wagon at the bottom of the sand hill and stepped out onto the sand. She knew the climb to the top would be difficult in the white soft sand, but the drive within her would take her to the top as it had done before. She made the climb and as she was nearing the top, she saw the most interesting and shocking sight. A sight she never expected to see.

It was Jason and Mary C. sitting on a blanket under the oak tree. Billy was lying between them. Mary C. didn't look up when she greeted Margie.

"Jason said the carousel would send you to us because you were the most worthy." Mary C. lifted her head and looked into Margie's wide open eyes. "We want you to be the next one."